Flat Out

An Apocalyptic LitRPG

The System Apocalypse – Australia / Book 2

By

Tao Wong & KT Hanna

License Notes

This is a work of fiction. Names, characters, businesses, places, events, and incidents are either the products of the author's imagination or used in a fictitious manner. Any resemblance to actual persons, living or dead, or actual events is purely coincidental.

This book is licensed for your personal enjoyment only. This book may not be re-sold or given away to other people. If you would like to share this book with another person, please purchase an additional copy for each recipient. If you're reading this book and did not purchase it, or it was not purchased for your use only, then please return to your favorite book retailer and purchase your own copy. Thank you for respecting the hard work of this author.

Flat Out

Published by Starlit Publishing
PO Box 30035
High Park PO
Toronto, ON
M6P 3K0
Canada

www.starlitpublishing.com

Ebook ISBN: 9781990491771
Print ISBN: 9781990491818
Hardcover ISBN: 9781990491825

Books in the
System Apocalypse Universe

Main Storyline

Life in the North

Redeemer of the Dead

The Cost of Survival

Cities in Chains

Coast on Fire

World Unbound

Stars Awoken

Rebel Star

Stars Asunder

Broken Council

Forbidden Zone

System Finale

System Apocalypse: Relentless

A Fist Full of Credits

System Apocalypse: Australia

Town Under

Flat Out

Anthologies and Short stories

System Apocalypse Short Story Anthology Volume 1

Valentines in an Apocalypse

A New Script

Daily Jobs, Coffee and an Awfully Big Adventure

Adventures in Clothing

Questing for Titles

Blue Screens of Death

My Grandmother's Tea Club

The Great Black Sea

A Game of Koopash (Newsletter exclusive)

Lana's story (Newsletter exclusive)

Debts and Dances (Newsletter exclusive)

Comic Series

The System Apocalypse Comics (7 Issues)

The System Apocalypse Graphic Novel: Issues 1-7 (limited edition hardcover)

Contents

To the Rainbow Room

You know who you are

Thank you for everything

Previously in Town Under:

The System Apocalypse hit Australia hard, just before midnight while most people were asleep. Kira Kent, with her kids Jackson (13) and Wisp (8) in tow are caught out at the Griffith University Nathan Campus when the System initiates.

Fighting alongside a group of strangers, the family manages to make their way past the already emerging mutations of local wildlife to the Garden City Shopping Center in search of a safe harbour. To their good fortune, they find a Settlement Orb which grants them a quest to gather an additional 1000 survivors together under one roof.

Completion of the Quest gives them a Safe Zone to begin rebuilding, effectively creating a small township that allowed them access to the Shop and their own Crafting Cartel.

But not all is well.

An intergalactic alien hunter group warns the humans about their impending arrival and demands they give up their settlement or face the consequences.

Faced with monsters outside, aliens on the way to take over their settlement and losses from the never-ending mutations, Kira and her family must Level up further or fall by the wayside.

Chapter One:

Three Days Early

13 days, 21 hours post System Onset

Gripping the railing at the top of the gate, I peered down, trying to make out what the hell was going on. Even with those flat and strange alien ships so close to us, I couldn't tell quite what was happening. Down the way, closer to where the OfficeWorx building was, I could see movement.

It had to be IRSHA, right? I could feel how restless the others were right behind me. Dale and Chris, Kyle and Evelyn, Dor and Sienna – all trying to figure out what was going on.

Apparently intergalactic species didn't care about making appointments and keeping them. There was being early, like five to ten minutes early for an appointment, and there was seventy-two hours of obnoxious early. I could already tell these guys were going to piss me off. Something in the pit of my stomach warned me, queasiness and all that maybe, just maybe, our defenses weren't going to be enough yet. I hoped it was just nerves.

Kyle elbowed me in the ribs. "What do you think this is about?"

"Didn't they say they'd be coming to claim unclaimed settlements? So they shouldn't even be here." Evelyn spoke softly, and I could feel the irritation radiating off her.

"Supposedly." There had to be something else going on here. After all, Evelyn was correct. We had claimed the settlement mere hours after our last encounter with IRSHA.

There was more movement, and while I could have walked all the way down the parapet to where they were, I felt like somehow that might relinquish some of the power dynamic. Make them come to me. That was all

I could think of. So that's what we did. We waited.

And it felt like my insides were roiling with ants.

I frowned at the sight of the spaceships above us. Shaped like stealth bombers, they were still much smaller than I'd expected alien space craft to be. It gave me a moment's pause. They also simply hovered, like they weren't attempting to land or park. Maybe I'd seen too many sci-fi movies.

Now that the gate was reinforced with metals, it felt safer up here. We'd made a lot of small yet effective changes since our Wombutant arrived and we'd fought off the harpies.

Maybe I could reinforce it with earth and stone and rock and magic-type things. There was a group of them approaching now, taller creatures than I'd been expecting. A relatively large group. Though from what I could see farther down, just a sampling of the people they'd sent.

A cold line drew itself down my spine like someone slowly lowering an ice cube. Even without settling on any one individual in that group, I could feel the danger right in front of me. Whether it was strength of Mana, or simply just towering levels above me, those people moving in on our gate, those aliens, creatures, whatever they were—some of them posed a severe threat.

And the mama bear in me wanted to rear her snarly head.

The first being to reach the gates made it with an entourage that lagged slightly behind them. They were tall, about half the height of our walls, and their feet splayed out like an upside-down hibiscus flower in full bloom. Four arms with ribboned flesh held in a way that made it seem like they were standing with their hands on their hips, and I realized it was, in fact, the exact same being we'd encountered before.

Dequasha stood below us, her eyes peering up out of her face that still vaguely resembled a flower. Something about her expression seemed perturbed by the sight of a rather large barricade that hadn't been there a few days earlier. I didn't need to be psychic to feel the irritation emanating off her as she realized we had, in fact, likely spoiled some of her plans.

"As previously mentioned, we are here to claim our property. Stand aside and allow us entrance," she said, quite hoitily.

Mum tone it was then. "What did you say?"

She blinked at me with all of her eyelids and cocked her head to one side like she was checking the translation or something. "I'm quite sure I spoke with the correct modulation. We are here to claim our property. We did warn you. Should you not vacate this property immediately, we shall be forced to slaughter every one of you. I do so hate to get blood on my parts directly, so could you be a dear and just clear off."

"No." Dale stood, pushing himself to the front and crossing his arms. He was decently tall, and as I was only just noticing, had a decidedly un-dad bod. It'd never thought of him as imposing before, but I guess he *had* coached teenage sports.

"Did you say no?" Dequasha asked incredulously.

"Yes. I said no." But Dale wasn't finished. Maybe he'd decided to take over Barry's role and be our representative to others. He was gruffer and not as friendly, but it felt like we might need that. "What gives you the right to think we would just hand our settlement over to you?"

Dequasha's eyes narrowed for a moment before she presented a projection to us. It flickered to life like an old television screen with nothing visible supporting it, allowing us to read the statement upon it.

Formal notice is provided that the order of the Intergalactic Rare Species Hunter's Alliance, IRSHA's exploratory and discovery team IRSHA Q-a593NP, has purchased from the Galactic Council first right of refusal and purchase of any and all yet unclaimed settlements on the continent of "Australia," on the Dungeon Planet "Earth," within the first sixteen days of System integration.

Please be advised that any illegitimate settlement squatters will be evicted by IRSHA.

Dale rolled his eyes. "And you are showing this to me because?"

Dequasha was about to speak again when one of her entourage pushed to the fore. This being was huge, much larger than I'd originally thought while he hid in the shadows.

His head was only a few feet below the top of our wall, so he probably hit like nine feet on a good day. The hair on his head looked like it had been molded into spikes by a rough, black clay, and there were bright markings all over his body like he'd been tattooed under a blacklight that glowed permanently beneath his skin even though his complexion appeared less soft and more like polished granite.

"Junior members of the alliance needs be educated more, it seems." His dark eyes flashed with a flame tinged with blue and I suddenly had no desire to figure out what his species was. He felt dangerous, if the Mana dancing around his body was anything to go by. And if nothing else, I'd learned just how badly I needed to pay attention to my Mana senses.

While he spoke, I took the opportunity to Analyze him.

Mon'swkinon
Third in Line
Dash'Kiri Clan
Warrior of Sound
Level 12

Warrior of Sound piqued my interest. I wondered what that was about. From his appearance I didn't think it would take him much punch a hole through our wall. So I appreciated the restraint he showed at not doing so. He inclined his head, and in doing so, briefly made eye contact with me. It took all my willpower to hold that gaze, however brief it was.

"We apologize, for we were assured given this continent's predilection for dangerous creatures, that local inhabitants survivability would be virtually nil. There are other settlements. We will proceed and claim those instead." He bowed his head as he chose to depart, and a warning sensation shot down my spine.

"Other settlements?" Kyle asked, his tone hard. My dear twin, ever the savior, ever the doctor. I knew why he was asking. If there were other settlements, then there were potentially other survivors, and if this deep granite-hued dude was about to go and claim a heap of these centers . . .well, that wasn't good. My only hope was that some of the others had managed to claim an orb too.

"But of course. For now, we will let you be. The System has estimated survival rates on this continent. You will be dead soon and fall beneath the minimum needed to maintain your town. As soon as you do, we will come and claim these premises. Maybe we'll even let your survivors live." His smile didn't make anything else twinkle; all it did was stab into me like someone was trying to tear my soul from my body.

That maybe let us live. Yeah, if that scenario happened, I'd be willing to bet we'd all be dead.

Out of the corner of my eye, I could see the spaceships hovering close by, and a ring of bright light up near where the Wombutant fought the harpies. Maybe the ships only brought some of them, or vehicles for them to use. Because that other thing looked suspiciously portal-like.

"Are your ears painted on or something, mate? We will be here, and we will be ready, and I don't give a brass razoo what you think you paid for. This settlement is ours." Dolores's voice rang clear and true across the gathering beneath us, like she'd somehow amplified it with her Den Mother abilities.

I'd check on whether that was a possibility or not later.

Slowly, the massive being turned to face us completely again, and even Dequasha took a step away. But instead of yelling or screaming, or hell, reaching out a pointer finger to tip our gate open . . . the rock guy drew himself up to his full height.

"My name is Mon'swkinon. I am the third of the Dash'Kiris and I will return to lay waste to what you think is yours. This is our continent now, and no human will hold onto what we have purchased the rights to."

His voice reached something deep in the earth, and it felt like the rumbling beneath my feet was trying to flee the hollow feeling his tones left inside me. Those words resonated on a deeper level, awakening a fear.

He continued, his tone about as reasonable as I suspected it got. "Humans are not rare enough for us to hunt, and we abide by the code of sapience. Your species are not our target, nor our prize, but I advise you not to come between us and our goals.

"You have been warned."

Every single one of us up there, including the few people who were on guard duty, stood and crossed our arms. Maybe it was because we'd otherwise be shaking, or perhaps to steady ourselves. I'd never thought humans were a particularly intelligent bunch when it came to defending our own, but I'd be damned if I was going to back down from some giant jerk who thought he knew all about our country and species after reading it in a damned report.

"We have our own goals," I called down cheerfully, not giving a rat's arse for those few seconds.

Dale piped up surprisingly to back me up. "We don't take well to alien colonization, thanks."

Mon'swkinon didn't even deign us another glance, probably already completely fed up with the likes of us puny humans. That was okay. I needed him to think we were incapable; I needed to have him lulled into a false sense of security, or perhaps "superiority" applied better here. Because there were several of his species in the IRSHA members I saw gathered behind Dequasha and him. And right now, we weren't any match for them. Not yet.

Even as they all began to make their way toward where the transports were unloading what I assumed were land vehicles I couldn't properly identify at this distance. There were some members like Dequasha, and many sort of Orc-like, maybe some vaguely troll reminiscent, and other creatures that my brain just couldn't wrap understanding around.

Sadly, they appeared too far away for my Analyze skill to reach too.

We watched as they moved slowly through the streets, out toward Carindale way.

"Oh shit," I said as realization dawned on me and things started to make complete and utter sense. "I bet the System designated all of the shopping centers as potential settlements."

Considering the way our shopping centers were laid out in distance from each other and the city center, it really made perfect sense. At least we'd know where to find other survivors. Maybe.

We didn't have a deadline, or a declaration of war. But what I did have was a clear path for the information we needed to collect on our invaders, and the Levels we had to get so we'd even stand a chance. At least we had direction.

For now, I called that a win.

❖

Back in the center, Sarah wasn't impressed with our report at all. She'd stayed behind, to ready the implementation of the damned Mana batteries. We couldn't all run off to watch the aliens from the city gates, after all.

"You can't be serious!" Sarah stomped her diminutive foot with much more force than I'd have given her credit for and stood right up to Dale, toe to toe. Chris hung back, biding her time, and from what I could tell, also trying to hide some level of amusement. "How can you all be so calm about this? They want to dispose of us. Displace us? In our own country?"

Dale put up his hands in the eternal "calm down, I'm backing away" motion. He'd never struck me as someone who liked confrontation, but it was good to see him standing up for himself.

"Look. This isn't our Earth anymore; it's not even our Australia. We've lost loved ones, children, spouses, family, friends. All of it. These creatures, they run by a different set of rules, and we've only just come into them. We have to dig in and do what we can to preserve what we've managed to start."

His words shot an aching arrow through me as I realized how much what he was saying was true.

"Frankly"—Dale sighed—"We're lucky we managed to fulfill the quota of people we needed for the settlement orb quest when we did. Who knows where we'd be if Kira hadn't claimed the settlement?"

That seemed to calm Sarah down somewhat. "Sorry," she said as she fiddled with several more glowing wires that defied my ability to Analyze. Focused on the task in front of her, she was silent for a moment before speaking. "It's just that . . . everything was finally starting to come together and then Jules, and the Mollecupai, and now the aliens. So much crap."

We'd all lost so much. I'd been too much of a coward to check on Mason or my parents' whereabouts. I knew it was possible, because others had purchased the information in the shop, but Kyle and I were remaining blissfully ignorant by choice for now.

Sarah's entire countenance had deflated and her face paled, showing her freckles in even more starkness against her white skin. She let her own hands fall and wiped her brow. "I just don't understand any of this. They have first right of refusal to buy any of our settlements?"

She looked up at Dale, as if hoping he knew the answers. But he wasn't versed in Alien Takeovers 101; he was just another guy with us trying to muddle through everything. What I wouldn't give for the internet on my freaking phone so I could just pull up answers to everything immediately.

So much for these aliens and Galactic Council being all powerful. Hadn't seen anything yet, not even in the hands of the IRSHA delegation, that compared to my damned cell phone's ability to get stuff done.

"I'm sorry, Sarah. I don't have answers." Dale's words echoed the wish that he could answer everything for everyone. "They can't just purchase this settlement, because it's already been rightfully occupied. I'm just hoping they don't get desperate enough to attack us for it."

Sarah nodded; her face now thoughtful as she mulled over his words. "I get it. It doesn't mean I like it. To have to fight to keep this home we've made when we already lost so much? This system is cruel. It's nasty."

A hush fell over all of us gathered there together. The library was filled to the brim, with more people than usual. Beanbag chairs were taken, as well as all the seats, including those meant for children.

Our whole tech department was in here, and by that I meant Jackson's little group of Techzards he'd gathered from the start and coerced into following his class. Sarah and Chris were here too, and a handful of adults I didn't recognize by name, but who I knew worked with them and the kids to start getting our electrically powered items online.

Shit. The quest.

"Are the Mana batteries installed?" I blurted the words out.

Chris paled. "Sorry. We'll get right one that."

The next moment all the Techzards were gone, and I breathed a sigh of relief. We were still within the window to at least progress to the next quest once this was done.

The world was a whole lot more reliant on modern technology than I'd ever realized pre-Apocalypse. I mean, Aussies were pretty good about water conservation, all things considered, our country being one of the driest out there. I remember distinctly back in the early 2000s having to ration water. Four-minute showers maximum. Use the run-off water for your garden if at all. Level six water restrictions, dams down to twenty percent capacity.

I shuddered.

It wasn't like we'd been wasting a lot of water, nor even that we'd been using as much water as Garden City usually would have used. But the process to ferry the water, treat the water, desalinate the water—all of it took electricity, and all the electrical gadgets had shorted out.

That initial plumbing quest saved us originally. And frankly, having one for powering our settlement was about to do the same thing.

"Kira!"

I blinked, not having realized someone was talking to me. At first, I thought Jules had called me, but a sadness washed over me reminding me none too subtly that Jules wasn't going to call out ever again.

Gemma stood with her hands on her hips, the sadness in her eyes enveloping her body in a tragic sheen of energy.

"Sorry. Brain sidetracked me." I straightened myself out, pulled myself up, and nodded at her. "What did I miss?"

Gemma leaned against one of the tables, her haunted eyes glancing back and forth between everyone there. "If they're out there, and we don't just fork over our little town, don't you think they'll just attack us?"

I shrugged. "Of course they might."

There was a small gasp from everyone around me, and I shook my head.

"You seriously can't be surprised by that; I know I wasn't the only one listening to Mon'swkinon. They don't think we're going to survive anyway, and that our population will fall below what our town requires to be considered the settlement we are. They might say they don't want to hunt sapient species, but that doesn't mean they won't just step in and take what they want once we no longer meet the requirements."

It seemed logical to me. From his body language to the way he spoke, I wasn't under any delusions that he was about to let Garden City go. I even had an inkling that he was under the impression he wouldn't have to fight for it if they just let the mutations and other creatures kill us off. Part of me thought he was right.

"Do you think it'll be easy for them to just come and take what we've built?" Ray's tone, contrary to how he'd spoken half an hour earlier on the wall, held a sense of apprehension I wish he'd shown sooner.

"I don't know how any of this works, but I do know how we can find out." I held my hand up as several others made to follow me. "I don't need an entourage in the Shop. Just leave me to it, and I'll be back with all the fun reading."

Now I just needed to figure out how to get what I wanted to get without the Shop fleecing me once they realized how much I wanted the information. I glanced into my Inventory and frowned. Well, maybe they'd be more inclined to be kind to me after I got a couple of these unique specimens out of my inventory and into their hands.

Chapter Two:

Infomercials from Hell

Two weeks post System Onset

12 a.m.

Ever watched one of those endless shopping channels at three in the morning on any type of regular or satellite channel? Yeah, that's just the thing. Where there's "But wait! There's more." Knives, jewelry, strange wraparound blankets with arm holes. All these things you never knew you wanted or needed, but now seem like you can live without.

That right there is the danger of the Shop, TM in my own mind.

The foyer was empty again when I stepped in. It still felt like I shouldn't be in there, like this was somewhere for upmarket shoppers to come and have their every whim catered to. And of course, in a way, it sort of was.

This time the greeter glanced at me, and their face broke into a million-dollar smile. Like they could sense the goodies I had and knew the potential wares I wanted. Damn it. So much for playing it cool. I needed to figure out the abilities of all these species so I could find a way to counter anything that affected me.

"Greetings again, Kira Kent. What might I be able to assist you with today?" they asked me politely, their words sugary-sweet and lulling.

I smiled back and pulled my hammer out of my inventory, equipping it. Immediately, a level of clarity hit me again as my mental defenses jumped back up to thirty-four percent. Yeah. There was a reason I should always at least equip my bloodthirsty metal friend. Needed that whole protection thing.

"I've got some items for you. Likely first or third of a kind to be found on this new Dungeon World of yours. So what's say we take a look?" I winked at my host, trying to soften the fact that we were now both aware their tricks weren't going to work on me.

Shi'enah's eyes narrowed almost imperceptibly, but the smile remained affixed to their face. "Let's see what you've got, then."

I think I liked the change of tone in their voice. They'd obviously been equipped with some sort of light mental manipulation so that they could get the best from their patrons. It made me cringe at how much I'd probably already lost out to them.

Still, they knew that they'd already managed to take me to the cleaners a couple of times, so I hoped that won me some goodwill. This time, I was willing to take longer in the Shop. I needed to find weapons that no other species would consider weapons. We had to find some sort of advantage.

"Mollecupai Mana secretion gland." There was a tinge of awe in Shi'enah's voice, like they were trying to suppress it. "You've already fought and defeated a Mollecupai here?"

As they spoke, my nice little Diviner skill kicked in, signaling that the question was most definitely of high interest. "Of course we did." I acted as though the matter was nothing out of the ordinary. Like we killed giant, weird ground-dwelling creatures that catapulted our friends through the air and left them as husks of smashed bones every single day.

Even while I separated out all the stuff in my inventory, I'd only had about twelve free slots left. Eighty-one was a much larger space than I'd started with, and I was still managing to fill it mostly after one expedition. I'd have to look into some form of inventory expansion even with knowing it would expand all by itself every five levels or so.

Shi'enah was being awfully quiet as they leafed through my wares. No one else was in the Shop with me, but from what people had mentioned before, not everyone appeared to get the same Shop or offering or . . .

experience as we'd had. Ironically, I felt like this mall-styled hall was a better way to go about it with humans anyway.

"There are several items I would like to discuss with you." They indicated several beaks, glob innards, and other random pieces of loot. Interestingly enough, they stayed away from the Mollecupai Mana secretion gland, one of its tentacles, and the eye I'd not been all too happy about acquiring as loot.

We haggled a bit, and I ended up with a lot more Credits than I'd anticipated from the more mundane stuff. "Sixty-three thousand credits for these." Shi'enah spoke tightly, like it was cash they didn't want to let go of, but I could feel like there was more in there.

Maybe I needed to take a better look at the Mollecupai's remains myself. So instead of saying anything, I pretended to be mulling over the offer in my head while inspecting the crap out of the other items we hadn't haggled about yet.

Mollecupai Eyeball and Stalk x 1

Type: Rare

> _Use: This is the baby brother of the more common all-seeing eye artifact. It can aid in divining Skills, but utilization requires a large amount of Mana. May be used in crafting items or as an accessory._

> _Warning: Mental Fortitude Resistances required for use. Minimum suggested levels of 54%._

Okay, so that might be worth keeping, though how I was going to find another twenty percent of Mental Fortitude, I didn't know.

Mollecupai Tentacle x 3

Type: Uncommon

>*Use: Can be crafted into ropes that can obey mental commands. Or string. Or anything, really.*

>*Requirements: Charisma.*

Immediately about five uses jumped into my head. Shit, what had I done pulling these out?

Mollecupai Mana Secretion Gland x 1

Type: Epic

Use: Crafted into armor or weapons to increase ambient Mana absorption rates.

What the fuck? What an idiot? I pulled it back into my inventory and gave Shi'enah a wink. "I'm going to hold on to a couple of these until we can figure out how everything works around here. I'd still like to sell a tentacle if you'll take it."

Shi'enah actually seemed relieved, and their shoulders relaxed almost imperceptibly. Maybe the price was too high and they'd get in trouble for buying it but also for not getting it. Two weeks into this new world and I still had absolutely no clue how these things were supposed to work.

Glancing at the tentacle, the host inspected it, frowned once, and looked at me. "I can give you thirty-two thousand Credits for this. But, should you get more, I would like an exclusive right of first refusal."

She was being truthful, and from what I could tell, sort of hedging a bet. I debated visibly for a second, mostly for show. "Deal."

I held out my hand and Shi'enah seemed surprised at first but then tapped me on my palm and bowed their head.

"Deal," they said, and a small smile played at the edges of their mouth.

Maybe I'd just made a business partner, but at least I hadn't angered the shopkeep, and that was a win for me.

"Where can I buy species information?" I asked casually as the exchange of Credits happened.

Shi'enah paused for a moment. "Third door down, as you know, has a massive collection of books. Go in, browse the catalogue, and type in what species you're trying to acquire information on. It should list them for you. Chjaveen isn't the best at communicating with his clients."

Being almost one hundred thousand Credits richer, I kept ten thousand to the side to transfer to the town later. Even though I knew the shopkeeps had to pay ten percent of what we paid them to buy things to the settlement in tax, the fact was that I wouldn't have a lot of the loot I had without the others who belonged to the city with me.

So I thought it was only fair that I donate some of the Credits I received into the town treasury. For now, at least.

"Done." Shi'enah glanced around themself, like they were afraid they might be overheard. "Just watch out. Mollecupai usually don't surface this quickly, even in Dungeon Worlds. Be careful out there."

Their voice was shushed and full of concern, and I wonder why Shi'enah had taken such an apparent liking to me. I didn't want to think about why those words made me expect complete and utter doom, but apparently something out there had the potential to be worse than an Apocalypse.

❖

Chjaveen sat behind a massive pile of books, languidly leafing through one of them. He barely even acknowledged my presence as I walked in. Good thing Shi'enah had given me some sort of direction or I'd be lost.

Except now my list was bigger. Mollecupai was smack bang at the top of it, because apparently if they popped up, you had a freaking amazing smorgasbord of crafting materials, not to mention a potential Credit. Now all we had to do was learn how to craft stuff.

Mollecupai and Their Inherent Destruction of Local Landmasses
Cost: 257 credits

The Mollecupai Myth: Do They or Don't They Exist?
Cost: 147 credits

I snorted at the second suggestion. Since I had very specific proof that they existed, the myth one didn't even cross my radar. First one seemed pretty interesting and was only a couple hundred credits, so I chose it.

Mollecupai: The Source of Their Power and the Downsides to Using It
Cost: 2,857 Credits

I raised an eyebrow at that one, but damn, it was tempting.

The Lonely Mollecupai
Cost: 65 credits

Mollecupai: Prolonged Clinical Trials of Mana-Bleed Item Usage and How it Can Kill You, Too
Cost: 3,682 credits

There were a lot of books, but so many of them were cheap, which in my eyes meant they probably didn't have much solid information for me.

Sadly, it seemed the more expensive the item, the more it would likely benefit me knowledge-wise.

I pursed my lips. Mollecupai weren't the reason I'd come to look for information, but they were certainly a good place to start. A few of these weren't going to hurt. Knowing your enemy was always a good start. Which was why I was here.

What I needed was information specifically on Mon'swkinon's species. Dash'Kiri or something. Searching for it brought up a lot less information than screens full of Mollecupai information and conjecture.

Maybe this species kept their secrets close to their chests. Even so, it appeared someone had been tattling.

The Secrets of the Dash'Kiri Clan
Cost: 14,852 Credits

The Dash'Kiri and Why You Can't Outrun a Death Curse
Cost: 12,894 Credits

IRSHA and the Legacy of the Dash'Kiri
Cost: 18,242 Credits

Okay, so. That was damn expensive. Maybe I wouldn't donate ten thousand to the city; I might just use it to get this information. It seemed like the more accurate or better researched the information was, the more it cost. So if these were that expensive, surely it had to have some good information in it, right?

Either that, or I was about to be made an utter fool of myself.

I took a deep breath and bought all the books I'd seen. Just shy of fifty-three thousand credits. I could practically feel the money just free-flowing out of me. Maybe I was a sucker about learning from books, but here we were, and the information just better be worth it.

Standing at the counter, Chjaveen handed me the books I'd bought with a raised eyebrow. "That's ssssome heavy reading you've got there."

I eyed the massive stack as I placed each of them in my inventory. The more expensive ones were thinner than the 147-Credits one. For a moment, I felt ripped off, except that book was very obviously someone spouting off, and I'd only bought it as a just-in-case.

"Thanks," I commented as I pushed out of the Shop and crossed the hall to the Skill Store. Now I only had forty thousand credits left from today's shopping, but I had a lot more left over from the previous days' combined. As long as I didn't spend the money on too much stupid stuff, I should be able to keep this up.

We hadn't walked into this particular department when I'd come with the kids the last few times. Wisp would have been reading everything, and I'd have trailed behind having to pay for everything and bleeding Credits in her wake.

This place was different.

Screens populated the place, in front of shelves that soared so high I couldn't even see the tops of them. Each of these had differing elements listed, or abilities. Like combat styles—broken into hand to hand, martial, sword, shield, gun, laser, pulse weapons, and so on. You name it; if there was a combat style in existence, it was likely here. Each of those categories were further broken down.

For example, pulse weapons fell into: pulse body armor, pistols, gloves, surgical eye implantations, and many more, some of which I wished I could wash from my memory. I didn't want weapons, though, nor did I want to look at styles of fighting just yet. Tempting as it was, I had other more immediate needs.

What I did want to do was find Skills.

Those I found along the very extensive back wall. I frowned, turning around in the store that seemed very Tardis-like. Much bigger on the inside than the outside. With its walls lined with books and screens at an appropriate eye level for a human, and the stacks that divided the room into different sections, it truly felt like a huge library.

Mana-based Skills and Abilities.

Yep, I was definitely in the right spot.

Mana Sense . . . I needed something on Mana Sense. To understand it as much as I could, to really know how to use the blasted ability. I was not expecting the sheer volume of information available on Mana Sense. Hundreds of thousands of entries.

From what Dolores had said, the affinity was rare, but apparently not galactically, as it were. Blew the wind out of my sails a bit, if I was honest. But I was nothing if not determined.

Thing was, I needed to refine the sorting. There was no way I could go through all of these. So I narrowed the search.

Mana Sense and Its Place in Your World
Cost: 6,482 Credits
Upon Completion: Mana Sense +1

That sounded oddly specific but also gave me an increase to the skill. Sign me up. I could read two hundred pages quickly. Frowning, I scrolled through the rest of the listing. So many seemed to say the same thing but be titled differently.

Understanding the Complexities of Mana Sense

Cost: 8,087 Credits

Upon Completion: Mana Sense +2

Okay, that one sounded about as good as I could hope for. The book hit maybe one hundred pages in length, and I frowned. It was so thin, and yet . . . I shrugged, deciding I was just going to dive in and go for it. Understanding anything about how all of my skills worked was only going to benefit me in the long run.

Mana Sense: A Cheater's Code?

Cost: 16,271 Credits

Upon Completion: Mana Sense +3

Note: There can be no partial credit allocated.

Now that one really piqued my interest, but that was a lot of money for something with little description and such a suspicious title. That one went in my maybe pile. I had plenty of other abilities I needed to check out too.

What about Mana Attunement? Ever since Mana Sense activated, I felt like Attunement sort of just . . . floated around in the background.

There was just so much in this damned Shop. So many abilities and so much Skill information. I definitely needed to upgrade some of mine. Maybe like Earth Barrier. Perhaps Implantation. From what I'd gathered, it was possible to purchase Skill Points, but the higher you needed it to go, the more they cost? Perhaps.

Although, on second thought, Implantation was already powerful enough. Dangerously so. It made me nervous, to be honest. I liked helping to defeat a creature, monster, whatever the hell these things were, but it felt strange to just implant something like that.

Seeds weren't supposed to be evil things. Even weeds had their own good qualities. There was nothing I could do except compare these things to my own experience with nature on Earth. Mana was like nature? Maybe? From everything I'd come to understand about it, Earth hadn't had enough of a Mana threshold before, and now it did and was overflowing, so we had become a Dungeon World. Right?

I think I needed to go back to the other side of the store and do some more research. Reluctantly, I forked over money for my Mana Sense books and headed back out. I'd pretty much blown all the cash I earned today, but I wasn't only protecting myself with knowledge, but my kids, my family, and hell . . . the whole freaking town.

Just about to leave the foyer, I paused.

There really was one thing I needed to do, one thing I had to check, because hanging onto the hope was unhealthy for myself and my kids. Just because I ignored it didn't mean it didn't happen.

Taking a deep breath, I approached the terminal to the side of the counter where Shi'enah appeared to be cataloguing something. Mason. I just needed to check. Sweat broke out along my forehead, and I could see my hands physically shaking.

Do you wish to receive information on: Mason Kent-Alon (Location)?
Cost: 232 Credits
Yes or No

That was odd. I'd heard checking on family members to double check they were dead only cost like fifty credits. Did that mean he was alive? And could anyone *anywhere* access information on individual players through the system?

Shit. That meant they could access information on myself and my kids. No. That wasn't okay, but I didn't know why I hadn't thought of it before. Surely there had to be ways for us to conceal our identities or at least parts of our identities from prying rich fucks.

Oh, hell.

Did that mean IRSHA already knew all of our information? I needed to avert the panic—that I'd just spent a lot of money on information and none of it on concealing my own. Mason. That's right. My ex.

Mason Kent-Alon

Status: Alive

Location: Gold Coast Australia

Class: Entertainer

Level: 19

I smiled despite myself. Of course he was alive. I could tell the kids now without having to hide anything, I could let them know their dad was still with us and maybe, just maybe we could meet up with him at some stage. The relief that rushed through me hurt. Like someone was squeezing my heart. Mason and I had a very amicable breakup as far as divorce was concerned. He'd always wanted to be a dad, but he wasn't good dad material. Don't get me wrong; he was great with the kids, as their friend.

But he didn't know how to be anything else. And he was a musician at heart, and being tied to one spot, it really just wasn't his thing. He loved our kids, and he'd been a great father, but I'd resented him for not being a parent.

Divorce freed up that resentment. He'd never missed a child support payment, nor had he ever missed a visitation until the Apocalypse hit. Even if he was halfway around the country, he would fly back just for that day, just to be with his kids.

The lump in my throat at knowing he was alive didn't really surprise me. He was, after all, one of my best friends. I took a deep breath and calmed myself down. Contemplating another purchase, I stopped myself. Knowing about mum and dad right now wasn't going to help me in any way.

One step at a time.

Now, I needed to take care of myself and my kids and protect the information about us that others could gain access to. I also wanted to see how much retrieving information on Mon'swkinon of the Dash'Kiri was going to cost me. Know thine enemy, right?

About to sit myself down and dive into these bloody expensive books, I heard a chime-like noise echo through my head and immediately received a popup. Odd, though, that I'd never had that sound before.

New Quest Completion!

A Habitable Safe Zone has been completed within the allotted time. Sadly, you took too much time and will not be receiving a bonus. Do better next time.

Part Two: Power

You have completed development of the casing needed to attract Mana to power your town, enabling the amenities you've lost.

You only used 22% of Shop items to manufacture your repositories. Well done.

Reward: 20,000 Credits and the ability to power your settlement. Access to the third and final Part of this Quest.

New Quest Granted:

A Habitable Safe Zone

Part Three: Staying Power

Congrats! You made it this far—well behind the rest of the civilized Earth, but then, look where you are. Considering your location, you should be proud to take this next step.

You need to make it three months into System Onset as a Township.

Goals:

1 - Gather 3,000 total inhabitants. This may include visiting species. Current population 1,423/3,000

2 - Build your defenses and successfully survive and remain in your growing township for three months from System Onset.

Time completed: 2 weeks/13 weeks

Reward: 45,000 Credits for your city Treasury, [unknown] reward

Time Remaining: 11 weeks

Good luck! You'll definitely need it.

Fucking hell. I flopped back down on the bed, pulled the damned book up to my face, and started reading.

Chapter Three:

Notifications

Two Weeks Post-System Onset

6 a.m.

"Kira!"

The shout ripped me out of my slumber and sent me tumbling off the small makeshift cot I'd been sleeping on to hit the hard tiled floor beneath me. I groaned, wishing for a moment that I'd have stayed in the department store on the plush beds.

"What is it?" I stumbled out into the corridor, scratching at the welt on my face I was pretty sure came from falling asleep on an open book. It was a good thing that Wisp hadn't woken up, though I did notice Dog eyeing me through the glass.

"We have visitors." Leena—Ray's sister, if I was remembering correctly—was out of breath and flushed. She'd probably run all the way.

"Not again." I swear aliens had no manners. But I moved even as the thoughts ran through my head, a sense of urgency guiding me.

"Well." Leena sounded unsure as she half jogged to keep up with my longer stride. "It's not the same aliens. These ones are different, not as scary, and specifically asked for you."

That piqued my interest. Directly asking for me was either going to be a really good thing, or a super bad one. The gates were open when I got there, and a small group had gathered beneath them.

And here I thought I was the only one having sleeping problems.

As I approached, I noticed a few things:

Kyle stood back, his arms crossed, his observing-everything face locked in.

Evelyn's hand rested loosely on her bow, but I could tell there was no real tension in her shoulders from the way she stood.

And thirdly, our visitors were short. Like super short. They had delicate features and cute snub noses and stood about four feet tall. They were too slender of bone structure to be dwarves, so they had to be gnomes. Or that at least was my opinion what with my vast knowledge of fantastical creatures.

What on Earth, and I guess in the galaxy, were gnomes doing right in front of me?

I blinked and activated Analyze on the one talking the most. He gestured widely while he spoke, and everyone around him hung on each word uttered.

Ginali Tomias

Species: Pharyleri

Clan: Gnomidarion

Master Artificer

Level 7

❖

Just as I finished, his eyes met mine and his expression lit up. "Kira Kent! I believe I need to speak with you."

Ginali wasn't wrong, and he was definitely filled with a friendliness that didn't inspire wariness. It wasn't fake, and I'd equipped my hammer on the way out the door, so I assumed it wasn't due to a Skill. His eyes sparkled as he approached me slowly, his entourage close behind. The others moved with him. There were around half a dozen at first count, several of them similar in stature to Ginali, dressed in tunics and pants. Some of it moved more stiffly than cloth, probably a type of armor.

One of them really caught my eye. Completely different from any of the others facing us.

She resembled an armadillo on two legs, with a human-like face. Her armor extended all around her, with differing colors that made it appear to be clothing, and yet I wasn't sure it was. Her eyelashes would have been the envy of every single cosmetics company on the face of the Earth before the Apocalypse hit. I could feel eagerness radiating off her, and it lent me a sense of calmness.

This group of beings was happy to be here. Excited, even. No deadly intentions lurking beneath the surface that I could feel.

"I am Ginali, the Coefficient Crafting Cartel representative in charge of overseeing this outpost." The Master Artificer bowed his head, paused, and then held out a small hand only somewhat hesitantly.

I shook it, a part of me amused that he seemed to have researched customs or something. His own shake was vigorous, reminding me of a happy puppy excited to meet someone new.

"I have brought crafters with me, versed in many of our main areas. This"—he motioned for the armadillo girl to move forward, and she did, although I could practically feel her nervous excitement radiating outward—"This is Malina. She is our Apothecary. Any type of potion you need, poultice, wrap, brew . . . she is brilliant!"

The pride in his voice was obvious, and it made me want to know more about how this new universe of ours worked. I held out my hand and Malina took it, while I used the opportunity to analyze her.

Malina

Species: Panodillia

Master Apothecary

Level 12

She smiled at me; at least I was fairly sure it was a smile. "It is a pleasure." Her eyes darted around, and I saw surprise. Perhaps she'd expected something different on this deadly continent, considering how much of a chance the System seemed to have given us.

"I cannot wait to see all of the new ingredients we find here."

Ah, there it was. Professional curiosity. That, I totally got. Ginali took that moment to clear his throat.

"Now, now. Let's get down to business then, shall we. I realize its early and you've likely got a whole lot of things to be doing, but you completed the System quest and thus have granted us the ability to set up our remote outpost. Thank you for that." He winked before stepping through into Garden City itself where he stopped short.

"This is, unexpected."

His expression was difficult to read, though it didn't set off any alarm bells. He appeared to be genuinely surprised about where we found ourselves. Maybe Garden City wasn't their run-of-the-mill usual settling ground. I guess even intergalactic travelers weren't used to entire town-sized shopping centers.

"Impressive." He nodded, and I think he was mostly speaking to himself. Then he clapped his hands together, almost shocking the crap out of me, and continued. "Now—where would you like the Cartel to set up?"

I glanced at Dor as she approached us, marveling at her impeccable timing. The older woman with salt and pepper hair never failed to amaze me. All bone and sinew, she exuded a strength I only hoped to emulate someday.

"I have the perfect place." She sounded efficient and businesslike. Less like she was going to tell us to get off her lawn. Relief started to flood through me because I'd had no idea where we were going to put the

Cartel . . . and then she motioned for us to follow her.

Fantastic.

I plastered a smile on my face, ignoring my brain trying to coax me to go back and get more sleep. I tagged along with the Pharyleri congregation as we all followed Dor. She took us through most of the main level and out past the Raybucks toward the courtyard.

Of course!

That made perfect sense. There would be enough room in the restaurants that spanned around for them to set up multiple different types of workstations. There were even outdoor spots where things like smelting that required more ventilation could easily set up and not poison us all. Or I assumed that was her plan, anyway.

Ginali's face lit up as he stood in the middle of the courtyard, just up from the AMC theater, and turned around slowly. His smile spread so wide I thought his face was going to flip open.

"This is an excellent spot. Easy access from multiple points." Then he frowned, like he was calculating some things. "Yes. Ability to expand as the Cartel grows in stock and influence. This is perfect for this end of the galaxy. Thank you!"

That flippant gesture about this end of the galaxy sent a couple of shivers down my spine. Sure, here we were, in my backyard, on the arse end of the galaxy.

I asked the question I'd been wanting to know since I realized this Cartel was an actual thing. "What do you need us to do?"

Ginali smiled. "Why, just bring us all your crafters. We will require apprentices—from cooks to armor workers, weapons makers, carapace shapers, cloth workers, metal workers . . . so many of us. We brought masters and several journeymen who are probably still making their way from the portal we opened."

He counted off something on his fingers, his brow pinched in concentration.

Portal? They opened a portal . . .

"Yes—they will be bringing all the necessary gear up so we can work on setting up properly. It'll take a few days. Then we'll be able to get the trading hub up and running. Now keep in mind, we will need crafting materials. We will pay well for them, but not always as well as the Shop. In return, you do receive a twenty percent discount on anything you purchase from us for the next five Earth years. We really hope that makes it a fair trade while we get set up and operating from this place."

He glanced around appreciatively. "It doesn't seem nearly as deadly as they made it out to be."

I wasn't certain, but I think he sounded disappointed.

And thus began a long morning of meetings and discussions and figuring out who could and would apprentice to our newly found friends.

❖

14 Days Post-System Onset
8 a.m.

Our quarters, in what used to be the old Body Shop, were small but cozy. Even the camping cot was surprisingly comfortable. I flopped down on it, determined to get through some of the meatier books I'd paid a small fortune for the previous evening.

Speaking of money, I was bleeding Credits. Kiddo's information had been protected under some System Act of Protection of Minors or something, but my own? Cost a whopping eighteen thousand to secure.

I desperately needed to go find me some more Mollecupai and harvest their organs. Because it was just that easy, of course.

It was nice and shaded inside here since the only light streamed through the glass windows from the skylights above. Somewhere along the way, Wisp had hung long-ass sheets from the glass windows at the front of the store, effectively concealing our little apartment, as she liked to call it.

The marginal noise reduction certainly helped, but I wanted an actual house sooner rather than later. That way we could use apartments like these for survivors and newcomers to Garden City.

Propping myself up, I reached over and pulled out my reading materials. So many books. I'd read most of the Mollecupai ones so far. After all, I'd always been a fast reader, but I still had: *Mollecupai: Prolonged Clinical Trials of Mana-Bleed Item Usage and How It Can Kill You Too* left. The damned thing wasn't even thick.

Opening it, I placed it against my propped-up knees and smoothed the first page with my hand. As soon as my hand lay flat, a spinning sensation assaulted me. Like I was in one of those Gravitron rides, being slammed against the meager padding with centrifugal force. Knowledge exploded in my head like I'd opened a floodgate.

Suddenly I understood how Mana-bleed items could potentially kill you or others around you. Pulling too much or too little, standing in the way of rushing Mana and channeling it through your body.

Holy crap.

When my head stopped spinning, my breath came to me in ragged gasps, and I felt like a truck had just run over me. But above all—I knew what the book had contained. Why the hell didn't the others do that?

And I realized—those books were cheap. This one was super thin and basically just a scientific study on about eighty pages of parchment. Yet it had cost me close to four thousand Credits.

I glanced over at the other books. Especially those about the

Dash'Kiri, and eagerly plucked them from the pile. These ones had cost an arm and a leg, and while a few hundred pages long, I was pretty certain I was about to get the same information injection as the others had.

Reaching down, I grabbed a half-empty water bottle from next to my bed and chugged down what remained. Thirsty for knowledge? Sure, I'd take that pun.

Except . . . I really wanted to understand my Mana Sense on a whole other level. I put that book back down and picked up the *Mana Sense and Its Place in Your World* one. I mean, realistically, it would give me enough information that I could skill up, right?

At least I hoped so. It had cost a pretty penny, and it wasn't a thick book. Taking a deep breath, I placed my hand on the first page of the book. Information flooded my brain, making it momentarily difficult to inhale.

The information felt like it was just out of reach of comprehension though, which didn't seem right. This wasn't about the differing levels of Mana; it was more about how Mana came to inhabit the world and how it worked as a force in the universe. At what point saturation was reached . . .

Once the deluge of knowledge stopped, I received a popup.

Congratulations you have gained a new skill.
Mana Sense (2) +1

What. The. Hell? Quickly, I opened my Status Screen.

Status Screen			
Name	Kira Kent	Class	Ecological Chain Specialist
Race	Human (Female)	Level	23 (4,252 XP to next Level)

Titles			
Diviner			
Health	300	Stamina	300
Mana	650	Mana Regeneration	44 / minute
Attributes			
Strength	27	Agility	27
Constitution	32	Perception	58
Intelligence	70	Willpower	47
Charisma	25	Luck	18
Class Skills			
Mana Attunement	2	Earth Barricade	2
Blood Transfer	1	Mudslide	1
Water Siphon	2	Mana Transfer	1
Rockslide	1	Implantation	2
Skills			
Leadership	3	Mana Sense	4
Blunt Weapons	4	Mana Sense (2)	1
Combat Spells			
Shield of Power*			
Perks			
Diviner		Analyze	
Mana Cloak 2			

That didn't even make sense. How . . .

It couldn't be translation problems, could it? I mean, there had to be a plethora of intergalactic languages out there, and we'd only recently been incorporated. Maybe it was a translation problem. As annoyed as I was, I couldn't change the fact that I'd absorbed the knowledge now. It wasn't exactly what I'd wanted, but it was sort of related.

I needed to figure out the translations before I attempted any more of this Mana Sense information absorption. Because the last thing I needed was more skills with that bloody name.

I deliberately pushed the rest of the Mana Sense books to the side and focused on the others. For now, I needed those even more anyway.

A couple of deep breaths later, I gently placed the first of the Dash'Kiri books on my lap and opened to the first page. This time when I placed my hand flat onto it, the rush didn't surprise me as much. But the turbulent circles my mind twirled in still happened and still took my breath away.

The Secrets of the Dash'Kiri Clan
The Dash'Kiri and Why You Can't Outrun a Death Curse
IRSHA and the Legacy of the Dash'Kiri

These three books cost me almost forty-five thousand Credits. And from the information pouring into my brain as it agitated like an upright washing machine, every one of those Credits was well spent. Death curses would require a little more research to understand fully. I wasn't sure why I seemed to be retaining this with pinpoint clarity; perhaps it was my Intelligence numbers, but my brain felt almost computer-like.

The Dash'Kiri clan was pretty screwed up. Their involvement with IRSHA wasn't just partaking, but an integral part of their heritage. If their children didn't make it into IRSHA, which apparently had pretty strict hunting capability guidelines, then they were banished from their families and doomed to roam the galaxy alone.

With Mon'swkinon as our enemy, we had to best him or kill him—or align with him. There was no possibility of reconciliation beyond those three options. Not exactly what I'd wanted to read. He hadn't seemed like the reasoning-and-same-side type.

Overall, potentially dealing with Mon'swkinon was starting to be my least favorite thing to consider.

There was too much information floating through my mind. Just because it was all in there didn't mean I'd been able to process it all yet.

At least my kids were protected. The familial protection provided by the System in order to foster whatever it was it wanted meant that minors were protected by searches. Their dad was alive, my info was hidden, and I'd passed on that tidbit to everyone else after the Cartel meeting a few hours ago, so what was bugging me? Why did I feel so damned uncomfortable?

Evelyn knocked on the door and I looked up, motioning her to come in. There wasn't really any privacy in any of these apartments, but I guess Wisp had done her best with ours. She was off right now with Dog and Wombie or whatever she called that slowly growing marsupial. Evelyn stepped inside and let herself fall on Kyle's bed.

"This is such a clusterfuck," she said to no one in particular. I knew she meant the whole Apocalypse situation, but you know, after two weeks, I was sort of over it. This was the new Earth and we either got used to it, or we died.

Still, I did agree. "Yes. It's a prime example of a clusterfuck too," I said it with all seriousness, and she burst out laughing.

"Did you picture it like this?" she asked, waving her arms as if to encompass the entire world.

I shook my head. "No. No, I did not."

We sat in silence for a bit. "Just got some info on IRSHA and what we might be facing. When I've had time to process it, I'll fill everyone in."

"Good, good."

She didn't sound like it was good. Evelyn sounded positively off on a totally different train of thought. I waited for a couple of minutes, but growing silence never sat well with me.

"Well?" I asked and waited.

"Your kids are happy. Not like they sing and dance or anything, but you can see their relief in knowing their dad is alive."

Ah, that's what was getting to her.

"Did you check for yours?"

I'd asked the question softly, and at first, she didn't respond, though I could see her eyes welling up a bit. I guess that answered it for me. She was braver than me though; I'd not even managed to work up the courage to check on my parents yet.

"Mason is about forty kilometers away. If he can get here, he will, but with what's out there, I'm not counting on anything." I'm not entirely sure why I felt the need to soothe her about Mason. Evelyn and I were . . . what we were.

Comrades-in-arms, friends, more things as yet undefined. Rocks for each other to lean on. We were stuck in this shithole together and had fought through losing friends and battle mates, and somehow remained alive ourselves. What we had was necessary.

This new world didn't require definitions. It was enough that we existed.

She turned to me and smiled. "This end of the world just isn't what I'd expected."

"Nope. Definitely not. No zombies, for starters."

"Not yet, anyway."

I smiled at her, happy to have found someone that I felt comfortable enough to talk with about aspects I might otherwise bottle up. "Yeah. Not yet, at least. For all we know, there could be necromancers."

Evelyn laughed. "I hope not. That's not a nice visual." She squeezed my hand and stood up to leave. "Hey, Kira?"

"Mhm?" My mind was already halfway off again trying to figure out how I could predict what our new opponents might do.

"Thanks for listening." She hesitated, and I watched her, wishing I could read minds better than body language. "Just thanks for stepping in when we first met. I'm pretty glad I'm not a casualty."

She left the room, and I couldn't help but hear the echo of a yet at the end of what she'd said.

Strange, how an unspoken word could leave me cold.

Chapter Four:

Bookworm

Two Weeks Post-System Onset

1 p.m.

The Dash'Kiri were truly terrifying. They weren't so much a species as a cult of interwoven species from what I could tell, crossbreeding deliberately to produce the most stout, terrifying warriors they could. No two Dash'Kiri appeared to be exactly the same, and thus, neither were their weaknesses nor strengths. You know, just to complicate things.

The only weakness I could find was pride. But I just wasn't sure if needling them enough to make them explode was a good way to go about having them make a mistake or a really, really stupid mistake on my part.

I guess they did seem to be rather honorable. For the hunters that they purported to be, I'd assumed they'd just steamroll us and take the settlement. But they appeared to prize honor and the sapience of those that they fought.

We were lucky that they considered us too intelligent to hunt.

With any luck, maybe we could leverage that to our advantage. Though I had no idea how to just yet.

Next time I was going to search for a book on: *Hi, my world just got taken over as a Dungeon World. How do I avoid dying to a hunting group's claim of ownership?*

"Mum?" Wisp pushed through into the room, followed very closely by Dog, who appeared, for once, to be highly concerned. I didn't think he'd grown anymore, and for all appearances was about the height of a large Great Dane now, though fluffier and bulkier, sort of like Lassie. He'd definitely mutated into his own creature.

The lumbering and clumsy Wombie followed, half rolling, half moving as he clambered behind my daughter. He was around the size of a Shetland pony now, and I wasn't certain how much longer he'd be able to stay in the center with us before he needed to go out and join his Mum.

"What's up, Whisper?" I asked, holding out my arms with the sudden need for a kid hug to warm the cockles of my heart.

She ran in and squeezed with all her strength, which was considerable and hadn't diminished since the shit hit the fan. "Mum hugs are the best hugs."

"I know, right?" I ruffled her hair and looked down at her. "What's up, buttercup?"

"Oh. Nothing? I mean, Dolores sent me to find you. Apparently they all want a meeting soon."

"Define 'soon' and how long it took you to get the message to me?" I tried to be stern, but I couldn't stay that way.

Wisp was a curious kid. Always had been. There was no doubt in my mind that she'd stopped along the way to chat with others, find friends, and follow any type of insect that had managed to get into the Center.

"Maybe thirty minutes?" She really thought about it and nodded, as if to reinforce the time's accuracy. "And after dinner. Which is like almost now."

I really needed to read those Mana books. But I wasn't doing that until I'd figured out this whole thing with a second Mana Sense skill. Those books might be my last ones, but if they weren't going to increase the Mana Sense skill I wanted them to increase, I'd see if I could get a refund. To say I was unimpressed was definitely an understatement.

I was going to have to stop by the Shop so I could figure out exactly what was happening with my skills.

That, and my head still felt like it was spinning occasionally. Maybe there was only so much information I could take in at a time.

After dinner, and after the meeting. I'd get to it then.

Though I had a sneaking suspicion that our dear IRSHA friends weren't just going to let us sit here and power up our skills. We needed to stay on top of defenses and figure out how best to utilize our new Crafting Cartel friends in order to protect our town.

"Okay. Okay." I grabbed the Mana books and popped them in my inventory, snagging a couple of the others for good measure. Wasn't sure others would just get the brain insertion of information, because I doubted it would be that cheap, but maybe they could at least read the information and absorb it in the old-fashioned way.

Calling my Warhammer out of inventory, I equipped it so that it dangled heavily at my side. Even though I know she didn't mean anything by it, I couldn't afford to let Sienna's Charisma affect how I tackled issues that could impact my kids.

Damn, did I need to up my Mental Resistance.

What I liked about the Garden City Council Library was how airy it felt. From the paned windows that let in plenty of light, to the brown flooring interspersed with multiple blue-hued tiles, it felt like we weren't necessarily indoors. Although, let me tell you, the air conditioning a hundred percent gave that away in the summer.

I digress.

The kid's area was filled with arched window paintings and had a gorgeous secret garden vibe to it. It's why Wisp often came with me and just settled down, nestling with one of the thousands of books she had access to. I don't think I could express adequately how grateful I was that my kid at least got to experience some of the library fun of childhood.

The usual suspects had showed up. Kyle and Dale, Sienna and Dolores, Evelyn and Ray, Chris and Red, myself and now some members of the Cartel, it seemed.

I was never much of a Risk player. The board game, that is. Never got it, never understood it, got bored with it way too easily, but my brother? That was his thing. I watched him as he stood there, frowning at the digital map of the surroundings as it cast itself in the library in our meeting place. It turned this and that way as Kyle, Dale, and Mike instructed it to, casting off different shades of light here and there.

Strategy games were everything to my brother and father. At least he could still have that.

Kyle's dark curly hair was finally less disheveled. That must have taken some doing since it took a while to get it back under control. He was clean shaven again, too. Lucky us, with all of the stocked items in the stores, it allowed us to portion out everyone's favorites, giving everyone a fair go at getting something they loved. I was so glad Dolores put several people under Red who was in charge of inventory control.

My twin had lost weight, his cheekbones hollowed out, and I felt a stab of worry in my gut for him. There were shadows under his eyes, and his clothes, while clean, were in disarray. It was such a far cry from his usual sophisticated doctor persona.

Walking all the way here from the hospital, dragging the survivors with him, had laid nightmares at his doorstep. Still, he was in his element here, treating the surrounding defenses like an open chest on his operation table.

Even so, striding around the table, muttering to himself, he seemed younger than ever. That old Aussie Rules injury he'd sustained in high school wasn't stiffening up his right knee like it used to. Different but the same. He'd always been able to fly through the sky when going for a lob, but that one waist tackle as he came down from a jump had put him out of commission for three weeks. He often lamented it was the whole reason he became a doctor instead of trying to play for a club.

All I could think was that the System was keeping us alive for a reason, patching all our injuries together and grafting Mana bits onto us to make sure we survive. I just didn't know why it felt the need to be a Frankenstein to us all.

Our town funds were getting low, and while donations were pouring in from most people, not everyone was able to contribute that much, considering the majority of our people weren't Adventurers. Still, with an average of a thousand credits per person and a population of 1,423, we had almost one and a half million credits to use for upgrades.

"Kira? What do you think?" Sienna asked, her tone all full of business. Even though I had my Warhammer equipped, I could still feel the underlying tug of her Skill Coaxing Shadows, a Skill I knew she wasn't trying to actively engage. Politician-type Classes probably all got that Charisma boosting, trust-me vibe going for them.

"I think I have no clue about defense stuff. That's more Kyle's area of expertise. Though I do know we have to fend them off for as long as we can. I just wish I knew when or if they were heading back here." I strode over to the table, staring absently at the map but not really seeing it as I mused out loud. "I wonder if we can figure out if any of the other settlements are owned?"

"Of course we can." Sienna sighed and shared a portion of the settlement interface with me. "See? Easy. But it costs. Like every damn thing. Credits for this. Credits for that. I'm surprised they haven't though to charge us for air yet."

"Don't you go givin' them ideas, dear." Dolores piped in; her tone dry. Thing was, I thought she was only half kidding.

A mild chuckle echoed through the room, but I could feel the discomfort underneath it. Reaching into my inventory, I plopped my Dash'Kiri and IRSHA piles of books onto the table next to me. Not the Mollecupai, though; those I wanted to share with a select few until I could talk to Ginali alone about how the crafting elements were going to work in this hybrid brave new world. "I've been trying to find out exactly what we're up against."

Dor raised an eyebrow. "Hitting the books. Would never have thought of it." She laughed a bit ruefully, like in this weird apocalyptic wasteland, searching for information in the form of books was the last thing she'd considered. "Got a TLDR version for us?"

I laughed despite the pit in the middle of my stomach. After all, knowledge of and building defenses against something were two entirely different things. "IRSHA aren't interested in Galactic politics or ownership or what happened to Earth or Australia. They're not interested in anything other than finding the rarest, most dangerous mutated creatures and bringing them back as trophies. That—and acquiring rare items from those corpses for trading or sale purposes—is their only goal. As far as I can tell, anyway.

"Well, the trophies are taxidermies, and the innards of those rare creatures sell for stupid amounts of Credits. That's what they were banking on, as far as I can tell. Australia happens to be classified as 'not survivable' on a brand-spanking-new Dungeon World. That apparently ups our potential number of unique mutations and, of course, the danger factor. None of us were supposed to survive the initial few days."

Shrugging at that uncomfortable thought, I attempted a smile to soften the fact that we were just considered dead people walking. "So basically, we could probably, like, buy the information from the Shop, I guess? Feels like you can just buy anything there if you have the Credits. Anyway, it seems IRSHA purchased the rights from the System or from the Galactic Council—I'm still not sure what the difference is, or if there is one—to claim, and thereby purchase, our unclaimed settlements."

"Wait." Sienna pinched the bridge of her nose. "The System predicted that we would not survive the onset of the Dungeon World in sufficient quantities to own settlements. Because of this, and the fact that we have high levels of rare mutations here, this IRSHA group bought the rights to purchase unoccupied settlements in Australia. So they thought they'd be able to buy them all and claim a monopoly?"

"Sounds right." I nodded.

Kyle piped in. "Guess we put a spanner in their works. Or something."

Dale waved a hand. "Wait. Wait. What are they going to do? Like are they going to siege us?"

I shrugged. "From what Mon'swkinon said, they apparently respect other sapient creatures and thus won't hunt us down? But I'm not sure that applies to all of them. Wouldn't it be better for them to consolidate what they can still purchase and just worry about us later?"

Kyle began to pace. "Maybe? I mean, all things aside, they're trained hunters of rare monsters. Can't they just race us to rare spawns and beat us every time? Isn't that why they're here in the first place?"

Dale cracked his neck from side to side, appearing more restless than before. Maybe he felt like I did—I'd finally got my kids to safety and had a potential new home, and yet here we were . . . potentially under siege, in danger yet again. He ran a hand through his brown hair and eyed Kyle. "No clue, mate. But standing and chatting about it isn't going to make us any stronger, right?"

"Right." Kyle nodded, and a gleam of determination entered his eyes. "Right . . ."

Ray clapped his hands together, and I noticed that he too looked marginally younger, not that he'd had far to go. His short black hair no longer had that disheveled look like when I'd first met him, and I had to think the System had made him a tad taller than he'd originally been, topping out around six feet tall. Any younger and he'd be a toddler in diapers. Still, he'd grown into his Ice Mage Class over the last couple of weeks since meeting him. "Do we reckon they're coming back any time soon? Now? Later? Tomorrow?"

Dale shrugged. We all echoed the motion. Not as though anyone of us had an Alien Mind Reading Skill.

How useful would that be?

"Probably? We need to get stronger, so we can't just wait around for them to come to us. We need to be watching out for them, making sure we have advanced warning," Dale finally said.

"There are security options for that." Sienna piped up, fiddling with something in front of her, A second later, blue light bloomed on top of the table so that everyone could catch a glimpse. "There are options in this whole City Management software or whatever it is that adds external perimeter alerts for different distances. The further they are from the actual gates, the more expensive they are. Not to mention that we can get turrets for the walls, and more offensive defenses."

She paused there for a second and looked at Kyle. "That's what we were fiddling with before, trying to figure out what all of it did." She exhaled suddenly, sounding tired. "There's thousands of options in here. Many are still greyed out because we don't have the funds or the prerequisites, but this is city planning on a whole different level."

There was such wonder in her voice, I found myself smiling. Maybe we would be okay, at least for a while. Dale mulled over her words while Kyle spoke up. "I think we should reinforce what we have and take a look at the best options. I mean restrict things out of our boundaries to that which we can't visibly see. Things that might pop up behind buildings just beyond our boundaries. That sort of thing."

Dor pursed her lips and folded her arms, and if I squinted, I could almost see the thoughts racing through her head. "Solid train of thought." She activated a preview several lines of defenses deep, so much that I couldn't follow what her train of activation was, and then she frowned.

"We need to account for stealth, like that Rigoll creature did when we sent our scouts out. It might be best to make sure every person in here is registered and anyone else who crosses the threshold and is not registered has a five-minute window to become so? Or to have a delegate from our welcoming committee greet them."

"How would that make any difference to what we're already doing?" Dale said.

Dor grinned. "It's not really different, but when we have survivors approaching us now, they come to the gates and are greeted by one of the committee. They're accepted and begin processing the moment we discover them, so the System identifies them already as members of our little town." She took a breath, like she was trying to find her bearings in her train of thought.

"But for anyone who enters without permission . . . this would include harpies flying overhead and getting into our airspace. Birds, flying transports, and the people on them. Stealthers scaling walls." She waited a moment while she let the words sink in. "Basically, we automatically categorize anyone who isn't greeted as enemies. And that gives us a burglar alarm, if you will."

It really was a simple—yet brilliant—concept. But if what I was seeing on the screens that Dolores called up was correct, it was also going to cost a lot of Credits. I found it so strange that we'd gone from being a capitalism-corrupted society to having an alien invasion that ended up being by another capitalism-corrupted society. Way to let me down, intergalactic evolution.

"So wait." It hit me, and I had to stop myself from giggling with overtiredness. "IRSHA purchased the rights to buy settlements in our country, but each settlement orb would still cost them once they got here. That means they'd already have to put in defenses and whatnot. There must have been some Credit benefit in it for them. I wonder if they have a minimum percentage of settlements or control that they needed to fulfill."

"Wouldn't surprise me. If they got a contract giving them such broad requirements, there was probably a pretty big catch to it." Dolores' eyes sparkled. "Nice to put a dent in their plans, right?"

"Yeah." And I meant it, but at the same time I couldn't help worrying about just how they'd react to that rather large dent. Because there was no way in hell that we were the only Aussies who'd survived.

"Might be an idea to have a fundraiser?"

Every single person looked at me and I could feel the parent-committee soul rising in me. "No fucking bake sales. For the protection of everyone in here, people need to look through what they can afford and donate to help up our security protocols. Taxes for the Shop are set. And I know a percentage is sent to the treasury from buyers and sellers. Do you think we have the time to raise the funds that gradually?"

"I'm not sure. . . . I can cast projections though and figure out what we'll need when." Sienna pursed her lips thoughtfully. "Leave it with me. I'll figure out a way to get everyone on board. Pretty sure no one in this settlement wants us to lose it."

I nodded, happy to delegate community management to Sienna. Dor made her way over, the pair of them putting their heads together to properly manipulate our populace. In the meantime, I glanced around as the rest of us gathered to figure out how best to Level, gain strength, and defend our home.

"I think we're about done here." Mike spoke up in that quietly confident voice that always managed to span the entire room. With his sturdy physique and lean muscle mass, he'd been a great choice for our security chief. "Dale and Molly will finalize adventurer teams and set you all out on leveling rotations. Gather in the carpark near the northeast gate."

I could feel the excitement in the room at that announcement.

The library had turned into an excellent administration hub. Enough seats, enough reference material, and enough room.

I watched as people filed out. Chris and Sarah were heading back to their little tech hub. Dale and Kyle had their heads down as they walked, probably discussing more about the healing teams. I was glad my brother had found someone he could connect with.

Ray, our Ice Mage, and Tasha, our Fighter-Mage, walked side by side. Maybe they'd found a sense of solidarity in each other. Molly and Sange, our Tank and Healer, respectively, were as close as ever.

Even Drake and Gary, former enemies until we thwapped them over the head, had become contributing members. They were here on good behavior, representing the people who'd come with them.

In fact, they both really seemed to be trying to make up for being such dicks during our first encounter. For their conscience's sake, I hoped they were genuine.

I hadn't even noticed that Morton and Eritia—from when we'd fought that the Rigoll slug—had been in the library too. Gunslinger and fire girl. Yeah. His hair was closely shaven, and probably had been black at one stage, but white salted it now. Sort of like gunpowder. And Eritia's close-cropped chestnut hair reminded me of the fiery glow of autumn leaves during sunset. Their appearances matched their Classes.

We were an odd bunch.

"So. What's got your goat?" Dor elbowed me in the ribs as I stood watching the others go on their way. She'd already gathered a couple of the books I'd left in her arms.

"What?" I turned to her, rather perturbed. I thought I'd been hiding my irritation better.

She shrugged. "Books and stocking up on info. Not going all gung-ho into the void. You don't seem nearly as excited about the Cartel as I thought you'd be. What gives?"

There was an uneasiness in my bones that I couldn't pinpoint or put a name to, but she was dead right. Something about this whole situation, not just the apocalypse, but the rest of it. The settlement, the fact that they'd assumed our continent would be wiped out.

There were instances of information that trickled through to us that made absolutely no sense at all. "It really pisses me off that this System discounted us without a true understanding of the country and our creatures. I'm not a violent person usually; I like to research, assess, and plan a course of action. But that IRSHA and the System—they make me inordinately angry."

Dor watched me for a few seconds, her face thoughtful. "We need to get you higher mental protections. You working Willpower? My Den Mother Class allows for me to basically protect everyone around me by knowing how to see through bullshit. Sure, it's a lot more complicated than that, but working on that Willpower attribute will do you wonders."

"Already doing that, Dor. But thanks. Maybe it's just my impatience. I was doing fine until these bastards didn't understand how to keep an appointment they had arranged themselves. But now .. now I'm just irritated. Hell, I'm worried about my kids and their safety." I gestured around, hoping she realized I meant that I was angry at the entire universe.

"That's not new though, is it?" Again, that gentle prodding.

I shrugged. "You know, I was meant to go on a trip into the Amazon to examine flora and fauna in four months? Total dream expedition. Mason was even going to step in for the six months I'd be gone."

"Sucks, sure. But that's not all." Dor prodded again, more gently than I'd ever heard her speak.

Damn it. I hated it when people saw through me when I was still trying to kid myself.

"No. No, it's not." The thing was, I still wasn't entirely certain why I was so irritated. "Something out there decided to drop us all into this, without our choice in the matter. I've spent my entire life fighting against stereotypes, fighting against the unfair workplace treatment of women. Being a woman in STEM . . ." I shuddered theatrically—well, maybe not so theatrically.

Dor made a sympathetic face, though something flashed in her eyes. With her age, perhaps she'd faced even harder, bigger—or maybe just different—problems.

I kept ranting. "Well, right now, it turns out humans are just the women of the universe, because this is some trippy stuff. Here we are, in an unenviable position, and nothing out there cares that our species just got blasted off the face of the Earth. Quite literally. Forty percent of us left, and you know it's got to be even fewer than that now."

I took a breath not having realized quite how upset I'd really been about everything. "So yeah, you could say I'm just done. Done with all this crap. But I'm not giving up. I have two kids whom I adore and want to see live and succeed in this new hell, no matter how hard that might be. And I have a family, my twin, my kid's father—if I can ever get to him in this wilderness.

"But I'm tired. Instead of just lying down in defeat, I have to drag myself up every day and figure out things I'd never have contemplated if life had gone on the way it should have. I should be working on my plants, not killing monsters. I'm a scholar, not a fighter. A biologist, not some Adventurer!"

I hadn't realized it, but my voice rose a bit toward the end. More than a few of the people left milling in the library looked my way, but the rest looked away. Meltdowns, even justified meltdowns, weren't exactly unusual.

The System, the idiotic Classes or Willpower or what have you, might have been helping with our mental state, but all this was still a little much.

"Plants are still important here, you know?" Dor nudged me again, her smile soft with understanding. "Your love of nature might do you better than you thought. Might be a great idea to go out there and immerse yourself in it and see just how much or how little has changed. Take a few moments for yourself. We got this far together."

I blinked at her. "Those are some wise words, lady. I might just do that." I couldn't help but smile wryly. "After I make sure the kids have eaten, Wisp hasn't decided to find more pets to adopt, and I figure out a bit more about this damned Mana ability of mine."

Dor couldn't help but smile a little too at my codicil. Being a parent never stopped, not even for the apocalypse. "Shoo. Get going, young whippersnapper."

With a smile, I left the library, knowing Dor was just about to dive back into all of the intricacies involved in organizing a settlement that was growing day by day.

From the sadness that flushed over her expression every now and again when she thought no one was looking, I got the feeling she'd lost her family when all this started. Maybe we could fill that void for her. Maybe we already had.

Chapter Five:
Understanding Mana

First things first though, I needed to find out what the hell was up with multiple skills titled Mana Sense. Unsure how exactly to go about it, I headed to the Shop. Surely Shi'enah would have an inkling, right?

I was surprised to see Jackson talking to the Shop host when I walked in. He glanced up, equally as surprised, and a sheepish look crossed his face. "Hey, Mum."

He stepped over and gave me a tight hug.

"What you after?" I asked him, squeezing back.

"Trying to figure out how many modulators the tech department can afford. Chris and Sarah have been whisked away by Ginali for the moment, and we're trying to refine some of the projects we're working on."

Evelyn had been right. He wasn't typical thirteen-year-old boy happy, but he was post-apocalypse happy. He'd found something he loved and was good at, and he'd thrown himself into it wholeheartedly.

"Good. I won't interrupt you." I gave him one last squeeze before relinquishing my hold.

"Oh, you didn't. I'm mostly done here." He smiled. "Thank you for your help, Shi'enah."

The host inclined their head as Jackson hefted a few things from the counter and exited the shop.

"How may I assist you today, Kira." Shi'enah inclined their head again, waiting for my response.

Suddenly, I felt awkward, not entirely certain how I should approach asking for this. "Why am I getting multiple versions of the skill Mana Sense?"

They just looked at me, blinking, and I wasn't sure why that made me even more uncomfortable. "Multiple versions of Mana Sense? Could you show me an example?"

I shared my Status Screen with them before I could consider potential ramifications. Wasn't sure that would make it into my memoir, but if it did, it would be in the list titled: ten things not to share with alien species who might want to wipe you out.

They balked for a second. "How did you get this?"

"I bought a book from Chjaveen, and it was titled Mana Sense, and it gave me a Skill Point, but made a new Mana Sense Skill, apparently." I really hadn't thought the System that took over my world would glitch. Apparently, technology sucking was a universal thing. I pulled out the now mostly useless book and handed it to them.

They fiddled for what seemed like forever, frowning as they did so. Then they looked up at me, and I have to admit, they seemed almost ill at ease. "It seems that several of the System translations have . . . misfired."

"Misfired?" I asked, wondering if I'd successfully managed to raise the eyebrow I felt this situation warranted.

"Translation-wise. This would be closer to Mana Understanding . . I think. And the one that is higher level is more of a . . . Mana Awareness enhanced by the Skill Mana Attunement, allowing for Mana Recognition and Tracking." They looked up at me. "Would you like me to force the System to adjust how it refers to those skills?"

"No. I mean. Can you make the second one say Mana Understanding? But just leave the original one it called Mana Sense as that. I'm not having another long-ass name on my Status Screen." I pondered the other books as Shi'enah nodded and adjusted my information before my eyes.

Pulling out the other Mana Sense books, I took a breath and asked, "So will these increase Mana Sense or Mana Understanding?"

She perused them briefly. "Mana Sense. Those are what you're wanting."

I couldn't help my huge sigh of relief. "Thanks."

"Sorry for the System translation issue. Mana Understanding might behoove you to have anyway, given your other skills, but I can see how it must have been frustrating."

I laughed a bit self-deprecatingly. Trust me to get the faulty System item. "Yeah. That it was."

❖

I had to admit to feeling relieved that Shi'enah had vetted these books and that they hadn't been a complete waste of Credits.

Understanding Mana Sense
Upon Completion: Mana Sense +2

Mana Sense: A Cheater's Code?
Upon Completion: Mana Sense +3
Note: There can be no partial credit allocated.

What if actually soaking up this magical knowledge affected me differently? I hadn't told anyone about it; what if it knocked me out?

Which was why I sat myself on my cot again. At least that way, if I fell into unconsciousness, I wasn't about to smash my head against anything less forgiving than a pillow. Then, the moment I sat down, I found myself changing my mind.

Wouldn't it be more fun to go sit in the sunlight, out in the mutating gardens and soak in our evolving nature? I mean, it was within the Safe Zone, so I was fairly certain it wouldn't suddenly eat me alive. I could always take a small pillow with me.

The *Cheater's Code* was the one I was most hesitant about. I mean, what did it mean, no partial credit? I couldn't read a couple of chapters and get a +1 instead of the +3 if I didn't like the content?

Besides, if the other books were anything to go by, this one wasn't going to gradually filter into my brain. All or nothing. That was the way.

With all my fears in mind, I gathered the books from my apartment, my pillow, and traipsed out into the courtyard. Most of the cobblestones were pretty fucked up out there, but some of the planters had survived.

They sported small trees and shrubs, some flowers. Nothing usable for survival, but nature didn't have to appear useful to be actually useful. The plant life appeared to still be able to provide us oxygen, which was a bonus. It was just that their growth, the way they photosynthesized now? Well, once I got a chance to study them in more detail, I was excited to see just how that process had changed.

Pulling *Mana Sense: A Cheater's Code* onto my lap, I sat cross-legged on the lip of one of the stone planter areas and leaned myself comfortably into the plants with the pillow settled to nestle my head.

I opened it in my lap and rested my hand on the starting page.

Knowledge assaulted me, pummeling behind my eyes like a bass drum for a few fleeting seconds before it settled. It gave me a new sense of peace, as well as a notification.

Mana Sense: + 3

New Total Mana Sense:+7

Along with all those notifications was the information that gifted me the higher skill level. Mana Sensing, or Mana Awareness enhanced by the Skill Mana Attunement allowing for Mana Recognition and Tracking, as

Shi'enah had translated, was the ability, apparently, to see Mana and its strands as it interacted with the world.

Like I could see the gaping wound in the universe and how it bled into all the little areas of creation. It was raw, unprocessed power that was simply looking for a place to attach itself to, for something or someone who would utilize it and help its spread throughout the universe.

Mana was more than stardust. It was the thing that gave stars, dust, living, death, mutations, magic, and electricity its power. Mana was everywhere, always. Always had been, always would be. It wasn't unnatural; it was the dark matter we couldn't see, the uncontrollable randomness in quantum equations.

It was everywhere—from a gently flowing river as it helped the water along its way to the birth of a baby rhino who peeked its tiny eyes up at the stars above.

It wasn't life; it wasn't sentience. It was the building blocks of creation.

It had always been on Earth, but in ways most people denied or didn't pay attention to. When something seemed like bad luck, when it felt like déjà vu, when unexpected hybrids occurred. All of that was Mana seeking a way to find and produce life and to keep everything evolving.

My head swam with some of these concepts, and I mean, I'd understood interspecies grafting in record time. While I still didn't have the answer as to why especially *I* could see Mana, I did have an inkling, perhaps more of an understanding of why.

Mana Attunement opened the gate to this wondrous sense, but even though I could marvel at the beauty inherent in it, there was also a shadow of something dangerous.

All the work I'd done, the way I looked at plants and knew how healthy or unhealthy they were, and perhaps just how to save them, that lent me a part of this affinity I seemed to have with Mana. So when the world exploded into a Dungeon World and Mana sought out all of the paths it could take, it found me. Maybe because I was willing to look at plants, at life itself, at bending them to my will and how it all fit together gave me the leg up to this Skill.

Maybe the System, seeing my need and my Skills, gave me the Class that started my path.

Or maybe someone was having a laugh.

Yeah. This was not going to be an easy concept to explain to someone who hadn't already spent their entire life in the field with life-forces.

I let my eyes close for a second, organizing and reorganizing the information in my head. A part of me found it funny, threads about the Observation Effect. Quantum physics wasn't my thing, but the fact that I was looking at Mana itself meant that Mana was changing to what I wanted it to be was very, well, quantum entanglement thingamajig.

Eventually, I had the information sorted in a way that made me happy. I looked around for a second, making sure no one was waving me down, screaming about an attack or a giant wombat or a meal being missed, and then I picked up the next book.

I opened it and just stared at that first page. Trying to read the words made them swim in front of my eyes. Perhaps they weren't meant to be consumed any other way than magical insertion. Mana insertion. Or however this world worked now.

Another breath. In for a penny, right?

Steeling myself, I placed my hand on the first page. A flurry of information bombarded me. Cold, like a blizzard in my mind. Pain that soaked into all my neurons, down my nerves on the inside, the way snow stuck on a miserable wet day, but on the inside. Pain like I'd got my tongue stuck on a street post except, you know, the street post was every inch of my head and the tongue all my nerves.

Dungeon Worlds, man.

My head swam, and I was glad I hadn't tried to stand up yet while the world phased in and out of my vision. Just as I thought I wasn't going to throw up, another message flashed across my screen.

Congratulations! You have increased your knowledge of Mana. Don't worry, you still have a long way to go. This is only the first step of this wondrous journey.

Reward: Mana Sense + 2

Caution: Too much understanding might make you dizzy!

New Total Mana Sense: 9

Shit.

The world around me spun like I was suddenly in a salad spinner. My vision blurred, and I could feel myself leaning back until I fell, half into the bushes behind me, I think. Even sitting, I'd managed to fall over.

Lines of blue wavered in and out of my vision, of me. But the thing was, it wasn't just a single blue, it was all the different blues in the world. Pale and almost white like a clear day, right at the edges of the horizon, right through to deep and dark blue, as if night was falling but the moon and stars had yet to come out and brighten it up. So many hues, so many colors, all of them shifting and moving, and I swear, some of the bits even waved at me; it sent my head into a spiral.

Awareness assaulted me; words whispered so close to me that I should be able to grasp them, but they slipped out of my fingers just before I comprehended their message. I shut my eyes tightly, clenching my fists as the assault continued. Chill air swept in like someone had turned air conditioning down to zero and left me in the freezer. None of which was possible, considering electricity didn't actually exist. Everything now ran on Mana.

Not now. Always.

Mana.

I started laughing, and the sound was foreign even to my own ears. Like it came from someone outside of myself, outside of the building, raining down their very own panic completely on me. But at the same time, I knew it *was* me.

I'm not sure if I passed out or not, but the next thing I knew, I was half slumped over the planter I'd chosen as my safe spot. Righting myself, I wiped the offending drool away from my face and slowly looked around.

Nothing seemed out of place; the area looked exactly the same as it had before my little episode, though the sun was further set than I recalled. Everything was the same. Except for the Mana visibly running through all the things.

Everything, nothing, running. Hah!

I might have been a little delirious.

I watched as the changed world in front of me. It was so different, like a fog flitting through everything, soaking every object it touched. Ever since this whole thing started, I'd realized that Mana was everywhere, but I'd only caught glimpses of it here and there. Out of the corner of my eyes, when I was stressed or about to die.

Now I could see it, and I wasn't sure how I missed it before.

It moved around the whole planet like a sentient root pattern, touching everything, encompassing us all.

I eyed the books still sitting innocently next to me. Upping my Mana Sense was probably not a good idea for the foreseeable future, until I figured out how to better shield my eyes from this constant glow. Not that it actually shed real light. It was more in how I perceived things, filtered the information it gave me.

I wonder if I could see in darkness now. Or if this second sight, this second sense was just another way of seeing?

Like Daredevil, except he was blind.

Oh, hell. I *was* delirious, wasn't I?

So. No more Mana Sense books till I got a handle on what I was seeing, a handle on myself. And, you know, figured out just what it was I could do with knowing how Mana moved and its purpose. Maybe the next step up would let me understand what it said, but I wasn't the biggest fan of getting actual voices in my mind no one else could hear.

Pushing myself up, I teetered briefly, still trying to refrain from squeezing my eyes shut to avoid the blue glare of Mana all around me. Would it even help? I wasn't sure I could handle the truth, one way or the other.

Anyway. I had a patrol to participate in, people to see, meetings to have, idiots to herd . . .

❖

15 Days Post-System Onset
2:30 a.m.

I don't know why I'd offered to take the night shift. We'd organized those before Jules died, and the aliens decided to arrive to their party early. Damn—was that just yesterday? Had I lost a day?

There was that voice in the back of my head telling me that hey, *if they'd arrived any earlier, you'd all be dead because you wouldn't have had a defensible city or a claimed settlement orb*, but I told that voice to shut up. I didn't need its common sense right now.

Thing was that even though it was nighttime now, nothing appeared dark to me. There was Mana everywhere, shades of blue illuminating my immediate surroundings, and pushed further out until it was all a pale haze.

Some of it tugged at my mind, pulling me gently in different directions like it was trying to point out specific areas or things to me.

By the way, if I closed my eyes, it was still there. I really was Daredevil.

My head spun, and I pinched the bridge of my nose. I wondered if any of those optometry shops had some sort of blue screen glasses? I mean, this wasn't a computer, but damn, that light was starting to hurt my head.

I'm not sure how long we stood on that wall. We being Evelyn and me. I'd been unaware that she'd signed up for the same duty as I had. Things weren't awkward, though; we were what we were, and she was by far some of the more pleasant company in this little town of ours.

Except even as we sat there quietly, even as I knew how much her friendship meant to me, I couldn't get all those little thoughts out of my mind. About our latest guests, the latest spoke in the wheel that was the Apocalypse. Frankly, I was surprised there wasn't a slogan or something like: "Give a rose to your favorite alien species—who will leave the planet?" Or maybe even "The apocalypse will be televised."

There was still so much we didn't know, even after having read books about IRSHA until the letters and information made my brain want to bleed, or about Dash'Kiri and their weird hunting yet honorable fixations. Though I was personally bloody glad they had that honor code.

But how was I supposed to know if IRSHA members in general could camouflage or not, get pass our defenses easily and such? After all, IRSHA was an organization and not a species, but it was filled with many varying types of creatures and Classes that could do the gods knew what. There was nothing I could be sure about their individual members, because all I had access to was the information I'd purchased.

And don't get me started on the sheer magnitude of different Class types that were out there.

A light dusting of dew began to descend on me, and I realized that I'd already been standing out here longer than I initially thought. Our shift was probably already up, or about to be. There were too many ideas running through my head, and I didn't have the time to just be standing here. But there it was.

I sighed—maybe a tad over dramatically.

"You ready to go in now? Or to talk it out?" Evelyn sounded a little bored herself.

"I don't think going inside is going to help anything except allow us to grab a few hours of shuteye." The light around me forced me to blink again, and this time I grimaced.

Evelyn put a gentle hand on my shoulder, and I could feel more than hear her inquiry.

"I'm okay. Just one of these Skills, Abilities, whatever it is we get in this weird new world." I paused, something that I read in one of those blasted books coming back to me. "Shit."

"What?" Evelyn glanced at me like she was worried for my safety or perhaps her own; I really couldn't tell.

My head was throbbing with this oversaturation of information that I hadn't had time to process. Or perhaps it was more that I didn't have the faculties to process it yet because my brain was still functioning with antique wiring—or so the books mentioned.

"Sorry. I'm okay, just upped a skill too much too fast, and now I'm having repercussions. Like only just remembering some of the stuff I read in the process to get to this stage and how if I'd remembered it before this patrol, I might have been able to prevent feeling like my head was going to explode." Lots of words fast. Which meant my brain was doing that overcompensating thing. Again.

Evelyn chuckled and was about to speak when my definitely-should-have-been-in-bed-and-asleep-for-hours thirteen-year-old ran up the stairs with Darren close behind him, panting desperately. He'd never been the sporty one, so I'd never made him do things he didn't want to. Even with the System, his cardio was taking a while to catch up.

Note to self: In order to potentially prepare for any future Apocalypti—yes that was it, my plural—make sure to push everyone's cardio further with the System.

"Jackson." I knew my tone told him enough. Mum tone had a lot of subtlety built into it. At least he had the decency to blush.

"No. Mum. I promise this is amazing. Totally worth the fact that I'm not asleep when I should be and things." He grinned at me slyly.

I crossed my arms and did my best imitation of a glare while having a migraine. Granted, it wasn't actually a migraine or I'd be curled up in a ball, but it was something definitely related.

"Fine. Fine. We've got the Mana stations finally tweaked, and they're drawing in the ambient Mana successfully." His smile shone like a thousand bright suns right then. Almost blinding my new vision. Weird, though—it wasn't just blue, but bright. I needed sleep and headache drugs as soon as I could get my hands on them.

My walkie talkie crackled "Kira?"

"Yeah?" I answered into it.

"Is Jackson out there?" Chris sounded frazzled, and more crackly than usual.

"Yeah."

"Tell him to come back inside and stop spoiling my surprises." Now she sounded irritated, and at least my son had the good grace to blush.

Darren turned a shade of red even I could see through my blue vision. He tugged at my son's arm. "C'mon Jackson. Told you we should have just gone to sleep."

My son smiled sheepishly, but he wasn't in the least embarrassed. It was nice seeing him obviously doing things he loved—even when the world we knew had essentially ended. Awesome parenting there, right? Happy and healthy kid.

"He's coming back in. To go to sleep." I emphasized the message to Chris who chuckled in response.

"Roger that."

I raised an eyebrow before leaning in and giving Jackson a huge hug, whether he wanted it or not.

He didn't pull away too quickly. Another win for me. "Sorry. Just got a little excited. I'll let Chris tell you the good news, I guess."

"Yes. You probably should, but I'm betting you've been tinkering your heart out, right?"

Jackson grinned up at me and I tousled his hair. "Thanks, Mum."

And then the two friends dashed off, just in time for my vision to lose them in the haze of blue Mana shrouding my eyesight.

Right now, my vision was tainted, and I couldn't really tell up from down. This wasn't a good thing if I couldn't get it under control, and the words I'd read in the book just before finishing it had addressed that, but I didn't like the sound of it at all.

The higher my Mana Sense got, the more I'd need to be able to filter through the information it provided; the more I'd require assistance that just wasn't built into my brain capacity organically.

Ocular implants. They'd allow easier integration with the System, allow more options for dealing with the System, and above all, they would allow me to define, categorize, and sort through all of the different—the thousands of different levels of Mana waves that would eventually accost me if I kept leveling this Skill.

Considering how much it leveled all by itself before I even read the books, I didn't think stopping it from increasing was an actual option. I'd obtained the skill, and now I was stuck with it. Just had to figure out how to protect my sight and sanity from it.

Other options that were apparently less intrusive included but were not limited to: genome treatments which just sounded like a zombie apocalypse variation waiting to happen if you asked me; ocular surgery—that appeared to be a lot less powerful than the ocular implants; and a few other things like meditation courses that I didn't think were going to help in the long run at all.

Or you know, leveling up to what they called Heroic Class.

Which, yeah.

Hell, and bloody hell.

Integrating my brain closer with the System might have sounded like the best option, but it scared the hell out of me. We were already its playthings, with Classes and Skills and Levels. What more control did it need?

I didn't know, couldn't know.

Exhaling, I realized our relief had finally arrived. So. First things first. I desperately needed a few more hours of sleep. Then, and only then, would I make any decisions about becoming a further slave to the System.

Chapter Six:

Spiny

15 Days Post-System Onset

6 a.m.

The shrieks that echoed through the halls of the shopping center weren't exactly conducive to that whole sleep thing I'd been aiming for. I'll admit it took me a lot longer than I'd have liked to rise from my bed and stumble out into the thoroughfare.

The corridors in Garden City weren't exactly dark and dingy. Up here on the upper level, there were skylights above the center portion, which was hollowed out in some places so you could look down and see the lower levels.

Here and there along the way there were small shops or coffee shops, stands, things like that. We'd already done away with most of those. One of them near the kid's indoor play area was now the home of the tech department.

Anyway.

I was still half-asleep, trying to figure out what the shrieking was about when I almost tripped over what appeared to be a knee-high dog. Or at least, that's what my eyes saw at first.

About a meter long and half that height, the creature was scaled all over with sharp protrusions jutting up from its hardened skin. I recognized the creature. It was a spiny leaf insect or *Extatosoma tiaratum*. I mean, it was, but it also wasn't from the way it snapped its not-so-tiny mouth in my direction, rising up like it intended to attack.

Thing was, I'd encountered these little guys so many times in the wild by accident that it didn't really scare me. Even though the size was way out of proportion, it just wasn't as scary as, say, a cockbat. But no, it also wasn't acting right. Spiny leaf boys weren't vicious. They were gentle and just scary looking, but this one . . . this one had fully backed up to charge at me, and all of my flight instincts kicked in at once.

"Shit." I scrambled out of the way, trying desperately to avoid the spines on its entire body, because upon closer inspection, these were truly sharp and dripping with a grey sludge not native to the original creature.

The screaming hadn't stopped. While people were closing themselves into their quarters and hiding behind glass doors, others were stuck in the corridors where it seemed a whole pack of these creatures emerged.

No more were they harmless, stick-like insects. These little guys had morphed into a nightmare type of Pokémon, complete with poisonous spines. Spines that knocked people out, if the way people were falling about on the floor was anything to go by.

I sent an alert to Kyle through our family chat, my brain finally awake enough to process that maybe I needed to do more than just back away from these creatures. Placing my hand on the top off my hammer, I pulled it out, never letting my eyes leave my spiny stalker.

Their multifaceted eyes saw so much, and there wasn't just one of them trained on me anymore. No, there were two others shuffling in their weird, stick-insect way over toward me to join their friend. Could they tell I'd just sent word for a Healer?

I shook my head—no time for this.

Running on a little over two hours sleep, I gripped the handle of my hammer and swung it at the lead creature, lobbing it away with what sounded decidedly like a crack of carapace. Thing was, I knew I could have hit it harder, but I couldn't disassociate these mutated versions from the ones I'd met crawling on plants in life prior to the apocalypse.

Stupid. Then again, shrieking late at night for me meant one of the kids had fallen out of bed and was tangled in covers. A hug, a kiss, and comforting words were what was needed. Not bloody mayhem. My brain wasn't firing on all cylinders, and from what I could tell, these little guys weren't stupid. The other two darted from side to side like they were daring me to take another swing at them.

Right now, all I had was my body, my cumbersome hammer, and the few Skills I might be able to use.

Erecting an Earthen Barrier in here was a bad idea in the middle of a shopping mall, especially on the upper level.

"Where did they come from?" Kyle asked, coming up to my left side.

I shrugged, still taking in the fact that I could see at least twenty of the little bastards inside the center as we backed our way down to the food court area near the shop entrance. My little escort of two of the mutations continued to follow us, skittering in defensive patterns the whole way. The mayhem down here was louder, and Mike ran over to us from the coffee shop area as we backed into the main gathering place. His face was a bewildered mask of confusion.

"What the hell is up with all of these . . . stick insects?"

Good question. So I Analyzed the little buggers.

Extatosoma Tiaratum Gigantus
Level 19

I really wanted to tell the System that these were not, in fact, the same creatures as they had been and it should have changed the names, but I didn't think it actually cared.

Drake and Gary were hot on Mike's heels, moving in a loose formation as they watched out for more of the dog-sized insects to hunker down and attack. They all had a bit of a wild look in their eyes, not that I could blame them.

"Isn't this supposed to be a Safe Zone?" Evelyn rubbed her eyes as she joined us, her bow raised with her right arm as she attempted to focus on one of the creatures. Their skittishness made targeting decidedly difficult.

By now we'd managed to form a little bit of a group that was surrounded by approximately eight of these mutated insects. They moved in a disjointed way, darting from side to side, back and forth. It was as if they knew just how difficult it was to keep them in our sights.

And then they basically pounced on us all at once.

The one slightly to the left front of me jumped high into the air, making me swing my hammer in a haphazard attempt and slogging it through the air. I only managed to clip the thing's tail-like appendage, sending it careening into another group just beyond us, briefly bowling over several more of their kind.

While I was distracted with that, I heard Kyle scream to watch out, but it registered with me too late that he meant for me to do the watching.

Maybe because I'd picked these things up when they were the size of my palm, I wasn't expecting the pain that rammed through me when the spine on the second creature's back smashed into my left-hand side. Agony ripped through me as I felt my flesh tear under the sheer force of impact.

But no sound emerged from my throat but a cough of expelled air as it winded me in the process. The next thing I knew, the insect was flying through the air, lifted into it by Mike's baton, and was then riddled with arrows before it could hit the ground where it lay twitching in death throes.

Kyle's healing hit me before I could seriously inspect the damage to my side, visibly now only through the thirty-centimeter bloody rip in my clothing that it left behind. I righted myself, picking my hammer back up from where it had fallen, and gripped it tight.

"To the right!" I called out as two of them launched themselves at

Evelyn.

Suddenly, as if out of nowhere, Molly's shield was there, taking the brunt of the flying insect attack. And we began to fall into a rhythm of fighting. Since so many of my abilities would tear the very foundations of the shopping center apart, I opted for my hammer.

I needed to get better at swinging it anyway.

Off to my left, I noticed that Kyle had a type of pistol and I frowned. Not that I wasn't fully aware of guns being available from the shop, I just hadn't thought my brother would get one. It might have to do with the fact that some of his own Class abilities scared the crap out of him. I'd talk to him about it later.

What it did do was drop the creatures effectively if he managed a headshot. After several missed shots though, he put it away. Seemed he hadn't been able to afford a self-targeting one.

I smashed my hammer into my third little menace, now used to the sickening crunch of the carapace as it gave underneath the weight of my weapon. If I looked down at them, these once-cute plant insects still appeared mostly adorable.

At just above knee height for the most part, the spines on these usually harmless creatures had mutated into something hard and dangerous, with oozing goo I'd hazard a guess was poisonous. Coming into contact with them like I had only minutes ago was definitely what we aimed *not* to do.

The only creature so far I hadn't seen completely subverted by the damned Apocalypse was our little Mumma Wombutt and that . . . well, there were always exceptions, right?

These little spinies reminded me of corgis, or miniature dachshunds with their tenacious herding of us all. They snapped and prodded, coming perilously close to stabbing a lot of us. It meant that either shielding like Molly had, or distance weapons like Evelyn had were the best possible avenues of attack.

Those Garden City inhabitants who weren't prone to fighting locked themselves in shops or stood on tables. Several of them orbed into the Shop itself while more of us tried to figure out ways to control them.

There were no alarms to let us know that our Safe Zone had been quasi-invaded. Perhaps these had been inside all along, quietly mutating in the plants and their planters—in here with us the whole time.

Dog ran up to my side, snarling as he pushed me away. I hadn't seen one of the stealthy little things skittering over to me rapidly. I reached down and petted Dog on the head, glancing to see if Wisp had followed him and was relieved to find that she had not. At least not that I could see.

Kyle lanced out with one of his offensive abilities, striking directly through the insect with a sickening crunch of hardened carapace. It split mostly in half, oozing green and grey goo out onto the tiled floor with a slightly acidic sizzle as half of each side plopped open.

We hadn't split one of them open before this, and damn how I wish we never did.

A foul smell leaked into the air, making me cover my mouth as I began to cough. The sudden death of one of their own caused the nearest half-dozen of the creatures to back up for a moment. Here they were, fully cognizant of one another, and now, instead of just attacking us blindly, they were wary of us.

More of them appeared, skittering down from the walls, the ceiling, over the railings of the escalators . . .

Now we knew a thing about them. They were mutated, didn't set off perimeter alarms, and there was more poison in their spikes than I'd initially given them credit for. And there were a lot more of them than I'd initially counted.

❖

"Spread out. Use Shields where possible," I yelled out through clenched teeth as another splash sizzled its way through the denim of my jeans into the flesh below.

Sure, the acid wasn't as strong as I'd initially anticipated, but it still hurt like buggery.

The thing was, these spiny mutations weren't that hard to kill, they were just difficult to lock onto so you could kill them. I still felt guilty for doing so too, especially after so many years of treating them like they were my gardening friends.

Then again, they'd been about the size of one of my hands back then, so it really wasn't comparative.

"Shit!" Mike bellowed as he literally punched one of them off his thigh with a closed fist. His security-oriented Class certainly reinforced his skin from what I could see. There wasn't even a break in his flesh for Kyle or Dale to patch up.

Gary and Drake weren't so lucky, but at least the acidic poison wasn't like what killed Kylie's mum those weeks ago. Normal healing appeared to take care of the wounds it created.

The main food court and gathering area were vacated now, even as we closed in on seven in the morning. We managed to pull everyone who was unconscious back into safe areas, their bodies slowly clearing out the poison and waking them up. Now, more of the people hid behind closed glass doors as we Adventurers out here did our very best to antagonize the Spiny Leaf Mutations into attacking us instead of going after everyone else.

Taunts were only something a few of us could manage. Molly, and it appeared Drake as well as a few others I didn't know well. Making something focus on them helped a lot, but even so these fresh mutations were skittish and volatile.

Molly always surprised me. The way she leaned forward in all her diminutive glory and bellowed with a sound wave that basically said, "look at me, look at me" worked every time. Sometimes the duration differed, but it was always good for at least a distraction.

The Extatosoma Tiaratum Gigantus differed in Levels from the 18. Levels 18 and 19 were some of the toughest that arrived. Others were much lower Level, which helped. Even so, I was beginning to think the System had no imagination whatsoever. Or maybe that was just for when it took already existing creatures and mutated them within an inch of their former glory.

We'd managed to weed the creatures down, having already killed a good dozen or so. More seemed to stream out from around the shopping mall, so there were still about ten left. Ten of the nastiest, highest-Level fellas. Their agility continued to surprise me, and now they were learning; they'd shown us just how fast they could move. The increased size only seemed to have magnified their natural speed.

Their usual swaying movement patterns served to half hypnotize an opponent if they weren't fully aware of how a spiny boy usually moved. And the twisty way the eyes and head rotated made me gag more than once.

A sickening clicking sound accompanied each rotation of the neck, and what used to be tiny pincers at the end of each leg echoed resoundingly through the tiled halls of the center. Splashes of red and white, blood from them and us shifted in the surroundings, marring the clean tile.

Dog stayed by my side. Perhaps he thought that helping me to defeat these creatures would keep Wisp safe. A perfectly sound assessment, from my point of view.

We approached another spiny, me wielding my hammer with more confidence than I'd ever felt before, now I'd been able to use it more. So much better than any type of bat.

Dog nipped at the backs of their legs, causing the spiny to turn around briefly and give him attention, giving me enough time to Water Siphon it. It was one of my only abilities that wouldn't demolish the center.

There was a split-second timing involved that I'd missed the first few attempts, but I was getting better at it now. If I got it wrong, the damn creature spun around and stuck its spines into me, leaving me poisoned and ouched. I refused to keep relying on Kyle to watch my back. It was with a twinge of sadness that I managed to suck the life-force and hydration from my fourth victim in a matter of moments.

The carapace crumbled in on itself like the body inside got sucked out with a vacuum, making the outer shell suddenly appear brittle and dry. I didn't have the time to touch it and see it my supposition was correct, so instead, I looted the monster and then placed it in my inventory along with the others I'd already gathered so I could show them to Ginali later on. Surely there had to be some benefit to this other than a complete and utter lack of sleep.

Once we managed to coral the remainder and no more appeared from the depths of the mall—even when our Warriors used their taunts—we finally got the rest of the infestation under control. All but the last one.

I could almost feel its sadness, see the blue lines around it jittering in what I think might have been fear, or loneliness. It wasn't at fault here—the Mana had taken the docile little creature it was and turned it into something it was never intended to be.

It made me angry all over again that this System could come in and just wreck a whole lot of lives. Lives that included an insect whose worst offense before this was eating some leaves I might have tried to graft.

Its death was quick and as painless as we could make it, or at least I hoped so. If we weren't at least compassionate to those beings that deserved it, then we'd lose all of our humanity and be no different from the aliens seeking to dominate our world.

I crouched down, examining the empty husk of the creature who'd fought us until its last breath. The team swept out, not needing me to tell them otherwise. But even when Molly and Dave let out another Taunt, nothing happened. No more of them crawled down the walls, or up from the lower level.

Eventually, I could hear doors opening and footsteps coming back out onto the tiled surfaces as people realized they could exit their havens again.

I was glad we'd managed to give our people some peace of mind, but several things bugged me.

We were in a Safe Zone, so shouldn't it have alerted us to the presence of these rogue mutant insects? Or was it because the insects were in here already when the Safe Zone declared itself, did that mean they, too, were covered under that zoning? Didn't it already say that mutations couldn't happen in a Safe Zone? If that was the case, did these things come in from outside?

Dog butted the back of my arm, and I reached over to scratch his ears somewhat absentmindedly. Size of a pony, I swear. He wuffed hot air out at the nape of my neck like he was trying to reassure me of something and trotted off silently.

Out of the corner of my eye, I could see Wisp throw her arms around him and snuggle into his fur, and I forced myself to correct my previous assessment of the way mutations affected different creatures.

We had Mumma Wombutt, baby Wombie, and we had Dog. All of those hadn't been affected in a violent manner. Each of those had somehow chosen its own sentience over a driving factor of violence. Now if only I could figure out why, perhaps I'd feel a little safer.

Chapter Seven:
Eyes of the Storm

15 Days Post-System Onset

8 a.m.

Thanks to the absolute Spiny Leaf Mutation fiasco, I'd gotten even less sleep than I'd originally wanted. And there really wasn't more time for me to invest in it right now. If the glare around my eyesight would just ease up a little, I'd feel much better.

The Shop and I were getting far too well acquainted. I had savings, almost a hundred and fifty thousand Credits, but I needed to figure out exactly what I could use and what I could do.

"Um." I found myself unsure of how to ask for what I wanted. Wouldn't it seem really weird if I was asking about ocular implants?

Shi'enah raised their head and looked at me, their own eyes blinking slowly.

"Yes?" they asked like she wasn't sure I really wanted help. Which was right, because I had no idea if this was even something remotely viable.

Not to mention it had to cost a fortune. And the only reason I had a decent stash of cash was the two rare monsters I'd managed to help kill. Still, if I wanted to make sense of all this and Level up, so to speak, I needed to dive into it now.

Taking a deep breath, I nodded. "Implants and body enhancements?"

Shi'enah seemed to be putting all their effort into refraining from raising an eyebrow. For a couple of seconds that seemed like a lifetime, they just stood there and blinked at me. Maybe it wasn't a common request, or perhaps it was, and they were wondering why it had taken me so long to ask. Whichever it was, they ended up nodding right back at me.

"If you want cybernetic variations on body modifications, then you need to go to the third door on the left. If you want System-enhanced devices with direct brain modifications, which can include cybernetic attachments and neural interfaces, then you want the fourth door on the left." They smiled at me, or at least I think it was a smile. I was still learning how to tell. "Is that sufficient information?"

I nodded nervously. So much had happened in the last twenty-four hours that I wasn't even sure if I should be considering such a huge decision, given my severe lack of sleep. But Kyle had his eye on the kids, and right now I couldn't keep my eyes on anything. It was like I had Meares-Irlen syndrome on acid. All of the lights around me danced constantly. Letters, words, nothing stayed still. The Mana brought everything to life.

Along with a dull and very persistent headache that was like a constant bass drum rhythm played by a group of enthusiastic three-year-olds. And if you haven't been to day camp with a group of three-year-olds given a drum kit for the very first time, you haven't suffered.

Navigating my way down the hall wasn't even without its dangers. Stepping one foot in front of the other as blue beams of light ran rampant all around me was precarious at best. At least I could still count.

Fourth door down, since I didn't think anything not hooked up to my brain was going to help me. Holy crap, did that mean I'd be essentially getting brain surgery? I stopped, my hand on the knob, like I was frozen and couldn't figure out if I really should enter the room.

The decision was taken from me when the door opened, revealing Gemma. I almost fell onto her, and she let out a surprised squeak that sounded nothing like her assassin self.

"I'm so sorry," we said at the same time, and then laughed, and then I felt awkward because this was decidedly so.

"You okay?" I asked her since she looked like she'd just seen a ghost. Her skin was paler than usual beneath her sun-freckled nose, and the darker parts of her sun-bleached brown hair seemed duller. She no longer looked like the fresh and inquisitive young girl we'd encountered along with Jules. Loss had marked her.

"Yeah, just—been getting myself some enhancements." Her visage darkened briefly, and I knew all the things she was thinking about. "Not letting an arse like that monster fuck up me and mine ever again."

I could feel her regret, and her sadness. Jules's death would have torn her up a lot more than it did me, not to mention the fact that she had still been recovering mentally and hadn't gone with us when the Mollecupai ambushed us probably made her feel guilty as hell about her best friend's death.

"I totally get that." There were darker strands of power that wove themselves around her, through her, attached in some areas more than others. I was starting to wonder if those darker strands didn't depict strength of Mana, but type. "Dog-eat-dog world, right? Make ourselves stronger, because we can. How, uh . . ."

But I wasn't sure how to finish the question.

How did I come out and go: *So was it painful, do you feel like you have brain damage?* but I think she got what I was trying to ask.

"It's surprisingly painless, and fast, and virtually no healing time." She grinned, but it was a controlled expression and didn't reach her eyes. "Whatever you're wanting done, if it makes you stronger, if it makes you able to protect those who depend on you? Do it, Kira. Don't hold back."

She clasped my shoulder tightly and headed past me without another word. She'd been maybe nineteen when I met her, but now, as I watched her walk away, she seemed far older—like the weight of the Apocalypse was dragging her down.

Her and the rest of us.

Taking a deep breath, I pushed the door open fully and stepped inside.

❖

I'm not sure what I was expecting. Maybe some backwards little dive with dirty floors and mirrors, where they took money under the table and did horrible backyard surgeries. Maybe more like those organ-harvesting, genetic-opera type shows and musicals that had been all the rage in the early 2000s. I'd obviously watched far too much cyberpunk TV and played too many post-apocalyptic games.

I mean, this was lightyears ahead of that sort of thing, right? Aliens invaded us, so we should have access to all their stuff.

I found myself laughing despite the situation, mostly out of nerves, but also tiredness and just how much Mana ran rampantly through this space. It shone off every surface, and I had to shield my eyes before it died down slightly and I could start taking stock of my surroundings.

White, with a hint of blue. Everywhere I looked. White tiled walls and stainless-steel appliances. Not kitchen gadgets, no. But medical-grade stuff everywhere, partially curtained off by white drapes. The desks and chairs, white with stainless steel legs. White. White. White.

If I hadn't already needed something to help acclimate to the brightness constantly assailing my senses, I would now.

As I was about to take a couple more steps into the room, a pedestal rose out of the floor, presenting its screen face to me. This screen form of shopping menu was pretty cool, but only if you knew how to narrow it down, to find exactly what you wanted.

You had to think at it pretty clearly, directly, and not hum and haw about it.

So, you know, crap-all useful for anyone neurodivergent.

Ocular implants gave me way more listings than I would have thought, so I narrowed it down to ocular implants that were compatible with human genetics.

That list was much shorter than the first. There were a disturbing number of them with little hashtag marks which led to tiny little legalese indicating their compatibility was all via Skill or computer modelling. It took me a second to realize perhaps the ones without the hashtag marks were even more disturbing.

Looked like live human experimentation was not off the menu for the Galactics.

Fuckers.

It did leave me only a few options once I got over the moral quandary of all that. And yet, the number of options were still surprisingly larger than I'd have imagined.

Mana Definition Implants by Divine Sight (requires a Tier III neural link upgrade).

Cost: 18,000 Credits

Note: Connections limited to 2

This implant by Divine Sight allows for those pesky Mana waves to tone it down. It has the ability to differentiate between twelve different varieties of Mana waves in order to classify them so you can better keep yourself and your allies alive.

Be aware that Divine Sight offers no guarantees that your brainwaves will function with this implant. Divine Sight cautions that the Tier-III neural link upgrade is not included in this package and must be otherwise obtained.

Ocular Mana Implants by Fortieth Sight requires a Tier IV neural link upgrade for installation with further upgrades available.

Cost: 32,000 Credits

The Ocular Mana Implants by Fortieth Sight offer the discerning Mana interpreter a new view of Mana like they've never seen before. Once in effect, this implant will let you see the galaxy in an entirely different way, allowing for multiple avenues to interpret and understand Mana waves and their complexities.

Note: Limited to 5 connections.

Caution: Fortieth Sight does not guarantee the level to which the Implant will differentiate varied Mana waves.

I blinked at the options it gave me and frowned. None of these sounded right. In fact, there was something off about both those descriptions. Nothing like ordering from a screen instead of a person. Still, maybe this way it was less expensive than getting fleeced by someone face to face. I didn't trust either of those options, nor the others available that I'd already skimmed.

So I guess I needed to try another search term.

Human-genetics-compatible ocular implants for Mana sensing.

There, let's see how it dealt with that search inquiry. Instead of being its usual fast self, the process to find what I entered appeared to take a long time. Well, like, at least a few seconds. But it felt so long that I wanted to start twiddling my thumbs.

Sadly, the previous two popped up again, but this time there was also a longer one.

Mana Sense Complete Ocular Implants by Neural Divergence

Required: Tier-II Neural Link - Upgradable

Required: Active Ability - Mana Sense

Required: Mana Sense - 9 or higher (15 recommended)

Required: Intelligence - 65 (80 recommended)

Required: Minimum of one Mana fiddling data storage device connected to Neural Link.

Description: Neural Divergence's ocular implant stands out from the rest of its competitors by being individually crafted by high-ranking Artisans. This Implant is specially crafted to work with the Mana Sense skill to enhance its projection abilities and as such, each implant is uniquely tailored to the individual.

The Implant comes with an automatic filtration and storage options, allowing the user to process and view Mana waves.

Warning: Should you choose to utilize this Implant before Mana Sense reaches 15, you could experience headaches, dizziness, nosebleeds, hallucinations, and other more debilitating side effects such as brain hemorrhaging or death. Incidents of death and incapacitation have been reported on a highly irregular basis.

Cost:

Tier II Neural Link: 95,000 Credits

Ocular Implant: 100,000 Credits

Mana Fiddling Data Storage Device: 25,000 Credits

Total: 220,000 Credits

❖

I grimaced, seeing that my Credits were short. By a really decent chunk, too. I could potentially sell another one of those tentacles and some more of the Mollecupai parts, but I really didn't want to yet.

This one gave me the feeling that it might actually be what I needed. It didn't try to sell it to me the way the others did. It felt more legitimate. I hoped my gut instincts were right.

However, I was way below the recommended Levels and

hemorrhaging just didn't have a welcome ring to it. So many possible drawbacks if I got it before Mana Sense hit 15.

Plus, we'd be going out on patrol soon, pushing ourselves further than we'd been so we could go and find more people and see just what the world had done further out. I'd be able to find this again, and I could get it then—once I could properly afford it.

Leveling in the process would allow me to receive the implant with less immediate death danger, too. A thought hit me, to tide me over until I had the cash and slightly better stats, and I searched for another option.

Mana Sense Glasses v 29.11 by Neural Divergence

Required: Active Ability - Mana Sense

Required: Mana Sense - 9 or higher

Required: Intelligence - 65

Description: The Mana Sense Glasses are a highly portable filtration system for Mana waves as experienced by those with less-than-optimal control of the ability. At Neural Divergence, we recommend that the user secure the Mana Sense glasses to their cranium for optimal portability.

As with all of Neural Divergence's premium products, the Mana Sense Glasses v29.11 come with upgraded filtration systems, decreasing Mana glare experienced by the user. Our patented optimal fit molecular binding system allows for comfortable fit in 98.4% of all races and we offer 2,000+ color and design flares within the glasses, including an automatic "best look" feature.

Cost: 9,000 credits.

Glasses it was, then. Plus, they were made by the same company that produced the eventual massive upgrade I wanted. If these were decent, then odds were the expensive version were too.

They fit around my face surprisingly well once they finished adjusting, the colors of the glasses flickering till it ended up on intra-bio-dorn Level 625. The fact that it flared upwards, giving me a little of a bookish look as part of their "best look" feature was kind of amusing.

More importantly, the glare from the Mana faded, easing back on the headache I'd been developing. Though I guessed I probably looked like an idiot wearing them, these were going to have to stay on my face as long as they could. I was sure there was a sunglasses shop somewhere that would have sport bands in it. Ray would know. He seemed to have the stock down pat.

As I made my way back out of the store, I almost ran face-first into the glass door. This was going to be a problem. Though I didn't require corrective lenses anymore, differentiating through sunglasses at night would take some getting used to.

Now I had a goal, I needed to get out there and kick alien, mutating-animal-and-plant arses. We all needed the Levels; we all needed the practice. By now, we had weapons from the Shop, new armor, and I knew some people had even purchased Skill upgrades from it. With everyone having dumped their points into new Class Skills, we were ready.

We'd made it through the tutorial stage.

Now, it was time to get out there and level. I was going to make it to max Level one day.

Endgame, fuckers. Endgame.

Chapter Eight:
3 2 1 Oh

15 Days Post-System Onset
11 a.m.

Wisp sat in front of me as I prepared the stack of items I needed to take with us so my team could go find some more survivors and kick some more butt. We still hadn't heard anything about the other shopping centers, nor had we been attacked by IRSHA. Though from how they'd phrased it, that wasn't something I expected any time soon.

Thanks to the signs Leena insisted on hanging several days ago, off larger buildings they'd encountered while clearing areas, we had an ever-present trickle of newcomers entering via the gates. Our numbers definitely weren't dwindling. Yet. And that definitely brought us more time.

Still, a lack of a concrete date of attack was killing my schedule-happy brain.

Sitting here and waiting for both of those things to happen wasn't doing us any favors.

Our fighting forces needed to level. Toohey forest was a decent way away, as were several other possibilities. But considering the amount of people we'd been sending out already, the Levels there were low, and we had to start branching out further from our comfort zone.

We now had a few dungeons popping up around us, which made the whole "Dungeon World" thing much more relevant. MacGregor Highschool's upper levels were the only solid option. Most teams were avoiding the oval for fear of another Mollecupai. Though I wouldn't say no to those crafting items.

We were fairly sure another one was beginning to form in Toohey Forest too, close to the university I was in when this whole shitshow began.

More scouting was needed, and for that we required more people and higher Levels. Conundrum extraordinaire.

Go in search of bigger and badder trouble and hope we didn't bite off more than we could chew.

"Mum. They just don't suit your face shape." My daughter was still inspecting my face and I watched as lines danced all around her.

From what I could tell they were feeding her body, her strange bond with Dog and Wombie, and just her in general, she seemed stronger than before too. The System might not have let her choose a Class yet, but the Mana certainly made her subtly stronger.

Just like it did for all of us. Like those of us that survived were being beefed up so we could be devoured later. Pretty fucked up right there. Like a huge play on Hansel and Gretel. Devoured by what? That I didn't know, didn't want to know either.

As for the glasses, well, it seemed fashion sense for Galactics and humans didn't exactly mesh. That was probably the *least* surprising aspect of having humans around. Even if decades of sci-fi shows said otherwise.

"Well, I didn't really have a choice of shapes. I just grabbed the first ones I found." I hadn't explained why to her, and I could tell she knew I wasn't being completely honest. Even though I'd tried for most of my life to be.

"And they help with headaches?" she asked, fishing for answers.

"Keeps out the bright light," I answered, immediately regretting it as she looked at me in triumph.

Her smile was smug when she spoke next. "Knew you were keeping stuff from me. It's not even bright in here. It's okay, Mum. I'll know you'll tell me when I'm ready."

She jumped off the table and kissed me on the cheek and ran over to play with Kylie, Aisha, and Rolo.

Sometimes I wondered who the parent was. Right now, just me, but Wisp was an old soul in some ways, and I wasn't always sure that was a good thing. She had a kid's curiosity wrapped up in some next-level observance. Great.

"What's with the shades and the glum?" Dale stood next to me suddenly, creeping up on me when I'd not been paying attention.

I raised an eyebrow at him before I realized that the glasses were probably too oversized, and he had no idea I was giving him a stare. "Shades for one of my abilities, and glum because no one wrote a parenting book for the Apocalypse. I wonder if the Shop has any copies of *Parenting in an Apocalypse: It's Not the End of the World?*"

Dale laughed, and maybe making someone else laugh was just what I needed right then, because I certainly felt a bit lighter for it.

"Maybe you should write it," he quipped.

"Sure." I sighed and pushed myself up from my seat and glared at the too-acidic coffee I wasn't drinking. "I'll get right on that. As soon as we've figured out IRSHA's angle, killed a gajillion more monsters so I can retire on Credits, and raised my kids through an actual Apocalypse."

With a shrug of his shoulders, we fell into an easy walk out toward the eastern gates. "There are thousands of books out there preaching at you, why do you have to be an expert? Most of your readers won't live long enough to sue you anyway."

This time I laughed, and the band securing my glasses around the back of my head felt a little tight, but it'd do. Dale's crack would have been funnier if it wasn't so accurate.

"Let's just be thankful reading is probably not on everyone's minds right now. We won't have to worry about sales." I ended up muttering the last of it as I digested what was happening before me. Even now, I was unsure of what exactly was going on.

Jackson stood, gesturing emphatically, while Gemma and Ray looked on skeptically. Seconds later, Chris and Sarah zoomed past me on their way to join my son. Their excitement was palpable, and blue waves danced around them all, charging up with the energy they released. Ambient Mana and I needed to sit down and have a chat. I didn't even want to imagine how bright seeing this would be without my glasses.

Damn. I needed to kill monsters so I could afford those implants. If we survived IRSHA and Mon'swkinon's threats and promises, then we still had giant mutant creatures and magpie dragons to contend with. We finally got close enough to the group that we could hear some of what they were saying.

"No, seriously. It works. We have two of them!" Sarah's arm flailing one-upped that of my teenager's. It was nice to see an adult equally as enthused.

Ray crossed his arms, his expression one of pure disbelief. "I don't even see how that's possible."

"Considering everything we've seen lately?" Chris slid in easily, standing with her arms crossed, mimicking him. "I'd really think your levels of impossible might need reassessment."

Ray colored slightly and let out a pent-up breath of irritation. "Sorry. Things have just been so surreal, and we have . . . I know you know what's going on. So show us this mobile battery accumulation device."

Chris's eyes lit up again, and I could feel the excitement feeding what was to come, but Jackson beat her to the punch, and I had to stop myself from laughing out loud.

"That's just it!" He pulled out a paper diagram, obviously drawn by hand, but full of intricacies. "See—this is essentially how it works."

Eavesdropping on the conversation left me entirely too confused. I was glad we'd finally arrived and could see what he was talking about. I had to do a double take, remove my glasses—which was a total mistake, but we learn from those, right?—and double check.

"Wait." Dale interrupted the murmurings going on around the diagrams. His voice filled with incredulity as he attempted to work out what it was he was seeing. "You figured out how to capture ambient Mana and combine it with solar energy to power up the batteries in these cars and allow them to drive?"

"Well, it's not quite that simple." Sarah stepped in, her face glowing too. "But in a nutshell, that's pretty much it. Tweaking it so that solar energy functioned too was pretty tricky. Mana doesn't behave like the normal methods we use with electricity, so getting them to work together took me leveling enough to gain a special ability with enough points invested in it for it to work.

"But essentially, yes. This will slowly recharge with both solar power and ambient Mana, thus allowing the vehicle to operate using either-or. Think hybrid engines but completely battery sourced from two differing inputs." She seemed so proud, and I couldn't blame her. Whatever Classes they'd all chosen had been brilliantly thought out.

"What about petrol?" Gemma piped in, and I could see the enhancements she'd made to her body. Where she'd been hurt the worst in our last encounter, it appeared that her skin was now fused with a Kevlar type material making it more difficult to puncture, probably almost impossible.

Well, it was a weird new world. Maybe *impossible* was a bit of a stretch.

Now Chris hesitated. "Yeah, that's the one thing we don't have down yet. Not that we couldn't get the motors to take petrol, it's just that getting the pumps to work in order to distribute the petrol is more challenging than just getting a car to power back up. Plus, the tanks will eventually run dry, you know? We need better solutions for long term."

"Not that we couldn't just buy stuff in the Shop," Sarah interjected. "But the cost of that would end up astronomical in the end."

"So, for now," Jackson interrupted, like he didn't want to share the secrets of how everything worked with everyone, "we've managed to wrangle several electric cars we've found in the immediate vicinity and begun converting them."

"Several?" My ears perked up at that. If we had multiple cars, we could reach further destinations, send our teams out to really kill things and Level up. Maybe even go on multiple day trips to harvest for crafting items and potential money drops.

My son hesitated, momentarily looking like I'd deflated his balloon, but he perked right back up and drew himself to his full height before continuing. "We managed to get several of them into the Center carpark, but keep in mind, right now there's no easy way to set them up. We only have two operable vehicles right now."

Two. My enthusiasm waned a bit, but still. In a world where I hadn't thought anything electric would ever get turned on again, this was good news. And two cars was a fantastic start. "So we have two cars we can use. What's the downside?"

Because there had to be one, right?

Sarah hesitated. "We haven't fully tested them yet, but you're probably not going to be able to do more than about forty kilometers on one charge to begin with. Granted, if you get somewhere and it's almost empty, but it's bright outside, it'll probably recharge in several hours. Like say six to eight. For now, anyway. You'd be able to bring it back. But right now, we're basically limited on range until we get more tests and trials in."

"Only because the Skill is low Level though, right?" I looked back on my Skills. Leveling up was basically the answer to everything. Money to buy books, levels to gain Skill Points . . . "Like when you get it up higher, the effectiveness with which the batteries hold the charge should amp up too, right?"

"Yes!" Sarah's eyes would have shot stars out of them if it was humanly possible. "Exactly. It's just another one of those time-consuming and leveling-balancing things. The components to make the batteries are also pretty expensive, relatively speaking, anyway. None of us have all that much money right now."

She continued as if thinking out loud. "I mean, you could buy vehicles in the Shop too. I don't know about you, but my monetary status isn't going to extend to a vehicle purchase any time soon. But this stopgap measure will help, and eventually I'll be able to create long-term solutions for travel for us."

I chalked that up to city maintenance too. We were going to end up having to create a pot. Where if people wanted shit developed, they needed to contribute monetarily. More than just the taxes. First to contribute would be first served, I guess. That was going be a nightmare of logistics, and I'd lump it on Sienna and Dor later, if they hadn't already thought of it themselves.

On top of that, of course, maybe we could do public transportation. Though, then you'd have things like monster attacks on trains or mage lifts, so maybe not? I wonder if anyone had a Taxi Driver or Bus Driver Class?

There were probably millions of variations on every single Class or potential job someone could have.

In the end, the Shop had everything, but it was all for a price. Hefty sticker prices.

"You should talk to Ginali about all of this, you know." The thought occurred to me. Sure, the Cartel had only been here a day and was only just beginning to build their hub, but I'm sure they'd have some sort of barter or trade system—maybe things wouldn't cost us as much as the Shop always asked.

"Yes!" Sarah's eyes lit up. "I totally forgot."

"Having a trading hub is still something I'm getting used to." Chris shook her head, the long side of her short blond hair jostling as she did so. "I feel like we've gone back in time, and forward in the same instant. I did not expect the world to end this way."

Sarah's silvery laugh echoed through the shopping center. With her bright red hair she just had this way of making everything feel lighter. "It's just a new beginning, Chris."

I instantly knew they'd had this conversation multiple times before.

"So we might have patrol cars, eh?" Dale seemed thoughtful, and I knew almost instinctively that he was thinking about creating ambulances down the road.

"Next up is how to get petrol up from the stores?" Ray asked the question, and I wondered why he couldn't see the futility of it.

Chris shook her head. "No. I mean we'll figure out how to get it, considering it's got more uses than just for cars. But like we said, we'd prefer to concentrate on creating electric cars that we know we can sustain powering through sunlight and ambient Mana. Petrol, without us traveling far and wide in order to retrieve the petroleum? That's just going to be something we don't need to do. There's enough work involved in reviving fully electric cars, considering we have to get all of the navigation doodads to work again and turn off those that aren't completely necessary for driving the vehicle."

"And then probably look at converting the other vehicles into electric ones?" I asked, quietly trying to add up how many electric vehicles might be around this area. Probably not that many. Lots of people took busses.

"Exactly." Jackson ran to me and threw his arms around me in utter excitement. "Isn't this great?"

"I'm proud of you, kiddo." He glanced up at me with huge brown eyes, reminiscent of how he'd been as a little kid. It made me want to hug him and squeeze him and never let him go. "Yeah. Yeah. This is fucking fantastic.

❖

Gearing up to head out, Dale grabbed the backpack he always lugged with him. I'm not sure why he found it necessary, considering the amount of storage we sort of automatically had; maybe it was a comfort thing.

Gemma had donned armor obviously purchased from the Shop. It barely let the augmentations she'd had done to her arm and body show through. Ray had a short staff, or maybe it counted as a wand slung through a belt loop. It'd never really seen him with a weapon before; perhaps this magnified his abilities.

Evelyn carried her bow in that loose way that said she could fire off several arrows at a moment's notice, and I grabbed my hammer.

I didn't like the idea of heading out with fewer than ten people. Tasha, with her whirling swords that sometimes made it looked like she was dancing rather than fighting, was someone I'd trust my life with. Slinky and Big Guy—a.k.a. Gary and Drake, our erstwhile enemies—came along with us, armed mostly with daggers. At least that's what I thought they were. Swords weren't only a foot or so long, right?

They'd been trying to prove they weren't complete and utter dicks for several days now, and I just hoped they were good enough that they didn't accidentally get us all killed. At least I knew they could hold their own in combat.

Molly and Sange ended up coming with us as well. I was always grateful for our Tank and Healer duo.

Ten people. All good at their abilities, but it meant my twin wasn't going with us. There was a part of me that didn't want that to happen, considering I'd been worried I'd lost him for several days. But I knew he was here, and considering he was a Healer, even if he was a bit scared of his abilities right now, meant that I'd be hogging three Healers if he came along. Not a good look, not good planning.

Worse, we were down a Healer since Jules. Her death still sat uncomfortably, even if I knew there was nothing I could have done to stop the Mollecupai from catapulting her up through the air with one of its tentacles to smash into the ground when she landed.

The thud her body had made as it impacted the ground rang constantly through my head. Such a sickening sound. It made my blood boil and fed my anger so much I found it hard to think straight. It wasn't even as if I'd known her for long. Circumstances just made it feel like forever. But she'd been so impactful. Saved so many lives with that damned healing shield that losing her the way we did without being able to do anything just . . .it was a crock of shit.

Still. None of that was going to help any of us right now.

It was so tempting to take one of the cars and pile in it like clowns so we could get to where we needed to go sooner. Thing was, that didn't always work. If we found people, we'd have no way to bring them home safely. If we ran into mutations unexpectedly, then it could easily destroy one of the few modes of transport we'd managed to revive.

I could wait until they had enough for every patrol to take two of them. Six patrol groups out and earning what I hoped was a crap-ton of experience, finding more survivors and perhaps even managing to kill some rare monsters? Now that was what it was all about.

We needed Levels, experience fighting enemies bigger than us, and money. Venturing out past our previous safe areas was all we could really do.

Just not too far . . . yet.

It wasn't until we'd biked over fifteen kilometers that I realized just how bad having these glasses on was. Even with the sports band attaching them to the back of my head, they still felt loose, like they'd drop at any moment. There was no real way to filter any of the information I was receiving, or the non-verbal whispers I could hear in my head.

If I wasn't completely still, then reading the Mana waves was nigh impossible. Which meant that utilizing my abilities was next to useless with these on. But I needed the dimmer so I could stop being blinded which I wasn't going to get without the glasses.

"You're worried about something?" Evelyn asked quietly as she rode beside me. I could hear the undertone to her voice. She thought it might have been her, because we had this sort of unspoken agreement that we'd not make things more difficult for one another. Right now, we both needed someone to lean on.

I shook my head, though even that minor gesture of concern made me feel a little better already. "No. Definitely not you. Just these glasses."

"Oh, I meant to ask you about those. Not very flattering."

This time I laughed. "Thank you. Everyone says that."

She smiled, of course, not having a clue what I was talking about. So I filled her in. "Couldn't afford the optical implants I need in order to use one of my abilities without sending myself insane or into migraine hell. I got these as a stopgap measure, and they're mostly useless."

Evelyn looked like she was mulling over what I'd said. "I would have lent you the money, you know. I've sold some pretty kooky shit myself."

"Yeah. I know." I hoped she realized that I really did know, and that I truly did feel that way. It's just I'd been independent since I could remember and always fought to do things my way. Taking money from people during an Apocalypse, well, it just seemed like such a dick thing to do.

Plus, owing friends money was a sure-fire way to stop being friends.

Or maybe something more. In the future.

If we had a future.

Chapter Nine:

Bravado

The thing you have to understand about Brisbane is that it's not just a city or a suburb. It's a sprawling mass in a circular sort of pattern from the central business district. And when I say "sort of circular," I mean that's probably how they originally intended it. But as people flocked to the coasts, the greater Brisbane area became well . . sprawling.

Like, there's no other word to use for it. Untidy, irregular, sprawl. It's the only adequate term to describe it, really. So riding down from Garden City, past so many abandoned vehicles, under overpasses that no longer functioned as such and through the occasional bushy areas, it felt like we were passing through ghost towns.

Daily Hill Conservation Park had been on my list since we discovered the school turned into a dungeon. Because there was no way Daisy Hill was going to be anything but a massive dungeon. There was way too much wildlife there, way too many possibilities for playing with Australia's already fucked-up fauna. I couldn't see the System passing on it in any way at all.

The Mana was going to gobble that stuff up.

We pulled up under the gum trees. Silly little koalas and their very specific diet. The entrance to the park was lined by the tree, but there was already something darker about it. I could already see the changes underway. Mana was alive in here, rampant even. For it to be showing this blatantly on the outskirts, it had to have changed profusely inside already. It made me itch to go and visit places like Lone Pine and Currumbin. I could only imagine just what those areas were going through.

"Here." Evelyn surprised me, handing me a strange sort of hairband contraption.

With my own hair already in a ponytail, I raised an eyebrow at her from behind my shades of doom, asking just what it was for.

"Your glasses? Even with that sports band, they're constantly slipping. This way at least maybe you'll avoid them falling off your face at an inopportune moment." She glanced at me pointedly.

"Thanks." I looked at the contraption she'd made and was at a loss. Finally, with a sigh of what I hoped was mock irritation she walked behind me and did whatever was needed to attach them together. It pulled the backs tighter, forming around my head in a smoother fashion than the sports band allowed.

Shaking my head from side to side, I could feel how much sturdier they were. "Thanks. That was a damned brilliant idea." Now maybe I wouldn't trip over all the Mana lines. I squeezed her shoulder briefly to try and convey that I was really glad her brain hadn't failed where mine had.

"You owe me," she said, her eyes twinkling. I had to admit to not being afraid of what I might have gotten myself into.

We all rolled slowly along the road underneath the canopy of trees, an odd bunch to be sure. Gary and Drake didn't quite fit on their bikes, but they'd been the only size we could find for them. Even my legs had difficulty.

Molly and Sange scouted out front as usual, ever alert, working as a team. Tasha and Gemma slunk in and out of my direct sight, even though I knew they were on bikes and that they were there. Those stealthier Class Skills sent shivers down my spine, but Mana Sense made so much more visible to me now.

Not that the surroundings helped either. I could feel Mana-fed sensations roll through my bones. We'd entered a hefty saturation of Mana even before I saw it. My entire vision lit up and I'd have hated to see how bright it looked without the glasses. I jumped slightly, glad for the elastic braces that kept them attached to my face.

"It's alive here. Teeming with Mana and . . ." I didn't like the pit I felt forming in the middle of my stomach. It was like doom and impossibility had met in there and decided to make a baby named Why the Hell Are You Walking Into Danger?

We'd been pretty lucky on the ride up—out, wherever this was—but now I felt like that luck was draining away from us all. Even as we coasted slowly along the road, I knew everything around us was watching and waiting.

This had nothing to do with being controlled by a Rigoll or anything. No, this was far more about intelligent creatures made more observant through the System and just waiting us out. Stalking us, if you will.

This is where I needed a butt-crushing wombat helper. Wish I'd thought to see if I could get a makeshift saddle and ride her into battle. Hindsight was always brilliant. If this was the way in, I was trepidatious at best about what we'd find when we finally reached the actual koala center.

"I don't like this," Gemma muttered under her breath, but the words carried anyway like they were ringing on the wind. She activated stealth mode, and I noticed as she moved from her bike how the Mana she used disrupted the ambient flow around her, allowing me to "see" her.

See invisible. Sort of. Not a bad Skill. Probably couldn't see camouflage unless it engaged Mana in order activate. The thing was, if I was watching for more than one person at a time, I could see even the Mana disruptions bleeding together until I couldn't differentiate things.

Still. There was so much potential for this Skill, it was sort of scary. I really needed to get myself the cash for my upgrade. More perception of what was around me meant more survivability for me and my kids, and others. Aim number one. Get those damned implants.

No aliens were taking more from us without a huge-ass fight.

"We've got this. Stick to the road and be aware of everything around us." I sounded a lot more confident than I felt, but I had to.

Molly's nod was barely discernable in the dim lighting. "On it."

"Righto, Mum," Drake said, but there was a grim smile on his face, and I knew he was just heckling. "You got it."

The last was full of seriousness, because I wasn't the only one with eyes and a brain. We all knew we'd walked into danger.

These weren't my kids, but no one, absolutely no one, benefited from someone else's panic. So the best way to get through this was for us to all fool ourselves into believing we could do this. Welcome to a new level of bravado.

❖

It was darker under the canopy than I'd thought it would be, especially considering the number of gum trees that made up this forest. The road wound around like I'd always remembered it, and would eventually lead to a parking lot and a decent-sized building with a wooden ramp and metal railings meandering up to the koala sanctuary.

What had become of all of the creatures kept inside of the building's walls?

And what of the koalas? They usually sat in their little boughs that rose out of the ground, with tubes of gum tree branches right there for the taking so the little buggers only had to eat and sleep. The path wound around them just far enough from them to keep prying hands away.

They were adorable, and I couldn't count how many times I'd been to visit them, seen their sleepy little eyes, marveled when they actually moved like in slow motion, their claws digging into the soft flesh of the trees.

Just what were they now?

There was still a bit of a ride to the sanctuary. It was only early afternoon, but the gum trees weren't themselves anymore. Subtle differences leaked through, changing the bark ever so slightly. The veins running through the leaves glowed with a sickly green blue.

The Mana in here felt like algae took root and made it sluggish, sickly, infested. Even the air was thick with something I couldn't place, and only the trepidation that made me slow down my bicycle saved our lives.

If a tree falls into the middle of the road for no other reason than Mana ate away at its base, will it still kill you?

Fuck yeah, it will.

I stood there, mere centimeters from where the trunk came crashing down. Even as the rush of air it created ruffled my shirt and hair as the shock to the ground reverberated through my feet, all I could focus on was the sap oozing from the tree and how it was like no sap I'd ever witnessed in my life.

Milky in appearance, it ran more green than blue, that bile tint leaking through what could have been beautiful.

"Don't let it touch you!" Evelyn screamed, jumping back in obvious pain as part of her shoe dissolved right in front of us. Just like the tree was dissolving.

That former gum tree hadn't been small, either. It plummeted down from stories above us, its trunk thick enough for its age to be somewhere over fifty years. I gulped, emotions assailing me as I stumbled back. What about the koalas? Eucalyptus leaves were their only form of sustenance. How were they going to survive?

At first, the shadow that fell over us confused me. We were already in a shaded area, and the smell of eucalyptus wasn't enough to overshadow the deep scent of *wrong* that filled the area. The shadow, while not technically towering above us, was definitely larger—and furry.

I followed the line of its muscular body up, from the small, human-sized claws on its feet, and the way the sturdy, stump-like legs bulged with rippling power that flowed up the entirety of its body. Its nose and teeth looked massive from my vantage point. Don't let anyone ever tell you that an up-the-nose camera shot is flattering.

The claws on the ends of the Koaladude's hands were sharp and about as long as my eight-year-old. They hung to its knees just above my head. It stood there, only some of the fur on its body moving in the light breeze as it sniffed around for its prey.

Koalas are usually herbivores, but whatever Mana had done to this creature nixed that. A glint from the light shining through the forest canopy left nothing to the imagination of how sharp those teeth had become. I could practically feel the lethal pressure in its jaws as it worked its mouth, jaws that would crush bones almost to dust.

I tried to motion with my hands for the others to stay back, not that I thought anyone was going to be stupid enough to creep closer and check on the mutated koala. It raised its claws, deathly sharp claws that could rip open my skull on a whim and I prayed it continued to be ignorant of our presence.

Even its breath as it snuffed in the air held a rancid stench to it, like it forgot how to clean its teeth and had week-old meat stuck in-between them. My gag reflex worked overtime and it took all my considerable Willpower to not throw up, to not move a muscle.

Its eyes alert as it gazed around the area, I could feel how much power went into fueling it, what it drew from the tainted earth around it. There might have been more connections, but my head began to buzz and throb, and I could already feel the pain coming on from a migraine that might have been avoidable otherwise.

Shit.

Suddenly everything else in the forest stopped. No crickets, no birds, not even the rustle of leaves against each other as the wind became perfectly still. Then, like I was watching some blockbuster giant beast movie on the big screen, that face looked down, focusing directly on me, and I almost shat my pants.

Ever see the photo meme of that drenched koala in the trees, the infamous dropbear? Take that and multiply it by about a thousand. The sheer terror I felt running through my soul at that moment could have leveled cities.

Around its face, the fur stood out at odd angles, except it wasn't wet with water, it was very obviously blood, and a lot of it had dried, giving the creature a macabre, spiked facial hairdo. Where the white bits around its mouth were, the whiskers were hung with dollops of red viscera, like someone decorated it with a Halloween theme in mind. Right then, a drop of still-liquid guts fell and plopped at my feet with resounding finality.

My gag reflex finally won out, and I vomited things I swear I hadn't eaten since this whole apocalypse started.

That one specific movement sparked a chain of reaction I could barely follow.

The Koaladude, which I'd inspect later for actual reference when I wasn't running for my life, opened its mouth and roared. The sound was so loud it shook the trees and set everything in the forest running for its life, including our little group of ten.

We spread out and dove into the forest, which in hindsight was the worst thing we could have done, but right them all that mattered was getting away from the surprisingly agile, rotting-flesh-faced monster.

We only had a split second lead on it, too. Bikes abandoned, we bolted into the nearby brush. The thing was, gumtrees don't provide a heap of cover low down, so dashing into the forest was more detrimental than beneficial. Bushes lined the ground in some places, but for the most part, the ground cover consisted of dead leaves and sticks that crunched in our wake, stealing any possibility of stealth from us.

Australia wasn't known for its damp ground cover.

Koaladude didn't appear to care about awakening anyone, and I had to wonder at its lucidity, and whether or not it had banded together with others, or just eaten them all in order to gain that amount of stature it had.

The answer practically hit me in the face in the next thirty meters of running, as two more mutated koalas dropped down from the trees they'd been using to hide in or on top of . . . whatever. Foliage all around us shook as they dropped, their own muzzles but a shadow of what their other friend managed to produce. These guys had dried globules sticking to their fur and whiskers, and there was something about the desiccated nature of it, making it browner, that at least gave them less of a semblance of a devouring monster.

"Surrounded." I could practically feel Sange gulp as they pushed their short, dark hair out of their face. Their eyes darted all around as if seeking out somewhere to flee, and suddenly I realized there was a lot more to this, because as a group we'd already faced some shit.

This? We should have been finding ground to make a stand on, and worrying about exactly what strategy to use to kill these things, and instead we ran away. That wasn't like us at all.

Success!

You have successfully resisted the mental influence of the Koalzilla.

"Guys," I called out, still trying not to groan at the System-generated mutation name, "it's using a fear tactic on us. Snap out of it. We need to approach this like we would any other mob."

Sange and Dale, then Molly and Gemma, were the next ones to resist the effect. Surprisingly enough, the Koalzillas in front of me no longer seemed quite as intimidating. Don't get me wrong, fifteen-feet-high creatures that could probably bite or swipe my head off with their claws? Still intimidating, but just not as bad as I'd originally thought.

They now seemed . . . mildly terrifying.

We stood our ground as the rest came around. Tasha and Ray, Evelyn, Gary, and Drake. We stood in a circle back to back. Drake could take some hits too, and with Dale there, we were in a good position as long as no one lost a limb. Finally, I had time to inspect the creatures.

Koalzilla

This mutant Koala has been pumped full of Mana and has decided to pursue a carnivorous diet. Bulking up by lifting trees and eating meat, the Koalzilla is a far cry from its now-distant koala bear beginnings.

Note: Koalas were never bears. Deal with it. They're now able to vent their rage at their mislabeling.

Level: 25 Elite

Fan-fucking-tastic. It felt like someone was watching over Australia and getting far too many kicks out of coming up with annoyingly phrased descriptions for pretty much everything.

Well, they wanted a fight? We were going to give them a fight.

I cracked my neck from side to side and pulled out my hammer. My sports-holder-jimmied glasses picked up on several aspects of my weapon that I'd need to examine when I wasn't being considered as a meal. The Koalzilla was far more complex than I'd originally imagined.

At least now I knew I needed to be careful of how much it got a hold of me and my emotions. Keeping them in check when I had a weapon that was actively trying to draw them out? Not exactly conducive to survival.

Damn, I loved this weapon.

Warhammer of the Orbtralon Chiefs

Congratulations, you have gained the Warhammer of the Orbtralon Chiefs. In order to access this item, an Orbtralon Chief, also known as Officer, must undergo several punishing trials which include besting his seven training officers in combat.

Weapon Stats Modifiers:

+10% of Strength

+5% of Constitution

+12% Mental Resistance

Weapon Requirements:

Strength: 26

Intelligence: 60

Perception: 50

Weapon Ability

Note: Weapon must be actively equipped for this ability to be available.

Mana Forge

This hammer was forged in the Mana fires of the Orbtralon Ancestors longer ago than your piddly planet has existed. How a lowly Orbtralon Chief got a hold of it is a testament to how far they, as a species, have fallen.

This Warhammer blesses its wielder with the ability to take the Mana flow they can see and mold it directly into physical elements that this Warhammer will then utilize as it is wielded.

Warning: Be aware of the lure of Mana. It can grant you great power but demands a high cost in the process. Most Mana Forgers lose their minds.

I hefted it in my hands, luxuriating in the weight. It was time to get some more experience. After all—I wasn't going to get strong enough to protect my family if I didn't level up, was I?

Chapter Ten:
Childhood Trauma

Molly screamed with rage as she bashed her massive tower shield into the kneecap of one of the two remaining Koalzillas. Bone crunched audibly, echoing throughout the forest with sickening volume. She wiped blood off her forehead and swung immediately back into the reverse move, swinging the shield around to finish the blow on the opposite side of the knee, thus causing the massive creature to stumble to its other one.

She heaved a ragged breath and looked back at Sange, who'd taken a tree to the head. They were fine, or they'd be fine at some stage. Dale had already begun healing, and I was taking all the pressure off that I could by trying to heal myself with Blood Transfer. Gary held off the other one with surprisingly spry attacks that kept him moving, which meant he constantly avoided taking any damage. Lucky for us, his Monk-type Class managed to avoid ninety-five percent of all attacks. Still though, when he was hit, he got clobbered.

Earth Shield got a lot of use; smacking it up in front of where we stood gave the Koalzillas one more thing they had to break through in order to, well, break us. It took a couple of smashes for them to get through my barriers completely. But it wasn't the best for those of us who needed to get into melee range with our weapons.

With Implantation and Water Siphon being my only real damage spells, my Mana was often better used protecting and enabling others.

Drake was surprisingly good at what he did. His Knifeblade Class sounded oddly specific. Similar to Gemma's assassination-type Class, he would flash behind an opponent and appear on the opposite side to where he'd initially been. He sliced at tendons, launching himself high up to plunge dagger guns into the neck joint of the creatures, thereby releasing a charge which let loose small explosions into the creature's body. Not devastating damage to something the size of the Koalzillas, but effective enough.

I guess he'd had the funds to buy those dagger guns as soon as he got access to our shop. Lucky bastard. Decent weapons, useful even if the bullets ran out.

Both Drake and Gemma's dual attacks on the separate Koalzillas were the main thing that saved us. Tasha's brand of Spellsword or Fightermage or whatever she was didn't pack enough of a punch to be truly useful in this type of fight. Though she did contribute to the overall downward spiral of the creatures, she was better served by her distance abilities in this fight.

I based myself between both of the creatures, darting in when a lull in my own casting rotation presented itself to swing my Warhammer up into kneecaps. The satisfying crunching against the bone beneath the fur lent my bloodthirst toward these creatures an edge I wasn't sure I liked.

I wanted to disable them. I wanted to kill them.

Sange sat up and shook their head, a look of pure irritation overcoming them. Luckily, while they'd been out of it for all of twenty seconds, Dale really stepped up. He didn't have anything like Jules's shield, but he did have a fantastic group regeneration Skill that helped all of us at once, just enough to keep topping us off, or to help while he readied another heal, or else someone used a tonic or something.

Of course, healing potions or tonics were expensive. No one had figured out how to make them back in the mall yet, not with any major points. Our Crafting Cartel was still too new to have this sort of thing on hand.

Since there was a maximum use—something about diminishing returns that varied depending on quality of the product and volume of healing, no one wanted to use the cheap stuff. Which meant the Shop got more of our business. That still didn't sit well with me. But for now, it was what it was.

With Sange back in the game, Molly switched from defensive to mostly offensive tank. She was fearless, and I wished I could have a bit of that nerve for myself. With her leading the charge, the Koalzilla she'd already kneecapped was being whittled down fast. It lumbered as Gemma darted in, severing its Achilles just as Molly smashed the other kneecap.

I was in the midst of the fight too, ducking in and out and lashing out with my hammer. Since Mana was low, just beating on things with my hammer was the best DPS I could pull right now. Every single hit, I dug in deep to pull on that anger. Even when my shoulders should have been screaming with exertion, that emotion served to fuel the fight in me.

As long as I could keep a hold of that, use it the way I needed to, I shouldn't have the breakdown I almost had back with the Mollecupai.

I really wished these creatures we were fighting didn't look like the koalas I'd held and petted over my lifetime. Even though they often stank to high hell, and even though their claws always could have ripped holes in anything they wanted to, the little buggers had always been so high and sleepy, they'd been cute as hell.

These guys, once their faces got low to the ground, seemed exactly the same. Cute and sleepy and cuddly, even if there was dried blood and guts around their little mouths. It made me so glad my kids weren't here.

Right then, one of the fallen creatures' flailing claws managed to rip through my side, right through the skin armor I wore, and I suddenly found them not cute at all anymore. Sure, it was about to hit its death throes, but that didn't mean that injury didn't hurt like buggery and make me bleed profusely.

I screamed and spun my massive hammer around, sweeping in like I was about to hit a six and smashed it right in its blood-drenched-but-cute little face. The bone gave way beneath my hammer, jolting up my arms and reverberating through my body as it crashed to the ground. I barely jumped out of the way in time before the Koalzilla crushed me, my wound already healing thanks to Sange's quick reflexes, and I turned to find only one Koalzilla left.

It was the first one we'd encountered. And it was pissed.

The roar it let out made the ground shudder again and had me seriously rethinking my life choices. I pulled all the power I could from my coat, all 175 Mana of it, and pushed out a sizable Earth Barrier, as sturdy as I could make. Even the trees around it got sucked up into it, making the whole construction a weird mix of clay, dirt, and wood.

But it didn't matter, because our opponent swatted it away like it was a fly annoying it on a hot summer's day, and for the first time since realizing it had influenced my fear, I was *actually* terrified. This wasn't induced by some sort of fear pheromone; this was my logic trying to beat my skull into submission about how crazy it was to be out here fighting when I could be back in Garbo snuggled up with my kids and ignoring that any of this had happened.

Logic brain apparently didn't work well with *oh my god, the world has been taken over by mutant Mana which subverts all my childhood loves into horrific, killing creatures.*

So logic brain needed to take a break, while I screamed at the creatures and summoned the fuck out of Implantation and threw in Water Siphon. Effectiveness cooldown be damned. Whatever it took.

"Let everything loose. Everything you've got left." I amended it belatedly because I knew most of us had already blown our Mana load with the others. Whatever we had left was either subpar to what we'd already used, or else needed serious charging up.

Still, my teammates impressed me. Tasha shot out multiple magical daggers that dug into its chest, sending its own blood to mingle with that of all the creatures it destroyed in reaching this level of bloody hell.

Gary and Drake jumped in, cleaving and fighting like their lives depended on it. The determination with which they attacked left no consideration for their own safety, but Dale was there to make sure they had heals over time, HoTs, on them, and any type of shield defense he could muster.

Gemma dove in too, working with the other Knifeblade to blink in and out to confuse the senses as much as she could. All while Molly drove that damned shield into its knees and groin whenever she could reach. Ray's Ice Lances pierced holes where there shouldn't have been any, allowing blood to come sluicing out like floodgates had opened. And it was only then that I realized that his Ice Lances were more like straws and were effectively draining the creature's entire contents out onto the ground below it.

Standing too close meant getting covered in the thick liquid. Even as the fluid fell, as we stood in it, slipped in it, and fought the now-dying Koalzilla. Mana sparked around it, life leaking out of the magic itself as its creation died, seeping into the ground until it could find something else to either enhance or corrupt.

The thing was, Mana itself didn't appear to be anything but a life force looking for an outlet. This koala had simply not been well enough to use it wisely.

Finally, its drained and wounded body crashed down, taking another tree with it in its wake. I felt pity well within me as it lay convulsing on the ground. After all, koalas were a national treasure, an endangered species, and downright cute when not wet.

And here we were killing what remained of a species we'd had so much pride in, an internationally recognized breed of cuteness that would never be seen again. Mutated beyond recognition, so far from what it had originally been. All of this death, all of this blood . . . at that moment, nothing stood out to me more.

Mana had swallowed our world, and was in the process of wiping out all of the creatures that made our country unique, replacing them with monsters because they didn't know how to harness the power in a way that would leave them even a fraction of what they'd been.

Only our Wombutants and Dog back home had retained any of their original persona.

I looked down at my blood-spattered body and wondered just how many humans there would be after all of this—would we, too, be wiped out like this beloved species? More importantly, just how much of myself did I have left?

My goal in life had always been to help the nature around me, to understand it and figure out ways to help it thrive. To take back the portions of it that were dying and give nature a way to climb back from the brink. But now . . . now I understood how Kyle felt about killing with his healing gift.

A sudden chill wafted over my back, like something was watching me, something predatory.

"Not the cleanest kill. You could improve your techniques."

The voice that lingered over the area with those heavy words made the hairs on the back of my neck stand on end.

I turned, slower than I'd have liked but at least not fast enough to whiplash myself, only to have my eyes fall on Mon'swkinon of the Dash'Kiri. His gaze lingered on me, those stony lips pursed in deep thought.

How long had he been there? Movement in the corner drew my gaze and only then did I realize that he wasn't alone. Shadowed by the trees, there were at least four other aliens gathered with him. I couldn't quite define their appearance, though one other of them appeared to have a similar stature to that of the Dash'Kiri.

The brightness of Mana that reflected off all of them dulled whatever senses I had left to tell them all apart. Damn it, these glasses were almost useless.

An attempt to pull up their Status information gave me nothing. Either I couldn't see enough to get their Levels or they were hiding it. Just another trick we needed to learn.

"What is your childhood trauma?" I blurted out, the anger and shock at seeing them fueled by fear for my life. We hadn't even heard them. They could have wiped us out before we'd even noticed they were there.

That sort of recognition? That sort of vulnerability? Yeah, that sucker punched me right in the gut.

Mon'swkinon cocked his head to one side, like he was trying to interpret my words. That was fine. I took a sliver of pleasure in being able to stump them.

"This does not make sense," he finally said.

"In what world is it okay to sneak up on people and scare the crap out of them?" I asked, my heartrate calming down now that I realized they weren't here to kill us. Not that I understood the why of it, just that it didn't appear to be their current driving force.

"Ah." He glanced around, and the other few hunters with him gathered closer. "We watched. Humans are not a well-known factor to us. You are sentient and thus . . . we do not hunt you."

He sounded confused, like he wasn't entirely sure just how sentient we might be.

"Sapient. You mean sapient. We're not animals. We possess intelligence and wisdom. Technically, anyway." I was proud of how steady my voice held considering I was shaking so much on the inside I was surprised blood wasn't leaking out of my ears.

Mon'swkinon just looked at me, his dark eyes gleaming with that same light they'd showed when we met him. He had to be all of ten feet away, but

I felt like he was breathing directly into my face. Just a flick of one of his massive hands would be enough to break my neck, shatter my bones, pulverize me.

There was nothing I could do, nothing any of us could do.

If they could sneak up on us like this in this damned dry underbrush, then they could take out every hunting party we had. The realization had always been there, but now it came rushing to the fore like a brick wall hitting me head on. Right now our existence, our Safe Zone and our survival as a species—it hinged on the fact that these aliens lived by a code.

"Thank you for watching," I found myself saying. After all, couldn't they have just stepped in at any time and taken the kill for themselves?

"We do not interfere in the kills of others. That would not be . . ." He paused for a moment as if listening to something someone else said. "It would not be sportsmanlike?"

I suppressed a nervous giggle, all too aware of how still my entire team was. Good to know I wasn't the only one barely refraining from shitting myself.

"Is that your honor code?" I asked, belatedly realizing I'd said it out loud instead of in my head.

"Yes. We would not interfere in the kill of another. Once engaged, it is a fight to the death. Taking on something above your skillset would be its own punishment."

Okay, I could see that. So I nodded, slowly understanding that there was a lot more to this IRSHA group who'd landed here in our country. Hopefully it was enough of "a lot" that we could survive it.

"We'll abide by the same," I offered, hoping I'd read his words and body language right. Plants had always been so much easier to read. Give it a bit of sunlight, have a happy plant all reaching toward that nice food. People, though? Much harder.

Mon'swkinon nodded very slowly, a flash of something passing over his gaze the I couldn't interpret. Perhaps it was grudging respect? More likely it was the suppression of the urge to kill me where I stood. I'd take either or both.

"To not abide by our code would bring dishonor to my species. You humans are surprisingly resilient." Again that massive pause that gave me goosebumps just in case he was considering being something else, or changing his mind. "Truce for now. Do not get in our way. We will not get in yours."

He turned as if to leave, not waiting for my response. Not that I blamed him, considering I wasn't about to tell his nine-feet-tall ass to stop. What little light filtered through the trees gleaned off his rock-like skin, and he half turned back as if he'd had an afterthought.

My breath stuck in my throat as he did so, hoping against hope he hadn't decided to just destroy us then and there. I could feel Mana gathering around me even as he paused. There was no way anything was taking me away from my kids without a hefty fight.

"We will see you soon. There is much here that is different than anticipated. Much that is not what we were led to believe."

And with that cryptic remark, the bastard disappeared into the trees as if the air simply swallowed him up.

❖

"Well." Dale breathed out as our visitors left us. "That was interesting."

Molly barked out a laugh, easing the tension that held us all hostage. "Good word choice."

We turned around and looted the Koalzillas, the killing of which had given us enough experience to boost up to the next Level for most of us.

Level 23. I wanted, no, *needed* more Levels than that. What with that looming visitation from IRSHA and not being entirely sure how friendly they'd remain—I wanted to be able to defend my own. To tell where they were coming from and know what sort of trouble we might get into. I might not *want* to kill anymore mutated national treasures, but they weren't themselves anymore anyway.

We got plenty of weird innards, skins, and several serrated claws. Plus a few items that were unclassified—I guess new and unusual mutations produced crap like that. We'd be taking those to Ginali.

Now we just needed to find our bikes and get to the actual sanctuary itself. I was fairly certain it was a perfect spot for a dungeon to form. At least it was obvious now we weren't going to be looking for cute and cuddly koalas to save.

"Kira?" Ray sounded far less confident than I was used to from him. I nodded and waited for him to continue.

"That was pretty fucked up."

I glanced at him and contemplated the words. There was a lot to unpack there, as my mother would have said in all her psychiatrist glory. She would have been right, too. "Yep. Koalas—no longer just cute, high, and cuddly; they're deadly, too."

He looked around, and I suddenly realized how haunted his gaze was. Much younger than myself, he was barely out of his teenage years, and this entire debacle had really affected him. The wombat we'd fought with cemented his world view. Wombats were smart, cute, and cuddly, and of course they were on our side. Mutant Magpies and whatnot, they were always evil to begin with, but here we'd been faced with our childhood plushies come to life as horror movie inserts and he didn't know how to deal with it.

"Hey. We couldn't foresee any of this. You realize that, right? There's no right or wrong reaction. Our brains are dealing with all this as they see fit." My words came out more clipped than I intended, because I didn't want him to feel bad. It made me cringe that it might have come across as snapping at him, but he looked at me, this newfound realization in his eyes, and he nodded.

"True. We can only protect what we can protect, right? Only preserve what is possible." The sadness didn't leave his face; in fact, it appeared to sink deeper and give him a prematurely aged thing despite the fact that I was pretty sure the System actively worked against that.

Alert: Your son wishes to make a Shop purchase that requires your permission. The item below is perusable at your leisure for approval at any time. Should you decline or approve, your son will be notified.

Item:

Human Genome Treatment.

This treatment adjusts . . .

I didn't read the rest. First up, I didn't have time, and secondly, I was going to wait and talk to Jackson about this in person. There was no way this was safe for a kid only just starting puberty, and I wanted to know what had brought this up in the first place. Sighing, I managed to dismiss the notification and hoped that I would have time to deal with it later. This was all getting too complex to manage.

It would be such a massive help if Mason were around to give me a hand. Although, he'd probably approve it because he was always the lenient one. Right now, I could do with some of that frivolity—I ached to not have to be serious all the time. Every feeling I'd had in the last two weeks, every friendship, they were all embedded in death and need and desperation.

A bit of levity right now would be a nice change of pace.

"Protect what's possible, and get out of it what you can for yourself."

I spoke quietly, and I think Ray had almost forgotten I was there.

He nodded and I knew the thoughtful look on his face would give him that inevitable crease between the eyebrows no matter how much the System tried to fight it.

We collected our bikes and made our way back to the main road, having completely cleaned out any and all loot that we could off the creatures. Maybe mutant koala meat was something we could end up eating. We definitely couldn't cuddle them anymore.

Chapter Eleven:
New Plans

I'm not sure what I expected as we made our way along the road that wound through Daisy Hill. There were no cars in sight, this area not being conducive to night joyriding. Made me wonder just what Mount Cootha Lookout would have been like. How many of the couples up there had survived? What about the cafe? That overlook was certainly something that'd give a sobering view of our city.

As we rounded the final bend in the road to where the sanctuary had always been, Mana leaked up to us like a turbulent river daring us to cross.

Just before we got to the Center, I noticed something in the distance, through the trees. Shading my eyes, I blinked, but whatever I'd seen wasn't there anymore.

Maybe these glasses were interfering with my regular sight, too.

"Everything okay?" Dale asked, pulling up next to where I hadn't even realized I'd stopped.

I nodded, although not entirely sure things were okay. "Yeah. Everything's fine." I pushed off, and he followed, but now I was even more determined to get myself those upgrades.

The koala sanctuary was no more. Instead of the nice, green-roofed little building that had once stood there, the underbrush and ground had instead begun to reclaim it as a cave on its own, pulling the structure back into nature.

While Mana morphed everything else in its path.

Dozens of other possible dungeon locations flagged themselves in my mind. I'd slot them away for future reference. Level up or die—the new way of life.

"It's in there, isn't it?" I could hear the trepidation in Molly's voice.

Like, there was a hint of excitement in there too, but I could tell she was scared. I didn't blame her.

"Yeah. It's right in there. Or I assume it is, since this is where the Sanctuary was," I murmured, not really wanting to admit it.

I'd spent so much time in this area with different plant grafts and studying the way the trees and plants around here grew without any direct sunlight under the canopy, how they thrived after koalas had been released and eaten so much that regrowth was stimulated.

I'd really hoped, for some obscure reason, that this area might have been spared. I could daydream though, maybe write stories about how the world used to be. Perhaps sell them through the Shop in a series about: Earth—in the times before.

"Are we going in?" Dale sounded eager, like he wanted a chance for payback, even if he knew it didn't quite work like that.

"We can try and see what it's like." I looked over the area, and even through the glasses, I knew that this was different from the dungeon at the high school. Hell, they probably all were. After all, everything was constantly evolving.

I took a deep breath, smiled at my friends and stepped off my bike. "Let's hide these and see what we can and can't kill. How's about a few hours before we head home?"

"Home before dark, though." Ray stated it more than asked.

I nodded and no one else spoke, not that I blamed them for remaining silent. Frankly, I was scared to walk in there. I wasn't an Adventurer despite the amount of time I spent outdoors. My obsession was with nature and how it worked and intermingled, how it produced the oxygen of life that fueled us all, and how we could better preserve it.

Now I was stuck with figuring out Mana's intricacies, how it mutated things, and just what this meant for the longevity of my own species, for myself, for my kids, and every single person we'd gathered along the way.

Especially considering the System hadn't even given us a chance at survival here on our little continent.

That made all of this frankly terrifying, but at the same time, it was also invigorating, a challenge—proving a point that we would survive. Stubborn. Sort of like cockroaches. I'd never really admired their ability to survive until we were the ones being squashed.

Where once the ramp that led to the entrance of the koala sanctuary had been a beautiful wooden structure, it now seeped with black ooze that bubbled out of the ground and up through the slats. Blue strands of power barely scratched the surface around here, replaced by the thick and oozing mess. Maybe it was a type of blue, but so dark it appeared black?

Maybe I was reaching.

Even the canopy overhead lowered itself to reach us, to push through and block out any sunlight. Once inside the structure, I had a fairly good inkling there'd be a brand-new tunnel leading underneath everything to drag us down into an actual dungeon. Not that it had to be underground, considering how the MacGregor High dungeon developed, but I was fairly certain this one would be.

It was the first time I hesitated, and I know the others saw it.

"Rethinking this?" Sange asked in that quiet way of theirs that hid ten thousand other questions and opinions.

I shrugged, not entirely sure of the answer myself. "I just want to get back tonight."

Because I wanted to sell the stuff we'd gotten, or barter for it. Talk to Ginali and see just how this trade hub was going to benefit us. If my constant throbbing head was any indication, I needed those damned implants. And I really needed to hug my kids.

Dale nodded. "Two hours and we head back, then. Set a timer?"

"With what?" Ray barked a laugh, his dark hair brushing over his eyes as he did so. "It's not like we have phones anymore."

I could see Dale fighting back his own bit of laughter. It made me feel old. I wasn't sure I'd be dealing so well with the apocalypse if I was only in my early twenties. There was a time before phones. Still though, the EMT got control of himself and was far nicer than I felt it in myself to be.

"The interface. It's a system, a computer in our heads. We can use it as a timer." His words were so matter-of-fact that I blinked. Why on Earth hadn't I thought of that before? Of course it kept time. I'd even used it more than once.

"What are you thinking?" Molly's interest was piqued. She leaned on her shield that I noticed now she never put away regardless of fighting or not.

"Two hours in? Alarm. Let us decide if we want to give it another hour or not depending where we are—and otherwise, we retreat at four and head home, or else we retreat at five and head back. We should make it back before nightfall that way." Dale was so logical, almost like he was dictating a play.

Way to go, coach. I couldn't help smiling. It helped that I wasn't the only one with kids to get back to. Thing was, if I didn't have that anchor, I could see this pulling me deeper into danger, like a drug, a need to know what lay beyond and if, just maybe, we could beat it all.

Ray nodded slowly and then his whole demeanor lit up. "I get it. Okay. Let's go see what rare crap we can find."

I just had to quash my overactive imagination and its doomsday scenarios. The odds of the entire settlement being vaporized before we got home were minuscule. IRSHA wouldn't, shouldn't be waiting to fight us when we got back, right? Mon'swkinon hadn't sounded like that in our meeting but an hour ago.

We needed Levels though, so this was it. This was our option. Scout it out, pare it down, so others could make their way here for Leveling purposes. Maybe more than ten of them.

"Check over everything first. Make sure you've got all the supplies you need, your Mana is topped off, and you haven't forgotten to activate, choose, or apply a Skill."

I knew I was set. Needed another Skill Point before I could grab my next Skill. There wasn't anything else for me to do but go and get that remaining seventy-five hundred experience. Let's hope I didn't have to lose any of my newfound friends to Level again.

It was beginning to get old.

Black sludge in the form of a speeding projectile spitball careened through the half-formed dungeon hall. The pale, greenish walls, lit with flickering lighting, that had once been the entry hallway of the koala center still offered good footing at least. I didn't think they'd had snakes in here as exhibits, but that didn't mean there hadn't been plenty outside.

Or at least the creature *looked* snake-like.

If snakes had stubby multitudes of legs, and their spit corroded the metal support beam right next to my head.

Too fucking close.

It moved almost like a cobra, but we didn't have any of those around this area, or we didn't prior to the apocalypse—maybe it migrated everything shitty here. I moved slowly, watching its eyes never leave my face as it swayed in an oddly hypnotic way with its centipede legs perfectly still. Why it focused on me, I had no idea, but at least I didn't get the same sense of terror from it I'd gotten from the Koalzillas.

Thing was, Mister Eastern Cobra Mutant Centipede wasn't your average size anymore. Height-wise he swayed about as tall as Dog, but his body extended out the back. If I had to guess, I'd say there were four or more meters of him in total, roughly twelve feet long. And he was a whopping Level 30.

Pseudonaja Centificus

Level 30

At least the bastard wasn't an Elite.

The Level-30 Centificus reared back on tiny hind legs. Its lips peeled back to reveal fangs that didn't appear as if they could possibly fit in its mouth and even as the jaws elongated, the head grew. I scrambled back, away from the still-smoking hole in the iron girder, muscling my Warhammer as I did so.

No mind tricks here. The terror I felt was all mine.

And then its head bounced on the ground in front of me, the tongue still flickering and those now-sightless eyes full of surprise. I looked up to see Molly staring at me with a grim grin, her sword still following through with the motion that had cut the head clean off the still-twitching body.

"Kira. Snap out of it. You're going to orphan your kids."

Her words stung, but they weren't wrong. Shaking myself, I hefted my Warhammer over my shoulder and followed the rest of the group. Two weeks and this area was a fucking train wreck. Level 30s growing from the ground up, having eaten everything in sight.

If we didn't level up and get ourselves out here to extend our safety net borders, we were going to wind up with a lot more dead people. Surely wildlife wasn't supposed to level this fast.

We worked through the rest of the main floor methodically. All of us together. My cloak filled with Mana far too slowly for my liking, only sitting around fifty Mana again a couple of hours after having taken on the Koalzillas. My own Mana Regen was decent, given my Willpower and Mana Transfer, but it still wasn't enough.

It was never enough.

There were far too many snakes around here—half of them mutated with something else. They'd grown five times in size, fattened themselves, unhinged jaws snapping like nature hadn't intended. Venom spitballs, tail lashes . . .

We jumped over them, ducked from them, got hit by acid balls that tore through armor and started melting weapons and flesh. It all passed in such a blur of speed and experience I didn't even notice at first when the timer went off.

Blood coated everything we carried, all of our clothes and weapons, hair and skin. Drippings of black sludge that passed for the blood of the creatures we killed ran down our bodies and made weird, splotchy noises when we stopped.

We hadn't even gotten to the lower levels yet. Full-day expeditions, that's what we needed. To get serious about this, to complete the next quest, we needed to expand our reach and survive—and find others who had too.

I paused, holding up a hand to signal that we stop for a moment.

Even with the System's help rejuvenating our bodies, I could hear us panting as we regained our equilibrium. I wondered how much of it was mental, how much physical. We expected to be tired, so we were. Or thought we were.

Something like that.

Hissing still came from several feet away, signaling more attackers just waiting for us. They weren't too difficult to kill, just dangerous if we let them overrun us.

"This isn't going to work. We need full trips to clear these to a point where they become manageable. We need to reach out further, find any survivors we can, and make it our priority to bring them back with us." I knew I stated the obvious, but people weren't speaking what they thought. Someone had to put it into words.

"Yeah." Evelyn pursed her lips, looking around the dimly lit forming dungeon thoughtfully. "The more things are left, the higher they'll level, the faster they'll be able to branch out themselves. These were never stupid creatures to begin with. I feel like our wildlife is leveling on acid. Everything around here is higher than us already . . and I think it'll only get worse."

"Great." Molly scowled. "Let's get back and put together some solid patrols. We're getting more people all the time—we need targeted leveling strategies, Kira."

Dale nodded his agreement, crossing his toned arms. "You need to hold a meeting."

I choked down a laugh and shook my head. Not because I meant to say no, but because I couldn't believe I'd managed to become the PTA mum despite avoiding it all of Jackson's and Wisp's lives previously. "Fine. Let's get back. We have shit to do."

As if on cue, there were multiple slithering hisses from all around us. We'd stood still for too long. Drake and Gemma activated stealth, making the Mana zing right in front of my eyes, and we turned to face another five Centifici before we could even think about heading home.

❖

Twilight was already falling when we managed to trudge back into Garden City. In hindsight, it hadn't been the best idea to venture out late morning. As much as I feared coming back and finding everything leveled and our newly instated overlords presiding over us, everything was about as apocalyptically peaceful as it could get.

The center bustled when we stepped in, and I chose to head toward the showers downstairs rather than straight to our little apartment because, and let's face it, I was covered in flakes of dried blood from head to toe. I couldn't imagine what I smelled like from the outside, but from in here I was constantly fighting my gag reflex.

The only people not complaining or commenting or giving me the side-eye when we got back were the very same people who arrived with me.

Thing was, I didn't make it that far. Apparently I was nowhere near repellent enough, even with globs of meat flaking off me and my weapons.

Red stopped me in his tracks, his eyes lit up with excitement. "Kira! You've got to meet Paul! He, like, knows how to cook with everything in an animal or creature."

I raised an eyebrow and smiled at the aforementioned Paul. He was shorter than me with closely cropped black hair and shining dark eyes. His warm golden skin stood out against a pristine white shirt he'd probably just got from our store allocation. "Nice to meet you. Think you can help us keep up feeding our hungry horde, then?"

"Definitely. My grandmother taught me how to cook everything. Never let a piece of animal go to waste—respect what is given in death." His smile never waned, and the seriousness in his expression was only outweighed by what felt like joy emanating from him at having discovered a way to be helpful.

"You should talk to Ginali. I'm sure he'll be able to help with extraction tools, et cetera." I smiled and turned to Red who was almost vibrating out of his skin. "And you're so excited because?"

"Because I needed some serious help in the kitchens, and this frees me up to help oversee rationing our stock, so I can make sure we don't run out. This gives me more time to work with Ginali on what we need as a settlement, and what we can trade to keep ourselves ahead of the curve." He smiled a bit sadly. "Besides, it's weird being here without Barry. I need more than food to occupy me."

I gave him what I considered an awkward pat on the shoulder. Yep, had no words for right then. "I'm glad you've got the help, then." Glancing at the time, I realized we'd need to do the meeting sooner than later.

"Hey—let everyone know we need to gather outside near the Northern Gate at 6:30 p.m. Have lots of information we need to discuss." That gave me an hour to find Dor and Sienna and tell them everything our little hunting party had found. Or maybe slightly less than an hour. I still had to get the stench off me.

Which took a lot less time than I thought. These System-sponsored shower adjustments really made short work of the mess. Maybe that was deliberate, but either way it was welcome. Freshly cleaned hair and body—with a set of clothes that wasn't crusted over with mingled species' blood—felt like a world of difference.

Industrial clothes washing machines. I felt like we could really use some of those. As far as I knew, we were just taking advantage of the ones from the department stores and using the fuck out of those.

Wisp joined me as I exited the shower bays, Wombie and Dog following at a not-so-discreet distance. "You didn't come and see me straight away." Her accusatory tone wasn't lost on me, and I felt a stab of guilt right in the gut. Very well aimed.

"Sorry, sweetie, but I knew you were safe, and I had to get the blood off me." Not a lie in the slightest. She wasn't ever far from my thoughts.

I reached over and gave her a tight hug which she didn't relinquish in the slightest. Walking with someone clinging to your waist who is about fifty centimeters shorter than you is never comfortable, but at the same time there was a different kind of comfort to be found in being able to hold my eight-year-old at all.

"Yeah. I get that. I don't like blood." She paused and pulled away slightly, still holding my one hand that wasn't busy trying to rub a towel through my hair.

"Mum. Can I ask you something?"

She sounded timid, which was very unlike my little Wisp. Timid and yet sort of determined. "Fire away, kiddo."

She paused, mulling over the words and trying to find the specifically correct ones. "Jackson is upset because you didn't okay what he wanted to buy at the Shop. But . . . I don't want you to okay it. I'm worried."

Her gaze focused right on my eyes, holding my expression so tightly that I stopped our walkup and dropped down to her level. "Thanks for the heads up, love. But what are you worried about?"

"Some of the guys here—the people, not just the other older boys—they don't even look like humans anymore. And I don't want Jackson to not be what he is. It's my favorite thing about him." Her lip quivered, but I watched as she physically stood straighter and stopped herself. "Everything's changing, Mum. I miss Dad. Do you think he'll make it to us?"

I enveloped her in another hug, and this time she clung to me like the kid she was. For all that she acted so mature and always had, she was eight, in the middle of a fucking apocalypse, and she was scared despite the bravado. Guilt ate away at me. Who was I to be going out there and trying to protect all these people? I should be here with my kids . . . but that wouldn't make me stronger, and strength was what I needed to protect us all—them included.

Damn those Catch-22s.

For a moment, I wondered how soldiers, policemen, those who used to put themselves in the way of danger for their work, did it. The ones with a family, obviously. We hadn't seen much of them, but the suburbs weren't exactly the place you got a lot of soldiers or policemen. And I bet many had gone out to do what they could.

Did we just lose the majority of them, then? Or had they established their own camps?

"It's okay, love. I'll talk to him. He won't stay angry for long." I knew he wouldn't. Teenager he might be, but he was cursed with our family's logic gene.

Dog head butted my back, like he was agreeing with me, encouraging me. Damn it, but I liked that animal. I reached over and scratched behind his ears, marveling at how he was the size of a small pony now. I was willing to bet he could cart my kid away in a pinch, and I was grateful for it.

"Thanks." Wisp wiped away a tear and smiled up at me. It was an expression tinged with sadness, but somewhere in there was an element of hope, too. I'd fight to keep that there.

"Now, do you want to come with me to talk with Dolores and Sienna?"

Wisp wrestled her hand out of my grip and laughed suddenly. "No. Why would I want to talk to old people who aren't you?"

And the next thing I knew, she was dashing away with Dog and Wombie trailing after her. Children.

Love them, want to strangle them, still have to take care of them.

Chapter Twelve: Organizing

15 Days Post-System Onset

6:30 p.m.

Lights from the four vehicles that our little tech department had managed to convert to Mana batteries lit up the area we met in. While we could have fit the odd fifteen hundred people out here in one spot, we didn't need to. Many just sent a representative of their group. Most of our residents came from initial small batches of people.

From couples to family-type groups, even if there was no blood relation. Safety in numbers, comfort in familiarity. And right now, we all needed some of that.

I'd never been excited by public speaking, but I'd never balked from it. While Kyle was the outgoing twin, I was the pragmatic one—the one who did what needed to get done. Just like I was about to do here.

Dor cleared her throat and spoke over the makeshift PA system the tech team set up for us. "So, loves, we have some not-so-happy news for us all. But we have ideas to make our situation better and not worse, so listen up and don't be a dick."

There was a terse undercurrent of laughter scattered throughout the crowd. Probably a hundred and sixty people, just above ten percent. Mostly made up of the Adventurers from every group and then some pocket change.

Dor's voice rang out clearly, with that gruff undertone I'd come to appreciate so much. "We will spend tonight drawing up adventuring groups. Those who are Level 15 and higher will need to take their combat expertise and gain more of it. Thing is, those monsters out there aren't about to stop spawning, and this Mana isn't about to stop mutating the creatures we've grown up fearing or revering."

Mumma Wombutt managed to bleat out a punctuation note that luckily undercut tension while driving the point home. Not that it was planned, but I appreciated her involvement.

I continued the information. We'd not wanted people to feel like they were being preached at. "We need to clear around our area like we have been doing, but also to rotate further out. The more we leave the nearby areas to flourish on their own, the higher Level the creatures in them end up. Either spawning or mutating, or whatever they do.

"If we're not careful, we 'll end up getting overrun by monsters that we can't fight or even defend against because we don't have sufficient Levels." I paused for a moment, looking over at everyone. Bearer of bad news it was. At least I wasn't telling them about the vegetation yet. Dor hadn't thought it a good idea.

Dale cleared his throat and spoke in that deep voice of his—it resonated through like an umpire you didn't despise. "We encountered Level-25 Elites, and Level-30 average mobs in areas that would have been easy pickings for us early on. Now that they've been let go for two weeks, the creatures there are going to outlive us easily if we don't get some tight control over them."

"To that end . . ." Evelyn stepped in, her bow held at her side in plain view. It was a *really* nice bow. "We will be putting together parties and pushing leveling. If you have any combat abilities in your Class, then we urge you to step outside your comfort zone and Level. The lower Level we are, the less chance we have of making it much further. The stronger each of us gets, the stronger we become as a whole."

I could hear the subtle shake in her voice, but she stood strong even as the Mana whipped around her tightly, like it was trying to force its way down her throat. Damn it, I needed those implants and I needed them yesterday. I needed to be able to understand what it was all the Mana dancing around me was doing—to differentiate between bad and good. And maybe help those incomprehensible whispers from trying to inundate my brain.

"We are dividing up the surrounding areas, trying to reach through to Carindale Shopping Center, and maybe eventually the Hyperdome. To bridge the areas between us." I paused, letting that settle in before continuing. "Most of the Settlement Orbs that we know of are based in other shopping centers around the city. The closer we can get to keeping most of the monsters under Level 30 between those settlements, the better chance of survival we Aussies will have."

A soft murmuring rose up.

"Bloody oath!" someone yelled from the crowd, causing a round of raucous laughter to cut through the tension.

"Too right! Can't keep Aussies down."

The sheer indomitable will I was used to from the people in my country let me smile. We weren't about to back down from a fight.

Sienna stepped to the PA, the crowd mellowed out, and I was glad I'd chosen to equip my hammer on a newly minted belt at my side, because even with that added mental protection, I could feel her Charisma trying to grab a hold of me. Bloody politician perks. "Tomorrow morning, we will have groups allocated in order to keep the best chance of survivability and success at leveling and gaining more strength in place. Please note that you may not be paired with people you know. Right now, we have to concentrate on surviving, and to do that, we need to get stronger faster—"

"Like that Daft Punk song!" someone shouted out I the crowd, and even I felt the smile tugging at my face.

"Yeah, like that Daft Punk song," I found myself answering. Maybe there was some hope. "This isn't going to be easy. And I know it's hard for some of us to work with people we don't know, or to even care about people we don't know. But the thing is, we're what's left right now. And we need to find any other survivors that we can, and bring them here to be safe with us too. We can't protect ourselves and our town if we don't work on our Skills."

A muttering of agreement rose from the crowd, even if there was an undercurrent of fear. None of which I could blame anyone for. But they weren't devolving into screaming fits or angry mob mentality. Frankly I think some of us were so exhausted that we just didn't have the energy to do anything but go along with others.

If we were lucky, that would keep us alive.

Jackson and the tech crew hadn't been at the meeting, but I knew Ray had already headed over to them to let them know what the plan was. Not that Ray was my first choice for that sort of thing. He was quick of temper, and slightly volatile most of the time. Give him six months and I think he'd weather that youthful trait.

My son didn't notice me at first, and I felt a swell of relief to find him completely absorbed in the soldering he appeared to be doing. At least, I think that's what it was. His hand glowed as he held the device, allowing him to create the seams along what I assumed was a Mana battery.

Whoa, did I ever not want to go and look at the current town treasury balance. I had a strong suspicion a lot of the items this ever-growing team was tinkering with had been purchased by our little settlement.

Still. Worth it.

"Mum." He looked up, a smile tugging at his lips, and I could tell how tired he was. Proud, but tired.

Still, he was just a teenager. He needed more sleep, even in this self-rejuvenating world. "You're not sleeping enough, silly boy."

Absentmindedly, he reached out with his right hand and gave me half a hug. "I'm sleeping about six hours a night. There's just so much to do, and it's a lot cheaper if we do it ourselves with relatively few components from the Shop."

Shop. That's right. I needed to see Ginali and sell to him or the Shop. Hell, I needed to understand the difference between selling to the Cartel and the Shop.

Instead of saying everything that ran through my head, I focused on my main reason for coming to see him. "Kind of like human genome treatments?"

Jackson at least had the good grace to cringe. "Yeah. Sorry about that. I wasn't *actually* trying to purchase it. I was trying to see if it had more information about it than what it listed. Which it didn't, and I didn't feel comfortable asking the Shopkeeper exactly everything it entailed." He looked up at me, obviously somewhat embarrassed, and something else as well. Something I couldn't place.

He put down his tools and rubbed his hands off on his jeans. It felt like he'd grown again, not in height, though. Just in age. Maturity. My babies weren't babies anymore. All I could do was guide them, right? Could they still become good people when apocalyptic death was everywhere? What kind of people would they become if they had to kill, on the regular? To survive?

I didn't know. But I'd do my darndest to help them.

"Hey, Mum, do you think we could just—like all have breakfast together or something tomorrow?" His huge eyes looked up at me like that puppy dog I almost bought him for his tenth birthday.

Guilt crashed down on me like a tidal wave of my own making. "Of course." I reached out to hug him and felt tension drain out of his body as I did so. Oh, my big little boy. We were going to crush this thing.

136

Backing up, I held him at arm's length, really looking at him. Either I let him go out with other groups, or I couldn't let him go out at all. He was a few Levels below me now, despite the crafting Leveling, and I just couldn't take him with me into that much danger yet. I'd be second guessing every move I made, every spell I cast, every bomb I planted. But he could go out with the twenty-and-under groups. And gradually work his way up.

Mind made up, I gripped his shoulder tight and looked him dead in the eyes. "You up to going out to Level? Got any gadgets that will help you kick ass?"

Jackson's whole face lit up. "Well, now that you mention it, Darren and I have been working on something."

A small wave of relief swept away some of my guilt. Stronger. We all needed to get stronger, even our kids. As I sat and listened to him go on about his inventions, I mulled over the last stop I needed to make before I let myself get what would probably be my last sound night of sleep for a long time to come.

Ginali and the Shop.

Because I needed a plan for this overwhelming headache that was my Mana Sense. And despite thinking I could probably afford the implants after I sold what we'd gained out there this day—I had a bad, bad feeling that the recommended Levels were far more important than the bare minimum. It was going to take time to get those Skills to a point where I wouldn't melt my brain by getting the implants.

Damn it.

❖

If the System had taught me one thing since activating in front of my vision like a pain in my arse, it was that sometimes I just hated being right.

"No. No." Ginali shook his head emphatically, peering at me with his eyes that saw through every excuse in the book. "Never, ever go on the minimum specifications. You want recommended at least, if not higher. What you have to understand is that this technology wasn't specifically engineered just for humans."

He frowned as he leafed through something while we stood in the pristinely white Shop together, browsing through the options I'd found previously. "You do not order this until you have everything you need—and you will require specific genome treatments in order to enable your body to readily take on some of the modifications necessary to allow your ability to reach its fullest potential."

"Why doesn't it say that?" I was already overtired and irritated. The System not giving what I considered full information made it worse. Not that I should have expected better.

"Because humans are not an old species." Ginali shrugged like it was purely matter of fact. "You came along several hundred millennia ago, and didn't even evolve properly for such a long time. Your data is lacking in the System, and you're all just awfully fragile. You need to beef up your genetic sequences specifically within human ramifications so that the tech you need to handle your Mana Sense won't . . . well . . . won't damage your fragile brain."

He smiled at me, about as sweetly as he probably could. And I had to forcibly make my blood not boil. Ginali wasn't my problem and taking it out on him was a bad idea. His Cartel allowed for us to purchase cheaper from the Shop, to barter and trade, and well . . . I mean, it was obviously going to be beneficial for the Cartel in the long run to have a foothold here or they wouldn't have done it.

But this was helping us.

"Anyway," he continued like I wasn't having a total mental meltdown all on my own over here. "You will need to add a human-specific neural genome treatment. That should help you the most. And, since you are wanting me to be completely honest with you, this is something you should get at least a few days before your operation. It will boost your Intelligence scores, and it's best to give your body time to acclimate to it before you add everything else into the mix."

The worst thing was, he made complete and utter sense. I nodded slowly. "Guess I'll grab that once we're done. Will the glasses I'm using in the interim still work?"

Ginali nodded, smiling brightly. "Of course!"

I had enough to sell that getting the human-specific neural genome treatment wouldn't be a problem. It made total sense this way, too. "Thanks. I appreciate the rundown."

"Of course, of course! We have a mutually beneficial business relationship here." He pulled his gaze away from the menu he was perusing and turned to me, his eyes gleaming with eagerness. "Now, did you say you had some rarities for me?"

I grinned at him as we left the implant room and the Shop with it, waving at Shi'enah on my way out. She nodded at us both, and I could see the sides of her lips quirk with what I thought might be satisfaction. And for a moment, I thought there was just so much more going on with the Cartel and the Shop than I'd ever imagined. I wonder if they'd gained any more footholds in the direct vicinity.

And then I got down to haggling with Ginali, before I'd sell the rest to the Shop and go over to Sienna, Dor, Dale, and Kyle to arrange the Level groupings for tomorrow morning. After that, I was going to get that treatment.

Be damned whether people wanted to adventure or not; I was getting them to at least be proficient in their abilities. I wasn't leaving any more Aussies behind if I could help it.

Chapter Thirteen:

Open Mind

6 Weeks Post-System Onset.

8 a.m.

I stood in the Shop as I waited for Jackson to get done selling the items he'd gained on his adventures. Now he was Level 27, I felt a lot more confident about him going out with his own patrols. Mostly, anyway.

The Settlement was thriving, having just reached over two thousand people. Not a peep out of IRSHA yet . . . unless we included the encounters in the field, the way they watched us fight. Yeah, that wasn't unnerving at all.

I watched my son but didn't really pay attention to exactly what he was up to. We'd had another report from last night's patrol that just didn't sit well with me.

We couldn't be sure if Mana was subverting creatures faster or something, but over the last week or so it felt like we were constantly being watched. Fleeting shadows, figures in the distance.

All of it could be chalked up to stress, but even I'd managed to catch a glimpse yesterday, and there'd been so much Mana interference I couldn't identify anything about it. It could have been a mutating tree for all I knew, but my gut told me it wasn't.

My glasses didn't help at all. In fact, they pretty much made it worse with the blur of abundant blues they gave me instead of information. The damned whisperings of the Mana were only getting louder. Now I'd finally levelled my stats enough, it was time for me to get the damned implants.

Jackson was kitting himself out. Staff, like a true mage, but one that allowed him to utilize specific elements of his technological abilities. He'd been saving up for the components and the base staff for weeks, and now he was gleefully selling things so he could take it over to Ginali at the Crafting Cartel and finally put all of the pieces together to help enhance his spells.

I didn't even pretend to understand how his Class worked. All I knew was that he could tinker with technology, wield electrical elements, and magnify his powers through his crafting abilities.

Wisp, Dog, and Wombie waited their own turns patiently. The kids had taken to scouring around with some of their tutors under Jan's guidance after classes to find scraps they too could sell. It helped us all, keeping the immediate vicinity around our walls clear, and allowing the younger kids glimpses outside the walls we'd fortified to keep them safe.

Because outside the walls . . . well, let's just say that Mana-infused nature took over more than it let go. Nature had always been hungry to reclaim its territory, as evidenced by abandoned theme parks and hotels even before the apocalypse hit.

But this . . . this was something else entirely.

Vines that moved and grabbed at low-Level monsters—or the random kid who got too close. Plants that dispersed hallucinogenic or sedative pollen, so that people or monsters just lay down to sleep and never woke up. Trees that used to be bushes, that flowered and offered fruit that was actually edible.

Not all bad, not all dangerous. Surprising, how fast the children had learnt not to touch anything without proper precautions, to use long sticks to prod things. Even to carry pocketknives to cut their way out if they made a wrong decision.

That little, suburban-mum part of me was quietly screaming in horror at the risk the kids ran. Some of the other parents had done the out-loud part. We had to squash that, when we pointed out how dangerous life was going to be from here on out. There were still parents, kids who refused to go out, who weren't allowed out. Others had been traumatized to the point they weren't willing to do so.

Wombie and Dog did a lot of good there, acting as chaperones. But as much as I hated it, as much as we took precautions to keep them "safe," risks—and dangers—had to be taken. It helped, I guess, that System-infused healing meant that injuries weren't permanent.

Just death.

Jackson was taking longer than I wanted, and I'd already bartered with Ciago and Ginali. Ciago was the gourmet cook attached to the Cartel and was busy helping Paul adapt all of the recipes for heart and liver, lungs and tongue, and more parts of animals that his grandmother had taught him.

The less I knew about how we got what we ate, the better. I had enough on my plate. I tried not to laugh at my own joke.

Anyway, we didn't always get Credits in trade, but we always got things we needed, and I had more than enough to pay for my surgeries finally. I'd just been waiting for my damned stats to catch up with me, and I was so close I could taste it.

Impatience taking hold of me, I pulled up my stats.

Status Screen			
Name	Kira Kent	Class	Ecological Chain Specialist
Race	Human (Female)	Level	30 (2,380 XP to next Level)
Titles			
Diviner			
Health	400	Stamina	400
Mana	900	Mana Regeneration	12.2ps

Attributes			
Strength	30	Agility	30
Constitution	40	Perception	65
Intelligence	90	Willpower	60
Charisma	25	Luck	20
Class Skills			
Mana Attunement	2	Earth Barricade	2
Blood Transfer	1	Mudslide	1
Water Siphon	2	Mana Transfer	1
Rockslide	1	Implantation	2
Treesong	1	Planted in Place	1
Top Soil	1		
Skills			
Leadership	3	Mana Sense	12
Blunt Weapons	4	Mana Sense (2)	1
Combat Spells			
Shield of Power*			
Perks			
Diviner		Analyze	
Mana Cloak 2			

A quick glance had me review the Class Skills I'd picked up, refreshing their uses in my mind. It wasn't like my older Skills, ones that I'd gotten so used to that I never even thought about it anymore.

We'd been leveling so hard, I sometimes forgot that I *had* the new

Skills.

Tier Three (Levels 20-29)

Treesong

Effect: Your affinity with nature and the life around you allows you to be at one with the trees. Sort of. The System and Mana have made vegetation come alive. Duration of Skill varies dependent upon strength of Mana Affinity.

Command Vegetation to attack your enemies, or just leave you and your friends alone. Assistance arrives with a price. The more time you spend in the clutches of Treesong, the more likely the voices will speak to you voluntarily.

Mana Cost: Commands: 12 per second

Requests: 60 per request.

Topsoil

Caution is advised. Too much power could go to their heads. Too little could shrivel what you hoped to help thrive. Practice makes perfect—Mana Sense lends understanding.

Effect: Supply nutrients to those plants around you and they will be more likely to come to your aid. Increases nutrition levels and ambient Mana levels by 15% on each use. Requires a period of 72 hours for nutrition levels and ambient Mana to collect. Repeated uses within the collection period will extend timeframe and provide a prorated fraction more level increase in effects.

Mana Cost: 10 Mana per second of Topsoil Treatment per plant.

Tier-Three Hybrid Ability (30)
Planted In Place

Exactly what it sounds like. Call on the roots and branches, vines or leaves, of the plants around you to aid in your adventures and root your enemies in place. Effect:

Employs vegetation to grasp a single target with roots, branches and vines. Length of rooting dependent upon strength of vegetation used and ambient location.

Mana Cost: 30 Mana per instance

I wondered if it was a bad thing that I was itching to get out there and try out Planted In Place. Either way, I had my eye on some direct Skill downloads I could purchase from the Shop to increase my offensive and defensive lineups, not to mention that one book that was going to cost a ton, but it would get Mana Sense to 15, to where utilizing the implants wasn't going to be as dangerous anymore.

Leveling it up without the optical advantage I needed was painful . . . but I'd made it to 12—the Level I needed to buy the next Skill-Up book in the first place. Now my only question was whether I should get the implants now or once I hit 15. There were so many . . .

"Kira Kent?" Shi'enah's head was cocked to the side, and I realized Wisp was tugging on my hand too. I'd got too caught up in my own thoughts, my own plans.

"Sorry." I stepped forward and pulled forth everything I wanted to sell . . . and it was a lot of stuff. Some of it rare. I could practically see Shi'enah salivate, if that was something she did. Like genetically? Speciesistically? I gave up.

"Mum, can I go with Jackson?" Wisp tugged again, her other hand caught up in Dog's fur like a security blanket.

"Yeah, love. Go keep an eye on him and make sure he doesn't get into any trouble." I winked at her and she laughed.

"My plan exactly. Plus! He said he'd buy me things." She skipped away like this was any normal mall in a totally non post-apocalyptic society. Grounded or delusional, I wasn't about to judge. At least Jackson spoiled her. He was a good big brother.

Plus, any purchases that could modify or potentially endanger him were run through my interface first for approval. We'd been over this a lot in recent weeks. The last few had seemed like a blur.

"You have a nice haul here." Shi'enah almost purred approvingly. Since I'd come in several times with Ginali, I felt like my prices had improved. Not massively, but significant enough that I noticed when making larger quantity sales. Savings. While I still contributed significantly to the overall kitty that the city had, I'd managed to amass just over half a million Credits.

440,280 Credits to be precise, even before this run.

Thing was, around half of that was needed for the procedures I wanted, not to mention another fifty thousand for the book which would give Mana Sense the final boost. And yes, I'd double checked that it was the *right* Mana Sense.

"You've got more Mollecupai components. It's really not nice that you're keeping them from me, though." Shi'enah raised what I thought might be her eyebrow; I still couldn't tell. Her beautifully fox-like face would have been enchanting if I wasn't fairly good at reading body language. Well, sort of. Needed to get better at it.

"Already promised those to Ginali. You know that." There were crafted armor and weapon components, not to mention potions that I desperately needed. The Cartel gave me better bartered deals on several of those indispensable items. Trades made for a decent potion haul.

"Besides, I know you're an extension of the Cartel." I winked at her and she sighed.

"That whole quest deal was the worst idea ever. It has severely cut down on my profitability." Except she didn't seem upset—quite the opposite, in fact. It made me wonder if it just meant she didn't have to work as hard for what she got out of everything.

"Well, since you won't give me that damned spleen you know I want, it's only going to come to 168,975 Credits." Shi'enah did manage to sound slightly put out, perhaps a little pouty.

"Excellent." I could feel the excitement washing over me. Ocular implants were just around the corner. Especially now that my human-specific neural genome treatment had had time to settle in.

I just hoped the implant relieved the damned headaches once and for all, and maybe let me understand what the hell I was seeing in more detail than the mess of lines and interpretations I got from the blur all around me.

❖

I stood in what had become one of my most-frequented Shop rooms. Books, and books, and more books. The System even made it possible to find pretty much every book that had ever been written on the face of the Earth.

How they'd managed to pull from databases or, in some of these cases, from books I was pretty sure were only available in paperback, I had no clue. But I loved the fact that they had. At least some corner of our human culture had been preserved. Fiction.

I wasn't looking for fiction, though. Specifically, I needed one book I'd seen and been unable to purchase before now because I didn't meet the requirements.

Mana Sense: Reaching the Next Level

Cost: 47,825 Credits

Requirements for Purchase: Mana Sense 12

Requirements for Use: Mana Sense 12

Upon Completion: Mana Sense +3

>*Caution: Take measures to ensure this book is consumed in a safe*

environment for both yourself and others.

Well, that right there was heartwarming. I could feel myself hesitating. Buying the book wasn't the question. How and when I should consume it, if I should absorb it before or after the ocular implant—those were my concerns.

I purchased the book and the overwhelming situation really began to nip at my nerves.

Kyle would be here shortly. He'd promised to come with me for this, but for just a wee second right there, I was getting cold feet. Changing some of my genome sequences to allow for the ocular implants to take full effect in my fragile human cortex? Yeah. That stuff was next-level science fiction right there.

Shooting him a message because I knew he was in the center and the family chat would reach him, I asked him to meet me outside the bookshop now, and not in twenty or so minutes. Maybe he felt the urgency through the twin bond; perhaps he'd just been standing outside the entrance orb, wanting to give me space for a bit, but he was there much faster than I'd anticipated.

"You okay?" he asked quietly, giving me one of those side arm hugs that always worked so well.

"Okay, yes." I shook my head. "It's not like that. I can't make this stupid decision. Do I absorb the book first and run the danger of killing my head with brightness, or do I get the implants first and run the risk of death first?"

Kyle chuckled. "You're seriously asking that? C'mon Kira. You're much more logical than that."

And he was right. It wasn't just nerves. I was a bit excited too. I wanted to know all about this stuff, because I had that same damned gut feeling that knowing what I'd be able to read was going to help us all tremendously.

"Absorb book, hit the recommended threshold for implant success, and then initiate the processes." I smiled. "I mean, I knew it, right? It makes the most sense. And the center does have pods or beds I can lie down in. Perhaps a delayed initialization."

"Sounds perfect. I'll come with you. Jackson has Wisp, and we'll take care of each other until you're done. Probably by dinner tonight. This shit is fast. You're not going to have to rest up for a week after laparoscopic surgery." There was a wistful tone in his voice, like he wished he could witness all of this amazing technology under a different set of circumstances. Not that I could blame him.

I'd been working toward this for weeks. He'd been wanting to save lives his entire existence. I couldn't help but feel the pain he felt at how many humans had died so far. More humans the world over were dying every single day. They didn't have to be directly involved with us for us to feel the pain of that loss.

The implant room was exactly like I remembered it. Activating the screen, I pulled up the implants that I needed and frowned. Yeah, there was that, and the Tier-II Neural Link might work, but after speaking with Ginali, I'd made sure to obtain the neural treatment a few days in advance so that it would strengthen and fortify my feeble human brain so I wouldn't . . . you know, fry it.

It had set me back a pretty penny, but I didn't regret it.

Neural Human Genome Treatment by Neural Divergence
>*Specifically targeted to strengthen and reinforce the neural web of human brain cells allowing for more robust Neural Link Tiers and attachments. This Genome treatment will also adjust subtle elements in the target human body to*

assist with longevity as well.

Required Intelligence: 85

Required Willpower: 50

Cost: 85,000 Credits

In fact. I kind of thought of it fondly. Still. As I gazed over the rest of what I was about to do, I felt this insurmountable stab of caution. Something this invasive, this cybernetic -- it felt surreal.

Mana Sense Complete Ocular Implants by Neural Divergence

Required Tier II Neural Link – Upgradable

Required: Active Ability – Mana Sense

Required: Mana Sense – 9 or higher (15 recommended)

Required: Intelligence – 65 (80 recommended)

Required: Minimum of one Mana interpretation data storage device connected to Neural Link.

Description: Neural Divergence's ocular implant stands out from the rest of its competitors by being individually crafted by high-ranking Artisans. This Implant is specially crafted to work with the Mana Sense Skill to enhance its projection abilities and as such, each implant is uniquely tailored to the individual.

The implant comes with an automatic filtration and storage options, allowing the user to process and view Mana waves.

Warning: Should you choose to utilize this Implant before Mana Sense reaches 15, you could experience headaches, dizziness, nosebleeds, hallucinations, and other more debilitating side effects such as brain hemorrhaging or death. Incidents of death and incapacitation have been reported on a highly irregular basis.

Cost:

Tier II Neural Link: 95,000 Credits

Ocular Implant – 100,000 Credits

Mana Interpretation Data Storage Device – 25,000 Credits

Total: 220,000 Credits

Yep. This right here. Two hundred twenty thousand Credits plus the eighty-five thousand I'd already shelled out for the genome treatment. Not to mention the almost fifty thousand for the book. I was lucky I didn't have to put my kids through university anymore. I couldn't afford it in this apocalyptic, capitalistic hellscape any more than before shit hit the fan.

Not wanting to make a bigger deal out of it than it was, I made the purchase and was prompted to enter a pod. The pod slid out of the wall as if everything should be delivered that way, its sleek stainless steel appearance just another blip of perfection in the room of sterility.

Okay. I could do that. I hugged my brother perhaps a bit tighter than usual, and climbed in—only to be prompted for scheduling. Did I want to rest first, consume food, or go straight to the installation first?

Why, yes, good old pod; why, yes, I dearly wanted to do all of the above.

I wasn't the first person in our settlement to get a procedure. Gemma had several implants now, enhanced cybernetics for both her arms, allowing greater accuracy during fights. Others had genome treatments for hastened healing and rejuvenation.

But no one I knew had done any of the brain shit yet. So there was still an air of mystery around it for me, and to be honest, I had some very solid reservations about it. But Mana Sense wasn't taking a break, and if I didn't do this, I'd spend all my days rolling around with migraines.

Taking a breath, I set the timer for the procedure for four hours away, settled into the comfortable seat that molded to my body, and pulled out my book. This was the only other one I could find that would boost my Mana Sense in one go. Every other point I gained was going to be painstakingly wrought.

Time to activate that source of expertise and hope it didn't knock me out longer than I anticipated.

The rush of knowledge tore a surprised scream from my throat, and then there was only the brightness of Mana suffusing me.

Chapter Fourteen:
Different View

Unlike other surgeries I'd had in my life, not the least of which was a C-section, I didn't wake up in pain from this one. I blinked my eyes open and realized they still felt like my eyes. If I hadn't known better, I'd have thought they forgot to do the surgery.

Blue screen notifications assaulted me, bleeping off to the side and waiting impatiently for me to access them.

Fine.

Reward: Mana Sense + 3

Caution: You will need hours of rest in order for your brain to absorb and comprehend the information you have just loaded into your mind. Please allow up to six Earth hours for complete integration. It is recommended that you upgrade your neural net as soon as possible, if you haven't already, in order to avoid any brain or memory degradation caused by influx of new information sensations.

New Total Mana Sense + 15

Note: Mana Sense can no longer be increased by knowledge alone. Only experience and use will further increase your understanding from here on in.

Okay, I could get behind that. And I guess I'd been out a total of about six hours, so that was good.

Neural Human Genome Treatment by Neural Divergence

Integration: Successful

Congratulations, you can now correctly interface with your Tier II Neural Link without causing unnecessary damage to your existing biological neural processing unit.

Great. I couldn't help but feel the unease creeping down my back that I hadn't realized previously just how dangerous some of this stuff could be. I mean, logically, brain surgery and whatnot, but overall? Accepting that one, I swiped at the next.

Mana Sense Ocular Implants by Neural Divergence

Required Tier II Neural Link – Upgradable

Required: Active Ability – Mana Sense

Required: Mana Sense – 9 or higher (15 recommended)

Required: Intelligence – 65 (80 recommended)

Required: Minimum of one Mana interpretation data storage device connected to said Neural Link.

This implant will allow your brain to process the Mana waves you see and store the relevant data and information for temporary or permanent use and interpretation.

Recommended Requirements Reached.

Tier II Neural Link – Successfully Installed

Ocular Implant – Successfully Installed

Mana Interpretation Data Storage Device – Successfully Installed

Note: Please be aware of some disorientation as your newly augmented neural cortex becomes accustomed to its upgrades.

That was it for notifications. I sighed, refraining from the urge to rub my eyes considering I had no idea if I could even do that now. Time to adjust myself.

Except that felt a lot easier said than done. Even blinking felt like an effort right now. The sheer amount of information assaulting my brain felt heavy. I was picking up on details I couldn't even categorize.

This was going to take some getting used to.

Even with the pod dimming everything from the white room outside it, the glow contained within snuck in through the cracks and my eyelashes. I blinked rapidly, initiating what felt like a whir in my brain. Maybe I was being hypersensitive, or totally imagining things, but a rush of new knowledge began to cascade through my skull.

Even the level of light I could see, and the way I could now detect Mana in everything around me weighed heavily in my mind. My brain processed this information faster than I could tangibly understand. Light from Mana refracted through the pod, bouncing off the glow that was meant to slowly wake me.

My interface told me it was just gone two in the afternoon. Miracles of technology when this whole thing had taken, what? Not even six hours. I was glad I'd taken Ginali's advice and done the genome treatment earlier. There was enough new stuff floating around in my head.

No pain existed, not in my joints, skin, or even my head. The latter was a welcome change from the last few weeks of constant stabbing headaches while my mildly annoying sunglasses fought to keep the worst of the Mana leakage away from my eyes.

. . . approaching . . .

What the fuck?

But another moment later I could feel the approaching—person? Perhaps? Whatever it was, there was a Mana locus that was moving toward me in what felt like a gentle wave. Nothing hostile, though how I knew this, I still wasn't sure.

Decision made, I swung my legs to the side, activating the pod to open and almost immediately wished I hadn't. The light in the room burst into my otherwise-dim little bubble and smacked me right in the face.

It had nothing to do with Mana, just with the fact that this Shop was always sterile and bright. The Mana approaching me, however, it was almost here. And suddenly, even before the door opened, even before she ran into the room with her pets in tow and threw herself against my waist, I knew who it was.

Wisp.

Except now, with my enhanced eyes, I could see so much magic dancing around her. Mana lines attaching her firmly to her pets, to me, meandering off into the distance no doubt to meet up with her brother and uncle. Maybe even some of the kids she'd become friends with.

Joyous. That was the word.

Everything about the way reading her Mana lines translated into my brain brought happiness to me, but it was more than that. She was happy. In this strange and fucked up world, my kid was coping decently well.

Small mercies.

More power approached, probably Kyle, and I needed to get my head on straight. The information bombarding my comprehension wasn't easy to sort yet. I could tell it was there, but . . . this was going to take some getting used to.

Urgency.

I frowned, unsure exactly where that thought came from. Me, or my upgrades, or hell, even the Mana itself. I knelt down and enveloped the kiddo in a super tight hug. This whole new world—surgery, enhancements, whatever—I could see how Gemma might be getting addicted. Easy to do as long as you saved the money. Quick and painless. Not too much to get worried about.

"Mum." Wisp pulled back and eyed me critically. "You look a little different. But not much."

Then she smiled and enveloped me back in that tight hug. Even Dog buried his nose briefly against my side.

Great. Not *much* different? What did *that* mean?

"Kira." Kyle stopped just inside the doorway, and I looked up at him only to wish I hadn't. His Mana wasn't as friendly as Wisp's. That was the only way I could phrase it. Darker, thicker, almost like tar was stuck to some of the strands.

We'd rarely been able to hunt together lately, and I was beginning to worry just what lengths my brother might have gone to keep people safe. Still. Interpretation, right?

"Truth, mate. How do I look?" Because my eight-year-old wasn't about to give me a straight answer. Her vision of me was clouded anyway. I stood up so he could get an actual good look.

He cocked his head to one side. "I think you're a tad taller? Those few greys you had appear to be gone, and you're missing the start of crow's feet. Skin is smoother. Yeah, just like I told you after the genome treatment the other day." He paused for a second, approaching closer.

Nothing about him felt different, just this lingering presence of sticky Mana that I couldn't shake. I needed a few hours to sort through all the new information in my head.

"Yeah. Like it knocked ten years off you. Not sure why it made you taller, though. Might have to get one of those treatments myself so I can go back to my four inch superiority." He grinned at me and suddenly hugged me too. "Was a bit worried there. Not because I thought it was dangerous, but because it's always different when it's someone you've known your whole life."

"Silly sod," I muttered, pushing him away gently. I'd spent enough time in here when I didn't have to be. "I mean my eyes. Do they look different?"

Kyle shrugged. "Maybe if I look really close. Sort of steampunkesque, you know?"

I guess that was all I was getting out of him. "Don't we have that meeting to get to?"

He raised an eyebrow, and Wisp tucked her hand into mine, squeezing it as if to remind me she was still there. Like I could ever forget.

"You think you're up to that? I mean, you literally just had brain surgery." His gaze was skeptical, like he knew me well enough to know I'd be pushing myself. But the thing was, so did I. In fact, I knew myself better.

"I'm literally recovered. Sure, I'm a little tired, and some of the things I'm seeing and noticing aren't making any sense to me yet. But I'll be okay." I could feel my blood pumping, even if my newly depleted wallet felt like it was hemorrhaging life. "Besides, that damned quest isn't going to finish itself."

❖

The most noticeable thing about my new implants was the lack of blindingly bright Mana confusion trying to assault my senses. Just walking out of the Shop where so many people congregated around would usually have sent my head into a tailspin.

It was part of the reason I'd spent so much time with patrols and leveling groups over the last few weeks. Aching time apart from my kids. Necessary time apart from my kids. All so that I could keep hold of that sliver of sanity that didn't involve my world lighting up with people's Mana capacities.

But this, this was so much more.

Reasonable. Sensible. Compatible.

Every single strand I saw categorized itself in a way I half-intrinsically understood and in other ways I still had to process. Learning curve perhaps, but it made me ten times more functional. In fact, I simply felt better.

"Kira!" Dor smiled and got up as I entered the library with my brother in tow, and Wisp peeled off to dive into the kids' book section with her furry friends. Dog, for all of his border collie and whatever-else-was-there mixes, still looked like a medium-sized paint pony. Wombie, on the other hand, looked like one of those massive stuffed toys that could be climbed on. Except like his Mumma, his butt plating appeared on the outside. Though I doubted it had removed the inner layer, I couldn't be sure.

Eventually he'd grow too big to stay inside and have to go out into the carpark with his Mumma. But we'd cross that bridge and whatnot.

"In the flesh." I glanced around, my eyes automatically adjusting, calibrating. Wow, I knew I'd get used to it, but there was this machine-like quality to the way my brain processed the information it received. So much more to everything I saw.

Also, from the way Dor looked at me I think Kyle had been full of crap when he said there wasn't that much difference. Or else Dor hadn't really seen me since the genome upgrade. I couldn't quite remember.

"Might have to get me some of that treatment too," she muttered, turning around and gesturing for me to sit down with a grin. "It's like Botox on acid, and you don't even look puffy."

Now that, believe it or not, gave me a much clearer vision as to what potential changes treatment had wrought in my face than anything Kyle or Wisp said. Face lift, here we go. I'd take it. After all, it wasn't like the System hadn't already fixed my aching, almost-middle-aged knees, healed multiple sore muscle points, and helped close near-fatal wounds.

For all the shittiness of landing us in an apocalyptic Dungeon World—the System had definitely thrown in some perks for the survivors.

Jackass.

Sienna hadn't said a word yet, but I could almost feel her disapproval. Strike that. With her Charisma and my new eyes, that wave of disapproval could have leveled the center if she'd let it.

"You looked fine before this."

"I didn't do it for looks, Sienna. I did it so my Mana Sense wouldn't fry my brain." There were what looked like oatmeal bars on the table in front of us, and I grabbed one, suddenly famished.

Sienna had the grace to blush. I wasn't angry at her, but sometimes she could pull that judgmental air around her like one of those high-powered PTA mums who got manicures every week and spent way too much money on their hair. I'd had enough of that before the world went to shit. Didn't need it making me more stabby than our situation already did.

"Anyway," Dor broke in pointedly, taking a bite of her own bar. "Since you're here already, I'll give you a rundown. We'll have the rest joining us later, but it's always nicer to have more than just us two on the forefront."

Dor code for: Kira can take point because she has mum voice.

"The town really needs to level up so we can expand and increase our defenses. As it stands, we really only have the option to increase the quality of our defense construction. Which is good, of course . . . but ideally, we also need to expand our population. In order to do *that*, we need for people to begin buying properties in a sort of circular fashion around us." She raised an eyebrow, and I knew, right then and there that was our problem.

We'd put such an emphasis on leveling, on gearing up, on being ready to fight. And IRSHA still hadn't fucking shown their hands. It was like sitting on pins and needles the entire time—waiting.

"But we still have plenty of room for people inside here, right?"

The moment I mouthed my first objection, I actually started to think about it. Living in here was less than stellar. This was a shopping center. And we basically had to provide food and shelter for everyone inside here regardless. Sure, people contributed, but it was starting to feel like an environment that wasn't conducive for long-term survivability.

"Fine. That'll be my next task now that I can see in more than blinding white blurs." The sarcasm was even a little sharp for me. I massaged my temples, happy that I wasn't trying desperately to fend off a splitting headache, but still trying to soothe frayed nerves. "Housing, expansion to actual domiciles? Do we have a map? Do we need a percentage of land owned before it'll join with the complex like before? What sort of Credits are people looking at for buying houses and installing plumbing? Does anyone have any of this sorted?"

The questions came in spurts, and my brain categorized them all easily, slotting them into their own areas.

Perks of the upgrade, I guess. Not looking that one in the mouth.

By the time my little questionnaire was done, Dor was grinning, and Sienna appeared to be perturbed. I'd totally forgotten that Kyle was seated to my left.

He sighed heavily before speaking. "Red has a chunk of that info and should be here shortly. But basically, we have over two thousand people in here now. Sure, that's nothing on Christmas rush late-night shopping, but it's still a lot to always be in here. You probably noticed the crowding."

I had to nod reluctantly, and he inclined his head toward me briefly before Dor picked up where he'd left off. "The Crafting Cartel has helped some, but right now we need to look to expanding our borders or those walls out there are all we have. And while they might be super sturdy and hard to break down, we're also not nine feet tall and built like a brick shithouse. Those Dash'kiris? I don't think it will take a group of them any time at all to beat through our walls, and I don't even know what it is they're capable of."

"I don't think they'll be attacking any time soon." I sighed, knowing from our previous encounters that honor held the Dash'Kiri at least temporarily at bay. Defense was a weakness we had to address and immediately. "Fine. When are the rest of us getting here, then?"

"They're already here." Chris's voice always soothed me. She was one of those people who didn't need to say much, to be present. Sarah, her hair still that vibrant red that I hoped she never ran out of, toodled in after her partner, chattering with Evelyn.

Red came next, representing the organization of our stores. From food to clothes, to blankets, to sporting goods adapted into weapons—Red was our man. Dale sat down next to Kyle, our little medical unit represented as one.

 Ginali pottered in, his eyes only vaguely focused on where he was going. He'd started joining in on our meetings about two weeks ago once all the heavy lifting of setting up the Crafting Cartel was in place. But he usually spent his times in trading manifests and the portal crews he was trying to gather together.

I didn't even want to go into the complexities involved in setting up portals here.

Ray and his sister trailed in after them in a low-voiced but heated discussion. Our little Ice-Mage ran hotter than I liked, and the System adjustments happening to him didn't appear to be cooling him off any. Maybe we'd have to address that at some stage. Though Leena, in all her Street Smartist chic, did appear to be a good influence on him. When she was around.

Mike and his security detail trotted in after them. The ex-security guard was our in-house manager of problems, dealing with the domestic and civil disputes that over two thousand people, crammed into close quarters with superhuman abilities after an apocalypse, created.

In other words, he was very, very busy all the time. So busy, I was surprised he still found time to level outside the walls.

Mike smiled in my direction, and I nodded back at him. Ever since that very first night, Mike had shown himself to be one of the good guys. Had that really only been like six weeks ago?

Six weeks since I met and lost Jessica, Barry, and Jules? I frowned, not overly excited that Drake and Gary trailed Mike into the room as a part of his detail, but if nothing else, they hadn't caused any more trouble since the night we took them in.

That could have blown up in all our faces, considering the forced-labor type of situation they'd put all the people in their apartment complex into. At least now that they were here, on our side purportedly, they'd devoted time to helping those they'd put at a disadvantage get out from under it. Still, I'd keep my reservations.

Last but not least, Jan bustled in, her face a little red, probably from running here. She needed more help with the kids. While she had several former teachers working with her, she was still in charge of the schooling, for want of a better phrase. Kids had to go somewhere, and especially those twelve and under—well, they couldn't go out and fight yet because the System advised against them choosing a Class.

While everyone settled in, I checked in on our current city quest.

A Habitable Safe Zone

Part Three: Staying Power

You need to make it 3 months into System Onset as a Township.

Goals:

1 – Gather 3,000 total inhabitants. This may include visiting species. Current population 2,289/3,000

2 – Build up your defenses and successfully survive and remain in your growing township for 3 months from System Onset. Current staying power 6 weeks/13 weeks

Reward: 45,000 Credits for your town treasury, [unknown] reward.

Time Limit Remaining: 7 weeks

Good luck! You'll definitely need it.

We were getting there, but the people we were able to find now was trickling down. It had been so long, and yet such a short period of time. Even six weeks into this, I found it difficult to remember quite what life had been like before all of this happened.

"Penny for your thoughts." Evelyn's smooth voice snapped away at some of the reticence I felt. She rarely failed to help better my mood.

"Just trying to wrap my head around all of this." I gestured vaguely as the last of us settled in. The council was bigger now, more robust. A true working together of minds for the common purpose of stubborn survival. Tell us we were supposed to die and see just how angry we got.

"Your eyes have these tiny dots in them now," she stated, shocking me slightly. "Like cogs in wheels in a virtual simulation."

I hadn't had a chance to look at myself yet, not that I often felt the compulsion to be vain or anything, but I guess I had just had surgery. "I'll take a look later."

She pursed her lips. "And your skin is tighter, knocked like ten years off you."

"People keep saying that." I couldn't tell if she liked that or not, also couldn't tell which of them might have bothered me more. So instead of a response, I just shrugged. We had a lot more to worry about than some stupid backwards aging courtesy of my ocular implant necessities.

There was so much to go over. Who would have thought that a town of just over two thousand people required so much organization? But without infrastructure set up, that's what we had to do. Give a stable sense to everyone around us. Maintain public works and benefits. Take care of the kids and what elderly we still had.

And then Mike knocked me flat with a question from out of the blue. Nothing like when he'd half-jokingly asked me on a date all those weeks ago, no, nothing like that. "So, Kira. Wombutt Mum eats a hell of a lot of food. Do you think there's any way you can turn her into a combat wombat?"

Chapter Fifteen:
Everything Matters

6 Weeks Post-System Onset
7:30 p.m.

Wombutt Mum was one of the sweetest, massive, could-step-on-me-and-not-blink creatures I'd ever had the fortune to encounter. While she might not have initially been super friendly, the fact that we had saved both her and her offspring when we didn't have to do anything played in our favor.

She was fiercely opposed to anyone who might harm us, as evidenced when IRSHA approached our gates all those weeks ago. I often wondered if things would have gone differently if I'd let her out of the gates.

Yet she was so gentle the kids could clamber all over her in the carpark. Or so Wisp excitedly shared with me on more than one occasion. At least, the portion of the carpark that didn't contain our slowly growing fleet of Mana- and solar-powered vehicles.

Staring up at her, I breathed in deep. Wombutt Mum had a strange smell—not unpleasant, but a little musky and earthy, one tinged with a cobalt blue that swirled around her. I petted her nose and walked back to lean against her armored thighs and soak in some of that approaching winter I despised so much.

For just a few seconds, I could almost forget everything that had happened, and that I was leaning up against a massive wombat thigh. The stars in the sky shone so much brighter now the city lights weren't predominantly outdoing them. All we had were subtle lights that glowed more than shining bright.

A shadow fell over me and I refocused myself. Leena stood, her arms crossed, her face pinched in that overly excitable expression she got all too frequently. Ray's sister didn't resemble him much. She was short and petite with flowing, dark brown hair that she wore up in a messy bun. And she was all of nineteen. She crouched down in front of me, her enthusiasm written all over her youthful face.

"Since the signs I suggested have been working, I was thinking of other ways we might be able to communicate with survivors we haven't come across yet. Especially since finding them has become more difficult lately." Her voice barely faltered, but the hitch was there.

It was getting more difficult. Uncomfortably so. We'd had in excess of three million people in the greater Brisbane area. Where they fuck had everyone gone? "So what's the idea?"

Leena's smile lessened slightly and she squared her jaw. I noticed Ray's absence keenly. Probably meant he didn't approve of what she was about to ask me.

"Do you think we could take a couple of the fleet out and just scour the streets and buildings. Like, behind the patrols clearing the way for the day?" She waited for my answer, and I could practically see the hope flowing off her in cascades.

Leena
Street Smartist
Level 21

She'd leveled up some, but I still didn't feel comfortable just letting her go out further than ten kilometers or so. The mutations surrounded us, not to mention the already-alien creatures that began descending on us weeks ago. Keeping those at bay had become a full-time job for all of our patrols. Still, maybe there were some holdouts.

Just as I was about to open my mouth to speak, a strange sensation assaulted my vision. No, that wasn't right. My sense of perception, of the entire world around me. Essentially, it shook. Sort of like superimposing over an already developed image.

Maybe I needed to be more careful as I got used to my implants. I pushed past it, filing it away to think about later.

"Make more signs and drape them on any buildings you come across that might offer a different view or vantage point. I don't want you going out too far until you've leveled up more. And while I know your abilities aren't conducive to killing shit, you still need to figure out how to adapt them so you can glean as much experience as possible. We can't carry you. Not me, not your brother."

I held up a hand as she started to protest. There was no mollycoddling from me today. That got people killed, and we needed every single person we could muster.

"It's not open for debate. Level so you can help us survive, and help us find survivors. Stop weaseling out of the groups we put you into. Those leveling patrols are for your own good. If you're not strong enough to protect yourself, what makes you think you can save people?"

Leena blanched, and she nodded, her eyes downcast as she struggled with the truth of what I said. Thing was, when your big brother kept looking out for you, kept making excuses for you, and didn't really let you be your own person, it was easy to think you were invincible.

"It's not entirely your fault. None of us expected the apocalypse. But it's here, and you need to get stronger. I'm not a super heavy-hitting Class, which means I need my Levels in order to up my defensive and offensive capabilities." I stood up, reluctantly relinquishing my really comfortable Wombutt Mum perch. The creature harrumphed softly under her breath as I did so.

Offering a hand, I pulled Leena up from her crouch. "Don't sulk, don't get down. None of us have time for that. You have awesome ideas, but you need to get strong enough to help carry them out without endangering others."

Mana danced across my vision in thick, differently colored lines that attempted to punctuate my comments.

"Get Levels. Save more people. Prove they got us Aussies wrong." Because in a nutshell, that was what mattered.

❖

Night had settled fully around us, and I watched my kids eat as they glared at each other across the table at the front of Raybucks. The Raybucks where, to be honest, I'd kind of come to call my office home.

Granted, I was feeding them pretty late. But since Jackson had mentioned wanting to spend more time together, I figured we should start sooner than later.

I'd thought it would be the best place to silently study Mana strands and waves and get to know all of the nuances my newfound Skills could give me. And it was, I mean totally ideal. I'd learned that color variations didn't even mean strength of Mana, necessarily; instead, it often meant intention. The intention with which Mana was about to be used, or the intensity with which the power itself was being depended on or clutched at . . .

What I didn't expect was both my wonderful kids to use the dinner, where I was trying to concentrate, to bombard me with an over-abundance of sibling arguments I'd somehow managed to avoid over the last few weeks.

"Jackson is mean to Dog." Wisp crossed her arms, her face held in a fierce scowl. Thing was, I could see how tired she looked, and knew her best moods weren't prevalent when she wasn't getting enough sleep. But she really, really wanted to stay up with us.

Dog on the other hand seemed not to care in any way. And Jackson . . . he appeared to be positively nonplussed by the canine. Which meant Wisp was exaggerating, and Jackson wasn't responding to Wisp's attempt at getting attention from her big brother.

It all boiled down to sibling neglect of each other's feelings.

Yet, if it was just my kids, everything would have been fine.

The moment I'd given my advice to Leena, I'd opened the way for her brother to accost me. And thus it was that Ray stood next to me, glowering at my lack of response while my children death stared each other.

The Mana surrounding the Ice-Mage confused me. It was strong, powerful, and yet at its core there was something missing. Was it control? Perhaps true direction? I wasn't sure. Maybe his volatile temper lent a sinister overtone to his inner feelings. The thing was, I couldn't tell yet. I was never going to get the hang of these implants if I never got a chance to study Mana in all its forms.

"Ray. Leena needs to be able to protect herself. You won't always be there, and you can't be in two places at once." I snapped out the words, my tone clipped, because I was sick of trying to say the same thing in ten different ways to multiple different people. "Get on board. Help her level if you have to. You're sitting at 28, so you can choose to be one of the mentors of her group if you want to. But do something."

And that was it. My harsh words that stung finally managed to hit their target. About time. I was losing ways of saying it. A moment later, he had the gods-damned grace to look sheepish.

If only he'd managed that revelation before my bloody pasta got cold.

"Fine. I'll mentor her group until she hits 25 then." His face slightly flushed, I think it was one of the first times he'd taken advice and not just reacted to it.

Considering up until the meeting even earlier in the afternoon he'd been completely and utterly volatile, I found this change welcome. Even if the way the Mana danced around him still bothered me.

Why didn't Mana Sense 15 come with a bloody color wheel?

"Good show," I said and waved him off, dismissing him. He hesitated before nodding and finally, finally, leaving.

Jackson played with the food on his plate, using his fork to swirl it around and around before he finally spoke up. "How did you become the default mum, Mum?"

I shrugged, shoveling my lukewarm food into my mouth and gulping some of it down so there was at least something in my stomach. "I don't know. I mentioned coming here for sanctuary, people followed, then we picked up more people, and now we have a town."

My son pursed his lips thoughtfully, like he was figuring something out. Hope he shared it with me since right then all I wanted was food and sleep. Well, and a color wheel of handy "what this color of Mana means" explanations.

Even mostly cold, this pasta was good stuff. Bit of pesto, some tomato, and I wasn't about to ask Red what the actual ingredients were. The less we knew about how they got the food that fed us all was probably for the best.

Six weeks in and I was fairly willing to bet nothing fresh from the farm had survived.

Swallowing the last bite, I realized Wisp was partially slumped over the table, her head resting on her forearm as she dozed off. Jackson, still lost in thought—or so I assumed—startled me slightly when he spoke up.

"People listen to you. It's sort of like being the headmaster's kid, you know? Others listen to me, and Mum . . . I just don't know if they should." I almost didn't hear the last of what he said because he whispered, and I knew his confidence played a huge part in it.

"Love. This is *why* people should listen to you, even if they don't take your advice. The fact that you're not being a cocky teenager and automatically assuming you know everything—that's a rarity. Just keep being you, don't pretend to know things you don't, and keep pushing to become the person I'm seeing."

A softness enveloped his face, and the taut strands of Mana that hung around him diffused into a quieter glow. My brain filed it away as content Mana fields requiring little restriction. And I suddenly knew sleep would be difficult tonight, considering the amount of information my mind was disseminating.

"Thanks." He paused for a moment. "And I'm sorry. I should be paying more attention to Wisp. I've just got so many things I can do now, and so much that needs to be done. She's still so little and she doesn't understand the Class system or how all of these upgrades work. I don't even understand it, but she pesters me for answers and, even when I explain, she won't get it. Not for years."

There was a contemplative expression to my son's face, and I knew he cared. He was growing up a lot faster now than he had before. This wasn't tinkering for science camp, or the extra school credit he always pursued.

Everything we did here was required to be immediately real-world applicable. Some of it was life changing, more of it needed to be lifesaving.

"You know I'm proud of you, right?"

He looked up at me, like really looked this time, and there was something unreadable behind that expression. It smelled of hope and desperation, of a small part of him that might prefer to just be a kid, but of the other side that knew it was no longer possible.

"I know, Mum. I know." He paused, wolfing down a few more bites of food, his gaze now back on his sister. "We just need to make sure Wisp can be a kid for as long as possible. Even with the world falling apart."

"Right you are," I muttered, glancing around our new little world with reopened eyes.

172

There were kids up this late all around us. And yet Jan would have them all in her makeshift little school room in the morning. Grades one through four and five through eight. All of them. Anyone older than that had already picked a Class and were doing more than just schoolwork. They were specializing in other areas.

But Jan, no, she let those kids be kids. She organized the teachers, and the aides, and she made sure the hundred-and-eighty-odd school kids we had here were going to get the most out of their childhood that they could.

And damn it if I wasn't going to fight to make sure we maintained it.

Chapter Sixteen:

Strategy

6 Weeks, 2 Days Post-System Onset
6 a.m.

I stood out at the gate in the crisp morning air, my arms huddled around my side, not entirely sure what it was I was looking at. Flesh? Definitely. But whether or not the form was human, I couldn't tell.

"What is this?" I half whispered as the cold air snatched my words and made them fog. For a second, it allowed me to forget the more looming question of: what did this?

Dale shrugged, and I could almost feel the helplessness emanating from him. "Early patrol found it not far from here. Down the bottom of the hill close to the Gateway Motorway."

Gary had his hands locked under his armpits, like he was trying to fend off the cold that set in his bones. Brisbanites weren't cut out for this crappy, cold weather. "Heard a noise off into the brush of Bulimba Creek and just . . ." He gestured at the remains they'd schlepped back with them.

Yeah. I knew exactly how he felt. There was no Mana dancing or pulsing around the specimen, either, so I couldn't pick anything up from it. Not that I was good at that yet with all of my not-practice time.

"Can we get it in to our morgue?" Kyle spoke out of nowhere, almost making me jump. I'd been too preoccupied to sense his Mana signature. Everyone had one, but I'd only gotten used to a few of them so far.

"Sure." Gary took his hands out from his pits and motioned to a couple of guys I didn't recognize, directing them to take the remains away to be examined.

"Do you think it's human?" I asked Kyle pointedly.

"Humanoid, at least at first glance at the way some of those bones poked through what was left of the meat."

Dale was nodding in agreement while it was all I could do to control my gag reflex. Diapers, poop, kid vomit—all those things were no problem for me at all. But there were valid reasons I was a nature doctor and not a human doctor.

The chill air outside nipped at my arms through the new armor undershirt I'd hastily pulled on. Watching as they wheeled the thing away, I suddenly felt a jolt sweep through me like something heavy had been dropped on the ground near me. At the same time, there was a fraction of a second where my sight seemed to bright out.

Not black out, but go so impossibly bright that for that instant everything in my sight was white.

Glancing around, no one else seemed to have noticed the ground heave as I had. Maybe one of the calibration settings on the implant hardware needed fiddling with.

I rubbed my hands together, resigned to follow my brother inside with his specimen.

"It wasn't one of ours." Gary's voice pulled me out of my thoughts as he appeared suddenly in front of me.

Backing up a couple of steps, I blew hot air on my fingers, or tried to. Five fucking degrees Celsius was not my type of weather. Ever. "What we wheeled in, or whatever killed it?"

Gary paused for a moment, swallowing visibly, like he'd been trying to avoid exactly that thought. "The corpse. Not one of ours."

"You mean, if it was human, they didn't belong to one of our patrols?" I could feel the relief just waiting on the precipice inside me wanting to let go and give me that nice release of endorphins.

He pulled out a cigarette and nodded as he lit it. "Wasn't one of ours.

We're all accounted for."

"Thanks."

Did the rush of relief through my body make me a bad person? Then right now I was positively evil.

❖

Dale and Kyle's autopsy results disturbed me on a level I didn't fully want to acknowledge yet. Humanoid with canine elements. Mixtures of DNA neither of them understood. Ginali was helping them come up with a more concrete identification now.

That's what we got for being one of the newest species or something.

Instead, I stood in the library, poring over the maps we'd marked up over the last few weeks. Sure, we had all the information we could pull up in our brains, but for me, I'd always loved the tangible. Sketching out our progress by hand made it seem more real.

We'd been heading out in patrols for weeks, incrementally sending out higher Level groups and pushing ourselves. Level 15 and under kept the area immediately around Garbo clear of the low-Level shit. As much as they could. Then 15 to 20 and 20 to 25 . . . and so on and so forth.

Until we pushed right up to the mid-30s in areas like Daisy Hill, like the MacGregor dungeon and the rest of it.

We'd only encountered one more Mollecupai since Jules. They brought us cold, hard Credits, but there was also the vindictive part of me. I still felt Jules's loss keenly, and Gemma grew more distant, darker every day. And I had no idea how to pull her back from the brink I felt she teetered on.

Evelyn tapped her foot against the end of her bow. She never put the damned thing away. Not that I could blame her. After the Spiny incident, you just never knew when a flea or something was going to get into the center, mutate, and need an arrow to the knee.

She cocked her head to one side and I waited for her to speak. "This just doesn't make any sense. We're maintaining the areas around us, but not making a dent farther out. Those same creatures, with similar Levels, just keep appearing. Leveling up somehow as they spawn. Or have they like just designated those areas as those specific Levels and that's why and how those creatures are always going to stay that Level?"

Dale propped his feet up on the desk and leaned back. I think we'd been at the discussion too long for him.

"Probably. IRSHA told us Australians weren't supposed to survive. Maybe our country just has more Mana floating around and screwing things up." The defeatist tone in his voice was unlike him, but he had every reason to sound like that. Especially after he spent the last couple of hours with those remains.

As far as progress went, we'd ground to a halt.

My eyes zoomed in and out of the maps, like my vision folded in on itself. These things took getting used to that I hadn't anticipated. Though in hindsight, I wasn't sure what I'd expected from any of this cybernetic adjustment stuff.

"We should be pushing the dungeons." And Gemma was there, her forthright manner prevalent.

Gone were the times she joked, or the youthful enthusiasm she'd had at the beginning of all this. Her eyes were hollow and sunken, and the once-prevalent, sun-kissed freckles on her nose had faded like her liveliness.

"Go on?" Mike prodded her, his voice gentle. He didn't have his lackeys with him right now. We couldn't always take everyone away from their posts. It's why Ray wasn't here, nor was Red.

Gemma ran a hand through her now-pixie-cut hair, the light catching on the dark grey material that covered her entire left arm. She gestured in a way that all of us could see, to several positions on the maps.

"Our closest dungeon in MacGregor is seriously at bursting point. And the Daisy Hill Center isn't far from it either. From what my team has been able to scout out, even Nathan University Campus is on the verge of becoming another dungeon. They're all within close proximity, and we can't afford for them to leak over and interrupt the strict schedule of clearing monsters that we've been maintaining."

She looked at each one of us in turn, her expression serious. "We're barely holding onto keeping our immediate area safe. Or at least, within safe parameters. The dungeons are a problem we need to deal with. Our Levels are rising. We have two full 30 to 35 groups now. It's my suggestion that we push those groups to clear dungeons, and move the 25 to 30s up to clear the other areas left behind."

I nodded slowly, and Mike spoke up before I could.

"Which of the dungeons do you recommend first?" Mike's tone was even keeled, and genuinely interested. He was lower Level than I'd like our head of security to be, but he rarely left our base of operations for obvious reasons. 25 was still respectable.

Gemma hesitated only briefly before squaring her jaw and meeting his gaze almost defiantly. "MacGregor. It's the one in most danger of overrunning us. If that one breaks through, if those monsters level up too much—I don't see our defenses holding no matter how much we pump into them. I say we send one team in there, from the front of the dungeon, not the Oval."

The words hung heavy in the room for a moment, and then Mike slowly nodded. "Sounds like a plan. So MacGregor and?"

"Nathan. Because Daisy Hill has that upper floor being cleared regularly on our patrols, so that's at least being kept somewhat at bay. It's Nathan we've neglected. It's been weeks since the Eeshiriatmels over in that areas were mowed down efficiently. There have only been scouting groups thinning that herd. They've been gaining Levels steadily and are up to the mid-20s now despite the scouting efforts."

Evelyn piped up, a frown of concentration furrowing her brows. "They were what? Level 16 up to 18 or so when we first went out there?"

Dale stood up and stretched, and I could see the bags under his eyes despite the System's best efforts to keep us all rejuvenated and awake. "Usual clearing team out to the Daisy Hill area, and get two dungeon teams ready for Nathan and MacGregor. Got it."

I watched as he left the room, knowing he'd be going with one of the groups. Just like I would, even if I wanted to stay back and give my kids more attention. This was way more strenuous than any nine-to-five position I'd held in the pre-apocalyptic world. Long, dangerous, and deadly.

"I'll take Nathan." There, I said it out loud. I'd cleared the upper floors or MacGregor several times now, and I just wanted something new that didn't remind me of Jules, or of Gemma practically losing limbs.

She moved over to me, gesturing at several names she shared across . . . however these connections through the System worked. Gemma might have gone brooding, silent, and kind of dark, but she was solid at scouting. It was what she did best.

"You and me. Evelyn. Kyle, Molly, and Sange. That's a solid beginning. That leaves Dale to manage over the other group with Ray, Drake, and Gary?" Gemma said.

I glanced down our growing list of higher-Level members. "Oh— Tasha too, I guess? I know, Eritia our Fire Mage, and Morton our Gunslinger finally hit the 30s, let's take them with."

Gemma's face lit up and she nodded at my words. Though I couldn't help wondering if we should grab another tank; in the worst-case scenario I could always make the monsters pound through a wall of earth. "Maybe

Dannin too. He only just hit 30.”

I nodded, though I wasn't as familiar with that last name. A little digging in my memory and I was fairly sure he was a Ranger, just like Evelyn, only a few Levels lower. One of Kyle's crew he'd dragged with him. Ranged Classes were always welcome.

My spells were getting stronger, and the earth I packed denser—if all else failed, my support Class could definitely help reinforce the front line.

After several more minutes finagling groups for the best possible makeup to success of each of them, we were mostly ready to head out.

❖

Modes of transport were a godsend. Or tech-department-send, depending on how you looked at it. It was no time before my team and I reached University Road and slowed our pace so we could look out for potential threats along the way.

At least we'd been mostly able to keep the main roads clear. It made traveling to the monster dense areas easier.

We had thirty vehicles of varying types now. Enough to take our Adventurers almost anywhere. Not quite to the Gold Coast yet, though. Even if I really wanted to get there, just to double check, just to find Mason in the flesh. Right now we had bigger things to deal with.

The color of Mana as we pulled in through Toohey Forest deepened. There was this overlying green tinge to it all, but not the sickly pallor I'd seen in some things. No, this—this was all nature. I could feel the power as it suffused me, gently showed me where the concentrations were and made me fully aware that Gemma had been correct.

Nathan Campus was turning into a major dungeon.

Not even the trees were the same anymore. In the just over six weeks since System onset, everything had changed. The flora that covered the ground with its mossy texture now blanketed everything with a seething heartbeat that, from what I could tell, leached life force if you touched it with bare skin.

Drained not just from humans, from everything. Any type of creature that didn't do its due diligence when coming into land on the ground cover was going to be zapped of all of its living essence within several seconds.

The information seeped into my body, through my eyes and what they saw, an intuitive, knowledge-based mishmash that I wasn't going to question as I passed it on. "Don't touch the ground cover. Preferably don't even step on it. Don't go into the trees for anything. For now, just stick to the road."

Because in the instance I'd spoken up, I'd also realized that the trees themselves had completely changed. More and more information filtered through my gaze to my brain. The way Mana moved and recoiled, settled and lashed out—all of it meant something that my knowledge and implants interpreted.

In a way, I was just the messenger.

I hadn't been in this area for more than four weeks, not since our one encounter with those damned mushroom creatures.

Now, Toohey Forest had come into her own. She was fierce and protective, alive and vicious. And it didn't matter how much I loved nature, she'd gobble me up without a second thought if I tried to cross that line.

Road it was, then.

We continued silently, very slowly as our little makeshift jeeps trundled along in their almost-silent way. Mana had a way about it that meant we didn't need revving engines or noise, and these vehicles let us be stealthy.

Finally, we rolled into the carpark where I'd squashed that damned flying cockroach bug thing all those weeks ago. It was where I'd ushered my kids from my glowing lab and hoped for safety only to realize that everything electronic was currently dead.

There, in the middle of what had been the car park was my abandoned jeep. Except I only recognized it because I knew it should have been there. Where once there was metal and gears, it was now almost completely overrun with rampant foliage and leaves. Dirt erupted through the ground all around it, and the tires had practically melted to become one with the earth.

"Might want to keep our vehicles on the ground that hasn't succumbed to the wilds yet," Kyle noted dryly.

I'd have chuckled if I didn't have a pit of trepidation trying to eat away at my stomach lining. "Vehicles might be the least of our worries." I gestured toward the looming dungeon that had once been the Griffith University Nathan Campus and vaguely recalled coming to work for my first day here almost a decade ago like it was really part of a dream.

Nathan Campus had always been so pretty, nestled inside of the forest, treating its surroundings like the entire university was a fairy village trying its best to fit in with normal, everyday society. The concrete structures might not have belonged in amidst the trees, but I'd always felt that the builders, the architects, had made an effort to preserve as much of the wildlife around it as possible.

But now?

Now nature had mutated and taken it back. Vines and leaves, bark and trees, overtook almost every single building, leaving only glimpses of the grey concrete walls poking through the outside. Even here, in the bright mid-morning sunlight that filtered in to the campus, there was now a dank air about everything. That about-to-rot vegetation scent certainly stood out, lending a foreboding undercurrent to the whole scenario.

It reminded me of this morning's corpse.

The darkness of foliage had taken over and leaked through everything. Inky Mana strands wove through the structure, holding it all together with power, knitting it so it was imperceptible from the way nature had morphed.

Shivers ran down my spine, or maybe that was just a cold sheen of sweat as what stood in front of us became apparent. Gemma was right. Nathan was definitely dungeonifying. Except that it already had, and I wasn't sure we were prepared for what it had to offer.

"Should we really leave our vehicles here?" Eritia spoke up, a slight lilt to her voice.

I don't think I'd ever heard her speak before this, and I noted to myself that I could probably just listen to her talk for hours on end, because she had one of those voices. It wasn't an accent as such, but I was willing to bet one of her parents had one. That lilt was just unmistakable.

Just had to hope that her firepower lived up to the glory I'd imagined from a Level-30 Fire Mage. She'd definitely been in her element way back when we fought Rigoll. Or, more accurately, when my brother brought his life-saving crew to pull us out of the crap we'd fallen into.

"Well, we're hoofing it back if they get eaten by the foliage." Evelyn shrugged. "There's nowhere else to put them anyway. It's not like we can shrink them down and put them in our pockets or anything now, is there?"

I glanced around and noticed Gemma cracked a smile.

"That would be handy. I'm looking up shrink rays next time I get to the Shop." The rogue even cracked a small joke. Things were definitely looking up. Even if we were about to walk into the mouth of hell.

Queensland was a tropical state. So the fact that there were vines hanging over walkways, that there were staghorn ferns I was sure were about to spurt forth eerily alive creatures, wasn't a surprise to me at all. I mean the little plants that unfurled themselves from trees, spouting out their leaves—or fronds to be technical.

The humidity felt like it had dialed up a notch as soon as we hit what I'd call the mouth of the dungeon. Though in this ten-degree damn weather,

I didn't like that the air still felt humid. Rainforests would be rainforests, I guess.

Kyle and Sange were our Healers, Molly our sole Tank. I didn't want to think how nervous that made me. Eritia the Fire Mage and Morton our Gunslinger were mostly unknown to me, and I couldn't let myself focus on that.

Tasha and Gemma worked well in close combat together after so many patrols under their belts. Evelyn and Dannin appeared to get along well enough, so I hoped they worked well together too. He seemed around her age, mid to late twenties, tall and willowy like a typical elven archer with the blonde hair and blue eyes to match. Maybe that was a sign he'd be an excellent Ranger. One could hope.

I hefted my Warhammer in my hand, happy that I'd thought to put more into Strength and Agility. Not a heap, but enough that I wasn't at the bare minimum anymore.

"Let's go get me three thousand experience points," I muttered. Because if we'd come this far, and since the university I'd loved had changed so much, I wasn't leaving before I got something out of it.

Chapter Seventeen:

Nathan Campus

Saliva dripped down from my hand, making my hold on the Warhammer somewhat tenuous. The saliva was warm and sticky, a little thicker than you'd expect, and smelled rank. Like it had eaten its poop, its friend's poop, and then some of the vomit that resulted from eating it.

That first bite they'd delivered sucked. The colder weather should have rendered the Lace Monitors mostly lethargic, but I should have known better. Brisbane, good old humid-as-fuck Brisbane. The System didn't play by any actual rules of nature anyway. Mana bombarded every natural order and flipped it on its head.

Instead of solitary and partially hibernating, we'd encountered a group of Lace Monitors only two rooms into the campus dungeon.

These lizards, or goannas or however you want to refer to them, usually grew up to two meters in length on a good, non-apocalyptic day. Now? After over a month of Mana saturation and System messing around, these boys were about five meters long and came up to my waist.

At this size their jaws were formidable, and that only semi-recently discovered fact that they did, in fact, have venomous secretions? Well, it wasn't helping. Their greyish-brown skin wrinkled around their legs, making me think they looked a bit like grumpy old men.

At least until they moved. They were faster than I'd expected with their size having done little to change their speed. And they snapped at us so quickly, Dannin hadn't reacted in time at first. He'd received a nasty bite on his calf, pulling off an entire chunk of flesh in the process. His scream still echoed in my ears. Kyle's heals were still taking effect even now, and the Mana rushed in to do its job.

Lace Monitors had once been the second largest of their kinds in the country, but now . . . I was willing to bet they more than rivaled their supposedly larger cousins. And the brain natriuretic peptide that they secreted could increase blood clotting and send shooting pain through the body in its original form.

Now on System-acid, the creatures were *really* dangerous.

Molly's tower shield and my Earth Barrier were the only things standing in the way of total annihilation. Three of the damned things with their tough hides, fast reflexes, and venomous mouths were more than we could realistically handle at the same time.

They caught us off guard when we walked through the circuit after exiting the bus area into the university grounds now overgrown with bushes and ferns. The bleeding bark and moving branches had been startling enough, not to mention the monitors. Disaster had only been averted by some quick reflexes and System-enabled toughness.

"Down!" Evelyn called out, loosing an arrow almost immediately. I was glad I'd been on enough patrols with her that I automatically reacted to her command. Her simple shots with her bow didn't cost any Mana, and today was the first time I was witnessing the rush of power that soared through her as she utilized her actual Skills.

I was really starting to appreciate Mana Sense on a whole new level.

The shot catapulted from her bowstring, and I watched in almost slow motion as it plunged straight into the eye of the Monitor closest to me. The creature didn't drop dead immediately, however, even with half the arrow shaft embedded in its eye.

A squeal tore from its throat, causing the other two to swivel and focus on Evelyn as their partner writhed in agony on the ground. Its stubby little arms feebly reached toward the arrow. Its movements grew sluggish, and the other two bared their teeth as the creature writhed in pain.

An oddly guttural sound emanated from their throats, and I could see a bulge forming in the softer area of their jowls.

"Oh no," I muttered, suddenly all too aware of what was about to happen. Mana gathered around them—in them, in a way—and all I knew was that this was about to get ugly.

"Spit!" Gemma yelled before I could continue my thought.

Guess I didn't need my Mana Sense for that warning after all.

It was that split second between Gemma calling it out and the actual venomous saliva leaving the mouths of our opponents that saved Evelyn. Or at least saved us a lot of time healing her.

She ducked quicker than I'd have thought possible, and a surge of Mana noise echoed through my head at the sheer use of power by the monsters. The globules of spit landed on the concrete wall behind Evelyn with a sizzle that stung my ears, mixing with the hum of more Mana flooding into the body, warping the concrete.

While the Monitors recovered from their attack, Tasha and Gemma dashed in, using the mere seconds they had to dig daggers or blades into the softest parts of our attackers' flesh. I could practically feel the tension against the blades as they drove them in and out—three seconds later rolling away as the effort of the Monitor's spitball Skill finally wore off.

At least their Health dropped significantly from the attack.

In the meantime, the arrow-eye Monitor was getting hammered by the rest of the team, spells and Skills crushing limbs, ending its life.

Evelyn, hands trembling, stood against the wall, panting with the effort of her earlier Skill use. If I had to guess, it probably was a combination Stamina and Mana Skill, though the way her eyes looked, wilder than I'd ever noticed before, told me the near-miss was probably just as much of a problem.

Around us, the plant life moved, swaying in time with some sort of wind I couldn't feel. It gave me the distinct feeling that this entire place was restless and we'd caught its attention. Mana rippled around them, feeding them, helping them grow.

They moved in sync with the agitated Monitors, and I barely had any warning that the branches themselves decided to lash out too.

The two remaining Monitors bellowed into the air, sucking in breaths like they were skulling Mana down their long necks and into their bellies to better roast us with. At the same time, the vines hanging down and crawling across the walls detached themselves, pushing the bulk of our group further into the middle of the massive corridor, thus leaving us less room to maneuver safely away from the lizards.

Except there was something bubbling, about to happen, tingling all the way through my brain.

In a feat of "I have no idea how I suddenly managed to become that athletic," I dove across about three meters of space to push Gemma out of the way. A moment later, a stream of scalding hot air hit the spot she'd been less than a second ago.

Score one for foreshadowing from Mana Sense, giving me a heads up of what was about to happen.

There was no time to revel in the fact. Dannin stood on the opposite end of the wall, releasing arrow after arrow.

From where the Mana strands led, I knew a second blast was about to follow, straight toward Dannin, and there was no way he could move in time to avoid it. Kyle stood next to him, his back turned as he cut apart some nearby vines that were eagerly attempting to grab him. There was no way for him to see the warning signs.

Twisting around and lunging forward, propelling myself off the back of my legs, I hit Dannin in the lower legs. I felt-saw his ankle twist as he fell, knocking Kyle out of the target line as well. I winced a little, hoping I hadn't done too much damage to him. I landed hard, on my shoulder, turning it into a roll I swore I was far too old for. The pain from using my body to body slam two others away dulled almost immediately as Kyle reacted at last, pumping me full of a HoT.

At least I was already healing as I struggled up to my feet, still clinging to my Warhammer. I turned to the lizards while they stalked forward, their movements slower than I'd expected. How I wished Analyze could show me specific Skill effects.

At least we'd gotten them to show the full range of their abilities in the wake of their twitching partner dying. It felt so bad to watch this happen to a creature I'd once revered. Death throes weren't pretty in any of us, least of all majestic lizards. Whatever Skill—or item perhaps—Evelyn had used, it dealt ongoing damage to the creature over and above the embedded arrow. Otherwise, the damn thing would have popped out.

Stupid cheating System.

At least the first Monitor was dead. Trying to beat out the innate System regeneration was a pain in the arse.

"Watch out!" Gemma yelled at me, and I belatedly realized I'd forgotten about the vines clinging to the walls.

And the branches.

Pain exploded through my body as a sharper-than-possible branch stabbed down and into my leg. It hit just above the knee and completely impaled my thigh to the floor, pinning me far too near the wall.

My hammer fell out of my grasp while I grappled with another vine attempting to attach me to the stone wall at my rear, and a third glanced off the armor at my hip as I frantically twisted. The amount of things happening at once defied my ability to process and was fueled purely by reaction. I felt more than heard the scream tear from my throat.

I activated Water Siphon as my hands grabbed a hold of the branch-vines while enabling Mana Transfer to replenish what I was losing. Damned plants needed water whether they were running on Mana these days or not, and I could feel the limbs beneath my hands buck in utter desperation to get away from me.

Once I was sure Water Siphon was working, I let it go and began hacking at the branch that pinned my leg to the ground. Pain tore through my body with each strike, but it felt like it was something in the back of my mind, the entire ordeal experienced as if I was removed from it. My vision blurred with an abundance of blues, strands I still couldn't define holding messages I still had no idea how to interpret.

Suddenly, the pressure on my leg eased up, the branch breaking away underneath my grip, and someone pried my fingers away from the vine I held onto. Kyle gathered me up, moving me away from the wall while Eritia lowered her fire-gauntleted hands, keeping the rest of the living vegetation at bay. Morton appeared out of breath next to her, and his guns were smoking. I hadn't been able to spend much time watching for how he fought yet, and right now wasn't the time.

Damn it. I took a second to check on the rest of the team, to see what they were doing. Luckily, it seemed that the line had reformed and pushed the Monitors back, even inflicting enough damage that they'd backed off again.

The Monitors, now down to about a quarter of life each, seemed wary of us. We couldn't stop, though; the damned System would heal them back up if we weren't careful.

I scrambled, my leg still throbbing with each beat of my heart, blood flowing outwards in a constant stream even though the hole was already closing up. Though my head spun a little with blood loss, I knew it'd be replenished in no time.

"Stay away from the walls."

Maybe stating the obvious would help us all.

Evelyn began firing her bow, but her special Skill, Sniper, was mostly useless when creatures were aware of it already. At most, she could usually get off two of those shots before the damned things became cognizant enough of her that they knew how to deflect or dodge her sniping Skill.

There were differences in how Dannin played the Class that weren't all to do with chosen Skills. He tended to run mostly on his Autoshot, peppering in what appeared to be Headshots, and Snareshots in the midst of it all. More tactical than damage oriented. It meant they complemented each other well.

They were only three Levels apart. But one was a Ranger, and one was a Ranger of Sight. So I had no idea what the difference truly was.

Molly motioned for us all to fan out behind her and slammed her tower shield practically into the stone and earthen ground beneath her. It expanded out from each side, making an almost impenetrable wall in front of her. Level 34 suited her well.

Sange had gained a barrier along the way in the last few weeks. Nothing like the one Jules had had, but more of an absorbency shield for incoming overall damage. Like a sort of healing ward. They cast it around all of us, only letting our damage dealing Skills pass out of the dome. For at least a thousand or so damage, nothing would get in to hurt us.

Dannin, Eritia, Morton, and Evelyn proceeded to riddle the Monitors with whatever they could. Gunshots penetrated the creatures' skin with confident thuds, making me glad we'd brought the Gunslinger with us.

Fire didn't penetrate their skin as well as I thought ice might have, but it did the job and added to the ongoing mixed smell of crisped scales, charred flesh, and burning vegetation that surrounded us. Each strike sent them squealing more than once, the pair of Monitors charging into Molly's defenses again and again.

Each charge tore at the dome, pushed Molly back a few inches before she reset, caustic venom saliva dripping from the edge of her shield. Our attacks kept injuring them, but their health dwindled all too slowly, jumping up once in a while as their monsterized bodies healed themselves.

With Implantation to augment damage and assist with some group healing, I set about utilizing Planted In Place as well as I possibly could. The Monitors' legs were sturdy enough, and they possessed enough strength that my root didn't keep them in place for as long as I liked, but it definitely helped.

The vines didn't seem to like helping me, considering they'd just attempted to murder me, so I ended up juggling Treesong and Topsoil into the mix in order to bring them over to my way of thinking.

They still rebelled, but Treesong made them more amenable to my way of thinking, making it easier to force them into keeping the Monitors as restrained as possible.

There was so much I had to keep in check in my brain.

Sange kept Molly topped up, and I watched as Gemma and Tasha braved outside of the healing ward to stab the creatures at the best possible times. But it was Kyle I couldn't take my eyes off.

His face twisted in a mask of grief. Maybe he didn't know what he was doing, or perhaps he just didn't think anyone was watching him. The casting motions he made with his hands curled his fingers into claws, like he was dragging the life-force out of the creatures in front of him.

Just the concept hurt him; I could feel it from where I stood. Taking life, leaching it, it just wasn't something my brother did. And yet here we were, in the center of a battle, where he was pulling life force from the Monitors instead of gifting it.

I wanted to tell him to stop, but there was a grim determination around the stubborn set of his mouth that I knew all too well. He'd take what he was given and roll with it until it killed him. Ripping my gaze away from my brother, I had to push down the echo of pain I felt emanating from him and helped finish off these once-beautiful creatures before the agony overwhelmed me too.

❖

Two rooms of Monitors behind us, and we'd dropped down to the next level of the dungeon. Though the upper levels had clearly been the main thoroughfare of the university between buildings, the lower level was created beneath it, dug into the ground like a basement.

Definitely an odd thing to find in Brisbane. Even stranger was the fact that there were buildings all around us that I'd yet to see an entrance to. Maybe they were still forming.

As soon as we descended, a massive spine impaled the wall right next to my face, and I almost screamed at how close that call was. Spines being flung in my direction were definitely not the way I wanted to go, but apparently the short-nosed echidna mutations standing right in front of us decided I was the best thing around to practice targets with.

They blended into the dirty, stone-filled hallways. Here, beneath ground level, the plants devolved into roots and vines only. Branches were no longer in sight. Their writhing was less pronounced than in the level above us. And yet there was still a putrid feeling of dirty Mana leaking through to me. Tainted Mana with explicit death on its mind.

Short-beaked echidnas are so freaking cute. They hibernate, they're fast, and they're damned good at being what they are, which is a spiny-quilled anteater, an egg-laying mammal.

But when Mana comes and mutates the fuck out of them, blowing them up to ten times their size and making their spines that much more painful if they hit you, they're a part of nightmares I really didn't want to live through.

Not to mention the subversion of the natural order of things now the Mana had pushed the creatures out of hibernation and into defensive positions. Here we were, with a nest of the damned things, no motherly instincts in sight, and speed that shouldn't belong to something the size of a small hippo.

The only thing in our favor was that at least the size of the dungeon allowed us room to move.

Tachyglossus Aculeatus Giganticus

Level 34

Swarmer

The Mana hadn't just mutated the echidnas' size, but their proclivity for gathering in groups, too. Teamwork made the Tachyglossus really fucking dangerous. With the rest of the mutations at the fore, this usually solitary creature brandished otherwise-stationary quills as spines that detached with deadly aim. Facing three or four at a time upped the danger factor immensely.

A spine lodged into the wall right next to where Kyle's head had been but a moment ago. At least the creatures weren't elite. Yet. If that was how this worked.

My brother spun to the side and shot out another one of his Withering Shots, eliciting a squeal of rage from the Tachyglossus it hit.

Despite having been in this dungeon for a while now, we hadn't yet managed to find a boss, and I was starting to hope we didn't encounter one. The monsters here were far too strong, and I was feeling way too vulnerable for my own good. Phantom pain still smarted from the leg wound that had closed more than an hour ago, and my own mortality kept staring me in the face.

The Tachyglossus quartet we faced appeared to be studying us. Sure, let's mutate their intelligence too.

Molly let out a strangled cry of effort as she shield bashed a surprisingly nimble incoming foe. With their size increase, I'd have thought some of that agility would be gone, but that would be a no. I could practically feel the reverberation as the impact made her arm shake. Another roar tore from her throat, guttural in its intensity as she heaved the shield back, readying another attack.

I loosed Planted In Place twice in quick succession, making sure to tie two of our incoming attackers to the ground so we could at least maneuver more easily. Thankfully, all the mutated vegetation in here was working in my favor, making my Skills stronger than they would have been outside the dungeon. Lingering effects of the Topsoil Skill I'd peppered around earlier.

Point for me.

With four shopping-cart-sized Tachyglossus in play, we had to use some form of crowd control and the past few rooms had given me enough practice to make it possible now with my Skills. No one else really had any crowd control Skills, so it meant I was it.

My root didn't hold that well when the creatures were being attacked, but more often than not, it held long enough for Gemma or Tasha to get some attacks in there. Trying to mix it up with the free Tachyglossus when the others were firing into the scrum was just asking for friendly fire incidents. So they kept to hitting the rooted fellas, piling up the damage with well-aimed strikes.

Slow, but effective, with all our damage spread out. As long as I kept my Mana Transfer active and didn't use my Mana-based Skills unnecessarily. Wasting Mana was tantamount to losing battles in this new world, and while I had a few potions to chug down if I needed, the damned things were quite expensive, even when bartered for. And that didn't even take into account the lengthy diminishing returns.

"Do you think there's poison on those spines?" Sange spoke quietly to my left, multitasking their casting as they protected both Molly and the rest of the group.

Kyle, as we were coming to realize, was fantastic in a pinch and great at making sure we didn't lose limbs, but his Skills were slowly emerging as more damaging than healing.

Poor guy.

"I would err on the side of everything here wants us dead." I didn't mean it to come out in a comical manner, but Sange chuckled dryly anyway.

"Touché." But the concentration wrinkles creased their brow again, and a lightly green sheen overlaid the entire group. A new icon appeared in my Status at the same time, and I inspected it.

Shield of Poison Resistance

+20% to poison resistance for 5 minutes.

"Nice," I commented and belatedly noticed that Sange had leveled up to 34. Here I was still just shy of 31. I felt like I was lagging behind everyone. Soon I'd get passed to a lower group. Just one of the perks of owning the damned settlement. All the time spent in meetings wasn't time spent leveling. If I had the right Class for it, that settlement XP for owning might actually make up the difference, but since I didn't, it was all a net negative.

Another shake of my head, and I focused back on the fight itself. The problem with tying things down with spines was that they could still fire them, even tied down. With a lot worse aim, obviously, and my roots weren't invulnerable. They didn't last forever.

All of which meant that I had to manage my casts, switching out rooting as necessary between the four. Molly in the front kept the pressure up, blocking off as many of the spines as she could while the rest of the ranged fighters peppered them with arrows and spells.

We worked methodically through one of the echidnas, chipping away at its health while I desperately tried to keep the others at bay. It worked, but my Mana was almost down to half by the time the first was dead.

Having spines and fur all mixed together made the creatures more difficult to knock down. Arrow and spell aiming had the chance to glance off target. Even when they hit, innate System resistances seemed to reduce the damage we did. Surprisingly, our melee combatants with their damage-dealing Skills were the most effective—but we had few enough of those.

One down, I let another loose to rush in. Rather than attack us though, it turned and ripped the roots free from another of its friend and then another. I found myself reaching for Planted In Place, only for Mana Sense and intuition to tell me to hold off.

"Fall back!" I roared, wanting the team to retreat so that I could make use of new, clean, strengthened roots and vines for my Skill.

We fell back, Molly in the front, the two assassins harried by the newly freed Tachyglossus. Even experienced as we were with fighting, we weren't elite soldiers. We screwed up, opening up a space.

A space that one of the monsters made full use of, suddenly accelerating. Molly blocked it, but tussling with the Tachyglossus meant she had no time to deal with the second that shoved its way past her.

The echidna's long nose stabbed out, taking Kyle in the side even as he was shoved aside, the attack tossing him into one of the walls where roots began to reach for him. I snarled, throwing a hand up and used Water Siphon on them.

Keep the fear of dehydration in those roots—that was the way.

Kyle rolled to his feet, gasping as he clutched his side. I could feel anger rolling off him mixed with a heavy dose of frustration as a spine narrowly missed his head.

Again.

"You've got to pay more attention to that," Evelyn admonished him, slightly out of breath considering she'd barreled him out of the way with barely a second to spare. "Stop getting in your head. Be in the now. Pay attention to the meter-tall spiny thing that would like nothing more than to impale you against a wall. Wake the fuck up."

She was right to be angry. We all needed to depend on each other in here and even Dannin, our green little Ranger, was putting up valiant efforts.

In the meantime, while letting Evelyn dress my brother down, I cast Planted In Place and wrapped up two of the monsters. Molly fell backwards, getting hold of the creature that attacked my brother, the pair of assassins having bought us time by throwing themselves at the creature, wounds accumulating from their reckless actions.

My brother squared his shoulders and muttered a very curt "Sorry" before cricking his neck and taking aim.

Kyle focused whatever that Skill was—something that increased the damage done to the creature for a set amount of time. He didn't have a cooldown on the ability, but from what I'd observed, it had diminishing returns when used on the same creature constantly.

Still, with Dannin and Evelyn loosing arrows at the monster, and Eritia and Morton pumping damage via fire and guns, the creature's health smoothly ran down. Implantation in place, I ran in with my Warhammer since I was nearly out of Mana now anyway. I took a swing, knocking at its knees and head and anything I could reach.

As light pulsed over the pair of girls, Tasha and Evelyn healed up from their brief foray as front-line fighters before they returned to their backstabbing assaults on the monster.

Things began to move into place, our Skills clicking together at last. There was a rush of power through all of us, a feeling of cohesiveness that I hadn't experienced in any of our encounters so far.

It was heady and delightful, addictive. And the Mana danced before my eyes.

Concentrated fire power on the second of our opponents took it down faster, earlier damage causing it to fall much easier. It helped that the creatures were running out of spines, each of my Planted In Place Skill usages lasting longer than ever because they moved less without the preparation involved in firing their quills.

Our opponent was alive and then gone, twitching in death throes on the ground before we moved along to the next.

By the time we got to the fourth and last, I could practically sense the fear emanating from it. Gone was the boldness it gained in having fellow giant friends. Mana convulsed around it, almost as if it had given up on fueling the creatures.

Even the odd spine that managed to land a hit didn't stop our forward momentum.

This was what it should be like, working with a group. A fluid collection of people fighting in sync with one another. But as Evelyn's last shot took the final echidna in the group down, I couldn't help the sadness I felt.

Sure . . . that whole joy at being alive and being able to move on and see my kids when I got home definitely helped. But at the same time . . .

This is what life in the apocalypse boiled down to now. Be killed by once-cute creatures, or kill them before they got you. Kill-or-be-killed mentality wasn't precisely my thing. The apocalypse was changing us all in so many ways.

All those morose thoughts fled from my head while I was looting the damned thing, though.

You have received:

2 x Intact Tachyglossus Aculeatus Giganticus Spleen

1 x Intact Tachyglossus Aculeatus Giganticus Saliva Gland

3 x Intact Tachyglossus Aculeatus Giganticus Spine Fluid

3 x Intact Tachyglossus Aculeatus Giganticus Eyeballs

Even as I placed the items in my inventory, I heard a keening sound that made me shake in fear. It wasn't even necessarily that I knew what it was, but that from the sound of it, from the reverberation it made through the underground forming walls . . the creature was huge.

And it was very, very angry.

Chapter Eighteen:
Egg Protection

The keening from the mysterious creature below us was all the warning we had as the floor beneath us gave out and dropped us into a terraforming room. The dirt on two-thirds of the ground was still forming into a semblance of an actual floor. There was nothing solid next to it, and I knew instinctually that falling into that black hole would be deadly.

We crashed hard, our fall only softened by my reflexive use of Topsoil to cushion what I could. Not its intended purpose. I also didn't care. Truthfully, not sure how much it made a difference, but it was what it was.

Somewhere during the last battle, I'd managed to level, but I didn't even have time to allocate my points because the mother of all echidnas was careening in the corner of the large room as if it was about to pulverize all of us.

We scrambled to the one fully formed side of the room, though the rest of the floor was solidifying into place even as we moved. Dirt and roots cascaded down the walls like they were trying to bury us alive.

Tachyglossus Aculeatus Giganticus Mater

Level 34 Elite

Protectorate of the Egg

Oh, great. An elite boss with an egg to protect.

And that was all the warning we got.

Unlike the smaller versions we'd defeated in the room above, this one stood about as tall as us, and longer. The room's ceilings had to be about twelve feet in height, so at least it didn't feel as cramped as it could have, considering we were underground.

This short-nosed echidna, however, didn't much resemble their original form. Whereas the others just looked like enlarged versions, this one had a scaly appearance to each and every spine. Her nose had grown much longer, sharper, almost like an alligator's, and her feet sprouted claws that reminded me of the back heel of a velociraptor.

Even her bellow resembled what I think emus sounded like, less than the small warbling I'd come to expect from echidnas. She reared back, keeping her egg behind her in a well-protected nest of vines and roots, and hunkered down to charge us.

Her now-massive feet pounded the thirty-odd meter runup she had on us, and I cringed, immediately pushing up an Earth Barrier to dull the charge. But the wall I created was a flimsy reaction wall. I had to hope it would at least help.

Evelyn and Dannin's bows twanged at precisely the same time, smashing into the floor in front of the creature, leaving it glistening with what appeared to be an oil slick.

The Mater lost her footing and careened, slipping down to slide on her butt like an out-of-control bowling ball hurtling toward the Earth Barrier. Bits of hardened earth went flying around the room, only slowing her somewhat.

We stood beyond the now-destroyed barrier like bowling pins she was about to knock over.

There was barely enough time for us to react and dive out of the way as the Mater smashed into the wall behind them us. She roared, sounding much more like a lion than I'd ever imagined, managed to struggle to her feet and shake her head, bleating with irritation even as our ranged fighters bombarded her with everything they had, while Tasha and Gemma crept in behind to contribute their stabbing attacks.

All of our attacks took no more than ten percent of her overall health, despite her having smashed herself into a wall. Bloody thing was tougher than grandpa's week-old bread.

Shit.

"Fan out!" I called out, thinking of the only possible solution. We had to remain a less concentrated target for her. If she closed in on one of us, it gave the others the chance to attack for all they were worth, and I knew Molly was up to the challenge.

While our Tank dug her shield in, activating the best of her abilities, I tapped into Treesong, determined to get it to work for me. Along with Topsoil, I might even be able to subdue the plant life around us. Or at least get them to not to immediately attack us.

Treesong was like a lullaby in my head and took most of my concentration, leaving little room even for Mana Sense to leak in. Not great. I hope it improved in its capacity to allow for multitasking once I leveled it a bit, or I got used to using the Skill.

At least once applied, its effect stayed in place for a while.

Each of the roots, the vines, running through this underground room lit up to me. They glowed with life and Mana, with purpose—even if it was nefarious. It wanted to gobble all of our Mana up, to consume it and have us disappear in the process. All I wanted, all I asked of it, was to leave us alone.

Calming it with Topsoil, so to speak, brought us precious moments when none of us had to waste energy concentrating on a secondary damage source. If I kept this up, what with my slowly draining Mana pool, we should be able to make it through this fight.

Should.

Mater wasn't an easy opponent though. Where her earlier counterparts were fast, she was brutal. Her speed zoomed like she should have been in a superhero collection. Planted In Place barely managed to rip her out of her movement long enough that we could get in some good hits.

But none of us had infinite Mana. I could only do so much, and thus it fell to the Rangers to provide the distractions we needed in order to keep her attacks at bay. Except it didn't work like I wanted it to. She was intelligent and focused, protecting her once-a-year young like there was no tomorrow. And in her reality there might not be.

Short-nosed echidnas only mated once a year, only produced offspring once a year, and they did it all as a single mother. The mutation had taken hold of that survival instinct and magnified it. There was a part of me not wanting to hurt a single mother regardless of species, but then there was the other part—the logical one—that needed me to make it home to *my* kids.

Of course, that's when she took away my choices. For a brief instant, I felt like time stopped as Mana waves coalesced into the creature. Slow motion enough that I could understand the information my implants were sending to my brain. My head felt like it was about to explode, but the warning was what we needed.

Quillfire . . . bleed.

Shit.

I barely had time to smash up Earth Barrier. It rose from the ground, solid but small, only covering half of us in time. Mana poured from me as Mater's quills jettisoned out toward all of us. When I peeked over the top of my wall, I saw one of them stuck in Molly's shield, another in Sange's arm, one in Kyle's thigh, and another in Tasha's side.

There were also a few buried so deep into my Earth Barrier that cracks appeared. Time returned as the screams from my three injured team mates rang through the air. And while the bleed seemed hefty, the fact that only three of us were injured instead of all of us . . . it made keeping the HoTs on far more viable.

Those, and with the System's help, we should at least survive until the next attack.

There seemed to be so much I could do with my Mana Sensing abilities. I needed more time to practice and hone. In the middle of battle wasn't going to cut it for long. I was flying by the seat of my pants.

With my head throbbing, there wasn't much I could do but tunnel focus on the fight. Treesong required renewed application every now and again, but more practice allowed for defter control of it. Otherwise there was watching for Quillfire waves, paying attention to the Mater's Mana usage, and utilizing the Skills I had with caution and logical planning.

I really needed Mana Stone, but for that I required another ten Levels or so. Being able to increase everyone else's Mana Regeneration was damn overpowered, and I knew it, and I didn't care what I might lose in order to get it.

The Quillfire-like warning sensation flashed through me again, but this time subtly different. I realized belatedly that it wasn't the same Skill, just something very similar. Pushing my frustration to the back, I took a deep breath and dive rolled with no particular athletic prowess to the left, barely dodging the smaller spines that shot rapidly out of Mater in my direction.

Spine throw.

That Spine Throw was targeted, and just another ability we needed to be wary of.

Evelyn hadn't loosed an arrow for several seconds but made up for her slowdown now as she let loose a volley of arrows that planted down around Mater. The arrows each bore with them a layer of what looked like vines or something stringing them together, the arrows laying a net over the monster. An undercurrent of light or electricity ran through the makeshift net and as soon as all of the arrows landed in the floor, Evelyn dropped to one knee and smashed her hand down onto the ground.

Electricity sparked through a strand of netting I hadn't noticed and flared all the way up and into the rope that restricted the Mater. She squealed in pain as the static shot through her, hitting her nervous system violently.

Even so, the monster's own power reacted to the predicament. She writhed there, on the spot, her stubby legs of iron digging into the newly formed soft ground beneath her. Enough so that it gave me a really bad feeling about all of this.

The soil beneath her began to writhe, like she was leaching all of its energy from it, all of the nutrients, and starting to power herself up for another attack. One of desperation, a last-ditch effort to save herself and her egg.

Dangerous was all of the warning my Mana Sense gave me.

"Duck. Shields!" I cried out, scrambling to get the words out of my throat in time to make any difference at all.

Thankfully, Earth Barrier was still present. Even cracked, it gave a few of us somewhere to hide. What I wasn't expecting was the ground to betray us too. Even as I leapt in my own clumsy way to avoid the incoming tremors I could already feel through the ground, I saw Molly stumble. Her tower shield was the only thing that saved her, the massive weapon lodging itself in in such a way there was no chance for it to fail.

Still, I heard her shoulder pop and the muffled scream that tore from her throat as Sange's heal hit almost simultaneously. The healer's stability with a shaking floor was enviable and lucky for all of us.

Dannin and Tasha stumbled badly, Sange's wards doing little to allay the damage they took. Evelyn ducked behind half of the now-crumbling

Earth Barrier, her face pale as a ghost before she disappeared from my sight.

And then the only thing I could focus on was the heaving ground beneath me as the throes of the Mater tried to throw me to the ground. Shocks traveled through my feet and up into my body, blue light dancing in the edges of my vision as the monster's ability literally made the ground hurt us. Each jolt sent lightning up my pain centers for what seemed like an eternity, even if it was only a few seconds in reality.

Suddenly, there was less pressure against my brain as I felt a wave of Mana roll over us all, a push down the connection that was the System that emanated from the left.

Into the Fray
(Group Buff)
+20 to Physical Damage Resistance
Duration: 60 seconds

Tasha must have leveled it up significantly since the last time she'd used it. The relief that came with a significant damage reducer was all we needed to pull ourselves back together. Mater was down to ten percent life remaining, and we were going to use those sixty seconds to every possible advantage.

I much preferred fighting monsters that were completely alien to us. Those were monsters in the true sense of the word to me. But this?

As I watched the Implantation timer wind down, and my friends pumped all of their offensive Skills into the creature, I couldn't help but remember how cute these little things had been before.

She wasn't anymore, though, and she'd done her darndest to kill us.

Evelyn's and Dannin's Rapidfire shots resounded through my ears as each arrow thudded into the creature's soft, furry flesh. But it was Morton's gunshots that pounded in my ears. They thunked in a way that reeked of finality and sent the creature's squeals up to a whole new octave.

Her life ebbed away, and still the egg sat in the back corner, protected by the vine nest.

Eritia's fireballs made the fur on the creature catch on fire, which wasn't ideal for our melee fighters. But her aim kept it all to one side while Tasha and Gemma attacked the other.

Molly took the brunt of the Mater's frustration on her shield, but now as our opponent's life dwindled further, the attacks were fueled by sheer desperation. Sange healed; Kyle backed them up, tossing in offensive spells consistently.

My hammer felt far too heavy in my hands even as it thudded into her body, the sudden resistance she provided reverberating up my arms. Until the Mater made one final whimper and shuddered to the ground.

I stood there panting just as the buff wore off. It was amazing how long sixty seconds could take.

❖

Looting the corpse was highly anticlimactic.

Tachyglossus Aculeatus Giganticus Mater
Level 34 Elite Corpse

We got some spines, a liver, and several gag-worthy innards pieces. Enough to take and barter with, but not enough to feel everything was worth it. I eyed the egg, now probably doomed to decay and die.

"Should we take it?" Kyle asked no one in particular.

I could feel the fatigue in his voice. Hell, I could feel it in my bones.

This whole everything was inevitably draining. "Why not? It's not going to survive here on its own anyway."

Evelyn shrugged. "If it hatches, it's your problem."

I could barely decipher her words as she pulled at her bow, frowning at the string. Even I could see it needed repairing. I wonder if the electricity had damaged it.

She pulled out another string and quickly and efficiently restrung the bow. I raised an eyebrow at her and she shrugged. "Losing my weapon in a fight could potentially kill a lot of us. Not taking that chance."

I nodded at her. Not that I'd been surprised she could do it, just that I didn't know when she'd learned it.

Kyle picked up the egg, and it vanished.

"Oh no," I said. "You are not bringing that back with you. There is no way we're having an echidna monster hatch in the middle of our damned settlement."

At first I thought he was going to argue with me, but then he sighed and pulled the egg back out. "Fine. You might have a point." He was sulking, but I could deal with that a lot better than having to fight a baby mutant echidna.

We were a sorry bunch that clambered up the collapse of what had been the previous floor to exit the dungeon.

Even now, mere hours after entering, I could tell that nature was reclaiming its own. The dungeon beneath our feet morphed Mana as we moved through it. I could feel the way it twisted and utilized the power to create somewhere we'd no doubt have to come back to.

Mana didn't have a purpose as such as far as I could see. All it wanted to do was be utilized. And it was eager for that to happen. Always.

Our pace picked up as if we were dying to exit the dungeon. Some of these halls, now encroached by trees and underbrush, felt like they'd been haunted by the past.

Just shy of the exit though, shadows fell over us. Big shadows. Blocking-our-way shadows.

IRSHA shadows.

Suppressing the gasping gulp I could feel trying to break free of my throat, I squared my shoulders instead, trying to lend the most intimidating aura to my stance that I could. Given that I was clearly out-heighted by about three feet, I lost in every conceivable way.

"What?" I wasn't about to let them stop us in our path. There was no way I was getting blocked in that dungeon, not after the mutations we'd witnessed or the gleefully rampant Mana I could feel nipping at our heels.

Mon'swkinon eyed me contemplatively. At least that's how I thought he eyed me, but I could have been completely wrong. His stony expression was exactly what I imagined the dictionary definition to be.

Despite the granite-like appearance of his skin, the deep grey managed to ripple as he moved, even though he barely did.

"Well fought." He hefted what appeared to be a large spear in his right hand, like he was weighing more than just the possibility of how far he could throw it, but perhaps how well we'd all look impaled upon it.

"Thanks." I hedged my bets and just kept walking forward.

And it was only then that I realized there were several scaly creatures corpses scattered around him and his team. Some of them beneath his feet. It looked like those monsters might have been Monitors too, except even larger than the ones we'd encountered.

Our usual encounters had led me to believe that they wouldn't step in and take over a fight. But these had clearly been outside of where we'd been fighting.

Had they perhaps just saved our skin? Did I really want to ask?

The Dash'Kiri moved out of the way, barely stepping to the side at all. But given his imposing size, it was enough room for two of us abreast to walk past him and through to the . . . well, the more open courtyard portion of the university that hadn't been encased by nature yet.

I didn't trust the massive rock man as far as I could throw him, so I kept my eyes on him as the others filtered out behind me. Even if it might seem like they'd just helped us. We looked a sight. Dirt and blood clotted through all our hair, ripped clothing, broken weapons we desperately needed to get back to Garbo and to the Cartel to get fixed . . .

But we were alive, and I was starting to treasure that more than anything else. Mana darted around us, refilling the wells that were our Mana Pools, lingering around the Dash'Kiri and their ilk. We were all beings of Mana, of power, and this sudden well of realization rose in me.

"What do you want this time?" Because that was just it. They'd come to our walls and could have knocked them down, but didn't. They'd already shown up on numerous occasions after fights of ours, like when we fought the Koalzillas. Other patrols had also come across them.

So what were they really after?

Dequasha moved forward slightly, her movements so languid it reminded me of water lilies when their petals blew away. Fragile and dancing, yet stronger than they appeared.

She glanced up at Mon'swkinon, as if asking him permission. His nod wasn't nearly as surreptitious as I think he was aiming for, but I gave him the benefit of the doubt at least until I heard whatever it was she was about to say.

"Your hunting is not without its merits."

Oh great, we were starting off *really* well here. I could practically see my twin sprouting spikes at the comment.

"I'll make sure we tell people," Kyle commented dryly. Sure, he was usually quite personable. Just not after life-and-death battles.

Dequasha appeared slightly flustered, her long, petal-like appendages blushing with hints of color. "We have observed you to be competent. We are re-evaluating the assessment previously given to us by the Galactic Council."

Ah, that's where they were going with this.

"We're not about to budge, you know. We're staying here, in our country, on our world. It's not going to be that easy to get rid of us." It was probably one of the longest things I'd ever heard Molly say. Not quite in the vicinity of a speech, but damn close to it. Also, accurate.

"We do not expect you to leave." Mon'swkinon bowed his head; that, I had now come to realize was a sign of respect.

Still, though. All this respect, all of this dilly-dallying, and I just wanted them to get to the point so I could go home to my kids and sell the things we'd managed to find. A dull throb entered my head, and I couldn't tell whether it was because my eyes were trying to adjust to some of the excess light emanating from our foe-like friends, or because I was just done with the day.

To my surprise, the large, grey-skinned man nodded his head, and then dropped to one knee. Not like in an expression of fealty, but more so that our faces would be on an equal level.

Equal level not being equal in size. I swear his lips took up as much space as my entire face.

"If you are finished, we will be clearing the rest of this dungeon. Before it gains the foothold it seeks. Afterward, when there is time, we will visit." He took a breath, spreading one arm as if encompassing the entire area. "I think you will find that we have more in common than you realized."

I blinked. Okay so, they wanted to come and have a sit-down or something? Did I make sure we had scones? "Sure. You know where to find us."

He simply nodded but still waited, and I floundered on what to say. "Did you need us to do something?"

Mon'swkinon shook his head. "Be vigilant around your city. All of the cities must remain vigilant. I do believe we aren't the only alien delegation here anymore, though I have not confirmed it in the flesh yet."

"Okay, then." I mulled those words over in my mind, remembering the humanoid corpse we'd found on this morning's patrol and how we'd been unable to identify it as of yet. Was that what he meant? "Is there any way you can be more specific?"

He hesitated and then tried what must pass for more detailed in his realm of speaking. "Because of the situation we find ourselves in, we do not have the monopoly over this planet that we assumed when first arriving. This has given leeway for others to appear. Though we didn't witness the landing, we are certain it has occurred."

There was something in his eyes. Not just his, I was realizing, but among all of them. Not fear, but maybe concern? Worry, certainly. And something I had come to see all too often among the survivors—a look of someone who had the rug pulled out from under their feet, as what they believed to be true and safe disappeared.

That, the corpse this morning, the odd sightings our scouting groups had come across over the last few weeks? Yeah, all of that added up to something I didn't like the sound of.

My gaze narrowed, and I could feel myself becoming more irritated. Angry, even, at finding I had something in common with them. I was so glad that Molly stepped in, considering my brain had apparently turned to anger sometime in the last five seconds.

"We're done for today. Be careful down there. The rooms don't all seem stable. Might take you with it."

Mon'swkinon inclined his head again and rose to his full height. "Be well. Be careful. Be wary."

And then they were gone. Faster than I liked to admit, considering their size. Even my eyes couldn't quite follow their movements.

"So we made some friends?" Sange's tone held pure disbelief.

Kyle *tsk*ed irritably. I got the feeling my brother, the more perceptive and emotional of the two of us, had definitely picked up the same feeling that I had. Maybe even more. "Not sure they're friends. I get the feeling they're thinking more . . . the survivors of that which could not be survived might actually make decent allies."

His words, while likely accurate, lent a chill to the already-winterized air, and I had a sudden feeling he was all too correct. We might have a tentative truce right now, but that's all it was. I'd take it, of course, but we had to be prepared because if they were worried about something, it was in our best interests to be terrified.

Especially since the Dash'Kiri could crush my windpipe with a flick of their finger.

Chapter Nineteen:
Sitting Ducks

7 Weeks Post-System Onset
7 a.m.

Sleep had been fleeting since our encounter with IRSHA a few days ago. Not to mention that our discussion with Mon'swkinon had made me highly paranoid—so much that I was seeing shadowy spies around every corner.

Despite everything, the more I overanalyzed the situation, the Dash'Kiri had been concerned. And I didn't just think that concern was for us.

It didn't help that another corpse came in last night, so mangled it was unrecognizable. That one was human; it was one of ours. But the patrol it belonged to didn't stumble home until the early hours of this morning, exhausted and requiring immediate rest.

I'd seen how difficult it was for Mike to restrain himself from making them talk, but we weren't military. Not technically, even if some of us did go to battle every day. We were just people playing at being soldiers for the most part. I'd tried to sleep and managed a couple of hours, but my imagination was far too active.

And so it was that I'd been up for two hours fiddling with my ocular implant settings. It wasn't like I could reach into my head and turn dials or anything, but instead I needed to activate shit with my mind through yet another blue-screened interface.

There were settings that dealt with my ocular nerves, allowing me to adjust the severity and detail with which I saw Mana strands. Others adjusted my pupil sizes, the lenses within my eyes, and even dealt with Mana and normal light differentiation. Essentially, my eyes had sections allocated that could differentiate with the accuracy of a powerful microscope.

There were so many intricacies involved in how this worked, I was surprised there hadn't been a tutorial when I got out of the surgery. From heavy usage monitoring to lingering ambient flows, Mana fueled everything we were becoming.

There were so many questions left to be answered. Like how it had broken through to our world, how we'd reached this saturation cap that turned us from a normally developing world into this dungeon-forming mayhem? It was all something I wanted to find out.

My Mana quest remained silent. No new notifications or discoveries. Not even reminders that I had it. Complete and utter radio silence.

Small blessing. It left me with plenty of time to start getting used to just how these new eyes of mine worked. Utterly, annoyingly finicky, and yet completely necessary. There was this sense of urgency in the air, around every single Mana manifestation I could see. It was like the world itself was screaming at me, but I couldn't understand the language. Frustrating, and dread inspiring. Add this to wanting to hear from the patrol and no wonder I couldn't sleep.

At least it was getting easier to distinguish when others were using Mana either actively or passively.

Fascinating, really.

Almost as comforting as the coffee I clutched in my hands while I adjusted my vision. There were so many varied settings, I could have looked off into the distance for days and forgotten to consume any type of food at all.

Ginali, in his infuriatingly cheerful manner, came and sat with me. No inquiry as to whether or not that was okay. I looked him in the eyes, ready to scold him, when I realized he was much more serious than usual.

"Problem?" I asked.

He shook his head once, but then grimaced like he wasn't sure that was the right response. "I think those remains from the other day . . . are from one of two galactic canine species. One of which I really hope it isn't—the other of which I'm truly interested in why they'd be here."

"Is that all you're giving me?" I nibbled on the side of my cup.

He nodded curtly. "Yes. For now. But I wanted to soothe your worries and let you know that while humanoid, it was most definitely neither human nor a werewolf."

I raised an eyebrow. "Werewolf?"

His eyes twinkled as he stood up to leave. "You'd be amazed at how imaginative the universe really is."

I watched him go, pondering at the whirlwind he could sometimes be. Running an intergalactic crafting cartel appeared to require a lot of energy. I was glad it was him and not me.

Someone snapped their fingers in front of my face, and I reached out and grabbed their hand so quickly I surprised even myself. Nice visual acuity and hand reflex improvement there.

When my vision narrowed in on him, Mike stood there, his mouth open in a shocked O of surprise as he wrested his wrist back from me, massaging where I'd grabbed it. "You were staring off and didn't answer when I called your name like twice." He was defensive, and a little hurt. Completely and utterly reasonably so.

"Sorry about that. Still getting used to this. Lots to learn." I tapped the side of my head, hoping he realized I meant the implants. Then I took another swig of coffee, mildly annoyed to find it already cold swear I hadn't been nursing it for too long. "So, what gives?"

Mike motioned to two people I didn't recognize, standing beside him and looking like they weren't really willing to be there. Not truly a surprise I didn't recognize them, considering we had a constant dribble of people coming into the Center every single day. "Talia, and Tarin."

Talia had tightly curled black hair pulled back in corn rows that accentuated her beautiful square jaw and darker skin. Her eyes were bright with life and shone like polished amber. Yep, definitely some Charisma at work in there. My brain was going all purple prose on me. She nodded, a faint blush coloring her cheeks and then she smiled.

Tarin could have been her twin except his hair was short, maybe a three blade. He too had those polished eyes with a merry twinkle in the corner. I envied those able to maintain some semblance of peace with themselves in this state of the world.

"Kira." I held out my hand and shook theirs. They each had a firm, self-assured grip. Definitely twins. Maybe it was twinfinity or something, but it immediately made me like them more readily.

"What can I do for you?" I asked, motioning for them to sit down. Plenty of room around my four-seater table, the circular wooden table a common furnishing of the chain store. Nice place to hold my office hours in the morning . . . considering I didn't want to have office hours.

"I'll leave them to you, then. Don't forget we have that debriefing at 8 a.m.," Mike said. He was gone before I could respond. Not that I thought I'd get caught babysitting, but I did have multiple Adventurer groups getting ready to head out this morning, not to mention the debriefing he so offhandedly mentioned.

Our Adventurers were testing the distance limits on our newly enhanced walkie-talkies today. I couldn't help the sense of urgency in my stomach after last night. We really needed to get the radio waves up and running—radio towers? I was so bad at anything involving engineering. Didn't have the time to get it right, either, what with there being simply so much to do.

"So, you tell me what Mike wouldn't?" I gave them a half smile, tearing my mind away from all the things I needed to do. A part of me wished I could heat up my cup with my hands because my coffee was now lukewarm. Just past the place of skulling warm where I could have just downed it. Damn it.

Talia spoke up first. "Mike thought we might have a solution for you. We have . . ." She glanced at her brother, who nodded almost imperceptibly with encouragement.

"You're a twin too, so you might get this or not. I'm not sure. We've always had this sort of connection. Known things, seen things, shared things that we can't explain away. Well . . . in this really bizarre twist of the world now, we can actually share things that we see and experience over quite a distance. We've got a sort of built-in walkie-talkie of our own."

"Telepathy?" I asked, my mind suddenly doing two things. First of all—oh my gods, the sheer possibilities that could harness. And secondly, why the hell hadn't Kyle and I got that ability? Still, jealousy aside, this could come in really useful.

"Yes," Tarin responded, his eyes shining before he hesitatingly added, "Sort of, anyway. It was a Medium Perk that loaded for both of us."

"Explain." I was trying not to let my impatience get the better of me, but it was hard. Impatience and eagerness went hand in hand, right? I hadn't even contemplated anything related to my twin when hunting for Perks.

"When we communicate, it's faster than words. It's more of an instant connection. We've been testing it out since all this started happening, and we think we've got it figured. But it's still strange new territory." Tarin spoke more haltingly than Talia. Probably was the twin who spoke less normally. I knew *that* feeling all too well.

"What's your distance?" I was trying to think of things I needed to ask that could benefit the settlement as a whole. And not just fellow twin-interest things which was all the questions I could think of asking.

"So far we've been able to clock in around two kilometers. Pretty sure the more we use and level the Skill, the further we'll be able to send. There appear to be a couple of books in the Shop about it too." Talia's excitement was catching. While it wasn't going to be much more than we could do with our walkie-talkies right now, it seemed there was the potential to simply convey so much more information at once.

Oooh, maybe they'd even be able to project into other people's heads. First things first though. Couldn't get ahead of myself.

"We thought it might help more for scouting missions. Maybe get back information in more detail and faster with less static interference." Tarin's insertion made perfect sense and I perked up.

We were about there. Close to sending out a group of low to mid-30s purely to seek out other settlements and see if there were any that contained humans.

If we were correct and there were other settlements in other shopping malls, then we should be close enough to make contact with some of them. Provided we kept all the randomly mutating creatures out there at bay.

"Great. Thank you. Keep working on it and keep us updated?" While I wanted to personally know it all and be involved in every aspect of everything, I also didn't. I had far too many irons in the fire right now, so I really hoped they could be trusted to keep it going.

Talia smiled at me, her grin easily lighting up the area. It was nice to encounter others who were just trying to make the most out of all of this muck we found ourselves in.

"I have to get to a meeting now. Thanks again, and don't hesitate to let Mike know if you have questions. I promise we'll get you slated into some patrols." I gave them my best smile, fully aware of how fast the time was ticking down and getting near 8 a.m.

After grabbing another coffee from Red, I dashed down toward the library, relieved to see I wasn't the last one in. Mike was talking quietly to Drake, who leaned against a bookcase, wringing his hands in front of him.

His eyes were downcast, but if there was one word for how he looked, it was haunted. He glanced around, still muttering to Mike as they waited for the last few people to filter in.

I still thought we should have addressed this last night, but Mike had been right. It was too late to do anything constructive, and most of Drake's team were still in shock.

Finally, when everyone was here, Drake looked up, pushing himself away from where he'd been using the lower bookshelves as a crutch.

"We took the bottom route, the one down Priestdale Road, to the intersection at Ford and Kloske. Closeish to Daisy Hill, but not really— down toward the Koala Bushlands." He waited, making sure we all understood where he'd gone. It was only maybe six kilometers or so away.

But we were also all aware that no one had been down there for days, maybe even a week. There were just so many places we needed to thin out, it was becoming too much.

He took a deep breath and continued. "We had three vehicles, you know, in case we found a live human somewhere. It was all fine. They're silent and nothing hears us. But there were loud sounds over in the bushland, shadows that moved beyond us.

"I swear we heard fighting, a couple of gunshots, growls, and definite signs of combat." He gulped air down, like he was forcing himself to continue. "So we turned around to come back, thinking we'd get a double-sized group this morning and take care of whatever that was.

"Only we didn't make it. Something heavy hit the ground and practically bounced the cars off the road. Then a force smashed into us, sending us flipping. We were lucky any of us got out." Another super deep inhalation and Drake closed his eyes, leaning back for support again.

"Something grabbed Jason as he crawled out of their vehicle. The rest of us scrambled and ran. We could hear his screams for like a minute . . . and then they stopped." His breathing started to calm, and Drake looked up at the ceiling.

"From what Mike said, these things must leave remains to warn others out of their area or something? He said you found Jason's near the Gateway and Pacific Motorways again? Anyway, it was dark and we couldn't figure out our bearings at first. Frankly, I think we're lucky to be alive."

Kyle and Dale pushed past and joined Drake and Mike, only their muttered discussion breaking the otherwise silent room. I certainly didn't know what to say. If we were going to send out larger groups, we'd have to make sure there was a tracker or something with each of them.

Mike pulled himself away and walked over to me. "Any Mana inklings from any of that?"

I shook my head. "Only that it legitimately scared the shit out of him, and I never thought I'd see Drake scared."

Mike chuckled, but his eyes held sadness instead. About to talk to me, he was cut off when the library doors burst open and Dannin came to a screeching halt in front of us.

His face was flushed, and he was drenched in sweat. But even as the liquid dripped onto the carpet-tiled floor beneath him, I realized from the smell emanating off him that it wasn't sweat. It was blood—and lots of it.

I stood, almost flipping the table in the process, and only Tarin grabbing it saved it from tumbling. Grasping Dannin's shoulders with each of my hands, I made him look at me. Mana fissured through his whole body, like a shockwave had hit him and splintered it.

"Dannin. I need you to focus on me." This wasn't good. Where was Kyle? The kid was in shock, his pupils unfocused and his lip was trembling. "Focus on my voice. Tell me what happened."

"Patrol—they're all gone, Kira." And finally he looked me in the eyes as tears carved a path through the grime on his face. "They're all gone."

Chapter Twenty:
New Information

It took me longer to extract the information out of Dannin than I liked. Precious minutes, seconds even. But he was shaken, and a full patrol was lost. A full patrol of Level 25 to 30s.

A patrol we couldn't afford to lose.

The pain in my chest was only lessened by the sheer relief that my son hadn't been with that particular patrol. Jackson was safe, and my world could function as long as my kids were safe. I could function, I could help, I could research—as long as my kids were safe.

As long as my kids were safe. I repeated it in my mind.

I was slowly getting a little mantra going.

"How did he survive?" Evelyn mumbled, her head in her hands as we gathered back in the library trying to sort through the information we'd gathered.

I shrugged. "His shoulder is all sorts of messed up, claws that just . . . well." What was I supposed to say? He'd been in literal shock, not to mention trauma from the wounds to his upper torso. That lingering debuff halted a chunk of his System-boosted healing.

"The System kicks in and heals you pretty fast," Gemma piped up, her now-subdued tones ringing across the silent room. "Whether you want it to or not, unless it's a mortal wound, you're not dying. That debuff made a nasty stasis, but he'll be fine."

She would know, considering how many times she'd been ripped apart. I gulped, trying to envision the battle in my mind. Kyle walked over, ushering Dannin with him. Poor kid; even with the determined set to his pale jaw, he had to be suffering something bad.

"He wants to tell us in his own words." My brother was visibly shaken. Mana rushed around him, filling up his stores. He'd obviously healed Dannin of his debuff. Considering the way the kid's skin knit back together in front of my very eyes, it'd been effective.

Several of the people pushing into the library had been people with Kyle since the hospital—they knew my brother and the Ranger.

It took Dannin a couple of deep breaths and repositioning to get the words out, but once he started, they tumbled faster than anything I'd managed to pull from him.

"We were just on our way through Daisy Hill. Like usual for clearing, keeping an eye out for the dropbears . . . Koalzilla things. Whatever they're called." There was a nervous overtone to his words, a vibration that told me he was close to tears even as the Mana wove in and out of his wounds, repairing them like it was nothing.

"We kept formation, myself and Shazza bringing up the rear."

Shazza had been an Ice-Mage, if I remembered correctly, and I cursed having lost one of our more powerful mage types. Even if I hadn't known her well, she was human, and that was becoming a rare commodity around here.

"It all happened so fast. We rounded a particularly close group of trees and saw two, maybe three Koalzilla corpses piled on one another. Off in the distance, it looked like there were some more, but they were moving away from, not toward us.

"Suddenly, from all around us, things dropped from the trees, and I know it sounds crazy, but they were like dogs. You know?" He looked around beseechingly, caught my gaze and clung to it like a life raft.

"Those big upright dogs we all studied in ancient history? The ones in the pyramids. They had sleek sort of fur instead of skin, massive jowls and huge canine teeth. They wore armor, and a few of them had guns." Tears were having at it again, but he didn't seem to notice it.

Ginali's comment on the humanoid dog remains we'd found niggled in the back of my mind. I got the feeling I knew what that corpse was now.

"At first I tried. I loosed arrows, I aimed, and completely missed every single time because they were moving just too fast. Shazza screamed at me to run." He shrugged, wincing as he did so, belatedly remembering the wound that probably wasn't even visible anymore.

"One of them almost got me." His voice lowered to a whisper. "Its claws stung like a jellyfish, ripped right through me. Shazza . . . lanced him, distracted him long enough that I could pull away. I didn't care how much of my flesh I left back with it, with him . . . whatever it was. All I could think of was running. I ran, and I left them all."

He'd paled more by now, and Dale moved forward to shove a seat under the kid. Dannin sat down without fully realizing what he was doing if the dazed look in his eyes was anything to go on. His dark olive skin looked like it had pale green undertones. Kyle nudged me with a scowl on his face before he made his way back to the archer, and I knew he was about to take Dannin somewhere to rest. Best for him to sleep this off.

"I ran flat out back to the cars and I just grabbed one and came here. I didn't look back, and I didn't try to help. All I could think of was getting back here and telling you all." Finally he blinked, like he'd just needed to get it all out.

I knelt in front of his seat and squeezed his arm gently. "You did good. Now we know we have to prepare for whatever they are."

"Oh." He looked a little sheepish, like in all the horror he'd just experienced, he'd totally forgotten one of the most important things. That he'd acted how he acted in order to save others.

"They're called the Zarrie. I don't think there were many of them, but it felt like they were everywhere. They had weird Levels too. Like lower than you'd expect for all that power. Like beginners. Level 2 and a 3. But that doesn't make sense."

The exhaustion that overtook him now that he'd delivered his message to us in full was visible. He sagged a bit and Dale and Kyle propped him up on either side. Sure, the System might be able to heal physical wounds, but that sort of mental shit it just put the kid through? That was going to take years of therapy to fix.

Provided we still had therapy. Hell, provided we still had years of anything. After this, I wasn't so sure.

"Guess we have new visitors to deal with then. The IRSHA aren't the only ones here." Sienna leaned back in her chair, her Charisma somehow making the threat feel less imminent, less devastating. There were definite drawbacks to Charisma stacking.

"The Zarrie it is, then." Dor's businesslike tones cut through everything. "Do we think those were the same ones from last night?"

Drake shook his head slowly. "No. Not if the kid's description is right. Last night didn't feel like multiples, just one big thing. Maybe."

Dor gave him a stern look before backing up and giving him a brief nod. "Bit of research never hurt anyone. Our coffers are looking decent, though we still need to expand so we can reinforce our defenses more. I suggest we look into purchasing one of the longer-distance warning systems."

"Good call." Chris had been quiet the entire meeting, fiddling every now and then with something small she concealed in her hands. "Working on some longer-range communication devices—we should have them ready within a week or so. Also aiming to help those with telepathy-themed Classes be able to project a farther distance."

My eyes bleeped. Not like audibly, but a sort of whirring readjustment as ambient Mana boosted briefly in our vicinity. Nothing like a bright flash of blue to make you rethink your optical implant life choices. Something around us was building, reforming or whatever, and it was using a lot of

Mana to do so.

There was something we weren't considering, and I couldn't shake the feeling that it was going to bite us in the butt if I couldn't figure out what it was we were missing.

Gemma cleared her throat and spoke up. "You realize if they were lower Levels, they're probably Advanced or Master Classes, right?"

I turned to stare at Gemma.

She stood with her arms crossed, foot leaning up against the wall and a bored expression on her face. Like we all should have realized the blatantly obvious. I mean, I'd read about it briefly, but in one eye and out the other.

"Level 50 restarts, right?" Chris muttered under her breath, like she was trying to piece something together.

"Basic is what we all have, or should have. I don't think anyone blundered into an Advanced Class by complete and utter accident here. We can only dream." She sounded mildly annoyed. But she was rivaling Kyle for highest Level, so I kind of got it.

The stronger we were, the better our chance of survival.

"Basic, Advanced, Master . . . and well, if they're above that and fighting us at our low Basic Levels? We're entirely fucked anyway." She frowned for a moment. "So if they were lower Levels, it just means their Classes were more advanced than ours."

This whole Class system just made me tired. Couldn't we just keep leveling in our lowly little Classes up until like Level 200 and then beat the game? World? Existence? What madman created such a complicated System? Did he just like making everyone's life miserable?

I rubbed my temples, trying to ease the strain of constant Mana vision on my brain.

"So higher Levels, more potent powers, big creatures able to topple cars and carry off humans, things that vanish in the dark, ancient Egyptian Anubis creatures." There, I think that summed it up pretty well.

"Sounds like what we're up against." Even Evelyn sounded defeated, and I just wanted to give her a hug and make a pillow fort and never come out of it.

"Kira." Kyle's tone surprised me almost as much as his reappearance. "You'd better get out to the wall."

That didn't sound good. Not at all.

❖

The mess of Mana waves tangled around everyone and everything as I approached the gate made me have to turn down the brightness settings of my implants yet again. Still floundering to keep myself grounded with how to use them, their sheer ability to interpret data I—as of yet—couldn't understand, floored me.

But as the glare cleared, and I realized just what was in front of me, it was all I could do not to gag.

Kyle and Dale flitted about, with others from their little medical team in tow. Members of our parties limped in, were carried in, rips in their clothing, some still with rips in their flesh. Thankfully, though, it appeared that most of them were still breathing.

Most of them.

Two adults I barely recognized dashed past me, reaching for one of the guys on a makeshift gurney. He was convulsing, white froth forming at his mouth as Kyle tried desperately to save him. From the gashes to his abdomen and the shredded flesh of what had once been an arm, though, I didn't like his odds.

Even the Mana around him tinged red, began to leave, like it was abandoning a drowning ship. Nothing ambient seeped into him, and there was a sickly green ooze of thick Mana winding its way through what remained of his organs.

Poison. Venom. Whatever or however he'd gotten it, that kid was going to die.

My eyes whirred again, pulling me toward him. Drake, his own trauma pushed to the back burner, was busy holding back the boy's mother as she tried desperately to cling to him.

Purify Mana?

The question rang through my mind, and I didn't understand what it could mean, or what it did mean, only that I might be able to make it be something.

Sure, I answered in my head, to my eyes, or whatever it was that Mana Sense actually was.

It tugged at me, the Mana did. My vision narrowed, looking through the kid to his heart, even as it beat so erratically. To the perforated bowels that I had no idea how to fix, to the well of Mana that was trying so desperately to knit him back together and failing.

I didn't have an ability; all I had was Mana Sense. All I could do was follow the flow of the power to its source and see how sickly it appeared to be in there. My implants buzzed as they assessed the damage to the well in there.

Reaching in with my mind I sorted through the Mana, whirling around in it, slicing the bad components away from it, and making it be what it needed to be. Resistance fought me, like a toxin trying desperately to maintain its hold on the victim it intended to claim.

But I didn't know how to apply it, just what needed to be done. Looking around desperately, I grabbed Kyle's arm and tugged him over.

"Kira, what—" But he shut up as soon as I touched him, willing him to see what my implants allowed him to.

"Fuuuuuuuck." He breathed out as he engaged the healing he could, following my directions through to the bloodstream, picking the poison out of the Mana as we went with some kind of cleanse ability.

With its path cleared, the blue Mana shone brightly for a split second, rewarding me with a massive headache and a new notification.

Mana Purification Skill obtained.
Mana Purification
Level 1

Great. Another Skill to track, and spend money on, and perhaps adjust myself cybernetically for. Sudden tiredness overcame me, and that headache wasn't a joke, either. I could feel Kyle close to me, his frown very obvious in my mind, but I was just glad he was there to lend me sturdiness.

Kiddo was probably going to make it now, and I could hear the mother weeping sobs of joy. It washed over me, infected me. There was no way I could leave a kid just a few years older than my own to die if I could help it. Even if all I could do was show Kyle what he needed to heal.

"Kira? What the hell was that?" Kyle whispered in my ear as he helped steady me on my feet.

I shrugged, exhausted before midday. Fantastic. "Mana Purification, apparently."

He nodded, squeezed my shoulders, and left to go help some of the others heal faster.

Even as I blinked away all of the fatigue, promising myself I'd get to rest later, I realized that one little pitstop needed to become more. There were perhaps a dozen wounded people all around me, their auras not as bad as the kid I'd helped save, yet still worse than they should have been.

So instead of stopping, I soldiered on, following Kyle and helping him as needed. It led me to wonder just what the poison was that these Zarrie used, because without a shadow of a doubt, I was positive their claws were drenched in it—or else their weapons were.

Hell, it also made me curious about if all of this was these Zarrie. Some of these injuries and debuffs didn't appear to be just from these alien warriors.

We needed ways to protect ourselves from roaming huge monsters, and the strange canine Zarrie. Otherwise we were going to lose a lot of people fast. And that wasn't something we could afford in any way.

More discussions for our city council, more paper pushing and developing strategies, but for now, if I could help save people, I was going to do so.

I couldn't believe it wasn't even lunchtime yet.

Chapter Twenty-One:
Twenty Seconds

7 Weeks Post-System Onset

8 p.m.

I swear it had been one of the longest days of my life. All I wanted was to sleep, and I was trying, but my mind just wouldn't stop.

My hands were still covered in blood. Not the way you're thinking, though—I'd washed them. But under the fingernails and in the cuticles, some of the remnants of blood still stuck to those. It didn't matter how hard I tried, how much I showered, or thought about different things, I swear everywhere I turned I could smell the scent of congealing gore.

Wisp hugged me, leaning across from her own cot, even though we'd pulled them together. The drop ceiling above us wasn't the most attractive thing, but it was better than staring at my hands. She hugged me so tightly, Dog in his place at her feet, and Wombie snuggled into the pile of rugs in the corner. Though that was going to have to change. I swear we'd moved the cots closer because he took up so much room now.

That physical touch, the reminder that my daughter was still here with me, was enough to help the aching I couldn't get rid of in my chest. It was amazing how sadness could just weigh you down.

We were lucky. I wasn't dead. My kids were healthy. We even had pets. I'd made friends, none of whom had died lately even after today's body count. As far as the apocalypse went, I was in a good space.

But that didn't stop me from feeling like the weight of the world was on my shoulders. A weight that had been popped in a Gravitron and thrown to the side to throw up for everyone to see. This wasn't wallowing. This was breathing in my family, my luck, and using it to simply face the rest of the world outside.

Sometimes, I just had to stop and smell the roses so I could remember how pretty the petals were.

"Mum, you're stressing yourself," Wisp spoke softly, her head still buried against me.

She was right. And too astute for me to try and bullshit my way around. "Yep. I am."

Wisp squeezed me and pushed herself up. "We need a cupcake. Did you know that the Shop has like all of the foods ever? You could even get a burrito, or other stuff. Ray bakes too! Like cupcakes. Let's go get cake."

I blinked and then laughed. If sugar was going to be our solution, then so be it. Following her out of our little apartment was like being in a procession. Wisp, Dog, Wombie, and myself. People looked at us as we walked by, and the somber mood throughout the entire center followed us even as we made our way to the cafe.

Ray was bustling, yet so much more subdued than usual. Busy feeding us all, working to keep the morale up and momentum going. In the back there was a table occupied by a group of the Crafting Cartel, and I could see Ginali gesturing expansively with his hands as he explained something.

It wasn't *all* aliens hell bent on killing us apparently. Just some of them.

My seat was free, as it had been every single time I approached the place. I was beginning to wonder if it wasn't entirely arranged.

Did someone keep a watch for me to know when I was coming? Or had people just come to leave it empty for me?

I slid into my seat as my daughter disappeared into the Shop, and held up my hand to catch Ray's eye. An almost imperceptible nod and I knew I was going to get my nice bean water soon, even if it wasn't as good as I remembered it should be.

Inevitably, my mind turned to the events of the day. Sixteen people dead. Sixteen of our stronger people. Levels 20 through 30. Four groups, forty people in total, with only twenty-four who returned. These monsters were going to wipe us out if we weren't careful. With the size of whatever ripped Jason from the car and the Levels of the Zarrie, not to mention likely Advanced Classes, I had no idea how we'd manage to survive.

The irony ate at me. Here we were, surprising IRSHA with our whole not being dead, and yet—we were about to get wiped out by unknown assailants attacking us for reasons we couldn't fathom and with Abilities, Classes, and Skills that we couldn't even muster.

Maybe this is what they were talking about when we saw them at the Nathan Campus dungeon. A little more of a heads up would have been nice.

"Thank you."

I looked up, blinking to refocus my eyes on the human face in front of me. It was the woman whose son I'd helped Kyle save earlier. Lines formed around her eyes despite the System's best effort to rewind the aging process in most of us. She seemed utterly exhausted.

"You're welcome. I only did what I could." It wasn't polite to tell her I'd just been flying by the seat of my pants and that I had no real clue just how I'd helped the way I had. She didn't need to know that. All she needed to know was that someone else had given a damn about her son, and done what they could.

"Avery." She held out a hand in a very no-nonsense way. "I'm still getting used to all of this."

Her gaze flitted about, and I wondered how long she'd been in our settlement with us because I didn't recognize her right away, and her son hadn't felt familiar. Not that that meant much.

My ability to differentiate people based on their Mana signature was going to take a lot longer than a week with all of the people in our settlement.

"Sit down," I offered, not really wanting to, but hoping my daughter had given into her sweet addiction and grabbed more than just two cupcakes. I was tired and stroppy, and I didn't really want to have any company other than my kids, but this was a mother who'd almost lost everything.

If I couldn't take the time to have empathy for someone whose position I dreaded finding myself in? Then wasn't I as much a monster as the mutations we found ourselves fighting?

Avery took a seat, and I watched out of the corner of my eye as Ray nodded in my direction. He'd noticed. Frankly, he was really good at noticing everything, at organizing it all. In the wake of Barry's death, it was like he'd picked himself up and decided to be everything he could be. Sometimes, loss makes us stronger, as though the parts left behind have to be.

"How is he doing?" That seemed like the best way to start out any conversation with someone I didn't know.

She hesitated and looked down at her hands. I bet she could see blood all over hers too. Human psyche reinforcement. I was so searching for that next time I ran to the Shop.

"I didn't want him going out with patrols in the first place, you know. Nate . . . Nathanial is very stubborn. Just like his grandfather. He's a good teen. Hit his adulthood a couple of months before all of this. So I can't tell him what to do." She sighed and ran her hands through her sleek black hair. Her pale skin seemed almost translucent.

"His Dad is beside himself. He'd talked me into letting him Level. But the thing is, Nate survived. Maybe thanks to you and to things we don't understand fully, but he's alive." She looked up at me, and I could tell she was bewildered and just sort of lost. Like the rest of us. "Thank you for saving him. But now, all he wants to do is get revenge."

Ah, that might be why she was here. Revenge was never a good motivator to accomplishing goals. I mean, sure, it gave you that kickstart, but once you'd accomplished it, there was only that empty feeling of want. Not good motivation, not in the long term. It twisted and warped those who couldn't let it go, left them bereft of friends and family and in the end, hollow.

Fuel, however? Maybe he could use it as fuel.

"What's his Class?" I asked gently as Ray surreptitiously placed my coffee in front of me, and a lemon iced tea, if my sense of smell was still accurate, in front of Avery.

"He's a Machinist—which, as far as I can tell, is someone who develops gadgets and weapons that can fire projectiles and traps. He's always tinkered with things his entire life. Was in his first year as an engineering student . . ." Her voice trailed away and she gestured vaguely around us. "Was. Then all of this hit."

"Odds are he can develop ways to keep himself safe, then, and potentially others. Maybe steer his direction toward that instead of revenge? Or even as revenge? Definitely much more manageable to channel *that* revenge into saving others." Here I was, with my two kids eight and thirteen, giving life advice. This wasn't who I was, but for now it was who I needed to be. All I could do was hope I didn't scar anyone in the process.

"That sounds like a good plan. If he'll just listen to it." Avery sipped her drink, and it felt like she just wanted to break down and cry. Her shoulders were tense, and her brow pinched constantly, like she was giving herself a headache just thinking about everything she needed to.

I reached across on impulse and held onto one of her hands. "He'll listen to you. Just show him, let him know that things will get better if we all focus our efforts in the right places. And making sure we're stronger as a group, as a species, that's what we need in this new world. He can more than help with that."

Her eyes grew wide for a second and she smiled. "Thanks. How are you . . . doing all this?"

That was just it. I wasn't, even if I knew she'd never believe me. Everyone else was working together to get this done, but people needed to believe it was doable by one person. That way, it didn't matter who we lost, or how hard things got, maybe someone would always dig the survivors out.

Somehow, that person had become me.

As I was about to answer with a vaguely soothing platitude, Wisp saved me.

"Oh," she said as she sat a vanilla cupcake down in front of me. "I didn't realize we'd have company, but I came prepared. These are more expensive than I realized. You owe me money for feeding you, Mum."

Wisp sat another of the treats down in front of Avery and took the seat to my left side as she did so. Dog wedged himself under the table, and I had to wonder just how much longer that was going to even be possible. Sure, he'd slowed in growing, but he hadn't stopped completely.

His border-collie-mix ass had to crouch to get under the table in the first place now. And Wombie, who settled at my feet and could probably break my ankles if he moved in the wrong way, was going to have to live with his Mumma Wombutt soon because I was quite certain he wasn't about to stop growing.

"Hi. I hope you like cupcakes." Wisp's words caught me off guard. Here she was, halfway to nine with her dog and wombat in tow, getting us grown-ups cupcakes so we could wallow in our emotions.

Avery blinked at her, and a genuine smile finally crossed her face. No more half-scowling contemplation, just one instant of happiness. "I do. I love cupcakes. Does the Shop have them?"

And with that, my child had distracted a woman from her grief and filled my belly with sugar. I knew that she didn't do it deliberately, but I think our kids were worth protecting.

Even now, they still had this innocence that we'd all lost. This total faith that everything would be okay if only they were still surrounded by the people who loved them. We could all learn from that. I got the feeling we'd all have to.

❖

Wisp slept soundly as long as Dog was close to her. It still amused me, in that exasperated what-the-hell-happened way parents get that she had managed to get herself a dog, finally, even if it did take the end of the world as we knew it.

Figures, really.

I watched her chest rise and fall in even measure as she curled up on her cot with a unicorn blanket, dog weighing down the end of it all. There were so many ways this could all go bad, but right here, right now—this kid was getting me through it all.

"Got a sec?" Evelyn whispered from the doorway.

I'd barely had time to talk to her since word of the attacks arrived this morning. Dog glanced at me as I moved and nodded his nose subtly. Sure, now I could communicate with animals. Or at least with ones that gained a mutated type of intelligence I still couldn't wrap my head around.

"Everything okay?" I asked as I closed the apartment door behind me, wishing, not for the first time that we could just go and get an actual damned house.

That was on the to-do list. Always on the to-do list.

She laughed, a touch too bitterly, a touch too edgy, and I could tell nothing was okay. Silently, I moved closer and enveloped her in a hug. It was fairly quiet here at this time of night because most of our hub was now encased near the food court.

For a moment I wondered about tonight's patrols, worry eating at my stomach. But I nixed those thoughts and gave Evelyn the attention she needed.

She felt more delicate than I remembered, and she buried her face in the nape of my neck. There was so much we'd both been through, so much yet to come, but for those few seconds—everything felt like it might find a solution.

Locking her hands around my waist, I realized that this was one of the only times I'd ever seen her without her bow almost glued to her fingers. She held me tightly, like she was trying to squeeze the air out of me but didn't actually want to.

"Feel better?" I asked as she loosened her grip.

"Yeah. Sometimes, I just need a little reassurance, a little closeness, you know?" Pulling back, she eyed me critically. "And you could use some decent rest for once."

"Couldn't we all?" I didn't mean for it to come across as rhetorical, but it really was.

Thing was, sometimes I felt lonely, and Evelyn was wonderful. She was strong, decisive, independent, and a damned good problem solver. Above all, she was kind and caring, compassionate even. Traits that made us human, made us stand out from the assholes.

But she was also a complication that I couldn't afford, and I couldn't keep asking her to wait for when I was ready to move on. If you *could* move on from the apocalypse hitting your world and struggling to keep your kids alive. I squeezed her hand and glanced at her.

"You don't have to say anything." The words came out huskier than I think she intended, and it made me like her all the more. "This is all difficult, and new, and your kids are troopers. But they're troopers who need their mum. I'm not a mum. Never was, doubt I ever will be. But I am your friend.

And right now, even if that's all it is, I can at least help comfort you and listen, and be there when you need someone."

Evelyn was a decade younger than me, yet right then, I felt like she was far older and wiser than I could ever hope to be. I chuckled, a little ruefully, that she understood what I was wanting to say more than I think even I realized.

"Yeah. I think we all need someone, but so much has changed, and even what . . . almost two months in, we're now facing a new threat? More threats? I just don't have the spoons to keep my kids alive, try to maintain my sanity, develop these new and weird Skills, level up, run a settlement, and then make room for romance? I just don't have it in me. Something has to fall by the way." I squeezed her hand again briefly before letting it drop. "I'm sorry. Right now, it has to be me. You. Any of whatever this is."

She didn't seem upset in the slightest, even to the extent that a small smile crossed her face. "You're not the only one dealing with a lot. I'm still here, not just looking for a fling, or anything substantial. What I need is my friend, someone who gets me. So please, don't push that away."

Evelyn had a point. Except I didn't think she realized how tempting losing yourself in another human being could be. It would be easy to just lose myself in someone else, forsaking all my responsibilities. I'd seen it happen all too often to colleagues, friends in university, back in a less complicated time.

Thing was, I knew she wouldn't allow that. And the pragmatic side of me wouldn't either.

"So you're not taking my gentle pushing away, are you?"

She laughed, and the sound of it eased up all of the tension along my spine.

"No. I'm not taking the gentle pushing away. Right now you need an ear, and a shoulder and all of those good things. And frankly, so do I.

Nothing complicated. Nothing that's going to mess this already fucked-up reality more than it already is. Just be here, with me, helping me figure all this crap out." She shrugged. "Anything else we can address when we get to a point in the future where it might be viable to contemplate."

I pursed my lips. She made a lot of good points. Since we first met, we'd got on so well. Like one of those friendships forged in the fires of hell. This hell. "It's a deal."

She pulled me into a tight hug, ignoring the hand I put out to shake. That was okay. Hugs were therapeutic. Especially when they exceeded twenty seconds.

Science, bitch.

Chapter Twenty-Two:
Complications

7 Weeks, 1 Day Post-System Onset
10 a.m.

Coffee in hand, scowl on my face, fielding tight hugs from my eight-year-old is how Ginali found me that morning. I looked up as the shadow interrupted the perfect light I'd been viewing System maps in, ready to snap at the poor, unfortunate soul but found myself relaxing immediately.

If there was one thing the little Pharyleri did, it was always bring a smile to my face. Even when he was haggling and ripping me off to within an inch of my life. Except this time, his expression was grave, and not one I'd seen on him before. Alarm flared through me at the sight of it, at the sight of him being this serious about anything other than a monetary transaction.

"You better spill now before you give me a heart attack," I said drolly, prying my daughter from around my waist.

"We should go to the admin room. It'll be easier to explain that way." Even his tone held none of the jovial overtones that it usually did.

"Wisp, love. I think you're late for class. Jana has some cool stuff planned with Mumma Wombutt today." I pried her loose and hugged her quickly.

She scowled at me before rolling her eyes. "Fine. But I'm taking Dog out with me. I'm not leaving him inside this time."

Wisp didn't wait for me to respond but headed to where she knew she already should have been anyway. I counted to five, gathered my things and led the way to the former library, Ginali trailing after me with his unusually grim countenance.

He didn't even wait for me to be sit down or to call in others. Apparently Sienna, Dor, and I were plenty of people for him to start getting serious with.

"I received definitive results. The corpse is definitely Zarrie." He dropped the information on us without any preamble. Thing was, I'd already been pretty sure of that.

"We assumed as much. But thanks for confirming it." I smiled at him, a little irritated that I'd given up my comfy coffee morning for this. After yesterday, I needed all the comfy coffee mornings I could get.

He shook his head, and I think it was the first time I'd seen him exasperated. "That's just it. A Zarrie of that Level being unidentifiable means something big took it out. Something vicious. I would not think humans capable of it, so that means another species or something else did it."

"What about that magpie dragon thing . . . the Magon?" I asked, clutching at all the straws I could find.

He pondered that for a moment. "Plausible? Yes. Likely, no. Not where he was found. Besides, given the type of creature it is, I doubt it would have left remains."

I sighed. This wasn't the good news morning I wanted it to be. "So you're saying that not only do we have to watch out for these Zarrie that have turned up out of the blue and are intermittently attacking us, but we also have to watch out for another alien species or else super monsters?"

Ginali hesitated. "This is a little more complicated than that. I have to apologize. When we first entered into the Australian continent as an entity, we did so within a timed event notification. As in, we tossed our hat in the ring, so to speak, to allow us to gain a foothold in the first Queensland Settlement Orb gained. As soon as the Settlement Orb was obtained, our quest would activate." He sounded flustered as he paced back and forth, not making eye contact with any of us.

"We took the Galactic Council at their word and assumed we'd be the only ones with a vested interest." Then he sort of waved one hand as if dismissing that thought and continued. "They were technically telling the truth. When IRSHA claimed hunting rights, it had nothing to do with us. Even if they did claim a settlement with our attached conditions, everything we'd already paid for and agreed to provide would transfer directly to the new owners regardless of who those were.

"Given their proclivity for hunting down even the hardiest of creatures, there was never going to be an issue with that." He finally stopped moving, looking at each of us in turn. His ruddy skin was flushed, and he suddenly seemed even smaller than his actual stature. Like the weight of what he was about to say had shrunk him.

I took a deep breath, readying myself for the worst.

"Go on, mate. We don't bite. Much." Dor crossed her arms and propped her feet up on her desk as she leaned back on one of the swivel stools. "Can't be much worse than an apocalypse turning everything on its head."

At that, Ginali visibly relaxed. "Well, it's not another apocalypse, but it isn't good. You see, I've done some digging this last day, trying to figure out just why on Earth, pun not intended, the Zarrie of all groups would be here—and terrorizing you.

"To understand that, you have to understand that there are mercenary clans out there, full tribes of beings, full species whose sole purpose in life is to earn money through mercenary duties. Why, even the CCC is allied with such a species. But I digress." He took a deep breath and then spoke so fast I almost didn't understand him. "The IRSHA division who came here and tried to take your settlement, or at least wanted to claim your settlement, are one of their smaller divisions.

"Anyway. Because they are smaller, in order to fund the operation on this continent, they took out collateral against potential future kills and potential future ingredients. Which, had they been the only ones on an unsurvivable continent, would have been fine. New and unique mutations, rare creatures—such wonderful opportunities for riches."

"So they borrowed money to fund their expedition here?" I asked, a little incredulous that someone would think our creatures here worth such a risk. Although . . . given how badly mutating some of the things were, I could see it.

"Of course! This country, this world is out of the way. There are no portals built yet, no easy form of transportation to the greater Galactic community. The cost of such transportation, until Mana levels stabilize, is prohibitive. As it stands, only one-way portals are even vaguely viable. If not for the discount in using the Quest System and tying our chances to loss, counter-bets against yourselves and . . . well. I'm straying.

"Anyway, getting their ships and the other hunters here in such large quantities, in multiple different locations the continent over? This would have cost them millions of Credits to finance. Probably tens of millions."

I could see the other two nodding along, though Sienna was beginning to look impatient. So was I, really. Perhaps seeing it, Ginali sped up. "If my research is correct, the people who lent them the Credits are unhappy. Payments are in arears as of two weeks ago."

"So the Zarrie are here because IRSHA defaulted on a loan?" Sienna scowled at the thought as Ginali nodded and I could practically see her gathering her thoughts. "This monetary lender—"

"The Galactic Association of Monetary Lenders and Executors," Ginali provided. "GAMLAE."

Sienna glared at him and continued, a little puzzled. "So GAMLAE lent out a ridiculous sum of money to IRSHA. But since the System screwed up Australia's classification, the loan is being defaulted on because IRSHA hasn't been able to get enough Credits because of us? So they decided to send scouts to kill our people?"

Ginali half shook his head. "Well, I'm not sure that they're supposed to be killing you. But GAMLAE appear to have decided that the aid they gave warrants a visit to uphold their interests. Should IRSHA continue to default, GAMLAE will take the IRSHA settlements as theirs. Along with this, the current rights purchased by the hunters. Of course, they can't take your settlement—not legally. But violently . . ."

"So what? They want to soften us up a little?" I said, angry. "Doesn't that help IRSHA?"

"Only if you all die. If you become too scared to leave your settlement and Level, then it will make their eventual job easier," Ginali explained, a little apologetically.

"It does explain why IRSHA didn't start anything with us though," Sienna mused out loud. "Not much Credits to make, killing humans."

Ginali's next statement was quite hesitant. "The Dash'Kiri of IRSHA do have an honor code they uphold rather rigorously."

"Well, that's just fucking perfect, isn't it?" Dor slapped her knee and laughed. There was no mirth whatsoever in the sound. She was angry too; I could tell.

"I don't get why they thought so little of the humans who live here. You know Australia isn't really all that deadly, right? Unless you're an idiot and go wandering about in areas that aren't contained, that is. But the same could be said for anywhere." Sienna appeared to be talking more to herself than anyone else, but we let her.

"Now that we have to keep an eye out for mercenaries, I'm not sure how well we'll be able to keep the monsters contained. At least not to the level we have been." She ran her hand through her hair and looked up at me. I could feel the panic starting to set in. Not just for her, but me as well.

Damn, this wasn't looking pretty.

"All right," I continued. "We need to figure out ways we can still clear our monster population, level our people up, not die to these . . . scouts, and protect our home. Any suggestions?"

Because I was out of them. Running on empty and cold coffee.

"Well, there is something we could do . . . or *we* could do." Ginali's voice was much softer now, like maybe he didn't want anything to overhear what he had to say. "Our Cartel is now established here. Together we've made sure that we have the rare items in trade, in gear, and in through the Shop. We are heavily invested in this location. If you would agree to let us, we do have an alliance with a rival mercenary clan."

"Say what now?" I pulled back, almost wanting to scream at our little liaison. How could he have left this until the last minute to mention? "You have a mercenary clan?"

He nodded. "It's a little more complicated than that. We have a standing order for their gear and weapons, as well as potential groundbreaking technology or adaptions that we supply to them first. And in return, when we are threatened—or when one of our holdings is—we can enlist their protection."

"What's the downside?" Dor asked bluntly.

Ginali grinned. "Well, it's not really a downside, but the Hakarta just don't do anything without a clear benefit for them. So we're just going to need to find that benefit for them."

❖

7 Weeks, 3 Days Post-System Onset
9 a.m.

Brisbane gets one of the fewest days of rainfall in the entire world. So few that we often find ourselves with water restrictions on a regular basis. Overcast days were far and few between, and I remember growing up as a child to what we called electrical storms. No rain, nothing like that, just loads of lightning and thunder and the inescapable blackouts that plagued the city.

That is, until they redid the electrical grid in the late 80s. I don't remember blackouts after that. At least not many of them.

Now, with Mana powering everything we used, we didn't need to rely on an electrical grid, but those electrical storms sure as hell still existed, even in the time of the apocalypse.

Not only did I currently have to worry about these Zarrie, and IRSHA, and waiting for mercenaries to arrive . . . but we had to avoid being hit by lightning, too. None of this put me in a good mood as I ventured out on patrol wondering where the hell the visit IRSHA promised us about over a week ago had got to.

Thanks, guys, but we've already found what you wanted to talk to us about. In the form of killing us off, even. I should have known better than to expect something from them. I just wanted to go home and pretend this was all in my head. Not like that was possible.

"You're mumbling again." Kyle spoke softly, probably not wanting to alert any creature that might be within hearing distance. "What are you worked up about now?"

"I'm muttering about surviving this long enough to make it out so I can have dinner with my kids," I grumbled in delayed response as I scoured the underbrush for any signs that we'd missed. Another nice by-product of my implants was their ability to not only distinguish Mana quotients, usage levels, and direction, but also trace heat signatures and a plethora of other things.

Bionic woman, hear me roar.

248

"Having kids complicates things. Have you checked on Mason?" He asked the latter so out of the blue he pulled me out of my scan of the area.

It took me a few precious seconds of cricket-roaring silence, but I managed to pull myself together long enough to answer. "He's alive, and once we've got long-range communications set up—when Chris finishes it—maybe he can come see the kids."

Even saying it out loud made it feel more real, like he truly was alive and the kids hadn't lost their dad. Not like mostly every single other person in our camp.

A brief flash of heat in my vision with a streak of Mana following disoriented me enough to almost sit me on my butt. The flow of power around us was unsettled. As if something large was about to fill the space.

All of it was accompanied by a subtle rustling in the undergrowth and I found myself turning around to figure out which direction it came from. The sudden Mana rush, combined with that awful feeling of expectation, churned inside me.

"Watch out!" was all I had time to scream as I jumped backward, barely avoiding what looked to be a rancid claw. It was long and hooked, dark grey in color with a sickly brown tint to it, and the smell the attack left behind made me wonder if the creature had been traveling through the sewers.

And it was gone as quickly as it swiped at me.

I'm not sure what I'd been expecting when Dannin described the Zarrie. Maybe sleek and small like a Whippet, but not seven-foot-tall, lithe, armored creatures. Though I guessed, in hindsight, they were more like Anubis just like everyone who'd encountered them had reported.

I barely managed to get an Analyze on him before he disappeared.

Zyrilian

Zarrie

Ambusher

Level 3

That was all I got. There was nothing else, not even a whispering of leaves rubbing together. But the hairs on the back of my neck stood up.

Even the Mana rush around me was suddenly quiet, which made me even more suspicious. Mana was never quiet. It rushed into everything, filling it all up whether it wanted it or not.

But right now we had silence in every sense of the word.

In between one breath and the next, life returned to the wood. Leaves rustled and the breeze blew through, no trace of sewage left on the wind.

"So that was a Zarrie?" Molly put her shield down next to me, frowning.

"Apparently." The anticlimactic-ness of it all bothered me. But more so the fact that I couldn't figure out why they hadn't attacked us. Was that Ambusher just a lone scout not wanting to confront all ten of us in our patrol?

Suddenly, there was movement off to the left out of the corner of my eye. I spun, trying to follow the figure and only glimpsing it in the distance through the trees. A blink later and it was gone, leaving me to wonder if I'd really seen it.

Only my Mana Sense allowed me to feel like I hadn't just made shit up.

Foe

Ever helpful, it informed me that I had in fact seen an enemy, even if

I didn't think it was quite the same shape as one of the Zarrie.

Another thunder crack broke overhead, making me jump. I'd been so focused on trying to figure out what I was seeing in the distance that I hadn't noticed the lightning. Yet wasn't it odd that even with my implants I couldn't discern what the creatures had been?

"What's wrong?" My brother nudged me.

"Something is out there." I gestured vaguely toward the trees, still squinting and trying to see if I could locate it again.

"I'm not about to argue with your cyber eyes, but I think you're getting paranoid."

I scowled at him, even though a worm of doubt threaded its way into my thoughts. He could be right. Maybe I was just convincing myself that . . . no. I had seen it. "Shut up. You're just jealous you don't have implants too."

My twin chuckled. "That's better. Stop second-guessing yourself. Your gut has been right as long as I've known you."

He took that moment to move to the side, with Sange and Molly. All of us were on high alert now we'd found one of the scouts.

"Maybe we should head back?" Tasha suggested. She was a solid addition to any party, but I always got the feeling she wanted to be anywhere but out in the action.

I wanted to agree with her, but Mr. Zyrilian wasn't a Basic Class Level 3 out here. Not with the way he moved, not with the way he disappeared. We needed to know more about our opponents. The sooner the better.

Another flash across my vision and this time Evelyn and Ray both gasped. So much for it being in my imagination. It was huge and far away, and scared the shit out of me. How did something get to be so big, so close to our home base without us realizing it?

Except they had seen it. Drake's patrol a few nights ago.

"Shit. He wasn't exaggerating." Kyle backed up. "We should turn back—"

But he didn't get any further as two Koalzillas dropped down from above, landing in an all-too-human crouch in front of our group.

They opened their massive jaws, showing row after row of sharp teeth—yet another spin on the mutation—and roared. There was challenge in that sound, accompanied by the stench of long-dead meat and death.

Worry sprung through me, because I knew these weren't the massive shadow I'd been trying to track. No, there were, upon inspection:

Koalzilla
Level 36
Elite

We'd totally failed to maintain the Level caps around us. I cast Planted In Place on both of them and dive rolled to the side, fully aware that the others around me were getting out of the way as well.

"Left one!" Molly called out, focusing her attention on it. Her shield crashed into the ground with a resounding thud, activating its wall. Mana began to roll back into help her regenerate again and the whole circle started.

If I hadn't been so focused on locating the Mana signature of that shadow, I would have been able to give us more of a warning about the Koalzillas.

We began to methodically work on Molly's target while I maintained Planted In Place on the right one. I hadn't had this ability the first time we encountered them, and it made controlling the damage they did to us much easier.

Evelyn and Ray stood at range, firing arrows and icicles directly at the creature. Tasha and Gemma dove in as usual, with Gary joining them this time around. They went in cautiously but could be more effective because

I'd restricted the Koalzillas with my root and the creatures were unable to lash out at the rest of us as much as usual.

Tasha took a nasty swipe to her side, sending her tumbling into one of the gum trees. Her head hit the trunk, knocking her out cold for several seconds before Kyle could land a heal on her.

I'd never get over the sight of wounds knitting themselves back together.

Implantation and Water Siphon activated; I dashed in to smash at kneecaps while keeping Planted In Place active on the second Koalzilla.

Morton fired into the creature, several of his rapid shots hitting the same spot one after another. I didn't understand how his Class worked; all I knew was that he expended Mana a lot faster than most of us if he wasn't careful.

One of the trees about twenty meters away burst into flame, and I almost shat myself. Lightning split straight down the trunk, and Mana fled from the wound. The first Koalzilla fell at the same time, lending an eerie synchronicity to its death as we turned to mow down the second one.

Having been held in place for so long, this one flailed erratically, catching Kyle in the chest with a claw. A scream tore from my throat as another lightning strike lit up the darkening sky as I rushed to my twin's side. Sange's heal hit him at the same time as I made it. Checking him over, I was relieved to see him breathing and realized that the closing wound had probably just missed his heart.

I didn't like how close that had been. I didn't like that everyone continued fighting as if nothing had happened, but I was grateful that they had. And I didn't like that I knew I should have just kept on smashing its kneecaps too.

So, hefting the hammer in my hand, that's exactly what I returned to doing.

As the second Koalzilla plummeted to the ground, the hairs on the back of my neck stood on end. Spinning around, I saw *him* behind a group of bushes. Tall, pointy ears, snout that belonged on a statue.

Ignoring that I should have been looting, I dashed over to where the Zarrie had been. But he was gone, and the shivers that went up my spine made me suddenly realize we needed to get home.

"Loot up. Let's go." Because there was a sudden urgency about the way the Mana spoke to me.

Hurry. Leave.
Danger.

Yeah, I got it already. "We need to get back home before something else attacks."

I didn't need to add anything. Everyone got what I meant.

Loot acquired, we picked up the pace, jogging back toward the road. I could feel power behind us, Mana on a level I didn't know quite how to process. It followed us, getting closer as we ran, egging us on.

Finally making it to the vehicles, we dove in and drove flat out back toward Garbo. I knew I shouldn't have, but I took a look behind me. Two Anubis-like, clad jackals stood on the road where we'd been but moments before, and I thanked my amazing tech department that it didn't appear as if they could run at forty kilometers per hour.

Chapter Twenty-Three:
Enemy of My Enemy

8 Weeks Post-System Onset

6 a.m.

A Habitable Safe Zone

Side Quest 1

Congratulations! You have achieved a side quest directly related to your main quest.

Objective: Survive the wrath of the Zarrie until backup arrives and work out why they want you dead.

Remember: You're already beating the odds. No one would blame you for giving up.

Rewards:

Survival

25,000 Credits for the town treasury

???

Not my favorite notification to wake up to. Four weeks from completion of the third part of that quest anyway, and if our numbers kept being waylaid by Zarrie attacks, then we were never going to hit that three-thousand-resident requirement.

I rubbed at my eyes, belatedly realizing how different it felt when I did that as my retina tried to figure out if I was attempting to focus in on something. The back of my eyelids were eerily disgusting when zoomed in on.

Hopping out of bed, I grabbed clothes and dashed to the downstairs to the showers. I was done and dressed after a super speedy four minutes. The product of living almost my entire adult life with some type of water restrictions.

Clean and dressed, I stopped at Raybucks only long enough to grab a coffee and arrived at the library by 6:30 a.m. to face several of my fellow council members who'd beaten me to the punch. I was pretty certain Dor didn't actually sleep. Maybe she was part vampire.

Dale was quietly going over some numbers with Sienna, who had Rolo in with her today. That little boy saw things I wished I could, and I was fairly certain when it came time to choose a Class for him, that he'd end up having something to do with Mana Sight, or Mana Sense. Probably a variation of some form. Goddamn Skills.

He sat quietly in the chair next to her, his hands running over the bright pictures in the book on the table in front of him. Enamored with his imagination. Me too, kid. Escapism at its finest.

Ginali had brought Ciago with him. I was never entirely sure where I stood with the tiny Pharyleri woman. Her pale blue eyes never seemed to focus on my face on the odd occasion I'd spoken to her, and as far as I'd understood it, she took care of most of the inventory and cashflow aspects of the Cartel.

They were already there, deep in conversation with Dor. The two Pharyleri were gesturing expressively and I could see Dor's brow verging on that level of irritation we all tried to avoid. Ginali worked hand in hand with Ciago, but the latter was rarely at our meetings. I'd tackle the Pharyleri first then and save Dor some aggravation.

"Mornin'. What gives?" And only as I spoke did I realize I hadn't even taken a sip of my coffee yet. Well, needed to rectify that.

Ginali's face brightened up when he saw me, and I could see the relief coursing through Dor at the same time. Ciago, like I said, she was a bit of a mystery to me. I couldn't read her, and didn't particularly understand her well. She was super astute and businesslike, but she wasn't outgoing like

Ginali. I had enough irons in my fires; I didn't need to try and befriend everyone.

"Just the person I wanted to see!"

Ginali's infectiousness was a bit overdone. Which let me take two things from it: A, my Diviner Skill told me he was being genuine, but there were overtones of benefit to himself which made me keep my guard up; and B, well . . . it brought a smile to my face.

I genuinely liked Ginali.

"And, pray tell, why do you want to see me?" Because there was also that part of my Diviner Skill, gut instinct or whatever you want to call it, that was certain I didn't really want to know *why* he'd been looking for me.

Ginali snatched my coffee cup, smelled it, and gave me a grin. "Well, we have you and I and not a good cup of what you call coffee in sight. Kipatchya is so much better. I have some special beans for Ray. I will get him to make you a much better drink from my stash."

I scowled at him and grabbed my cup right back. "But for now it's what I have, so give it to me immediately or suffer my irritability. Why are you skirting the question?"

"Oh, that. I have received a communication through one of our intermediaries. You and I need to go to the wall. Now." Ginali was still not so clear on how to approach subjects with me and I had to remind myself that he hadn't been around humans at all until recently.

"Wait. Ginali. What was the communication? Why are we going to the wall? You can't just come and drop a bomb and expect me to follow without question."

He stopped short and blinked at me like I'd just said the most illogical things. "The IRSHA division is wanting to speak with you urgently. Or, well . . . with the settlement. Their Dash'Kiri made contact with us. We shouldn't keep them waiting."

"This kipatchya better be good," I murmured half under my breath, knowing he'd hear my thinly veiled threat.

❖

8 Weeks Post-System Onset
7 a.m.

Standing on the bitumen on the safe side of the gate as they opened it, I'd never felt so nervous in my entire life. Not before the wedding, not even when I'd had my kids. Nothing was like facing a nine-foot-tall being that appeared to have skin made out of stone to bargain for the lives of everyone under you to pile on the pressure.

The Dash'Kiri were a hunting species, one that prided themselves on their code of ethics, their strict moral compass, and their honor system. Even knowing all of that, having gathered as much information on them as I could reasonably afford, I still found it decidedly difficult not to be scared out of my wits.

Evelyn seemed surprised when I arrived, having just been on her way to fetch me. I'm uncertain how Ginali got hold of the information before she did, or how he knew that I'd be needed or called on to come out here. We'd have to talk about that later. Seemed there was a lot more ESP or telepathy going on around these parts than I'd anticipated.

Mumma Wombutt picked herself up as the gates opened and waddled her way over to stand closer to me. Her huge form trod lightly across the ground, only giving it a very soft thud with each step she took, as if maybe she was being careful not to break anything, or else not wanting to give away her presence entirely.

I appreciated her being cautious. It sure beat being knocked on my ass in front of our opponents by rumbling ground.

With her armor growing fiercer along her thighs, butt, and back, it actually *felt* safer to have her around. That and we had this little bit of an affinity bond. While I hadn't yet made the combat wombat I was secretly dying to create, I was starting to think it might be potentially viable and not just a pipe dream. After all, what was more fun than a wombat with plated armor body parts that liked to smush its opponents against tunnel openings?

By the time she was positioned, Mon'swkinon stood about three meters in front of me. On either side was another Dash'Kiri warrior. They were both maybe a head shorter than their leader, but still hugely imposing at over eight feet tall. Behind them in the formation was Dequasha on the left and a shimmer of what I could only describe as light on the right. Maybe it was a mirror image or something along those lines, but whatever it was didn't appear to have corporeal form.

The group gave off an imposing vibe, a "trifle not with us lest ye want to die" sort of atmosphere. Regardless of all the platitudes they could provide, I wanted to run as far as I could so that they never found me and my children again.

I took a moment to Analyze them.

Mon'swkinon

Third in Line

Dash'Kiri Clan

Warrior of Sound

Level 12

Nelv'isish

Dash'Kiri Clan

Warrior of Sight

Level 4

Ak'lumeter
Dash'Kiri Clan
Warrior of Blade
Level 3

Ever since our last conversation with them out at the Nathan dungeon where they could have killed us as soon as look at us, I'd been expecting to see them here. Something about the way Mon'swkinon chose his words, the way he carried himself.

Not exactly like this, though. Not as if they were equals wanting to talk about something that concerned the both of us.

Considering all the crap with the Zarrie, I'd actually been expecting them sooner than this.

Despite what he'd said when we met out there—talking over Koalzilla corpses, shooting the shit after killing mutant echidnas—I still had this fear of the unknown. A modicum of respect was all I thought we'd been afforded, but as it turned out, I was fairly certain they watched us and left wordlessly numerous times after that. As if they were maybe sizing us up, checking our potential to see if we were at all worthy.

I forced myself not to take a step back, to hold my ground instead as the mostly proud human I felt I could be. But the sheer force of Mana surrounding all of them shook me to my core.

Before these implants, I wouldn't have known. I probably would have just chalked it up to another gut feeling. Just like everything else when I'd seen them out there, I'd noticed that they glowed with a haze of power. But now, now I could see the thickness of Mana that wound through and around them, how it leaked into every facet of their beings. The power itself a slave to their whims.

Dark strands interspersed with light. Both from inclination and how their abilities were used, right through to the strength of each of them. My skin ran cold and it felt like the blood was freezing in my veins.

From everything I understood about Mana and how it worked within our bodies, how it worked inside the Skills it gave us, and what it bled from the land? These creatures could have crushed us from the very beginning. Like ants. Worse than when we'd managed to fend off our Spiny Leaf Insect friends those weeks ago.

They were all stronger than that Zarrie who'd chased us the other day. Zyrilian . . . at least as far as I could tell, Mon'swkinon being the highest Level IRSHA had brought with them. From what I could tell through Analyze, he'd brought the other higher Levels with him just for this meeting.

Not even all of the information in the Dash'Kiri books I'd absorbed what seemed like an age ago now had the same effect on me as the pure understanding I'd garnered through the implants in the last couple of days.

There was nothing about us that was equal. We were tiny and insignificant, and the only thing that had partially saved us was that we could think for ourselves, and thus weren't considered prey. How many other species would have treated us like this? How many of the species contained within IRSHA, even?

Right then, even as Mon'swkinon prepared to speak, as he inhaled from our Earth's atmosphere to voice whatever prepared statement he'd readied, I knew without a shadow of a doubt that the only thing keeping us alive was this being's code of honor.

"Greetings, Kira Kent. As promised, we have come to talk." Mon'swkinon's words didn't inspire any sort of grand confidence in me. "It seems that we are too late for some of this to be of news to you, but we have other information we hope will be of use in the circumstances we find ourselves in."

I cleared my throat as we began walking away from the gate. "Thank you for coming. Are you hungry?" It took a considerable amount of effort not to cringe after asking that since I had no clue what they might like to eat.

He saved me by shaking his head slowly. "No. We do not require sustenance."

"Then let us begin, shall we?" Taking a deep breath, I motioned them inside the settlement.

"We meant to arrive sooner, but we had complications."

Even in what I assumed was his quiet voice, Mon'swkinon's voice carried.

"Complications?"

He nodded. "Yes. Technically we were legally bound not to interfere, but we have ended that restriction." His expression grim, he stopped halfway to the actual shopping center. "We will sit here. Your sun is a welcome presence."

I had to stop myself from gaping as he folded himself into a cross-legged sitting position on the bitumen ground. Not the sort of comfort level I'd expected guests to want. At least Mumma Wombutt wedged herself in behind me to give me something to lean against.

"So I take it the Zarrie are here because of you?" I asked, not entirely wanting to give away that we were already certain of that piece of information.

"Yes. Technically."

I hated technicalities. "Maybe we can help each other, then," I ventured, not knowing exactly how to go about this sort of thing. It wasn't like negotiations were a part of my Class. Where was Sienna when I needed her?

As if summoned, I felt her Mana signature approach, accompanied by

Dor's. It helped me relax, to know that she'd understand any type of deal or negotiation that might take place on a much deeper level than I would.

The leading Dash'Kiri glanced at me, focusing that stony gaze on me for several seconds before responding. "That too is my wish. It seems we were all misled and now we find ourselves in a rather dire predicament that will affect everyone trying to live on this continent."

Considering our one encounter with the Zarrie so far hadn't given me high hopes of speaking to them on equal footing terms, I was taking this as the best opportunity to do something.

Plus, IRSHA had already proven that they weren't going to claw at us, kill us, or otherwise try to chase our vehicles down on sight. So I was going to go with the known of the two evils.

"So . . ." I pushed. "Where do we start with all of this?"

Even though I was fully on board with avoiding doom, we weren't good friends, and I frankly didn't like that state of affairs. These people, creatures, aliens, whatever . . . were trying. And I got the feeling that they weren't used to offering or asking for help.

Dequasha stepped out from behind Mon'swkinon, just as flowery and delicate as ever. It made me curious as to how she was in any way a lethal hunter. Guess you really couldn't judge a book by its cover. "Do you understand our suggestion?"

She was eager for me to understand it, I could tell. There was not even a hint of subterfuge in her tone, in any of their tones as far as my Diviner ability allowed me to see. None of these IRSHA members in front of me were trying to ambush us, either. There was no hint of them utilizing Mana in any way that might signify them attacking us.

So it was that I found it easier to trust what they were saying.

For all intents and purposes, this entire bizarre situation was legit.

"I mean, I understand that you'd like us to assist. I just don't know how or even if we can be much help. We don't have Advanced Classes, or Master Classes. We aren't high Level enough to be truly effective, and our money is all poured into our town." I raised my hands in helplessness. I still couldn't quite fathom just why they thought we could be of any help in the first place. We were barely keeping ourselves alive.

I could feel eyes on us as the watch switched, and as patrols began to return. So much curiosity.

Mon'swkinon let out a rumbling sigh. I liked the sound of it. Sort of like the sound of thunder in the distance on a stormy night. Far enough away that you could enjoy it without worrying about being struck by lightning. "The System made a miscalculation. The information our entire organization acted on was incorrect and thus the funds we borrowed in order to secure what we hoped would be a monopoly on several newly minted rare species never came about."

"But you received some compensation for that miscalculation, right?" I asked. Like as far as I could tell from the information Ginali had shared with me, they'd taken out a loan on false pretenses and were a bit in the hole for a heap of the money they owed.

Frankly, while I could fully see people becoming fully reliant on the Shop, this sort of miscalculation concerned me.

You know, not to mention that all of IRSHA's potential success was supposed to rest on the Australians being mostly wiped off the face of the Earth. Great shit to know. At least it made me enjoy being a stick in the System's wheel.

"As we've said before. We have managed to make some of our payments. But at this rate, it is doubtful that we'll be able to continue." He paused again, eyeing Ginali with an undercurrent of irritation. "Unfortunately, not having exclusive access to the mutations has seen an overall decrease in value of our kills.

"That you activated the Cartel means that the secondary, non-exclusive Credit value portions of our merchant contracts have activated. We were not made aware of the Cartel's interests. Given that it had to be triggered by the completion of a settlement—we can see how this came about."

Dale stood up, pinching the bridge of his nose with his hands. Though I got the feeling that his leg went to sleep or something. My hips were starting to give me hell, too. IRSHA, however, didn't appear to be uncomfortable at all.

We'd been out here most of the day trying to come to an understanding of just how we could truly help IRSHA. Even with Ginali's assistance, it was difficult to get over the species barriers. Some terminology that IRSHA used was simply confusing in context.

It felt so much safer to be conducting business out here, though. Where Mumma Wombutt could leap to our aid if we desperately needed it. But the more we sat in discussion with them, the more I realized that having these aliens as our allies might be a really good idea.

Inside the center were our kids and our elderly, our crafters and non-combatants. I wasn't about to bring potential danger inside our Safe Zone. Not yet, anyway. Not until we could be certain that we'd truly gained allies who weren't secretly plotting to betray us. So it was that we found ourselves sitting on the ground in the carpark.

"The fact that you owe money to one of our largest rival conglomerates isn't lost on me." Ginali's eyes flashed, and I could tell he was angry. Perhaps angrier than the situation warranted. "You wouldn't be in this problem if you'd utilized our old alliance properly before it fell apart!"

Now that was some baggage I had no desire to unpack. But just like six weeks ago, it didn't seem like the universe gave a flying fuck about my desires.

"That is not directly a result of my actions—" Mon'swkinon began, but Ginali cut him off.

"You'd have been able to claim benefit from our Cartel if your division hadn't backtracked." It seemed like the little Pharyleri was only just getting started.

"Enough. Explain. Short sentences. Now. Get to the point. Maybe you have long lifespans and don't mind meetings that should have just been an email, but we have work to do. Training to accomplish. Walls to fortify." Yep. I'd had it, and I could even tell that Mumma Wombutt was getting restless too.

It was amazing how much the presence of this Wombutt made me feel safe. I stood up, still leaning against her, and she let out a whuff of breath as I did.

Ginali sighed, opening his arms wide like he was asking the same lackadaisical universe that hated me to give him strength. Good luck with that one, mate.

"They borrowed money from the Capital Expansion Society Pool. Cesspool for short. At least that's what those of us in the know call them." Ginali then turned to me, and the expression on his face took me by surprise. "I've explained this before, I believe?"

He was serious. Not even a small portion of mirth entered his gaze at all.

"Basically, the Zarrie are here because IRSHA got greedy and gave them an open claim to everything. The Zarrie don't care if we're sentient. The Zarrie don't care about prior claims. At least not if they can get around it. Our one saving grace is that you humans who've held out here got multiple settlements together. Without that? We'd already be dead."

I cut him off, realizing that he was about to go off on a tirade. "Look. That's in the past and it doesn't fucking matter anymore. If we were going off the past . . . let's just say that *none* of you should be here." Taking a breath, I leaned harder against the oddly soft Wombutt fur. "Right now it appears that you think we can help each other. Is that right?"

Dequasha nodded and Mon'swkinon sighed. "Yes."

"It's not a good idea, Kira." Ginali was more worked up than I'd ever seen him and I might have to talk to him about that.

I held up a hand. "Right now we need to weigh all our options."

He glared at me for a moment before the equilibrium I was used to from him came rushing back. "Yes. This is a good plan. The Zarrie do not operate within the same bounds of honor."

Turning to Mon'swkinon, I gave him a tight smile. "Then we will have a truce. For now. Ginali obviously has concerns, and frankly, we've already been attacked by the Zarrie multiple times. Numerous corpses and losses and—"

Mumma Wombutt pushed herself up to standing and maneuvered behind me. I definitely appreciated it, especially since it had an obvious effect on our guests.

"When did these corpses begin appearing?" Dequasha's odd eyes focused on me, and I had to suppress the shudder trying to crawl up my spine.

"Oh. A week or two ago."

"Strange." She turned and glanced at the Dash'Kiri who nodded, his brows furrowing in concern.

"What?" My patience was wearing super thin.

At Mon'swkinon's nod, Dequasha continued. "It's just that two weeks seems a little early for the Zarrie to have been here. Maybe it was a lone scout?"

"You misunderstand." I cleared my throat. "The corpse we found *was* Zarrie."

Mon'swkinon drew in a breath. Not quite a gasp but close to it. "Have you had other patrols go missing or injured?"

That put my guard up and I didn't like the growing unease I felt. "Yes."

"We have had some patrols attacked too. There may be another species here, despite the System's allocations." The Dash'Kiri Warrior of Sound spoke softly, and his words were almost snatched away by the sudden breeze.

"Then let's all keep an eye out for whoever this is." I grimaced as I extended my hand for a dismissing shake. Zarrie, IRSHA, and now another potential alien foe. My brain was already hurting from all the possibilities. "For now, our settlements have a truce, agreed?"

They nodded. "Agreed."

Ginali clucked under his breath, like he had something to say and didn't want to say it.

"Out with it." I was so not in the mood.

He eyed me through his brief scowl and then cleared his throat. "It might be in all of our best interests if we have a contingent from IRSHA stay with us. Within the walls, that is."

I glanced at him, quite impressed he'd been able to put his personal feelings aside. "That might be an excellent idea."

Mon'swkinon nodded slowly. "This would be an excellent way to maintain communications between our two sides. It is acceptable."

"Great. That's settled, then." I put one hand on my hip and scratched the huge Wombutant with the other.

And Mumma Wombutt turned her head, nosing into the middle with a whuff of breath.

Yep. She had my back. Looked like I didn't even need to train my combat wombat.

Chapter Twenty-Four:
Re-evaluation

8 Weeks, 2 Days Post-System Onset
8 a.m.

The sun was shining, but it was definitely chilly outside. I'd take it ten times over, though. Two days into our tentative truce with IRSHA and nothing about the world had changed drastically.

Well, like, not again anyway.

With the cawing echoing in from just outside the gates, I could almost imagine being back in a less end-of-the-world time with my kids.

Wisp leaned up against me, chewing on a breakfast sandwich Ray had given us, while Jackson fiddled with some device absentmindedly to the other side. He'd barely touched his food.

Still, it had been his idea for us to have breakfast together. For us to spend some time together, and I watched as Kyle hurried toward us from the Center to where we sat leaning against Mumma Wombutt.

Wombie batted playfully at his mother's front paws. Occasionally, she moved one, and he pounced on it gleefully. It appeared to take relatively little to keep him happy. Dog lounged with us, completely relaxed for one of the first times since he'd joined us.

Wisp occasionally leaned to the side and scratched him behind his ears, and he twitched happily in his sleep.

"Sorry I'm late." Kyle plopped himself down next to me and eyed my seatback. Otherwise known as wombat body.

"Go on. She won't mind. The sun is up nice and high this morning and she's enjoying it."

Kyle raised an eyebrow at me but didn't argue, and instead reached for my cup of kipatchya. I promptly slapped his wrist and gestured at the other coffee cups. Ginali had finally introduced me to this drink, and it was the only one I had out here with me. I was not sharing, not even with my twin.

"You get your own kipatchya." I sulked at him, guarding the cup jealously.

Kyle laughed. "Fine. I'll go find something to bribe Ginali with." But there was a twinkle to his eye, something I hadn't seen much of late.

I watched another patrol walk out of the center, ready to go for the day, armed with provisions and equipment. A small portion of me felt guilt at that, but it was okay; I could take a morning to spend time with my kids. Our patrol would head out later on.

"Mum. Hug me," Wisp demanded, sidling up next to me. I obliged.

We all ate in silence for a while; even Jackson had started nibbling on his breakfast sandwich. I mean, the meat was of indeterminate origin, but the kid had had luncheon meat on his sandwiches in school, so I was pretty sure his stomach was hardy enough.

Kyle downed his last swig of coffee and I saw another two people approaching us from the center.

"This was a good idea," he said to me, watching as Evelyn and Chris approached. "With everything else, it's nice to just sit down with family and friends and remember what we can be grateful for."

I smiled at him, nudging him gently with my elbow. There was no need to say anything because he was right. So I raised my hand and waved at our friends. Their faces lit up as I beckoned to them, glad I'd thought to have Ray pack double the food I thought my teenage son would manage to eat.

As Evelyn and Chris grabbed their own sandwiches and sat down opposite my twin and me, my son finally looked up.

"Mum. Seriously. I'm starving. How can you give them my food?" He pouted, but I could tell he wasn't quite serious, even as he snatched himself a second sandwich.

Chris laughed. "Hey, it's not like you're wasting away, beanpole. I've seen the food you put away during tech hours."

Jackson had the grace to blush, right before he stuck his tongue out at his "boss." Evelyn joined in the laughter, picking up what I was pretty sure was an apple and biting into it.

If I closed my eyes so as not to see the perimeter defenses and changes to the shopping center, I might even be able to fool myself into thinking that nothing had changed.

I watched my kids and their interactions with their surroundings, their circumstances, and the people who'd become a new sort of family. This overwhelming sense of love for them, worry for them, and determination to keep them safe just smacked into me.

I gulped down my kipatchya and patted Mumma Wombutt gently, trying to convey how much I appreciated her safe presence. In another hour, I'd have to head out and patrol. I'd have to go out with a team, mowing down mutations and alien creatures, keeping an eye out for the Zarrie patrols, and hoping that no one close to me died.

But right now . . . for the next sixty minutes, I was determined to enjoy the small wins we'd had up 'til now.

❖

8 Weeks, 2 Days Post-System Onset
5 p.m.

The patrol hadn't gone as well as I wanted.

We'd encountered a lone Koalzilla and a nest of what I thought were vipers, but I couldn't precisely tell. Maybe they had been, once upon a time.

I shuddered at the thought of the hydra-resembling snakes with their multiple heads. Their green blood still stained my clothes and skin.

There was a part of me that considered the entire outing a lost cause. Because I didn't see any Zarrie patrols—and in the back of my mind that's what I'd gone out there to find.

Surely, since they were sapient creatures, we should be able to speak to them, reason with them, right?

Though there had been several creatures in the distance, through the trees. I'd thought they appeared to be too large, because of how far away they were, but I could have been wrong.

They moved so fast, too. Never toward us, only ever away. How was I supposed to be able to identify them? Training my implants to lock onto moving targets was a lot different from the intricate Mana-source tracing I'd been doing with them in the last couple of weeks.

Time, I just needed more time to figure all these things out. It was the one thing I couldn't buy more of from the shop. Although . . . with all this technology, time travel didn't seem quite so far-fetched anymore.

Silly me. Time travel made me laugh at myself. I could dream, right? About to strip down so I could get some of the sticky and sickly blood off me, I felt the ground rumble.

"Kira, we need you out here." Kyle's voice crackled over the walkie-talkie.

Though not immediately worried because I was quite certain the gentle shaking came from a particularly large marsupial exiting the gates, I pulled my filthy armored jacket back on and dashed out of my quarters, my Warhammer at my hip.

It was like Mumma Wombutt understood the whole predicament the other day with IRSHA and the sense of urgency that hung around the camp. She'd begun waiting at the gate first thing in the morning and trotting up and down the mostly ruined road, her massive nose twitching as she moved. Like a cute, cuddly, massively deadly guardian.

"Kira, you almost here?" Kyle's voice crackled over the walkie-talkie again. I didn't think he was panicking, just impatient, but I picked up my pace anyway.

"Yeah." I didn't respond more. Running really wasn't my thing. Running and talking—just a bad idea.

Dor handed me a coffee the moment I got to the makeshift medical bay in the carpark.

"What happened?" I asked, cringing as I watched the injured people on the beds being patched up by the System and our medics.

Dor shrugged. "Early patrol toward Daisy Hill, ran into some trouble."

"Kira, over here." Kyle motioned.

I scowled as I realized why he'd called me away from some rare potential downtime. I mean, he'd been out there with me until thirty minutes ago anyway, since Dale had stayed back at camp.

The man on the gurney had a sickly green Mana aura around him, just like Nate had however long ago that was. I swear days were beginning to run together.

Taking a breath, I put my coffee aside and guided Kyle's healing through the wound, helping him identify the crystalizing badness and kick it out. Sure, I bet there were better words to describe it with, but I hadn't even had time to skull down my evening coffee yet.

Done, I wished it was a Skill I could pass on to people. But as far as I'd been able to tell, it only activated because my Mana Sense was stupid high and could differentiate different types of Mana usage on an intricate level.

I downed the rest of my drink, sighing as I watched another group of people hurrying over to us from the gate. Coffee just didn't hit the same spot anymore, but I pulled myself up tall, ready to help with what I could.

The number of severe injuries we'd been fielding the last few days was starting to stack up. Sure, the System helped with all of that sort of stuff, but there was something about the frequency, severity, and the lingering elements of toxicity or poison lingering in and around wounds that lent itself to worry.

There was a panicked expression on the faces of the incoming group, and I only realized it as they pushed the body into place in front of us just why that was.

On our gurney, so tall his feet dangled over the edge, was the slender jackal form of a Zarrie. His appearance tugged at my memory and I inspected him briefly.

Zyrilian

Zarrie

Ambusher

Level 3

Guess that answered my question. He was unconscious, and my vision picked up a sickly winding of Mana running through him. We couldn't let him die. It didn't matter what their code of honor said; I wasn't about to let a sapient being perish if we could help it.

I glanced at my brother, whose lips were pursed in a hard line. He nodded once and I suppressed a sigh. Just my luck that I was the only one who could help fix this. I cracked my neck from side to side, and touched my brother's arm to guide him through again.

Damn it. I didn't like helping enemies, and I was all out of kipatchya.

The healing effect on the Zarrie took such immediate effect that I gasped. The wounds began to close, and within the next minute he sat upright, a very human scowl on his muzzle.

"You will not hold me." His voice resonated with a deep growl, setting the hairs on my arms on edge.

"Hey. Hey." Both Kyle and I backed up, our hands raised in that universal symbol of surrender.

"We just healed you. That's all we were doing." Kyle kept his voice even, his tone cool to some extent.

It was like he knew just what to say in circumstances where a patient woke up in shock. Like he'd been a surgeon or something.

Ah, dry wit in the face of panic. Never leave me.

Zyrilian pushed himself off the gurney in a movement so fluid I wished I knew where he practiced yoga. "Then I will leave."

I blinked as he began to walk away, turning briefly half around. While he didn't make eye contact, he spoke, his words, slurred perhaps by the way his jaw could move. "Thank you for your healing."

And then he managed to move thirty-odd meters in the space of two seconds and vanish through the gate.

It took several seconds for me to regain my composure, and Dor walked up to stand next to me, shock evident on her face as well.

"Well," Kyle said, turning to help the next person in line. "That happened."

"Yeah," I agreed, sudden tiredness overcoming me. I just wished I knew what in the hell *that* had been.

Chapter Twenty-Five:
At the Walls

8 Weeks, 4 Days Post-System Onset
5 a.m.

I was so done that being done could have learned from me. This whole last week had been a blur of one shitstorm after another, and I was totally over it. Except I didn't have that luxury.

Resigned to yet another night where I avoided sleeping for the most part, I rushed over to the gate, stumbling with my shoes not pulled all the way on. Damn it. Another Molotov cocktail or the alien equivalent lobbed over our twelve-feet-tall walls had hit the bitumen.

We really needed to be more on top of the defensive improvements. Dolores and Sienna were wrestling with the final upgrade options right now, but we needed to do something to stop our attackers sooner than later.

Concrete-reinforced walls and lookout towers weren't going to do much if our opponents could lob shit over to destroy us from the inside. At least they couldn't scale the towers, or so I hoped.

Even as I climbed the gate stairs, meeting Kyle up the top, I could see our small IRSHA contingent emerging from their makeshift tents. There weren't many of them. After all, we'd found out that only three of the shopping center settlements had been occupied by Australians.

Still more than the System predicted.

There was the Myer Center, as yet even unclaimed by IRHSA. Then Carindale, Chermside, Indooroopilly, Garden City, Hyperdome, North Lakes—then just outside of the Greater Brisbane area, there was Coomera, Pacific Fair, Robina, and Maroochydore.

That seemed like very few potential settlements for millions of people.

Which made the reality of just how little they'd expected us to survive really hit home.

By the time IRSHA got here, Chermside, Garbo, and Carindale had been taken by us resilient little Aussies. At least we'd shown the System that it shouldn't count us out. Even if it had wiped out two-odd million people.

So far.

Shaking off my thoughts of survival ratios, I surveyed the sight before me. The gasp that escaped me was entirely involuntary. There were at least twenty Zarrie out there. They stood like the statues in Egyptian tombs, their pointed ears making their elongated snouts appear more regal than I'd thought possible. Standing up straight, they appeared to be even taller than the one we'd helped. Even if I never really got to see him just standing.

Their Ambusher Classes used all of their abilities as a part-jackal species, including falling to all fours as a way to navigate terrain and remain close to the ground. Then there were their fighters, who were in full leather, or faux-alien-leather, armor.

It reinforced every aspect of their bodies, and the only weapons I could see was silicone-like gloves that spread over their claws. The toxins dripped from their hands, but even when they fell on their feet, it appeared that the Zarrie had a tolerance for it. They were immune to their own toxins.

Good to know.

"Surrender your settlement or we will be forced to take it from you." A high-pitched whine accompanied the voice that boomed through the dawning light. Like a dog who'd been hurt, squealing in the background. Such a horrible sound. "You have one hour to make your decision."

Damn. I hoped they didn't have amazing hearing like all dogs did. We needed to discuss this, and an hour wasn't enough time to do so. Not in the face of so much at risk. Besides, be forced to take it from us? That sounded all sorts of sus.

I know we weren't forcing them to do anything. Who was making them? The magpies?

My own joke made me smile.

Ginali clambered up next to me, his face grim. He closed his eyes briefly, his hands forming intricate patterns.

A shimmer appeared in front of my face at the edge of the tower. "They shouldn't be able to hear us now, at least not for a while. The Hakarta are still a couple of days away. They're pulling one of their clans in for us. We just need to hold out for forty-eight hours—give or take a bit."

I glanced at him, wondering why I'd never thought to ask him specifically what his Class could do. Then I looked around me at Dale and Kyle, at Evelyn. These were the people I entrusted this entire settlement to, who I knew would work with me no matter what. Molly and Sange finally made it just as I was about to speak.

"Forty-eight hours?" Sange asked, their tone guarded. "Hold the walls for two days?"

Ginali nodded. "Maybe even sooner."

Sange cracked their neck from side to side and looked at Molly with an unreadable expression.

"If you don't need me to stand on the front lines, I should be able to reinforce the walls. I'll need more Mana potions than you can shake a stick at, but . . ." Sange shrugged. "I haven't really had much of a chance to use the Skill yet. Just in a couple of those oh-shit situations. I don't always remember it in my rotation yet."

They smiled a bit sheepishly.

"Oh, that's right. You have that shielding spell now!" I tried not to get too excited. It had been six weeks without Jules and her magical healing shield. I thought we'd lost it forever. But my hopes were dashed when Sange shook their head.

"No. It doesn't work like hers, remember? It's Shielding. Reinforcement spell. It says it mirrors whatever defense the targeted object has." Sange frowned. "So if I use it to bolster Molly, it'll give Molly double the defense for the duration. As long as I don't have to heal, I can theoretically reinforce the wall constantly. Giving us just that bit more strength."

Sange held my gaze and I nodded slowly. Anything was worth a try. Because there was no way we were giving up our little town. I pulled up the quest, ignoring all but our current resident numbers.

A Habitable Safe Zone

Part Three: Staying Power

You need to make it 3 months into System Onset as a Township.

Goals:

1 - Gather 3,000 total inhabitants. This may include visiting species.

Current population 2,415/3,000

Time Limit Remaining: 3 weeks, 4 days, 17 hours

We still needed a lot of people, but if we couldn't hold these walls, then no one was going to have a home to come to.

"Sure. Tell us what you need." It was the only decision we could make. Because none of us knew how to defend against a siege.

Luckily, there were people we could ask.

❖

"Well." Mon'swkinon paused, his face thoughtful. "There are several ways we could bolster defenses."

He turned to me, a frown on his face.

"You can track their Mana usage, determine where spells will or could hit. If they're aimed at the wall, or within the walls, you will need backup who can follow directions and help halt the damage." He nodded, as if that was all I needed to know.

Maybe it was. After all, I'd been building up my ability to track Mana waves for a good while now. Just needed people I could rely on to follow my directions so we could head spells off. If I was understanding it correctly.

The large Dash'Kiri continued on. "The Cleric's reinforcement spell will work, but we will need to supply them with avenues other than Mana potions. Considering the diminishing returns on those, they'd be virtually useless."

Ah, battle experience at its finest. I'd have been marginally jealous if I wasn't trying frantically to dig through my abilities and Spells to make sure I could do what I wanted to.

"Do we need healing stations?" Kyle asked shortly before Mike interrupted him.

"What about patrols? Should we be sending out people to fight against the Zarrie?"

Mon'swkinon held up his hand, and a pained look crossed his face. "I am not your leader, nor your battle commander. But since we have a truce, we—this IRSHA delegation—will take over physical defense in front of the gates. We have the Levels and the weapons.

"Our reconnaissance tells us that out of the twenty-two Zarrie out there, only seven are Advanced Class. They do not appear to have anything more advanced than a Level 6. If it comes down to it, we can and will hold our own."

There was an undercurrent of Mana that jumped around him, erratically, like perhaps accentuating that underneath that commanding town, our new ally might be a tad nervous.

Dequasha piped up, her tone an attempt to soothe everyone's frazzled nerves. "A healing station would be a good idea. Have the Cartel make sure there are enough healing and Mana potions. They will suffice in a pinch if needed. Diminishing returns or not."

A thought occurred to me. "So there are only seven Advanced Classes in those ranks?"

Mon'swkinon nodded.

"What are we talking about? Melee Classes, ranged Classes?"

"Out of the twenty-two of them, eight appear to be close-combat Classes, and the other fourteen are ranged." He paused, as if accessing a previous memory or something. "Most of their close-combat Classes do posses some form of ranged attack, though."

"If seven of them are Advanced, what are the other fifteen?" I was just full of questions today.

Dequasha answered that one. "They're high-Level Basic Classes. Ranging from Level 40 through to Level 49. They have archery-based Classes, as well as what I believe are mages."

"We should be okay, right?" Dale piped up, and as a fellow parent I knew instinctively that he was worried about his son.

"I believe they have more members here than they are fielding for this attack. To be quite honest," Dequasha continued, her tone contemplative now, "I don't understand why they are attacking, let alone with what I believe is only half their force."

"Uncharacteristic indeed," Mon'swkinon agreed. "But we have a plan. Let us go and put it into action."

None of it made me feel safer, but at least there was a plan of some sort.

❖

My head pounded as I attempted to track the Mana flooding the region. There were strains of it I could push down and have running in the background as long as they were from friendly fire. But standing up here on the parapet, gazing down at the number of Zarrie beyond us, I had to wonder if I was doing any good.

It was up to twenty-five of them now, though Analyze told me Mon'swkinon was right. Even now with three more of them, there were still only seven Advanced Classes. I wished we'd have had more time to Level. Even out the field a little.

"Off to the left—mid-lower parapet." I spoke into the walkie-like receiver I'd been given to announce incoming attacks to those who needed to know. With two hundred and fifty defenders, we were doing okay. Not to mention some of our civilians who were specialized in creating weapons thanks to Ginali's guidance.

We had mechanical catapults, capable of holding acidic liquids I couldn't even pronounce. Our tech department had managed to finagle several different long-distance weapons similar to what only some of our people had been able to afford from the store.

Long-range guns that lobbed over Mana bombs, as Chris described them. I'd have to talk to her later; she had far too much of a Dr. Jekyll look in her eye when describing them. We didn't have many of them, but we did have some.

Several groups of defenders were gathered up the top with me. Not quite next to me, but scattered in intervals all along the wall. Many were armed with what I'd call pulse rifles bought from the Shop, but others had staves, wands, and other magical-based weapons that could help magnify their Class abilities.

Not to mention that the techies were also assisting Dor and Sienna in amping up the turrets they'd just installed up here on the walls.

The only limiting factor was that: all of this cost Credits. So many Credits.

We'd bought the alchemist out of hundreds of Mana potions, even with the discounted prices Ginali had given us, and even taking into account the considerable diminishing returns, it had wiped out a huge chunk of our reserves. There wasn't any way we were going to be expanding our boundaries any time soon at this rate.

I glanced over to where Sange was being protected by multiple casters underneath the main gate. There were four people around them; two of them were Mana users, similar to myself, from IRSHA. They could provide a small boost to his Mana Regeneration, as well as two defenders of our own. Level 28 each.

A part of me heaved a sigh of relief that we'd made that truce with IRSHA a few days ago. We were only a few hours into this fight, but having that handful of Advanced Classes on our side made the whole battle feel that much more manageable.

"Right upper turret!" I called out again as the focus of the next barrage of spells became clear. The throbbing behind my eyes increased, and I pulled some painkillers from my inventory, determined to fight this off.

"You okay, Mum?"

I blinked, almost losing my Mana-strand juggling at the shock of seeing Jackson up here with me. But then again, next to me was probably one of the safer spots to be if he wasn't in the mall itself.

"Fine," I responded, a little more clipped than intended.

"Sorry. I know you wanted me to stay inside, but I have Skills that can actually help, and I don't want to do nothing when I could do something." He had this quiet confidence that his reasoning for being there was sound and logical. He was right. Didn't mean I had to like it.

"Fine. Just be careful and take heed when I tell you to duck or move." This simply wasn't the time to be having an argument about whether or not he should be where he was.

A grin crossed his face, and I had to be thankful that he wasn't gung ho about it all. Soon, we settled into a pattern. I'd call out incoming attacks, warn wherever it was they were targeted with only a second's time for those people there to prepare. If he could, Jackson would lock onto my target and follow the spell, trying to set it off course, or explode it midair with his own Electrical Charge.

It was a first-tier Skill that enabled him to pull from static electricity in the air. Needless to say, it could be used for technology development and offensively.

While it didn't work every time I called out an attack, it worked enough to save several lives. It took away the need to everyone to be alert and switching concentration constantly.

Up here on the parapets, with the turrets and groups of ranged fighters defending our town, every bit of concentration mattered. Now all I had to do was keep Jackson moving around the wall with me every so often so that our opponents didn't end up concentrating their attacks on us once they realized what we were doing.

If I stayed in one spot for too long, I knew we'd become targets.

Eleven in the morning and my stomach was trying to eat my intestines. Or that's how it felt. No matter what anyone else said, using Mana and magic in this sense used up a lot of energy. Just as I was about to send Jackson for food, in fact even as I was readying myself for the brief argument about sending him away, Talia, one of the distance telepathy twins, appeared next to us.

She held a small box that she placed at my feet and righted herself to hand me and Jackson a water bottle. "Drink up. I have food in there, too.

I'm to stay with you so that Tarin and I can help you communicate easier with the main hub."

Relief flushed through me, and I'm not sure what I was thinking initially. It had felt like such a good idea to get up here on the wall and oversee the entire battle. Especially in light of Mon'swkinon's advice. But it felt so far beyond my current abilities, like I was striving to reach for something that required like another thirty Levels worth of power and experience.

"Got it. Jackson. Eat."

I could feel the glare he directed my way, but he didn't say anything and instead crouched at the box, pulling out what appeared to be a sub sandwich. He tore into it even as I called out another directional caution.

"Left mid-section. Fire, Ice Lance—incoming!" It was at least getting easier to read the waves, to feel the way the Mana moved. But damn it if I didn't understand how it had been weeks without an increase in Skill. Surely there was more I could see. Surely I hadn't capped the damn Skill out.

The impact that shook the wall and sent me stumbling came from right beneath where I stood. I grabbed onto the railing for dear life, dropping my water bottle and sending the liquid splashing over the floor. Damn it. I'd missed one. One right where I was standing.

Pushing down on the panic that tried to rise, I harnessed some of the anger at that shot instead. The adrenaline rush heightened my focus to such an extent that I could see the trace elements from the attack.

I followed it back to two jackals, Zarrie, little brats trying to take our hard-won settlement from us. All this "before we are forced to take it from you" bullshit. Not even IRSHA had done that. No, IRSHA had a bloody code of conduct. An honor code. These little shitstains didn't.

Narrowing my eyes, I hardly noticed myself raising my hand, tapping into my Skills, and exploding a fucking Rockslide down on their asses. I mean, I knew I was doing it, but it was so far away, and I had to dig so deep to pull the power I needed in order to do it.

There were no rocks, but there was plenty of stone, broken concrete, half-tumbled-down buildings and fences. Bricks and churned up bitumen from when our Wombutt friend had tunneled in the street. Oh, there was no shortage of shit for the spell to grab onto and use as ammunition.

The deluge of debris rained down on them, eliciting screams from the group of four casters who housed the attackers I'd let get past me. Even as I drained a third of my Mana bar doing so, elation hit me at its success.

My Warhammer fired at my hip, that tingle of power simply itching to break free, and I found myself grinning over at the buried Zarrie who'd dared to attack my new home. It was amazing how close about eighty meters was, yet how impossibly distant it felt. My senses sharpened, and the flow of Mana appeared to blind me for a split second.

The blue that flashed in front of my eyes gave me but a moment's reprieve from scouring these attackers for all their weaknesses.

Congratulations!

Your consistent use of Mana Sense, perhaps even to your own detriment, has allowed you to level it up. Combat usage is often far more potent than simply studying the latent Mana that exists everywhere.

New Mana Sense Total: 16

Note: Mana Sense can no longer be increased by knowledge alone. Only experience and use will further increase your understanding from here on in.

Caution: Mana Sense can lend power, but comes with great responsibility. You wouldn't want to let it consume you now, would you?

Well, at least it hadn't stopped leveling. Wish it had given me that caution earlier, though. Warning signals fired off in my brain, but they were things I didn't have time for while we were in the middle of a siege.

Kyle and Dale were nowhere in sight, their Skills being used at healing tents stationed on the ground between the towers.

At least the siege was mostly happening between our north and eastern gates. Considering the state of the MacGregor dungeon, I couldn't blame our opponents for not attacking from *that* vantage point.

Though we did still have a security detail guarding the southwestern gate just in case.

"How did you do that?" Talia's tone held just a little bit of awe.

I blinked at her, only momentarily taking my gaze off scouting out our opponents. "I overreached a bit. I'll have a huge headache tomorrow, but sometimes we just have to do what we have to. You know?" My Skills didn't really have a range, just a Mana cost that depended sometimes on duration, distance, or even like this one—reach.

Mana Sense seemed to expand that reach, so that I could actually lob it at anything within sight. I had a feeling it actually made me able to wield the Skills in a more flexible way than they were meant to. Certainly, everyone else I talked to couldn't do that.

Spells, on the other hand . . .

Not the time.

And what nonsense was I talking about headache tomorrow? The throbbing was already sitting in the base of my skull. I'd pay dearly in the morning.

Talia nodded, and I could see the way her eyes shaded over as she contemplated my words. Dangerous was dangerous, even if I was human. Jackson slipped his hand into mine, like he was trying to help ground me.

For just a second, I wondered if I was that transparent. I mean, it hadn't been difficult to just rain that much earth down on our very-sapient opponents. Should I be feeling guiltier?

Maybe, but I didn't.

And there wasn't any time to examine my conscience closer. There was only time to find the fuckers who were endangering my family and make sure they never did it again.

Chapter Twenty-Six:
Countdown

8 Weeks, 5 Days Post-System Onset
3 a.m.

We'd been at this so long I think my feet were going numb.

Naps were for the weak, or the decidedly lucky few. I hadn't yet been able to decide. Jackson was finally sleeping under protest—very loud protest, in fact. But I just didn't trust him not to hurt himself accidentally while trying to overreach with his powers and responsibility.

My eyelids felt heavy, dragging down. None of this made sense to me. Not to my aching head, or my voice that was growing hoarser by the hour.

Hell, I'd even been able to regen Mana, and Sange's reinforcements hadn't wavered due to their Mana being easily maintained. Something wasn't right here.

Sure, the Zarrie had been attacking. Sending in their ground skirmishers to harass the IRSHA patrol on several occasions now. Firing at the walls and the parapets. None of it felt like a true assault, and most of it gave me this sensation of desperation.

Several more Zarrie had joined the ranks about an hour ago, yet nothing other than a few more Fireballs, and several Ice Lances had shot out toward us. It was like they were waiting, but I had no clue for what.

"Shit." Evelyn stood up straight, her loose brown hair blowing in the night breeze. "Kira. They've been testing for holes in our defenses."

"What?" I asked, blood rushing painfully back into my feet as I took a step back.

"For whatever reason, they didn't have their full force with them. Now they've got over thirty people left. All we've done is trade blows. But they don't have city defenses because they're holed up in a makeshift shelter. They've been testing our defenses. Shit!" Evelyn dashed across the parapet and toward the reinforced gate where we'd set up our mission control.

Everything she said made sense. They hadn't even been trying. They were waiting us out, figuring out our weak spots. Nothing else made sense. And then the doubt started creeping in. Not about Evelyn, no, but about our supposed allies.

Weren't they supposed to be hardened fighters?

I guess, but they probably didn't have to worry about sieges when they were just hunting animals. Awake again now, I shook my head, downed half a bottle of the water that was sitting at my feet, and smacked my cheeks.

Evelyn was almost back when the first Fireball hit just below the top of the parapet, sending both of us sprawling. How had I missed it? Too caught up in my thoughts. No time to ponder, only time for action.

"Incoming. High Alert!" the walkie-talkies crackled out at everyone.

I focused on their ranged contingent, only belatedly realizing that they had about twenty of them now, not to mention twelve close-combat fighters who were making a beeline for our gates under the cover of ranged attacks against us.

"Left main turret!" I yelled out, but now the Spells traveled faster, and the impact happened only a split second after my yell demolishing its target.

"Left main turret—repairs." Talia spoke behind me, startling me. I'd mostly forgotten she was there, she'd been so quiet.

"Stay hidden," I murmured, focusing back on the line of casters across from me. They'd grown substantially now, maybe twenty-three of them. Nerves tried to eat at my braincells to make me nervous.

Not today anxiety, not today.

I let myself blink, drew in a deep breath, and hyper focused myself. Everything began to pick up pace. The main left turret was being rebuilt, now to save the rest.

Except over the next hour despite my best efforts, Evelyn's amazing reflexes, and Talia's relaying of information, we lost three more turrets and got a gigantic hole in the wall over toward where the OfficeWorx stood.

That, and I was so worn out. All of this concentration sapped at my energy, and protein bars weren't doing shit to replenish that.

And that was when allowing myself to take a breather quite literally got someone killed. It happened in slow motion. All I did was blink, but I missed a crucial cast, which sped at the speed of light, impaling one of our ground troops directly through the chest and to the gate itself.

The icicle lodged itself into the concrete before shattering. But there was still a moment where the surprised look on Torg's face seared itself into my mind before he was dropped to the ground like a sack of potatoes.

"Left—" I couldn't get the words out, and Evelyn stepped in for me, completing the order of *left main wall*. Damn it. Kira. Focus.

I hadn't even known Torg, except that the name stuck in my mind. He wasn't going to be the only death tonight, especially not if I let myself be distracted by it.

"Far right turret." Damn it, we didn't have many of those left. The System was still repairing everything. At this rate we'd run out of money before these blasted reinforcements got here.

I glanced down below during this short reprieve. I swear they had to be running out of Mana if nothing else. IRSHA had split their group into two and complemented it with several of our own higher-Leveled people. I could see Gemma and Tasha in the mix down there, Drake and Gary.

And I was watching right as they clashed with two Zarrie patrols, headed by Zyrilian.

Last time I saved a damned Zarrie.

"Kira." Talia spoke softly behind me. "Dor needs you to know the last turret is down and we still have two hours on repairs of them. Not to mention the holes in the walls."

"Got it." Compartmentalization at its finest. I turned my attention to glance over toward the gate itself when I saw an archer I didn't actually know plummet off the top of the parapet and land with a sickening crunch below.

The grappling hook that sank its blade into the top of the parapet now still had some of the tendons from her arm attached to it. "Center breach!" I called out, barely able to stifle my gag reflex. I was checking for something to stop that next time I got to the Shop.

"The settlement shield is down!" Talia called out from behind me, and it was the first time I think she'd sounded flustered.

If the shield was down, that meant Sange had either run out of juice or been hurt. I just hoped it was the former. I looked around me, my eyes taking in the people who'd been there but minutes ago. Some had fallen or been dragged over the parapet by embedded grappling hooks. At this point in time, I felt like they weren't even trying to get up our walls.

Large, reinforced icicles constantly stabbed massive holes into the gate, and before long, it was going to crumble too. Even the command center at the top of it had been abandoned. They'd had no choice.

My Mana was getting dangerously low too, and with the walls taking so much damage, I desperately needed to conserve what I could.

"May I take your hand?"

I turned briefly to find Dequasha right next to me. She moved silently, which was probably a large benefit while hunting.

"Sure." I was a little nervous about feeling her hand . . . petal . . . whatever it was.

She smiled at me. "It will be fine. I can link to what you are seeing and attempt to head off damage sooner."

"Ah. Okay, then." I guess she had a type of telepathy or kinesis or something. She'd been busy assisting Sange, so I knew either something had happened to my favorite Cleric, or else she was better utilized here for now.

Her petal-like hand was even softer than I'd expected. Like cotton wool met a cloud and had a baby. The sensation of her following my Mana Sense felt eerie, like someone was watching me in my head.

I guess she was.

Evelyn had even managed with her bow and arrow, though her reaction times were slightly longer, significantly enough that she didn't always deflect the attacks in time. Then again, we were lucky we had we even had people who could intercept spells in midair.

Dequasha's magic, on the other hand, had this soft, almost floating element to it. Like everything she did was a bloom of velvet, even if it was filled with poison.

I watched, through Mana heightened senses as she took my hand and activated her Skill. I didn't know its name, and now wasn't the time to ask, but damn was I curious.

Even with a front-row seat, I didn't fully understand what she did. There, within my enhanced close-up vision, I watched the Zarrie who fired the next ranged spell scream as that power returned, hurtling back into themselves.

Their skin peeled back, revealing charred edges and bone, crackling like some sort of firework exploded from the inside. It made me entirely too grateful that we'd reached a truce of sorts. The agonized scream that emanated from his torn-up throat only lasted as long as his life did, as the rest of the remaining defenders on the wall concentrated fire on him, seeing the opening. The sound held so much pain that I visibly shrank back.

"I apologize." Dequasha's voice was as soft as always. "My species has specific abilities unique only to us. I forgot that you wouldn't be familiar with them."

"What was that?" I whispered, still unable to tear my eyes from the sight.

"Flay. It's just called Flay. Not all of us are born with it, but when we are . . ." She shrugged.

Guess I had my answer for how something as delicate as her made a good hunter. I hoped with all my might that I would never be on the receiving end of having my skin melted from my bones.

And just as I began to feel some sliver of hope that we might just win this fight after all, the parapet shuddered as the eastern gate doors were destroyed.

❖

The stairs were gone too, which meant that all of us up here on the parapet were screwed. Then the ground rumbled, and I realized that my Wombutt was approaching. It was still a bit of a drop, but only five feet or so to land on her large, furry spine.

I didn't even want to ask Dequasha how she managed to get down. But as I slid down the side of our Wombutt and sent the creature a silent but love-filled thanks, I couldn't help but feel like I should have stayed up there.

Down here though, it was a battlefield. I could hear the sound of fighting just beyond where the gate had been and hurried over, emptying all of the Mana from my coat to refill my Mana well.

Earth Barrier needed to be as strong as possible. None of this easily break-through-able shit. I dug deep, wasting precious seconds to make sure I was pulling from the clay deep in the Earth to help bind all the pieces of soil with the bitumen remnants and concrete pieces.

Smushing it all together in my mind, I raised the Barrier in place of the gate. It only stood about eight feet high, and it wasn't perfect. It drained about 120 Mana, too, but damned if it wasn't sturdy as hell, and at least going to stop foot soldiers getting in here for awhile.

Dor and Sienna were pale, and I didn't like how close I'd come to losing my friends this time either. Ginali stood with them, his eyes closed like he was meditating. I wanted to smack him upside the head for sitting down on the job, but was fairly certain he was doing something Skill-based.

Where were these damned reinforcements we'd heard so much about?

I glanced around, watching in dismay as another Fireball breached our hole-ridden shielding and landed about ten meters away from me, totaling one of our precious Mana-driven cars.

Mumma Wombutt chose that moment to come back into range, and I ran toward her, calling to Dequasha. "We need to stop as many of those attacks as we can!"

I don't know how I thought I was going to get to the top of the wall from the Wombutt's back, but when she did a little bunny hop, catapulting me withing easy reach of the parapet, I felt like we'd arrived at a new level of understanding.

Dequasha met me up the top, and I focused my vision again, holding her petal hand. I wasn't exactly sure how much time had passed, but the horizon began to lighten as we fought, and my strength sapped even further.

Suddenly, there was a screeching bellow above us. Like all the magpies in the world had gathered in front of a megaphone and tried to mimic a lion's roar. I clutched at my ears, ripping my hand out of Dequasha's grip just as she pulled away from mine.

The sound reverberated through my ears, unsettling my stomach and making me retch. All around us, the sound echoed through and off buildings, rumbling into the ground like a sonic wave.

Every single attack stopped.

No one moved as we all looked up at the sky to see the Magon flying dangerously low. Even the Zarrie halted their attacks, practically freezing in place.

I'd never *seen* the cross between what I assumed was a dragon and magpie so closely before. Don't get me wrong, it was probably a good hundred meters above us, but that was all. Maybe it functioned like a T-Rex in those movies and wouldn't see us if we didn't move.

I'd never seen so many people involved in a game of Statue before.

The seconds grew longer, and a cold sweat began to form at the base of my spine as fear started to eat away at my resolve. As much as I pushed it down, as much as I knew fear wasn't going to do anything other than get us killed, trying to tell it to fuck off when I was frozen in place and couldn't actually act on anything was one of the most difficult things I'd ever had to do.

The Magon flapped its wings, dropping so low that I could feel the current it created as it tugged at my ponytail. And then as the sun crested the horizon, it roared once more and darted up high into the sky again, screeching as it flew in the direction of the bay area.

Still, it took a good thirty seconds before I gave into my screaming muscles and allowed myself to fall into a heap on the parapet.

"Turrets are active again." Sienna's voice shook over the walkie-talkie, scratching with the static as the sound echoed over to me from where I'd left it earlier.

As the Magon flew farther away, I sighed with relief, and Dequasha reached for my hand, only to frown as she glanced out over the devastation below us. "I think . . . I think the Zarrie might be retreating."

My equilibrium was already mostly shattered, and I stumbled to my knees as I watched our opponents across the road suddenly moving away from us.

"I guess dragons scare everyone." My words made my head spin all the more as I tried to gather myself together. There were only about twelve people on this portion of the parapet now, and I was glad no one else right here had died.

Didn't mean we weren't going to lose plenty more, even if I was scared to ask how many we'd lost over the last twenty-four hours.

And that, right there, was when our relief troops arrived. Just in time to not relieve us of anything. I wondered what it would take to get the Magon on our side.

Decked out in full war armor as far as I could see were beings that rivaled the height of our jackal opponents easily. They reminded me of orcs, with tusks wildly varied in size, not to mention skin in a heap of differently colored green variations. At least from what I could see beneath the armor.

Black-clad and uniform, they marched up to the makeshift gate, greeting Mon'swkinon and the IRSHA warily.

"They've finally arrived." Ginali suddenly stood next to me, and I wasn't sure how he'd gotten there, considering the stairs had been demolished, but upon glancing over, I realized that the stairs were already back in place. Maybe, since our repairs didn't involve complex turret mechanics, putting in an iron staircase had been a simple fix.

"We need you to remove the Earth Barrier. Makes it go quicker." He smiled at me.

"Yes." I sighed and pulled the Mana away from the Barrier, back into myself. Naturally, I got maybe ten percent of what I'd spent on it, but whatever.

"Those are the Hakarta?" I asked, even though if they weren't, we had way bigger problems than I realized.

Ginali laughed this time, and I wanted to steal some of that easygoingness. Laughing like we hadn't just all been fighting for our lives. Sheesh.

"Yes. Those are the Clan Pirra of the Hakarta—42nd Division. We should go down and meet them. Now that the Hakarta are here . . ." Ginali gave a vaguely gesturing shrug. "Well, we can hope that things will quiet down for a bit. Less frequent attacks from the Zarrie, at any rate."

Ginali paused, then rubbed his chin. "It'll be interesting to see the resulting investigations. In living memory, there has never been such a mistake. Someone, or something, must have altered the information."

I raised an eyebrow. Or I tried to; even that hurt the skin above my eyes. I didn't even want to contemplate what I might look like right now considering how my face felt.

"So . . . we're, like, constantly surprising you all, right?" I grinned at Ginali as we began our trek back to the gate so we could finally rest. So *I* could finally rest. I think most of the others had managed a brief nap here and there, but not me. Because I was stubborn as fuck.

Ginali didn't answer straight away as we descended the newly minted stairs. "You're definitely surprising, and unexpected. We never really thought that our little trading post would get a start. It was a tiny fee—relatively speaking—for us to opt into the first random settlement on this world on this specific continent. No one thought you'd make it this far. But you did, and I'm sort of glad you did. Considering the mutations we've been acquiring so far, I can't wait to see what else this Mana-rich area provides."

I wasn't sure I liked his words, but I did respect the business acumen. Something I'd never really had. Kyle stepped in and stood silently at my side, constantly stretching his right hand—opening and closing it.

"You okay there?"

He shook his head. "My body feels weird every time I use my powers. Every time I access the offensive portion of my Skills, the aftermath just makes me ill."

I reached over and gave him a hug, as worries about him tumbled through my exhausted mind. I wasn't sure if it was psychosomatic, or if his

Class was in fact drawing on his own body to pull off some of its feats . . . but he didn't need to hear doom and gloom right now. "It'll be okay. We'll get Dale to look at you, and I think the Cartel is about to open its apothecary to a wider audience. Maybe you can get some help there."

It probably wasn't what he wanted to hear. I wasn't as comforting as I might have thought to be, but I also couldn't lie to him. Whatever this Class was that he'd chosen, my twin just wasn't his usual self, and regardless of how many mercenaries or monsters we faced—that scared me more than anything.

My head was killing me, and my eyes felt like the lids had been dragged through hot coals and then run over sandpaper.

I pulled up one of the notifications I'd let side during combat while I waited for the Hakarta to make their way through and into our actual settlement. Something, anything to distract me from darker thoughts.

A Habitable Safe Zone

Side Quest 1

Congratulations! You have completed a side quest directly related to your main quest.

You have survived the initial wrath of the Zarrie until backup arrived.

Remember: You beat the odds and didn't give up. Again!

Rewards:

You have survived to fight another day!

25,000 Credits for the town treasury

You receive 1x Ring of Mental Fortitude 4

+5 to Mental Resistances

Only one of these can be worn at a time

I frowned at the reward. The money for the treasury was pretty much negligible, but an okay boost that would help start the massive repairs we were going to have to pay for. Couldn't get anything in the System for free.

Which is why these quests were starting to bug me. Like . . shouldn't we be doing this shit for free anyway? Why was the System being so accommodating? Or else . . . did someone up there just like watching us squirm?

Nausea began to overwhelm me as I realized just how long I'd been awake utilizing my Mana Sense with hyper focus almost the entire time. The pounding in my head intensified, and I dropped to one knee to steady myself. Damn it. I needed to sleep. Preferably five minutes ago.

apocalypses really were a special type of hell.

Chapter Twenty-Seven:
Broadened Horizons

8 Weeks, 5 Days Post-System Onset
12 p.m.

Sleep apparently healed all things System-related, including my eyes. When I woke after about five hours, I no longer felt like someone had taken a scouring pad to my corneas. My head still throbbed, but it was more like a light snare drum than a massive reverberating bass.

Except I didn't even remember falling asleep. Had I passed out or something? Rolling over, I blinked at the sight in front of me.

Next to me on a makeshift little table of a step ladder was a muffin and a coffee cup with steam still rising from it. The note next to it told me to come to the library when I woke up, and that not having coffee as an excuse wouldn't work.

Much love from Kyle.

Shit. The Hakarta. Scrambling, I grabbed a chance of clothes, realizing that I'd fallen asleep in what I'd been wearing during the battle. It didn't smell good and neither did I.

Still, a shower wouldn't take long. Damn it. I wanted our own place. That was next on my list. A house with two or three bedrooms. Or hell, an apartment. Somewhere I could shower without having to walk like a stinkbug through half a massive shopping center first.

I knew our house was out of the question. It was far too distant to be considered inside of Garbo's vicinity. That sort of made me sad in a way. After all, I'd never considered Wishart to be far away before.

Degunged and dressed, there was a bit of a skip to my step as I approached the library. People were huddled in groups around tables in the food court, and no one really paid me any mind. The atmosphere as I got closer to the library felt more tense than I'd imagined and I suddenly didn't feel a hundred percent about whatever I was walking into.

But then I spied what was in the library, and the weird feeling overlaying everything in the center was suddenly completely and utterly clear to me.

I could count about eight Hakarta inside, but that was just it. More of them wouldn't have fit. Along with Mon'swkinon and Dequasha and the IRSHA main contingent in there, there was just barely room enough to move. The library wasn't small, but the Hakarta had looked a lot tinier from above yesterday. Wait, wasn't that this morning? This was up close and personal—all like eight feet tall, towering variations of green-skinned orcs, if orcs wore body armor and used beam rifles slung haphazardly across their backs.

Bile rose in my throat as my fight-or-flight responses fought each other fiercely. Okay, so the fight response was like, maybe we should get the hell out of here right now or maybe twenty seconds ago. And my flight response was all for it.

But something stubborn held me back. Me. I was the stubborn.

Doing my best to ignore what my stupid brain was trying to say, I took a deep breath and pushed the glass doors open. The movement caused several of the Hakarta to turn around immediately, their hands reaching for their weapons as they did so. Silence fell over the room with a tension I couldn't have sawn through with a serrated blade.

Stifling the urge to scream, I forced myself to take deliberate steps across the carpet to join Kyle, Ginali, and Dor where they stood, majorly dwarfed by the size of our current allies. The Hakarta did not stand at ease or let their guard down, and I wasn't sure how to deal with that.

"Sorry for being late." I was proud of the fact that my voice didn't exactly shake. So there was that at least.

One of the Hakarta harrumphed and took his hand off his weapon, immediately diminishing the sheer terror trying to tear at my intestines. There was a fucking orc standing right in front of me. Tusks that were at least twenty centimeters long, thick and pointed at the end. Tusks that protruded from a large mouth with sharp teeth I could glimpse as he readied himself to speak. His skin seemed like it would be tough to the touch, and what hair he had was spiked in three-blade mohawk.

I Analyzed him instinctually.

Major Hirish

42ⁿᵈ Division Hakarta

Clan: Pirra

"You are the settlement owner then? Kira?" He spoke haltingly, like he wasn't used to doing so out loud. There was a gruffness to his tone that made his words sound thick.

"Yep. That's me. I was running on next to no sleep, and my eyes had to regenerate." I smiled, although it felt fully fake.

"I am Major Hirish Pirra of the Forty-Second Division. We are pleased to offer support. Ginali has explained the complicated situation." There was a slight smile to his expression, one that read as all professional, but it did nothing to put me at ease at all. Instead, it added a sense of danger to everything he said. Like he could rip your head off and laugh about it while he did so. Or shoot holes in you with a beam rifle and be perfectly calm about it all. Just another day's work.

Oh. My. Gods. Laser rifles, tough and green-skinned orcs, aliens everywhere. Now it felt real. Now the apocalypse really felt like an invasion—a colonization. And we weren't even in a galaxy far, far away. We were here, in our own little Milky Way.

Breathe, for fuck's sake Kira. Breathe.

"We appreciate your support. Let's discuss how we can further our working relationship." My insides felt like they were shaking so much, I was surprised I wasn't completely liquified yet. Still, my super businesslike manner apparently paid off, because Hirish watched me for a moment, and then nodded.

He had this oddly fatherlike softness to his eyes for just a moment as he looked at me. I wasn't entirely sure how I should take that, but then it was gone. We all got to moving the furniture so we could create a forum setting for us better to discuss this in.

Accommodating our large allies had this oddly massive-multiplayer-online air about it, and there was a small part of my brain totally freaking out. Thing was, an MMORPG or a VRMMORPG would have been so much preferable to this. Respawning, no permadeath . . . yep, sign me right up there.

"You okay?" Dor nudged my arm as we were moving the furniture, her tone low, even though I was quite certain the Hakarta would have heard what she said.

I nodded. "Eyes still adjusting. Might have overstrained myself a wee bit with all that focus over the last day or so. Feeling a tad loopy, actually. Going to try and avoid using them for a bit. Or . . . you know for more than preventing my own blindness."

Dor chuckled, and her relaxed demeanor helped me immensely. The way she accepted all of this bullshit was something I aimed to emulate. "Just don't overdo things or, like, fry brain nerve endings . . . not that I think that's how it works."

"Not planning to. Might need some more sleep and another one of those damn fine muffins." Even though I could still feel hunger gnawing at me, I was okay. We would all be okay. Maybe. At least for a few days.

Or until the Zarrie attacked again.

Or the Magon ate us.

Finally, with the area arranged properly and our guests held up by the smaller bookcases, we could get down to business.

"So. What are we facing and how can we deal with it?" I asked, since no one else seemed to want to say anything.

Ginali hesitated, briefly making eye contact with Hirish. "That's just it. As far as the Galactic Council contracts and rules, every single party in Australia at this moment has a totally valid claim. This settlement is legitimately claimed by you, and our part as the Crafting Cartel is cemented. This is also the same for several other settlements around the whole of the country. Carindale and Chermside, Pacific Fair, I believe, Macquarie Center, Sydney, Doncaster . . . the list goes on. There are about fifteen—maybe twenty if the information we've purchased is correct—town settlements. Assuming you all last, that's a significantly higher percentage survival rate than expected, and certainly not full settlements."

"Fifteen . . . maybe twenty? Is that all?" If there were only twenty towns . . . like.

I tried to keep myself calm, really tried. My chest was hurting, my fists were clenched tight. If I'd have been a berserker, then red would have flashed across my vision, and I would have gone ape shit. As it was, however, just breathing was difficult.

That was so few people. Comparatively. So many dead.

Ginali eyed me sympathetically, and he reached over for a moment, patting my hand as if we weren't in a room filled with other humans, aliens, and fucking orcs. "Kira. That doesn't mean there aren't other villages, just that there aren't other towns. There could be many villages. I don't have access to everything, especially if those other settlements don't have a Shop or a Settlement Orb to speak of."

I nodded slowly, trying to calm my brain down. Twenty by even an average of five thousand was only a hundred thousand people. What even the fuck. But I stopped the panic, because I had to. There was no other way for me to handle this right now. I could mourn or get angry later. But right now I had to focus.

"Sorry," I apologized for my slight break down. How many people were dead, how many kids? How many species were extinct now?

Again, I caught Hirish regarding me thoughtfully. Or at least I hoped that was it, because I didn't like the idea that he thought me weak. Maybe I was, but I'd take weakness via compassion any day over heartlessness.

Ginali continued. "There is room for the human species to grow here. That's the point. Even though the System had predicted an almost total wipeout leaving less than one percent of your population on this continent, suffice it to say you've exceeded expectations. But that makes all human claims valid, all Crafting Cartel claims valid, but also the IRSHA claim, and their financier has valid claims too. It's not unheard of, but usually not a miscalculation to this magnitude."

He shrugged and gestured around at the people in the room. "At it stands, three of us are willing to work together. IRSHA, our Cartel, and at least this human settlement. This will make it much more difficult for CESPOOL to do anything."

I stifled a laugh, the name still absolutely ludicrous. Loved it.

"What do you need from us?" Dor asked, her arms crossed and her business face on.

"From you?" Ginali smiled like he'd just been waiting for the question. "From you, I need contact with all other human settlements, and an agreement that we'll all fight CESPOOL together."

"What do you mean all fight it together? There's no way other humans would fight against . . . oh." Sienna stopped what she was saying and sighed deeply. "Yeah, I see that. Not the best history there. Still, though, if we prioritize reaching other settlements, we should be able to do that?"

"Or—does the Cartel have other stations?" I asked, suddenly thinking that there's no way they could have just bet everything on one location, right?

"We do have one other smaller hub down in . . . Victoria? But it's not the central trading hub we set up here. I can definitely relay a communication to them asking for their cooperation and for them to speak to the humans there on our behalf." He paused for a moment as if he was accessing some other information that was only available through his interface. Then he frowned before continuing.

"Their relationship with the settlement owners doesn't seem to be as smooth as the one we have here, but they're not completely hostile, so that might just take some time."

I mulled that over, unsure how any settlement owner couldn't be welcoming of someone who was going to offer them incentives. But then I realized that maybe they hadn't entered that state of mind. Perhaps all they wanted to do was survive. Surely, not everyone was going to adapt to the apocalypse in the same way.

Different groups of people with differing experiences and motivations.

Hirish cleared his throat. "We will work with Dolores and the rest of you to establish our presence in patrols and security. Ginali handles our payment details. Do not forget our deal."

The look he leveled at our little Pharyleri friend was more critical than I'd have thought, but I didn't have much time to contemplate it considering how fast he moved on.

"We will spare three Hakarta to accompany you once your people are ready to begin their patrols again. Three Hakarta per patrol. Maximum. I believe we brought more than enough." Hirish crossed his bulky arms and stared around the room as if daring someone to gainsay him.

Mike cleared his throat. "We appreciate the accompaniment, but we would also appreciate any and all feedback possible on how to tighten security and go about making our security division work as efficiently as possible."

I could see it took a lot out of him. He wasn't the most personable guy, and I got the feeling that confronting actual alien orc creatures wasn't something he'd taken in his stride. But he was dedicated to the security of our little town, and I was bloody proud of the way he handled himself.

Hirish nodded and walked the four massive steps it took him to land by Mike's side. They began their discussion in what would have been hushed tones, except the large Hakarta major didn't really seem capable of complete discretion.

"So . . . the Hakarta are here, then," I said to Ginali, my voice as small as I could make it without actively whispering.

"Yep." A shadow passed over Ginali's face, and I got the distinct feeling that something was truly bothering him.

"There's something you're not telling me." I didn't take my eyes off from following Hirish's every step, but I could still sense Ginali's hesitation.

"I will discuss it with you later, though it's nothing for you to be concerned with. Instead, it's something that I now have to deal with due to the situation the Crafting Cartel now finds itself in." He shrugged, seemingly nonplussed by his revelation. "What is good is that the majority of the Hakarta who are here will remain here in a protective capacity."

"The majority?" I asked, latching onto the word.

"See. This is why I sometimes avoid talking to you. You do that mother thing where someone can tell you perfectly innocent somethings and you find the one word in the sentence that means they might be sort of hiding another thing." He finally wrestled his gaze from the mercenary and turned his full attention to me.

"The Hakarta are very specific, a highly specialized species for the most part, and this—this whole mercenary thing they do. Well, they're damned good at it. But there are multiple clans and divisions, just like there are with the Zarrie. They sent us eight lower-Level Advanced Classes outside of Hirish.

"On the surface, it's not complicated, but now that they're here and facing off against a specific clan of Zarrie, while enacting their contract with us? Let's just say nothing is fully black and white anymore. It's got greys and blues and pinks and the gods know what else all mixed into one."

Ginali shifted, his brow furrowed in concentration. "The thing is, the Zarrie's withdrawal after the Magon, their strange declaration of attack, and the fact that we did have one of their higher-Leveled Ambushers in our compound for healing . . . it's making me uncomfortable."

"How so?" While part of me hadn't wanted to ask that question, the rest of me knew it needed to be spoken. Truth be told, I was having lots of gut feelings lately, and it was nice to know someone else might feel the same.

Ginali paused, glancing around. "It just means that while we have an alliance, there's always the possibility of a higher bidder. Because after all— Credits are third only to the System and Levels in driving our world. Not kipatchya and hugs."

Chapter Twenty-Eight:
Hakarta

9 Weeks Post-System Onset

7 a.m.

Coffee in hand, muffin half stuffed in my mouth so that I had somewhere to hold it, I was not expecting to be blocked by a large, green-skinned Hirish on my way to the morning meeting. Exciting stuff, the mornings, divvying out assignments and expeditions, discussing what else we were diving into that day.

Today was the first day we were setting out to take care of the surrounding monsters again, and I was dreading what Level some of the creatures would have reached. Almost a week of us not thinning the herd every single day. The nightmares had started coming to me and I was out of my depth.

Even the few sorties we'd done, just outside the barrier and well-within range of help had shown a definite increase in Levels. What else there was when we started exploring, who knew.

Not to mention the MMNs, my trademarked Mana Magpie Nightmares, were divebombing just outside of our town limits again. Like they'd fueled their Levels up into the low 20s and had decided to come back and haunt me.

Fucking magpies.

It felts like a timer was perpetually ticking down, telling us that we were running out of time. It was a feeling I couldn't shake, not when I was talking to the Hakarta, not when I was cuddling with Wisp at night, not when I rode Mumma Wombutt around the perimeter. We were running out of time.

"What's up?" I said around my mouthful of muffin.

Hirish did what I like to call an eyebrow lift—because an orc's eyebrows are not like a human's eyebrow. They apparently don't obey the general laws of physics, or maybe that was orc physique in general. The eyebrow actually lifts up, almost as if its angling away from the face instead of just raising slightly. Maybe even his follicles had muscles.

I clipped my walkie to my jean pocket and reached up and snagged my muffin from the hold my teeth had on it, with my now free hand.

"Did . . . you need something?" And then I cringed because that could have come out much nicer and didn't. I was tired. Sue me. "Sorry. What can I help you with?"

He smiled, or it was what passed for an orc smile as far as I'd been able to tell in the two-odd days they'd been around. And let's not go into how much Jackson fanboyed about them when he met them. Admittedly, they'd been just as amused by the pictures of orcs they'd found in the library and videogame stores.

"You don't know how to use your ocular implants properly," he stated. No beating about the bush there.

"Well, no. Thanks for reminding because I'd totally forgotten." Sarcasm and I were deeply bonded.

Which only left Hirish looking confused. "You're not functioning at optimal capacity. That ability you have can and will harm you if you don't know how to harness its intricacies properly. Who advised you to get the implants?"

It felt like he wanted someone to blame for what, as far as I could tell, he thought was a mistake? Maybe? I sighed and motioned for him to walk with me. Not like it was a long way to the library, but I was already running a few minutes late now, and the more time we let those unrestrained mobs out there run around, the less time we'd have to prepare for when they all attacked and ate our town.

"It was me. I advised myself to get them so I could filter the Mana waves correctly. How do you even know I have them? I know I don't look much different from the outside."

"My grandmother had them. Your Mana Sense as a Skill—that is rare."

"But everyone wants it, right? I mean, once I figure this out, I'm totally sure that it'll be awesome."

He hesitated before responding. "Not necessarily. Rare doesn't always mean good. It can play with your mind and thoughts, twist your own Mana and heart. You would be wise to be careful, Miss Kira."

I blinked, stopping short just before the entryway to the meeting room and turned to face my walking partner. "So you don't think it's good that I have this?"

He shook his head and contemplated his next words. "I've expressed myself incorrectly. You remind me of my grandmother when she was younger and full of hope. Don't let others twist that hope. And if you need assistance with your abilities, talk to me. I cannot help you personally, but I may know someone who can."

It wasn't a hard decision, or even one I needed to take time for. Since the headaches I got defending our walls still hadn't subsided completely, I needed to know more about this sooner rather than later. At least if I was going to be effective at all in future defenses. "I'd love to talk to them."

He seemed surprised. Maybe Hakarta didn't ask for help. Maybe he didn't offer it much. Or maybe I just reminded him of his dead grandmother. After a second where my thoughts ran rampant, he nodded in affirmation.

The atmosphere in the library had changed since we invited both IRSHA delegates and our Hakarta mercenaries into the planning stages with us. Dequasha was the only one of our new alien buddies who didn't dwarf us. She was accompanied by Mon'swkinon, who admittedly almost scraped the ceiling with every step, and another Dash'Kiri whose name I didn't know. Then there was the major and four other Hakarta who accompanied him. I didn't catch their names, probably because they didn't give them, and I was quite certain they disapproved of everything if their constant scowls were anything to go by.

I could have Analyzed them, but to be honest, my head was already full of too many names and faces I could no longer match.

Evelyn and Mike were working with two of the Hakarta over in one corner, undoubtedly laying out better security measures. After all, the Zarrie had just stopped attacking for now. They weren't gone by any stretch of the imagination.

Mon'swkinon was promptly joined by Hirish over with Sienna and Dor. They dwarfed those women even more than they did me. But as soon as Dale and Kyle joined them, coffees in hand, they all bent over something Dor pulled up to show them.

Ginali, Ciago, Chris, and Sarah all huddled around a table, arguing quite heatedly. Apparently our tech division needed more supplies, and Ciago drove a hard bargain. Ginali appeared to be acting as a mediator, which I thought was sketchy considering how much of a vested interest he had in the Cartel.

Here I was, mum of two, flying by the seat of my pants. It was enough to bring a chuckle to my throat.

"What's so funny?"

Gemma's voice close to my ear almost made me shit myself. Seriously. People needed to stop with the sneaking up on me. But worse still, why hadn't my Mana Sense warned me of her signature? And then I realized, I couldn't sense it at all. Was she cloaking it? I laughed softly, a bit of a delayed reaction perhaps, but I thought I covered my tracks.

"It's not funny, it's just uncanny. Look at us all. Groups of humans, talking to aliens or, you know, videogame creatures come to life. However you want to look at it, it's sort of bizarre."

"Give it two weeks," Gemma said, her tone dry. "Then it'll seem like normal. Day to day, even. All of it. It's our new standard. And we either embrace it, or we die."

"Aren't you just a ray of sunshine today. What's got you so irritable?" Her tone made me a little grumpy. This *was* life now. We either made the most of it, or we *did* die, but I didn't want or need a constant reminder of that.

When she didn't answer, I continued. "This right here, Gemma? This is proof that even though the odds are against us, even more so against our continent, that we can rise up and become better and show those fuckers we are stronger than they think. We will lose people, more than we've lost now, maybe even ourselves. But would you prefer going down without a fight?"

She was quiet for a moment before nodding, and I swear I saw the beginnings of a tear forming in her eye. "Yeah. You're right. I get that. I just don't have to like it all the time."

"None of us do." Because we didn't. Hell, I didn't like it myself. "But we don't have to let that define us. Even if they wipe all of us off the face of the Earth, wouldn't it be better to make them remember us before we're gone?"

"Oh, we're not going to get wiped out. That's not happening. It can't." But even though I could hear the bravado in her voice, I didn't have the heart to override that.

Tenacity was what we needed more than ever right now. Even with the Hakarta's help, I had a horrible feeling about the next few weeks that I couldn't shake.

And it was all Mana's fault.

❖

The closest massive mall shopping center, also known as settlement, was Carindale. From what information Ginali had gathered from the Shop and other sources, it was Aussie populated.

Carindale wasn't quite as large as Garbo, but it was still pretty massive.

Thus it was that we mounted the Carindale expedition. Myself, Gemma, Sange, Molly, Kyle, Eritia, Morton, and Dannin. We had Dequasha and Hirish with us, too. Which felt surreal considering they were literally aliens.

Although, I'd thought we'd get three Hakarta until I realized that when he said maximum three, he'd really meant it. Plus, Hirish was an Advanced Class, which was worth like one and a half basic Classes.

The jury was still out on how safe I felt with Dequasha, considering she could melt flesh from bones, but she seemed nice enough and not like she'd turn on us at the worst possible moment. All of these thoughts did a bang-up job protecting me from wallowing in the fact that several of my favorite people to scout with weren't in my group this time.

No Dale, no Chris, no Tasha, and above all . . . no Evelyn. It felt odd without the ranger there. Sure, we had Dannin, but it just wasn't the same. The other group better take care of her. She was headed down to the Underwood and Springwood Shopping area around the Pacific Motorway. It was close enough that the way should be clear of high-Level monsters, but far enough that we hadn't scoured it for survivors yet. I was more worried than I liked to admit.

We took five completely and utterly modified jeeps with us. Easier to sit in while observing our surroundings, with far more potential to cram a chunk of people into them if we needed. I was hopeful we might find some survivors on the way back. Once we'd made contact. Or attempted to, anyway.

After we'd established communication with the other bases, we were going to branch out toward Shailer Park where the Hyperdome was. Mon'swkinon said it was the one Queensland branch they had nothing to do with. They hadn't even approached it at all. The very notion left me a little queasy, because he hadn't been forthcoming about why. Maybe I could coax it out of my petaled friend instead.

The Mana around us, even as we made our way toward Carindale, was restless. Like there wasn't enough action for it to seep into. Mana was, in fact, everywhere. And while it wasn't sapient by any means we understood, I still got the distinct feeling that it had a type of awareness. That it knew what it wanted and that was bodies to leak into so that more of it could be absorbed and used. The more people there were, the more potential there was for Mana to be gobbled up and used, dispersed.

All of it. Mana needed to spread—like a weed, or a virus. Always moving, always adapting, always more.

At least, that was the way I was interpreting the waves of the world washing around all of us. The more time I had to spend in my head with the Mana Sense Skill downloads, the more I physically read about it and explored conversations about it with others, I was getting a feeling it wasn't universal.

My view of Mana, that is.

Some of it felt like a force that wove around us, no different than gravity. Always there. Constant. Or more like sunlight. Other times I saw the waves, but in a calmer fashion, like fractured light from a prism. The movements were more structured, less alive.

I sometimes wondered if it was the Skill or my Class. Or my own viewpoint. Or just that they didn't see as deeply as I did. It was quite the question, and asking about it had gotten me nothing but blank stares. Except with a single Hakarta who had grown strangely—and rather unintelligibly—philosophical.

We kept the jeeps at a nice soft twenty kilometers an hour. Nothing too fast, considering we were also keeping our eyes out for any survivor settlements. Carindale wasn't that far away from Garden City, even if there were tons of houses in between. The quickest route clocked in around eight kilometers, but just heading down Newnham Road didn't feel like the best idea if we were looking for survivors. So we'd take the long way back.

I might want humans to survive and was glad if they were able to do so on their own, but I also wanted Garbo to hit its three thousand people and move onto the next quest line. Gathering people on our way to another settlement didn't seem conducive to that goal. We only had three weeks left and another five hundred people to find.

Newnham Road was quiet. No other vehicles, unsurprisingly. But even as we traveled along the road, ignoring any stoplights, driving past small shopping centers and houses that sat eerily still in the daylight—many of them reduced to rubble—I could practically feel that something was off. Mana wasn't just floating around with nothing to do. Which meant it had to be going somewhere. There had to be people or creatures utilizing it.

Ambient Mana was everywhere . . . except on this road, apparently.

It made my senses prickle all up the back of my neck, like there was electricity in the air with such a dearth of power in the whole area.

Eerily silent.

Past so many empty houses, past empty vehicles both wrecked and not, eventually past the aquatic center where the once-blue pools that could be glimpsed were full of algae. Brisbane's hot sun didn't take kindly to pools of water that hadn't been chlorinated in two months.

Even if it was winter.

The fact that we were close to Creek Road, down a ways from where we'd met Rigoll, and that we hadn't even encountered a group of magpies or insanely large, swollen monsters was beginning to feel like we were walking into a trap.

Again.

But we crossed over Wecker Road and went through to the other side of Creek without a hitch, heading on the way up to Carindale.

Still further, past what smelled like rotten fish from a fish market, and then a dilapidated Aldi on the right, I finally spied the Golden Arches at the intersection of Pine Mountain Road and Creek. Along with a vague need to have some of those salty fries that wouldn't ever rot, a sudden sense of foreboding washed over me.

"Careful." I spoke to Kyle, who was driving my vehicle. "Slow it down. The Mana flows aren't right here. Everyone be on the lookout, there's something coming up." I relayed it over the walkies, knowing the announcement would reach the entire car conga line. Coming up very slowly on the right-hand side was a park. Donnington Street Park.

Lots of trees to hide in, and that's where all the Mana, as far as I could see anyway, seemed to have congregated. It wasn't being hoarded—no, it was fueling something over there. A pressure reached my head, making it begin to pound.

I wanted to shout, but my throat was suddenly parched and dry, and my warning turned into a scared whisper over the walkies. "Incoming."

Chapter Twenty-Nine:
Monsters

Something slimy dripped onto my forehead as what felt like a slime-filled ball used the top of my head to rebound off and divebomb the car behind me. I could feel blood bubbling beneath the wound it left behind, forming a stinging sensation in my scalp. Adrenaline already rushing through me, I jumped off the now-stationary vehicle, landing in a crouch.

My Warhammer dangling at my waist felt inordinately light.

Kyle was already out too, and I turned to take in the scene.

I was sure that thing had come from the small park. Opposite which there was a totally vacant lot. I swear there used to be all sorts of storage facilities there at some point in my life. Still, our team had vacated their vehicles and were backing away toward the empty expanse, past an erstwhile bus stop, giving our opponents less cover, and us more room to maneuver.

I'd imagined our assailant to be some sort of mutated wildlife, or maybe even one of those blob types that we'd come across behind Garbo during what seemed like a lifetime ago. Our opponents were hard to focus on in the mostly dead grass around the vacant lot, because they blended in so well. Light brown skin, bipedal, muscular back legs and smaller front legs, with eyes that were highly malevolent.

Fucking Christ.

Cane toads.

I glanced over at Kyle, who was already in his spot in the formation, and realized that he must have instantaneously healed me when he saw goop on my head because that shit—those toads were toxic as hell.

Make dogs severely ill or on occasion kill them in their usual size. But now they'd mutated, they could probably take a human out with little trouble. As long as the System didn't go heal the victim all up.

These boys weren't your usual kilo weight sopping wet, teacup-sized balls of ick. No, these were medium-dog-sized, agile pieces of death. From what I could see with the way Molly's shield was starting to sizzle, the toads were no longer just toxic, but had developed a way to shoot that toxin at specific targets from their shoulders.

Not to mention that their backs appeared to have ready-to-pop pimples situated all along their spine where the toxin used to find itself. Now, it was just a disgusting blister waiting to burst.

Molly kept herself planted against the ground, widening the defensive circumference of her shield. But I could see the look on her face. She didn't know how to combat the damned projectile poison effects that were trying to melt her shield like it was acid.

Taunts weren't going to work—they were already attacking us. I don't think her ability could make them close in, but she couldn't move, either. She was our defensive bulwark.

Sange dug their heels in, and I could see them cast the spell I'd become so familiar with during our little Zarrie siege fiasco. They were reinforcing Molly's shielding to take as much damage as it could, while we came up with something different.

At least this time they weren't trying to protect an entire city. Much more manageable.

Forcing myself to think straight, I looked around the rest of the fight, casting Planted In Place on three of the creatures to at least keep them confined to their area. Splitting forces was never a horrible idea.

I was used to seeing them being clumsy and somewhat cumbersome, but these guys were anything but. The two that remained free hurtled around the area, so fast it was difficult to target them with ranged projectiles, and the only defenses that worked were ones that remained locked in place. A quick toss of Earth Barrier had one side of our defenses shored up, but tugging on the ground was tough and draining, and staying on the defensive was no way to win this.

Dannin sped around the area in a sprint, finally managing to wrangle the attention of one of the toads. It locked on him and once it did, the Ranger snared it with his next arrow, enabling him to slow down a bit and concentrate on riddling it with more arrows, effectively kiting it.

Color me impressed.

As he whittled that one down, Eritia and Morton teamed up to do the same on the one not rooted by my ability. Morton's bullets had much the same effect as Dannin's arrows, except they didn't look as cool. However, theirs went down much faster due to the fact that Eritia scorched it with fire. There was a little worry about starting a small bush fire; but we'd worry about that after we got the killing done.

Everyone began to focus their fire on the creatures being kited, while Sange and Molly fended off the ones that remained Planted In Place. Their ability to aim toxin from their shoulders was just creepy.

With one of the toads down, Dannin fired upon another, just in time for it to finally free itself. It did not enjoy being attacked, so it was more than happy to chase Dannin. Followed by Morton doing the same.

Unfortunately, Molly's shield wasn't going to survive more attacks like that. If she couldn't hold the creature at bay, there was no way the rest of us could use this leisurely method to wear the others down.

"We need to speed it up," I called out. Dannin nodded, skidding to a stop. His lack of movement allowed him to fire his arrows even faster. A good shot took one of the toads in the leg, and the lamed creature held still long enough for me to use Water Siphon and suck the water out of it.

That messed it up even further, its slimy toxin attacks slowing down. Realizing they needed water to create the slime, I rapidly targeted the others. That became the real turning point, since the reduced rate of fire meant that

Sange and Molly could contribute to the fight itself.

"Nicely done." Kyle was panting, hands on legs but doing his best to stay upright. The last of the monsters were dead and the others were busy looting them, which was a job I was grateful to be able to delegate in this instance. Couldn't pay me enough to touch those horrid creatures.

I recalled vivid images of cane toads from my sixth birthday. There was no power on this Earth that could erase that.

Kyle had been both replenishing other's Stamina and Health and had tossed in a few of his own spells, but I wasn't sure what he'd done that had left him so winded.

It was only then that I noticed Hirish and Dequasha hadn't moved from their places in the vehicles and I scowled.

"Hey." I walked over, putting my hand on the jeep. "What gives? Why on Earth didn't you help us?"

"Why on Earth." The flower lady laughed softly. "That is just the cutest expression."

"What's the answer?" Kyle growled out.

She shrugged, but it was Hirish that answered. "We are not here to fight your battles for you. You were not in danger, thus protecting you was a waste of our time. You need to learn to defend yourself. My contracted work here isn't going to last forever."

While he was right, it definitely rubbed me the wrong way.

"Wait, so what? You're going to wait for one of us to die before you step in?" My sarcasm leapt out of my mouth before I could stop it.

The gaze Hirish leveled at me wasn't one I could read. "You were never in any danger of dying. We would have stepped in before that."

Well, that was good to know.

I wasn't expecting the low-pitched voice that interrupted us. Like someone was trying to impersonate a school principal.

"Put your weapons down, and step away from the aliens."

I confess to having jumped a little at the words, and at the look on Hirish's face as he watched whoever it was over my shoulder. It only took a second to gather my wits back together, but I still hoped it hadn't taken too long. Last thing we needed was an itchy trigger finger.

My hammer hung loosely at my side, and I realized I hadn't even drawn it in the fight, so I hoped they didn't mean me, because putting it down would involve drawing it first and I could see a lot of ways that was going to be misinterpreted.

I stepped away from the jeep, where I realized I'd actually sort of got all up in the aliens' faces, and turned around slowly.

Kyle didn't carry a weapon, nor did Eritia. Molly did not look happy to relinquish her shield, and Sange stubbornly held onto their staff, standing there like the regal Healer they were.

The guy in front of me had bright brown eyes, and a nice sheen of sweat on his dark brow. He stood about six feet tall and had what seemed to be a pulse rifle aimed right at Hirish. Behind him were four more people, two more guys, and I think at least one of the others was a woman, and another I couldn't identify and would ask them pronouns later. If they let me talk, that is.

All of them had pulse rifles, expertly aimed at us and our alien friends. But all of them were human. Here's to hoping they wanted humankind to survive more than they wanted to kill aliens.

❖

The Carindale shopping complex was almost as large as Garden City. Like give or take five thousand square meters. So not too much difference, all things considered. But it felt a lot bigger as they sort of paraded us through the center, not giving us a chance to say anything.

If *my* anger was boiling, I knew Kyle was about to fly off the handle. Inspecting them, however, gave some food for thought.

Jake Manly
Level 28 Rifleman
Head of Security
Carindale Settlement

Davis Johnson
Level 27 Rifleman
Carindale Settlement

Arian Harvey
Level 26 Rifleman
Carindale Settlement

And it went on. These guys at least were lower Levels than us. And they were holding us by pulse rifle, an idea I'd run past Mike once we got back if he wasn't already doing something similar. Those weapons had to have cost a pretty penny. Yeah . . . something was going on here.

Finally, we arrived at the admin section of the center. They seemed to have set theirs up in the library too, although I liked ours much better. Maybe that's just where all the Settlement Orbs had been placed. I could smell good coffee on the air, but I really wanted to know if they'd gotten their hands on kipatchya.

The more worrisome thing was that I had no idea where they'd taken Hirish and Dequasha. At any rate, they'd not brought them with us.

I mean, I wasn't actually worried about the aliens, more the humans.

They had no idea that Dequasha could essentially make their skin melt off their bones. I just hoped the humans didn't irritate the pair too much.

Finally, the door opened and we were ushered in.

A mop of red hair bent over the large desk in the back of the conference room we were led into. Kyle began to tap his foot and scowled at Jake when the man opened his mouth. The Rifleman closed his mouth quickly, obviously a bit intimidated by my brother.

I activated Analyze. That's what they got for keeping us waiting.

Joshua Harvey

Level 28 Settlement Administrator

Settlement Owner

Carindale Settlement

"Sorry to keep you waiting." Joshua looked up at us. His voice was almost breathless, but it was the smile that set alarm bells of in my head. Yet another settlement person who decided that Charisma was the go-to stat.

He stood shorter than me by about two inches, around my old height at five-eight. His bright blue eyes looked out of place in such a pale face, but the way his ears knocked up at the ends let me know he'd given up humanity in favor of what appeared to be half-elfishness. If I got my roleplaying tropes correct.

I doubted people could just choose to become a full-blooded elf via the System. Not that I'd even remotely considered it, but I was sure others had. I may not have studied up on elves specifically, but there'd been multiple mentions of differing factions and types of elf species enough in the books I had read that I didn't think trying to become that species was an overly good idea unless you had a supporter.

"It's so nice to meet you," he gushed, reaching forward to shake my hand, and I pulled it back to rest on the top of my Warhammer, still hanging at my waist. I wasn't going to draw the weapon, but even resting my hand on it was comforting as the mental boost from equipping it hardened my resolve. I was going to use that protection and my little ring for all it was worth.

"Is it, though? You stopped us at gunpoint while we were clearing away some cane toad mutations, and then you took our allies to somewhere that is not here." I gestured around, using my Mum-is-disappointed-in-you voice to its fullest.

Joshua blinked at me, like he was super used to his Charisma doing all the heavy lifting for him. A brief scowl flitted across his face before it was gone like it had never appeared. But I had kids. And kids try this shit too.

Didn't matter if it was sneaking an extra cookie or promising their homework was done when it wasn't and lying about it, you got a second sense after a while. It helped, of course, that most kids were just a lot worse at lying than adults, but exaggerated tells transformed into smaller tells were still tells.

He crossed his arms, his whole demeanor changing. "Well, of course I had to take measures. We don't allow aliens around here. They're who got us into this whole mess."

"So I take it you don't use the Shop out of protest, then?" Kyle piped up, his words droll, but containing a whole girder of steel in them. Especially considering evidence that they did indeed use said amenity.

Joshua blinked. "Well. Of course we use our Shop, but that's different—"

"How?" I asked, genuinely curious as to how this young man was going to justify his train of thought.

"It's their job to provide the Shop to us. They can't hurt us in there."

He did have a point, and I couldn't fault his logic. But I could fault his understanding of the situation.

"Aliens didn't make this happen. Mana and the System did. All the other species have done is try to fight for their own survival." It was clear cut to me. And I hadn't come here to discuss the moral ethics of them terraforming our world into a Dungeon World, but here we found ourselves. "We didn't come here to discuss our differing opinions on what happened, though. We came to see if we could open lines of communications between our settlements."

Joshua didn't appear to know how to respond. He looked all of twenty-five, but then the System sort of reversed aging depending on time, implants, and different procedures. My Mana read him as medium strength, so not with a huge repertoire of Skills that might kill me, but I still didn't want to underestimate him.

It had been so long since I'd been somewhere that had nothing to do with my own settlement. Since the only other people I'd seen weren't those who were coming to us for shelter. I'd forgotten that humans could be both greedy and obtuse.

Needed to make a note to myself for that for the future.

Warning, Kira: a lot of humans can be dicks.

"You didn't come here to take our settlement over?" he asked, waving at the guys behind us to lower their rifles, and I have to admit to the massive surge of relief that ran through me once he did.

"No. I've got enough on my plate with our own. I don't need any more responsibility, thanks."

"Well, that's a relief. We've had a hell of a time finding survivors for ours—I really didn't want to have to fight for them." He rubbed his nose and sat on the edge of his desk. "Sorry. Manners are failing me. Sit. Sit."

There were several chairs scattered around the room. Most of us grabbed one, but I had nerves running rampant through my system, and sitting wasn't going to make the Mana waves I was reading change, so I felt like remaining in complete control of myself.

"I'm good." I glanced around again. We only had two of the Riflemen and Joshua in here with us now.

"They'll go fetch your alien friends." Even as he said it, I could see the trepidation in Joshua's eyes.

"They won't harm you, as long as you don't attack first." Which was mostly true, or so I thought. I mean, I'd tried to tell them to be on their best behavior. Hirish acted like he wouldn't do any killing unless he was getting bonus Credits for it, and I trusted that creed. But Dequasha? She was a bit of an enigma.

Joshua ran his hand through his hair and looked up at me. "You seem to be doing better at this than we are."

Maybe he was younger than I'd originally thought. "Not necessarily. We only narrowly avoided having aliens claim our settlement first, so I'd say we're probably on a par."

Joshua shook his head. "No. We had the same problem. We have several Settlement Orb owners . . . sort of. Technically. But no one else wanted to, like, do anything. So I have to."

"All by yourself?" I asked incredulously. Because that right there was bullshit. I had heads of security, distribution, admin, recruitment, teaching, tech . . . because I was one person who'd just picked up a damn orb before the others.

He shrugged. "Jake helps. And I have a few others, but most people are . . . sort of stuck in denial."

"Still? It's been two months already. That's taking denial a little far."

Joshua shrugged again, and for a moment looked like a lost kid who'd bitten off more than he could chew. "A lot of our guys were randomly assigned Classes. We do what we can with what we've got."

"We could get Hirish to give them a wakeup call if you like." Kyle spoke gruffly, but I could see the story hit him. Still, I wasn't sure we could trust it.

The redhead clapped his hands together and pushed himself up from the desk. "So you came out here to check on us?"

I nodded. "Yeah. There's this whole thing where the System didn't think people would survive on this continent, and so I'm trying to make sure all of the settlements we have wrangled together can stay in touch and perhaps preserve the Aussie from extinction."

Joshua smiled. "Sounds like a plan, mate. What do I need to do for that?"

"Well, for starters, do you have a tech team?"

That was as far as I got because Hirish walked into the room, and Joshua promptly fainted.

Chapter Thirty:
The New Same Old

9 Weeks Post-System Onset

3 p.m.

"That was not my fault," Hirish said in his bored voice. He held up his hands and walked to the back of the room, sitting in a cross-legged lotus pose. It was kind of amazing to see a giant Hakarta look both bored and put upon at the same time. "I'll be over here until you settle these excitable humans."

We propped Joshua up on a couch behind his desk while his Riflemen just looked on. They didn't appear to know what to do. I got the feeling that things hadn't come so easily to the Carindale settlement.

"He's not going to last long in this world if he faints at the sight of a Hakarta." Dequasha's tone held disdain, and for a moment I wondered if her species was one of those survival of the fittest ones. It would make a lot of sense with her kind of abilities. "They're still oxygen breathers, after all."

"He's young, and not used to aliens yet," I muttered, suddenly curious as to when I became used to aliens. But that was a question for later. Also, oxygen breathers? I . . . nope. Another time.

Turning around to speak to our friends, I stopped as Joshua grasped my hand.

"Sorry. I'm really not used to all of this." There was another wave of likeableness just oozing off him. And I could see how his subordinates followed him with glee. The only reason it didn't work on me was my hammer and ring. That and the fact that as soon as I saw him, I knew he had a similar Charisma Skill to Sienna just from the way the Mana flocked around him.

Ahh, my trusty implants would take me far.

He pushed himself up and nodded back at Hirish. "Sorry. Your countenance startled me." I did notice that Joshua deliberately avoided looking at Dequasha. "Anyway, how can we connect? Is that what you said?"

It was, sort of. I did want to open communications and keep it open and regular. Chris had given me very explicit instructions on what needed to be done, but I did need a techie to actually do it. Damn Skills. "I need to speak to whomever you have working on communications and technology and we can get this all started. Then we'll head home and get out of your hair."

Something flashed across Joshua's face, and if I was making guesses, it looked like fear. Maybe I could get him by himself later and see if he'd open up. So much about his demeanor, the way he held himself, didn't sing out Settlement Owner, but Analyze was usually spot on about these things. And my Diviner Skill wasn't showing any signs subterfuge from him.

So it had to be something else.

I just needed to get him to trust me enough to see what it was.

Carindale seemed far less organized than our town, and that wasn't just my brain trying to brag on all our accomplishments. The atmosphere in here had this air of hopelessness to it too, and I wasn't entirely sure how to approach it, or even if I did, what to do about it.

One of the things about Carindale was the amount of greenery that had always been inside the shopping center. Except that now, as the plants dangled over from their perches above the seating area of the old food court, I had horrible flashbacks to the Spiny Leaf Insects who'd mutated in our home.

I wondered if they'd take friendly advice or not.

They'd made the main gathering area at the base of the stunning, curved double staircase, which was essentially a part of the food court, or at least, close enough to it if you went under the platform the staircases met on.

But the area didn't bustle like it did back home. And again, my Mana Sense tingled.

Joshua's big smile flashed as he introduced me to Lance and Para, the couple of Mana Engineers who ran their technological division, as far as I could tell. Except they seemed super stressed and appeared to be shouldering most of it by themselves.

They didn't have a group of older kids working together to trial and error things. Nor did they have other adults anywhere in the vicinity. In fact, it appeared that the only people at the station were the two of them.

"Lean pickings? Not many Mana Engineers?" Kyle asked, keeping his tone about as light as he could manage given that I was quite certain he was in a bad mood. He should trademark that thing. I swear.

Para smiled at us, his hair falling forward into his eyes as he did so. He pushed the sleek black hair back behind the headband that was utterly failing to contain it. "There aren't too many who chose to work with their hands and minds in this lot. Most of them are Adventurers."

That surprised me. We'd had trouble getting enough people willing to go out and level up. Still, everyone was different, right? Maybe it was the age of the crowd, since everyone seemed a little younger.

There appeared to be a complete and utter lack of teamwork here, mixed with total despair at their situation. That . . . and it suddenly hit me. I didn't think I'd seen even one kid since walking in here.

Call me stupid, but having the couple hundred kids between infant and twelve we had running around our center, going to school, being kids? It livened up the joint, made it so much merrier. Here, it felt like hope had been sapped away.

I'd also not seen anyone with white or grey hair in Carindale yet.

A creepy sensation worked its way up my spine. The System was good about rejuvenating our bodies, healing our forms of scars we might even have had for decades, but it didn't rewind the aging process completely. Just sort of slowed it down a chunk and reversed the obvious problems, like people who had been out in the sun too long without enough sunblock.

Huh. I wonder if the ozone layer had changed at all?

Now then, how had they managed to hide all of their aged people, and their youth? I kept the thought to myself, but I knew Kyle had caught onto something being off around here, too. Joshua just seemed to be too stressed for a settlement owner.

You know, because I had such a huge amount of experience myself. Or with other settlement owners. I rolled my eyes at myself and handed Para the device Chris had given me.

He mulled it over, turning it this way and that, until finally his face lit up with excitement. "Oh, wow. They did this really well. How did they know what to pick up from the Shop and what to mold themselves? Like, this is a bit of genius right here. It won't take me long to get it situated."

He ran off, showing the thing to Lance, whose eyes also lit up like all their Christmases had just come at once. Maybe having our tech-headed kids had spurred Chris and Sarah on or something. I wasn't sure, but I didn't feel like the people responsible for technologically hooking a whole settlement back up shouldn't be this excited about a communication module.

I needed to be able to talk to the rest of my team, maybe even Hirish, and see what they thought. Maybe it was my mum bones activating with the lack of kids or parents or, like, old people, but I didn't want to stay here longer than I had to.

And yet . . .

If there really was something happening here, then I couldn't let thousands of people just die, right? These were my fellow humans, my fellow Australians for fuck's sake. But I needed to gather evidence and get back to safety and work things out first.

Sound plan, if I did say so myself.

"Wow!" Para's exclamation carried over to where I stood by myself, oddly lost in thought. Even Joshua and Kyle had moved over to the engineers.

The others were hungry and had been taken to the food court by one of the Riflemen if I remembered correctly. Arian, I think it was. Inching closer, I glanced around again. There weren't any kids peeking their noses around corners trying to watch the strangers that had arrived. No distant giggles echoing through the tiled shopping mall.

There were no old people sitting and drinking together, or wandering the corridors to get their steps in like some of them did in our center.

No. There was nothing like that here.

Pushing down the wrong I could feel, I forced a smile and walked over to the others. "You there, Garbo One?"

I heard Dor snort on the other end. "Loud and clear, Kira. Loud and clear."

It allowed communications to operate somewhat like a CB radio, not quite a walkie-talkie, not quite a telephone either. The sound was crisper, clearer, and allowed us to communicate over farther distances.

"Mission accomplished then, Garbo One. We'll be coming home soon." I said it as cheerfully as I could manage, a huge smile plastered on my face while I made myself think of my kids so it didn't come off as too fake to the people who didn't know me.

Joshua grinned, so did Lance and Para. Kyle watched me, and I knew that he knew. "Great. It works. I was going to have to have words with Chris if it didn't."

And then I saw Josh glancing around, a bead of sweat gathering in between his brows. Something really wasn't right. Staying in Carindale wasn't an option for us right then.

"Great." Kyle clapped his hands, calling back to the other group on the walkie they had with them. "We have to get back home to the kids."

I don't think they meant to, but both Para and Lance looked startled by the words. Very briefly, but it was there. "Of course. Got things to do, places to go, families to feed, right?"

I nodded, trying not to seem rushed. There were no pets in sight here, either. And while Dog and Wombie were the main ones in my life, there were definitely several mutated cats and other dogs who roamed around with some of our Garbo families. The ones who'd resisted the feral call of the mutation.

Arian, Jake, and Davis came up, their weapons hanging loosely at their sides. I twisted my Ring of Mental Fortitude with my right hand, nervousness trying to eat me up. Other people, ones I'd not been introduced to, began slowly moving toward where we were, too.

Oh, not today. Fuck that.

And then Hirish was there, suddenly materializing in the middle of the group that began to crowd around us. Several people screamed, but Hirish just stood there, no weapon drawn. Also, how had he just gotten there? He and I were going to have a long talk about camouflage and what appeared to be invisibility once we were back on the road.

"Are we ready to go, then?" he asked. "I have to get back to my troop. They are already looking for me."

It wasn't my imagination, because every bit of movement in the place that didn't belong to our little group stopped. There was a part of me that wanted, so badly, to figure out what was going on. To figure out why they were acting that way. Then there was the self-preservation side of me that wished we'd never come in the first place and just left them to their own weirdness to start with.

Hirish backed us out, even as Dequasha materialized on our other flank. Maybe she'd just used a form of concealment, because I almost felt like she'd peeled herself off the wall closest to me.

Mana flitted around her like irritated fireflies, as if it was just waiting for her to harness it and obliterate something. But she didn't. Instead, she drew all of the stares and pulled back with us. No one outside our group moved at all.

I risked a glance at Joshua only to see the tears forming, and agony in his eyes. He was stuck here, and I got the feeling none of them were masters of their own actions. Or at the very least, something every single one of them loved was being held hostage. Only, we didn't have the time or the manpower to help them right now.

I couldn't leave my kids while I sorted shit out here. This had to be another time thing.

Not with the Zarrie out there focused very much on killing us to fulfill their own contract. Nor the potential other aliens out there. Not with the responsibilities I had to my own settlement first. But I'd be back.

I only hoped that when we could mount the manpower and the equipment we needed to help them. Of course, not only didn't we know what we were fighting against, but we had to hope that they'd last long enough so there was still something to save.

We pushed those damn cars as fast as they could go on the way back. Around forty kilometers an hour. They didn't have high speeds, not at all. That's not what they'd been built for. It wasn't until we hit Upper Mt. Gravatt that we slowed their roll.

Queasiness still lived in my stomach, and I felt decidedly ill. Out here, despite everything else, the Mana usage I could sense didn't appear to have a slimy overtone. Hirish and Dequasha had been oddly tight-lipped about the whole situation, and I wanted to know why.

Taking the back roads, we barely managed to pick up any new survivors, and I felt overwhelmingly guilty at the fact that I hadn't particularly slowed down to look. By the time we got back to the center, my head was spinning through so many different scenarios, I felt like I was in a bad movie.

I helped Ray log them into our system once we got back to Garbo, going through the motions while my brain still spun. apocalypse, Zarrie divisions sent by CESPOOL, Hakarta to fight them off, and I was starting to worry about how well we were thinning the herds around us.

"Mum." Jackson tugged at my jacket and I looked at him, blinking. My head wasn't in a good place right now, and I wasn't processing things properly. So much that I'd ignored him calling my name even though in hindsight I knew he'd probably said Mum about five times before tugging at me.

"Sorry. What's up, love?"

He shrugged. "Nothing much. I just . . . are you sure there weren't any kids at all over in Carindale?

Shit. I hadn't thought about that. He had several friends who lived over in that area, and when I thought about it, I didn't even remember having seen teenagers.

"They were probably all in a different part of the center. You know how huge Carindale is." I tried to put him at ease, but we'd always had this good level of communication. Where he could probably tell I wasn't being totally honest.

He raised an eyebrow and crossed his arms. "Really?"

I sighed, and tugged on my ponytail. "Look. The reception they gave us was weird, and we didn't want to risk being unable to leave and forced to stay the night. But I promise, we're going to figure something out."

It was obvious that Jackson had difficulty processing that information. After all, Tanner had been one of his best friends since they were seven. There was still a chance he could be alive, but checking the Shop surreptitiously might be the best option for me next time I went.

"Any theories?" he asked, hope filling his voice.

"Not yet. But when I have them, or you know, actual facts, I promise I'll tell you." I pulled him in for a brief hug, just to punctuate my words.

"Thanks, Mum," he said, pulling away, his cheeks blushing faintly with embarrassment. "Keep me updated."

I watched him go toward the tech area a pang of loss in my stomach. Stupid apocalypse ruining everything. Now I had to deal with the weirdness at Carindale sooner rather than later.

With a sigh, I turned and headed back to the library to find Dor and Sienna. When I got there, Mike was talking to them quietly. Bingo. Three of the four people I needed in one place.

"Can someone call Gemma? We need to get some eyes into Carindale."

Chapter Thirty-One:
Zarrie

9 Weeks, 6 Days Post-System Onset

7 a.m.

I refrained from rubbing my eyes. Barely. Thirty-eight years of habit were hard to break. Not that it hurt, it just made my eyes even itchier. Neither rubbing them nor breathing deeply was going to change the report in front of my eyes though. Neither was wishful thinking.

"How?" was all I could ask.

Gemma shrugged, and there was that guarded barrier around her again. Just like after Jules died. "I don't know. We had communication with them for three days after they were taken in by Carindale, and now . . ."

There was this helpless air through the library. Mike, Kyle, Dale, Sienna, Dor, and Chris. Most of the regular council were in here, and no one knew what to say.

Gemma had sent two well-trained Rogue Classes to keep an eye on the goings-on in Carindale. But we hadn't heard from them for almost twenty-four hours. Damn it.

It looked like our neighbors were going to become even more of a sooner-rather-than-later problem. Except, on the other hand, there were almost three thousand people here who depended on us and we had to put their needs first.

But what if Carindale put my settlement in danger?

This. This right here was why I worked in labs with my plants, mostly alone.

"We can't send in back up, Kira." Sienna didn't need her Charisma to make me see how foolhardy that black hole would be.

"At least not yet," added Dor, sending a *look* to the other town admin.

Sienna shrugged. "Look. I want to know what's going on too. But we are Garden City's council, and we have people who depend on us not to screw this all up. So yes. Keep an eye on them, but for now, while we have our own stuff to deal with, we have to gather what observations we can and deal with it if we survive all this Zarrie crap."

She was right and I knew it. We all did. That "let's try to save everyone" attitude was going to get us killed if we weren't careful.

"All right. All right." I held up my hands and focused on Gemma. "Let the scouts stay where they are and observe from the outside and we can wait and see if we get any more communication." Turning to Dor, I raised an eyebrow. "Have Lance and Para been keeping open communications?"

She nodded. "Yeah, but only mundane things. Just checking in every day. It's almost robotic. Hey, did you check that they weren't trying to become robot overlords?"

I laughed and then sobered up. "No, we didn't check."

I winked at her, but part of me wondered if we shouldn't have checked. I couldn't wait until we were leveled enough and safe enough to head over to the north side of Brisbane.

Mike and Dale began divvying up the groups to send out for the day's patrols. We couldn't make the groups too far in advance any longer because of fluctuations in our Adventurers. We'd lost a good fifteen people in the last ten or so days and it wasn't getting any safer out there.

While they talked and sorted, I pulled up the quest.

A Habitable Safe Zone

Part Three: Staying Power

You need to make it 3 months into System Onset as a Township.

Goals:

1 - Gather 3,000 total inhabitants. This may include visiting species.
Current population: 2,902/3,000
Time Limit Remaining: 1 week, 3 days, 16 hours

Just under a hundred people in, like, ten days. We'd been growing steadily, but it was starting to trickle in. We'd only had twelve survivors come in the day before. I point-blank refused to believe that this was all the humans left in such a populous city.

We'd been finding people in the weirdest of places, too. Clumped together often, though the occasional solo survivor popped up here and there. Obviously, apartments in tall flats were common, the height saving them from the monsters on the ground.

But there were also basement dwellers in some of the office buildings around here with lower Levels. We even found someone who survived in a septic tank out near Daisy Hill—Sewer Master was not a Class I would have taken myself, but circumstances made up a lot of minds.

There was even someone who'd turned their mobile van into part of their Class. Several Classes that were super odd, but at the same time had allowed these people to survive.

I didn't need to contribute much to the patrol sorting. They'd pop me in with a main group of people and off I'd go. Every time I left, I promised myself that I would do anything to come back.

It was a promise I didn't ever plan on breaking.

"Hey." Kyle nudged my knee with his own. "Stop daydreaming."

"Yep. That's what I do. All the time." I pushed myself up from the chair, my eyes adjusting as I did so. Bionic eyes. We were certainly living in the future.

I stretched my arms up to get the stiff feeling out of my shoulder. No injuries evident, just that I'd sat in that position a little longer than I liked. We left the library and turned to head up to our little apartment. I'd left my jacket in there and there was no way I was going patrolling without that extra layer of thin armor.

The Shop truly did have everything.

Wisp ran over to me while Dog bounded ahead of her, coming to a stop as he caught up to me. Wombie trudged behind, and I was quite shocked to realize that he was close to as big as Dog now. Almost pony-sized wombat. Excellent.

Yeah, we might have to look into him living outside like his mum did. We really didn't have the room in here.

Speaking of which. Almost three thousand people in the shopping center was really starting to get cramped. With almost five hundred stores here, around what . . . four hundred and forty smaller ones, we were up to almost seven people on average per shop.

There just wasn't enough room. Harvey Norman's with its beds and mattresses, and all the appliances was now just a refuge center for when we had newcomers before we could allocate housing. Ray had taken a group of people and completely reorganized it in the last few weeks.

Still, we had to extend our borders as soon as possible. Just another thing to add to the list that never ended.

My kid attached herself to my waist in that manner of awkward underarm hugs the entire kid kingdom is excellent at. Taking just those few seconds to recharge with some of that love was priceless.

Sadly, it really was only a few seconds.

"Kira, you got a minute?"

I looked up to find . . . Avery, I think it was, standing in front of me. My brain did that whole relating faces to incidences and pulled up her son that my purification ability saved. Right. Kid gloves on, I think.

"What's up, Avery?" I asked, really hoping I'd managed to get my memory centers working properly.

She smiled, a tight-lipped expression, and nodded at Wisp, who I hugged tighter. My daughter was pretty observant, and also a kid whose attention span wasn't always stellar.

"It's okay, Mum. Kylie, Rolo, and Aisha are waiting for me anyway." She gave me a kiss and turned to run, but not before Dog almost knocked me over in an effort to follow her, giving me a slobbering lick on my hand and making me wish I'd waited to have my shower.

Sighing, I motioned for Avery to walk with us. I could listen to whatever she had to say while we walked. I activated Analyze for shits and giggles.

Avery Daly

Level 30 Wrangler

Well, that was an odd name for a Class. Did she wrangle people, pets, beasts . . . ? The thing was, I really wanted to know, too. And I'd successfully just managed to miss everything she'd said.

"Sorry, I'm having one of those mornings. Can you repeat that?"

She looked a little irritated, but sighed. "I get it. You're always so busy. I just wanted to let you know that I've been helping Jana with the kids. Thing is, I think we're going to need to expand to an actual school or else build an extension on the center for one. We're sitting right at two hundred and fifty kids under twelve. And we've tried to accommodate them, even going so far as to use the carpark outside of Aldi and Coles, but there's just so many of them now."

"Oh." I glanced over at where I could see Wisp and her friends. Since Jana had taken responsibility for schooling them all, I hadn't given much thought to anything. Hell, I don't think any of us in the admin positions had.

Report cards weren't exactly needed in this post-apocalyptic setting.

Pushing away that wonderful onslaught of mum guilt that I felt, I nodded at Avery. "Thanks. We'll figure something out."

Avery smiled. "If you leave the school and teaching portions to Jana and myself, we've got your back. That's at least one aspect you can relax about. Don't spread yourself too thin, though. Remember. Wisp is just a little. Sometimes she might be brave just for you."

She had a point. More mum guilt. Fan-fucking-tastic. A part of me wanted to dig my heels in and tell her I was fine raising my own kid, thank you very much. But she did have a very valid point. "Thanks. Sometimes I get caught up in helping make this place work, and I forget how lucky we are to still have our kids."

Because the truth was, we might have a whole heap of them, but we'd lost so many more. And that made the weirdness in Carindale just that much more prevalent. One thing at a time.

"Thanks again, Kira. Nate is being much more careful since the incident, and I have you to thank for that." She leaned forward and gave my arm a squeeze before turning on her heel and walking back from where we'd come. I really needed to grab my jacket and get back to the library so we could finalize and send out the patrols.

I watched her go and glanced at the time. Almost eight in the morning already. Where did it all go?

Oh right. I eyed the next couple of individuals trying to edging over to catch me before I could escape into my apartment. There.

I pinched the bridge of my nose, wondering if I did it enough, maybe I'd black out and not have to listen to people bickering. How the whole library filled while Kyle and I went to get our gear for the patrols, I'd never understand. Except I did, because a five-minute duck out of the library inevitably turned into thirty or sixty minutes for me.

Enough was enough.

"Guys!" Mum voice activated.

The entire library looked at me. Well, not the library itself, but the people in it.

Ginali and Ciago were in the middle of a heated discussion with the Hakarta present. Hirish was nowhere to be seen. Dale was arguing with Evelyn about dungeon groups and what Levels we needed to clear out which areas.

Mike, Drake, and Gary were locked in a deep discussion with Chris and Sarah—so much that I could almost see sparks flying, and not the romantic type. While Gemma was arguing with Ray and Leena about their plans to find more survivors. And IRSHA wasn't even bothering to show up today. In fact, I hadn't seen them much since we got back from Carindale and Dequasha had disappeared, saying she had something important to do.

Leaving me to deal with this shitshow myself.

At least the room stopped short when I shouted. My eyes flared as Mana suppression glowed around them, waiting to be used.

"We have agendas. We need an actual designated school area. Housing needs to be extended, probably best to do that out past Logan Road and the main gate. We should send scouts that way. After all, we know the elderly home along Tryon Street stood up quite well a couple of weeks ago. That's where we got several of our residents. Maybe that would be a good place to start."

I frowned, going through my mental notes. "School. Housing. Border extension. Patrols. Leveling groups, Dungeon regulation groups, and monster Level controls. We don't have time for petty discrepancies, or for our own feelings to get in the way. So just fucking stop.

"If we want this to work. If we don't want whatever weird shit is happening at Carindale to happen here too . . . then we need to be on constant alert."

Though I might have been stating the obvious, it still felt like we'd all been acting like children. If no one else was going to pull the others out of the mud by smacking their faces, then I guess it was going to be me.

"Sorry." Ginali smiled up at me. "I am older and should be wiser. The Cartel just wasn't expecting some of these complications."

He nodded curtly at the Hakarta he'd been having his little tiff with, and the large orc's shoulders relaxed visibly.

"Basically. Now, take something off the to do list that specifically has to do with your own specialty, and get to work on it, please," I asked, hoping they couldn't sense the tiredness in my tone. Tiredness was one of those things I was used to shrugging off. "And we're late getting patrols out, too."

Had to pull a double shift for some obscure reason but your kid still needs to go to her gymnastics meet the next day? Smile, shrug it off, and pull up supermum powers. Guess the apocalypse didn't change everything after all.

"Sorry." Kyle nudged me softly with his elbow and I tried to smile at him.

"It's not you. Not this time. I just feel like we have so much more we need to get done. And we're not doing it. Bickering never got anyone anywhere." I shrugged. "Ten weeks into this thing and shouldn't we be farther along? Like shouldn't we have space ports and teleporters set up already?"

Suddenly Hirish was there, shaking his head. "No. Ten weeks and you are well within the correct parameters. Your technology was not at a stage where you would have understood things like space ports, and thus your ability to procure them is limited by more than just Credits. The knowledge of what to look . . ." He petered off. "Was that rhetorical?"

I nodded. "Mostly. But thanks for that. It's good for us measly humans to have some goals in life." My sarcasm was leaking out again. Luckily our little master crafter was right on time to rescue me from myself.

"Where have you been all morning? You left me to deal with Lousesh. You know we don't get along." I could hear the accusatory tone to Ginali's voice, but Hirish didn't seem to notice, or maybe he just didn't care.

The Hakarta major didn't deign to acknowledge Ginali's slight outburst with an answer. Or at least not an answer the Pharyleri wanted. "I've been speaking with our booking chapter, and CESPOOL lodged an official complaint against the Cartel and 42nd Division of the Hakarta with the Mercenary Faction."

"Say what now?" I asked, noticing as Ginali fell silent, and the room with him.

Hirish had a rather booming voice when he didn't try to conceal it. Now he had everyone's attention.

"CESPOOL claim that we have no right to infringe upon their territory under section 82-9bi of the Financier's Bylaws." He hesitated for a moment, before obviously realizing that most of us in the room had no idea what the hell he was talking about. "It means they're trying to use legal jargon to justify that their occupation is warranted and that we are trespassing, and thus they can evict us all."

"Are they right? Will they win? How would this sort of mediation work?" Kyle asked all the questions popping in to my head much quicker than I could blurt them out.

Lousesh let out a gruff laugh. "No water at all. It's a stalling tactic. This is a Dungeon World. Rules just don't apply like that. Sure, you can buy rights to things, but enforcing ownership? Evicting? Yeah, not going to happen here."

Hirish side-eyed his fellow Hakarta. "Exactly. Basically, what they're doing right now is attempting to gain a Safe Zone without us seeking them out and attacking. Since we weren't hunting them to begin with . . ." He shrugged.

A sly grin crossed his face though, and it felt like a brick dropped into the pit of my stomach.

"What aren't you telling us?" I asked softly, wondering if we should even try to expand our boundaries, beef up our walls, and find more survivors if it meant that the Hakarta were going to blow all our plans up at once.

He smiled.

Have you ever seen an orc smile? It's not all sunshine and raindrops with puppy dog tails. No. An orc smiling is one of the eviler things I've seen in my life. Their sharp teeth and tusks stand out in a way you wouldn't think possible just because their lips pull back. But they do—and it makes them look like nothing but teeth. Land sharks with tusks.

"Don't worry. Questioning our creed and understanding of a binding agreement is not something we tolerate, though we are not strangers to it." Lousesh might have thought he was being comforting, but he really wasn't. "The Hakarta are an honorable people. Sure, we're motivated by money, but essentially everyone is. Questioning our behavior within a contract's boundaries will not be tolerated."

He shook his head and smiled as well. Great. Two smiling freaking Hakarta.

"Spill it out. Explain in plain words." I'd thought beating around the bush was a human trait.

Ginali glanced between the Hakarta and sighed. "Well, he sort of did.

The Hakarta are contract bound to protect the Cartel's interests. We know we are well within our rights to be here. Our claim predates theirs because ours wasn't contingent on having a physically enforcing presence on the landmass at the time. It's all just words. In short: Dungeon Worlds aren't regular worlds. That's pretty much the crux of it."

"They have only bought themselves time. We weren't looking to find them in the first place, only to protect the Cartel's interests when under attack. You have bigger worries than them, from what I've seen," Hirish finished off.

"How long do we have to prepare?" Dale asked, and I could already see him trying to figure out just how much bloodshed all of this would entail. Pity we couldn't forecast that.

"We don't. At the most we'd end up facing a fine or something similar." Lousesh paused as if suddenly thinking of something. "IRSHA could be fined as well, though, due to their fiscal involvement with CESPOOL."

"How long do we have?" Sienna piped up, and I knew exactly what she was thinking. "Like, does this mean that they won't be attacking us for a while?

"Yes. Very likely," Hirish responded promptly.

"So they won't fight us, and we technically shouldn't fight them unless they attack us first?" Kyle sounded it out slowly. "Is that basically it?"

"Yes." Lousesh nodded for emphasis.

None of this made sense to me. Something was off about it. I held up my hand, trying to get it to make sense in my mind. "Wait. So . . . the Zarrie, who attacked us first, who killed several of our Adventurers, have basically asked for a temporary ceasefire? That makes no sense at all."

Ginali watched me, cocking his head to one side. "They obviously have reasons."

But there was something niggling at the back of my mind. "They said they'd be forced to take our settlement if we didn't fork it over, yet they didn't show up with all of their people. Not even when they made that big push."

Hirish eyed me thoughtfully. "This is true. I was led to believe there were more than thirty of them here. But did you not say you found a Zarrie corpse?"

Dale chimed in. "Yep, and it was barely recognizable. Ginali had to get a sample tested."

"Then something is definitely off about this. It is not how the Zarrie mercenaries act." His brow furrowed, making those massive eyebrows do squats. "These actions are strange. They may not be Hakarta, but I have never witnessed this behavior from them." Hirish shrugged and then looked around at all of us. "You are too small. You require more Levels."

Gee. No shit, Sherlock.

Chapter Thirty-Two:
Bulking Up

10 Weeks Post-System Onset

8 a.m.

Mornings had never really bothered me, but I was definitely not a morning person. The thing was, I'd had to become one, oh, say, about ten weeks ago. Still groggy, I'd practically stumbled into the Shop, clutching the kipatchya Ray handed me on the way.

My son was leafing his way through a whole pile of books he'd just conned me into buying. They'd set us back a pretty penny, but they were all about how to utilize Mana more efficiently as a power source. Something that in the end was going to save us a lot of Credits as a settlement.

Plus, I hadn't been fully awake at the time he'd asked if he could go purchase them. I'd have to remember that trick for future me.

I mean, we could buy vehicles and apparently even spacecraft through the Shop, but their quality was highly debatable if they were cheaper, and for those that were a hundred percent reliable? Nope. Those were ten times more expensive than my optical shit. So saving Credits in the long run? Yep. I was in for that.

"You getting everything you want there?" I asked, trying not to startle his concentration levels.

"Mhm." He looked up at me. "Sort of. I'll let you know."

Wisp on the other hand was curled up in a seat with some books of her own. She'd walked into the Shop and asked Chjaveen for three specific books. I got the feeling they were an Earth series. After which, without so much as a word, she curled herself up into a corner with Dog and Wombie, and dove into them.

Me? I was looking for anything I could find on creatures, aliens, any sort of species that might—and it sounded silly even in my own mind—that might maybe eat the young of other species, or siphon off their lifeforce or other gruesome things. I mean, we ate lamb and veal, right? The whole situation the way we'd left it in Carindale gave me frequent bad dreams.

Not being able to contact our spies didn't help either. And regardless of what the scouts Gemma sent out to maintain a safe distance and report back said, I was highly suspicious. And maybe a little scared for our own people here in Garbo.

I'd—briefly—looked into just buying information on the settlement. But since I didn't even know the right question to ask, the costs were ridiculous. I couldn't justify spending hard-earned Credits on hunches, not when the answers themselves might not even be particularly useful.

So, research first. Then asking the right questions.

I didn't even know what I was looking for, to be honest, and I didn't have long. We had to head out and do some herd thinning, not to mention some leveling up. Sunlight was a wasting. Still, information wasn't going to hurt.

Species Listing As Approved by the Galactic Council
Cost: 3,900 Credits

Species: Endangered and Dangerous—Just How Much Do We Know

Cost: 2,500 Credits

Okay, so the latter read more like a tabloid, but I was still curious. It would give me something to look at during the thirty seconds of downtime I managed to find in a day. Maybe after we'd dealt with the current issues, and I'd managed to level higher, and my kids were completely safe.

"Mum." Jackson stood next to me, two very heavy bags dangling from either hand.

"Mhmm," I asked him, closing the book and handing over the two of them to Chjaveen. It wasn't like I could stand in the Shop and read them, but I could leaf through their contents tables and double check that I was actually grabbing something useful.

"Mana Potions. Health Potions too." He wouldn't meet my eyes, and I knew why, sort of, in a way. He was going out to Level too. At almost 30, he was on the high end of our people.

"Of course." I smiled at him and gave him a hug because he couldn't move fast enough to get away from me. His relief at my not getting upset was palpable and tradable for affection.

Thing was, I just had to lock that mum part of me up. If I listened to her overprotective screaming in the background, we were going to lock ourselves in one of the bottom-level storage rooms and never come out. So, instead, I chose the marginally functional option. Support my son, help make him stronger, and that way we could survive together. Right?

After purchasing my own books, I walked over and kneeled down next to Dog's head. His side was supporting Wisp as she read her books.

"C'mon, buttercup. Let's go."

She glared up at me sullenly. Damn it. But at least she moved and came silently with us.

"Are you going to tell me what's wrong?" I asked as we exited the Shop and walked through the center toward the Crafting Cartel's station.

Wisp shook her head and grabbed at my jacket with her free hand. Okay, I wouldn't panic about it. There were probably all sorts of thoughts up in that head of hers. Instead, I gave her hand a light squeeze and continued on to the Cartel.

I didn't visit it as often as I'd like, but the courtyard area had transformed into this bustling and constantly busy area. We were growing by more than just our city inhabitants. The crafting delegation gave us a blacksmith, weapon-smith, apothecary, and tailor just to start. Not to mention that Ginali pretty much bought any rare thing for an amazing price, or else gave us trades that helped out more than Credits.

The only concern was where our own people were lined up, desperate to get their own hands on the materials we brought back to level their Skills. We needed to upgrade them too, but the quality of the work they produced just didn't make it very economical.

Luckily, Dor had figured out a way to share things out; and since we had so few crafters of our own, helping them upgrade was not a huge burden on our resources. And the Cartel were all for helping our settlement grow.

"What would you like today?" Malina smiled up at me. I still hadn't quite had the guts to ask her just what her species was, but I was constantly fascinated by her. She looked, for all my far-reaching attempts to find something to compare her to, like an armadillo on two legs, with a human face. Her armor never failed to throw me.

She had long and delicate fingers, and I could see how she might have been attracted to making potions.

"We need to top Jackson and myself up on Mana and Health potions for the next few days." I smiled at her, hoping I still had some Credits available to use with her, which I should, considering the amount of shit I constantly traded in.

She went over several of her boxes, and into a trunk she only dived into occasionally. "Two dozen each, do you think that is enough?"

As long as shit didn't completely hit the fan, we should be good. "For today, definitely." I only hoped I wasn't jinxing anything by saying that. Diminishing returns meant we shouldn't be skulling them anyway.

"Excellent." She handed over the potions through a trade option that allowed them to funnel straight into our inventory. At 36, my inventory now let me hold 144 items. So that was pretty nice, especially since Healing potions and the like stacked.

"Anything else?" She asked and I wished I could be one of those jokesters who asked for a million Credits because she had said anything, but instead I just smiled.

"I think we're good for now."

Just as we were about to leave, she spoke up again. "Be careful out there. Your wilderness is unpredictable."

I smiled at her. "Thank you." Because be damned if I didn't know that intimately.

"C'mon, Mum, we're late." Jackson grabbed my hand, tugging me toward the gathering area, and Wisp just trailed along behind us. I was starting to worry about her and how she was dealing with all of this, having been particularly quiet over the last few days.

"Give me a moment." I squeezed his hand before I let go of it and Jackson shrugged.

"Don't blame me if we leave without you!" he said, flashing me a grin before running off.

I bent down and stopped my kid from trudging around like her world had fallen apart. Apart from the fact that it actually had. Well, it didn't really get us anywhere, did it?

"Speak!"

She actually giggled but then sobered up and locked gazes with me. "I'm just tired. I miss Dad. I miss gym and my friends. I want the world to go back to how it used to be, and I don't want to have to deal with all this."

"Oh, my baby." I gathered her into a huge hug and lifted her to sit on my hip so we could continue walking. "How about when we get home today, we go up to the roof carpark and do a sleepover under the stars?"

She considered this and then smiled. "Counteroffer! How about we go sleep outside with Mumma Wombutt? We'll still see the stars and be outside, but she won't be alone either."

"Deal!" I held out my hand. "Pinkie promise?"

Wisp linked her pinkie with me, her expression somber. "Pinkie promise."

And we shook on it.

❖

10 Weeks Post-System Onset
2 p.m.

The more I'd tried, the more my combat wombat idea was only good in defense of the settlement. She was large and cumbersome and mostly preferred tunneling underground to walking over it. Sadly, I had to abandon the idea of her coming out on patrols with us, but that didn't mean she wasn't a fantastic part of the potential defensive capacity of our town itself.

Still, I really could have used her butt armor right about now.

Level 36, so close to 37 and another Skill Point. Really, I felt they should be giving those out every Level after 30. It took so damn long to kill enough. My newer Skills drained a lot of Mana. I couldn't wait to get to the next tier and become a Mana battery.

Evelyn moved to the outside of our circle, her eyes following the hulking mutation of what I could only imagine was a cane toad coupled with a fucking bull ant.

Have you ever been bitten by a bull ant?

My brain shuddered at the memory of sitting down on the oval for sports day and being assaulted by a nest of bull ants. Their bites stung like buggery and left horrible welts, sort of like hives. Their mandibles really packed a punch when they were a centimeter long, but this thing in front of us was huge. It stood about the height of a small horse, perhaps a large pony, right up to our chests.

Bull Toad

Level 42

Great.

Its mandibles jutted out of a swollen face, and though its beady eyes resembled that of a bull ant, the rest of the shape of the head was definitely cane toad. Just like the segmented body was of the ant, but the rough, warty skin was all toad. The toxin-secreting poison glands on their shoulders, though—those were there, and larger than they had any right to be.

I preferred the ones we'd found on the way to Carindale.

Slime gathered around its feet, and the fetid smell that wafted from it made me gag. Toads only fired their venom off when they felt threatened, but these were new and improved. From the way Molly's new shield began to smoke as she wielded it, the creature thing was obviously feeling majorly under attack.

With its legs all toad and very little ant, it swiped out at us, but didn't need to touch us in order to affect us. There was a wind component to its attacks that made its swiping extend and strike us when we didn't expect it. The only small mercy was that the wind-strikes didn't include the venom.

Mana flooded the creature's vicinity, lighting it up as it used the power every time it attacked. From what I could see it didn't have infinite power, just like we didn't. And I doubted the Bull Toads had their own version of a Shop . . . so it was unlikely it had access to Mana potions.

Kyle barreled into me, pushing me out of the way of a sudden gust of wind attack that would have smacked me straight in the chest if he hadn't saved me.

"Thanks," I said, irritated at myself. Less watching the Mana and speculating over what these monsters could and couldn't do, and more attacking. I hefted the Warhammer in my grasp as my brother nodded and cast another of his attacks.

A dart of bright red tore through the side of the Bull Toad, eliciting an alien-sounding squeal from its throat. Venom splashed out of its shoulder pouches, and only Sange's quick-thinking reaction of casting their barrier over both Tasha and Molly saved them from being eaten away by acid.

Maybe it wasn't only the quick thinking. We'd all been mostly fighting together for months now. We knew how to work around each other and how to support one another while fighting together.

"Pull back!" Molly shouted.

We moved as one, a well-oiled group, and stepped back. Evelyn and Ray fanned out to the right, while Kyle and I took the left. Tasha and Gemma were up with Molly as always, nice and in the fray. Drake tended to swap between close combat and ranged, while Dannin rarely stopped moving. Even for a Ranger he exhausted me.

Holding the Bull Toad's attention, Molly smashed her shield down in front of it, knocking it back with a wave of force that extended her defenses for about thirty seconds. It squealed again and had a hard time righting itself back up after the hole Kyle had ripped through it.

We all focused everything we had on it. Topsoil, Planted In Place, Mudslide, Stone's Throw . . . you name it, I focused fire with every portion that I could. Whenever there was an opening I felt confident about, I darted in, swinging my hammer with all my might.

It never did as much damage as I wanted it to. Maybe I needed to pour more Strength into my stats, but it still hit with a satisfying thud every time it struck. Ripping at the flesh through the sheer force of the hammer head, my melee abilities were getting better.

Just not as fast as my casting abilities.

Only real negative about melee? The smells. When I was behind my walls, fighting at a distance and just concentrating on casting, I never had to get a lungful of the creature's scent, the musky smell of unwashed fur or the repellent acridity of slime.

And in this Bull Toad's case—I'd prefer to wade through a sewer.

Evelyn and Dannin rained down arrows on the thing, while Tasha, Drake, and Gemma laid into it from every possible angle, giving it few options to stop and focus fire any of its own attacks. Knives and blades coming at it from all different angles made it squeal in frustration this time, and Molly's shield bash left it dazed and confused.

Ray and Kyle assaulted it from the sides, and slowly its health ticked down to nothing.

There were no fireworks or celebration once it fell to its side, its body twitching in death throes, just our own labored breathing from a hard fight with a creature that had no right to exist.

"Well, then. That mutated." Evelyn's voice held a strain of disbelief. Couldn't blame her. Some of the shit we were fighting was like two nightmares rolled into one and baked at high temperature.

We looted the beast and I sighed. "There are going to be more of these. I'm just surprised they weren't all together in the first place."

Kyle cringed. "Why did you have to say that?"

He had a point. But I shrugged instead of letting it get to me. "If there's one thing I've learned in this hell of an apocalypse, it's the end of the world as we knew it. Everything is jinxed."

My brother paused for a moment and laughed. I think it was the first full-throated laugh I'd heard out of him since all of this began. "Good point. Now check your stats, I think you leveled."

I glanced at the blinking notifications in the corner of my eye and pulled them up. He was correct. I had some catching up to do. All the settlement and parenting slowly chipped away at leveling time. He was already 40.

It was a relief to have leveled—I needed some of those damned Skill Points.

Congratulations!

You have gained a Level. Welcome to Level 37.

I frowned at it. Leveling past the twenties was such a damned grind. I guess if we went dungeon crawling every single day for hours on end, we might be significantly higher, but who had time for that? Quickly distributing my points, I took a look at the screen. There wasn't much time to peruse the information in the middle of a creature culling, but I did need to make sure I was at my strongest for any coming fights.

Level 37 also allowed for me to get my last 30s Skill. Now I had Stone's Throw, not that I really wanted it. I just wanted the skill above it, which I couldn't get without it.

Status Screen			
Name	Kira Kent	Class	Ecological Chain Specialist
Race	Human (Female)	Level	37 (14,252 XP to next Level)

Titles			
Diviner			
Health	500	Stamina	500
Mana	1120	Mana Regeneration	14.2ps*
Attributes			
Strength	32	Agility	30
Constitution	50	Perception	77
Intelligence	112	Willpower	70
Charisma	25	Luck	20
Class Skills			
Shield of Power		Leadership	3
Analysis	5	Mana Sense*	16
Diviner*	2	Mana Purification	1
Combat Skills			
Mana Attunement	2	Water Siphon	2
Earth Barricade	2	Blood Transfer	1
Rock Slide	1	Mana Transfer	2
Implantation	3	Treesong	2
Topsoil	2	Planted In Place	1
Blood Dispersion	1	Stone's Throw	1
Vine Defense	1		

Tier Four (31-39)
Vine Defense

Effect: Increase your Target's armor by 100% for 15 seconds by calling on the resilience of nature.

Note: Applying Topsoil and Treesong can boost the increase to 150%.

Caution: Fully effective only in vegetation-dense surroundings.

Mana Cost: 75 Mana (+cost of Topsoil and Treesong)

Blood Dispersion

Due to your devotion to understanding the world and mechanics of biological evolution, you are now able to corral the lifeblood of a target to aid your party. Damage done to the target is absorbed by this Skill and dispersed as health to you and your allies.

Effect: 5% of net damage done to target is returned as health to all members in the party within a 20 meter range.

Mana Cost: 95

Stone's Throw

Similar to Rock Slide, this ability allows you to form any single type of earth, from dirt to pebbles, into a projectile to be thrown at your opponent. Must have requisite materials on-hand for Stone's Throw to be used.

Be wary of where you choose to use this.

Effect: The Stone's Throw will cause 180 damage. If the stone breaks on impact, it has the potential to cause another 25% falling damage to those it cascades over.

Mana Cost: 75

Well, that was it. I had all of my Tier-Four Skills now. Abilities. Whatever they were. To be honest, I didn't really want any of the Tier-Four

Skills except Blood Dispersion, but since I wanted the Tier-Five Skills in the same branch, I had to get the pre-requisite Skill.

Stupid System.

Really annoying too, since my Class built upon itself, unlike some of the others I knew of. Like, the Ranger Classes were much more straightforward; with an entire Skill line just adding attribute points. But no, mine had to do weird things like dependencies.

Pulling my head out of my screens, I noticed something different. The Mana flow near us was amplifying. There was no other way to describe it. Near us, though, not like around us. Close enough that I was fairly certain the location was the shopping center. Home.

I couldn't panic, so I had to push that down. There wasn't time for that when lives depended on every single second. Closing my eyes, I felt around for the Mana flows in the area, and oriented myself with them. Definitely heading toward Garbo in a subtle flow.

It had to be the Zarrie, right? This was the same Mana signature we'd seen a couple of weeks ago when Zyrilian darted out at us. It had been all around him then.

Farther away from us. . . . Thoughts whirred through my head. There were just too many things that didn't add up anymore.

Injured Zarrie who weren't hurt by us. The occasional super high-Leveled mutant creatures out there. Not to mention the damned Zarrie corpse we'd found before anyone knew they were here.

I didn't have time for conspiracy theories. Whatever the signature belonged to, their target seemed to be Garbo. After all, it was our trade hub that stood in the way of everything, right?

"We have to head back. Get to the vehicles, now."

The thing about being a mum is that you to learn to turn off everything else and just do what your kid needs when they really need you.

Tired? Way too often, but Kid One is having a shit day at school and needs you to be there. Pushing away that exhaustion, putting them first for the duration they need you—that is just what we do.

I was already exhausted, my Mana low, but that didn't matter. Chugging a potion, I set off at a jogging pace I wouldn't even have contemplated had the System not shown up and rejuvenated that old knee injury of mine.

Apparently being a mum had prepared me for an apocalypse. Put all the exhaustion behind you and be there for those that need you.

Now that I'd seen the Mana signature, now that I could feel the unsettled frequency of the waves, I knew that we didn't have much time to make it back.

My Communicator flashed with a message from Jackson. Which meant he was close enough to me, close enough to Garbo for his communication to reach me. It made my blood run cold for a split second.

We're heading to Garbo too. Lousesh got a notification. Love you, Mum.

Be careful. Don't be overconfident. Love you too. I sent my message back and prayed that the pit I felt forming in my stomach wasn't a premonition.

Chapter Thirty-Three:

Garbo

10 Weeks Post-System Onset

3 p.m.

Smoke billowed from the top of our parapets as we came into view. The closer we got, the more difficult it was to navigate the terrain in the vehicles at any significant speed. It might have seemed like a good idea at the time to let Mumma Wombutt tunnel around, thus making the road difficult to traverse, but it had disadvantaged us too.

We ended up having to leap out and abandon them back up on Logan Road so we could make it to the walls in time.

The ground shook the closer we got, and I realized the massive hulking shape moving toward us was Mumma Wombutt. She got to me, nosed my hair briefly, and somehow didn't manage to knock me down. She looked straight at me as she stretched a stumpy and armored little leg out.

I kind of wondered what she was doing out here but didn't have time to give it more than a fleeting thought. I climbed up onto her back, gripping her coarse fur desperately. Kyle and the others followed, all of us gripping for dear life. I suddenly understood why she'd done that. Not only was she trying to help us get past the torn-up road, but she knew what I was only just realizing.

We couldn't get to the gates, not with the number of jackals I could see just over the other side of the road, using the shops and the houses as their own defenses. Yet another reason we needed to expand outside of the center.

It was still up the roads a ways, so she took us to the southeastern section of the parapets and harumphed.

"I get it, girl." I petted her gently, unsure if she'd be able to feel that.

But sitting on Mumma's withers, we could almost reach the wall—with a little help from our friends, that is. The others clambered over with assistance from those already up there.

"You got this, Sange?" I asked, knowing they'd understand what I was saying. Their response was a curt nod, as they were already worrying at their lip and I knew just what they were thinking.

Damn it, I really needed that Mana Stone spell.

Wombutt remained on the ground beneath us, traveling with us as we ran up toward the gate as if daring anyone to hurt us. I was definitely taking that night under the stars with her as soon as we sorted all this crap out.

An explosion went off right next to Mumma's feet, and I grew worried for her, but she snarled, her body shaking with what I think was rage. A part of me wished I'd have risked riding her. That would have been a hoot.

There was anger in this Mumma, and I was behind her a hundred percent. Finally, we made it up to the gate. Mumma gave me a look that pretty much said "about time" and took off, barreling toward our attackers.

At the last minute, she spun around, letting her legs skitter across the ground as she plowed into a whole group of Zarrie. One of them, their Tank, even managed to activate an ability that made her rise above the glowing shield he angled, a couple of his friends sprawling face down under it for protection.

That did little good, since that meant her entire armored butt was above them when she activated a Skill or something. One that suddenly had her lower body flexing downwards, slamming said armored butt onto the three remaining platoon members that hadn't bounced backwards.

Strong or not, getting squashed by armored Wombutt was probably not a nice way to go.

Kyle threw a spell toward the Mumma as more attacks targeted her, a warding or something—I wasn't sure. But I shot him a grateful look before I set myself up on the wall to track incoming attacks. Hirish jogged up to us, a concerned look pinching his face. I don't think the Hakarta were used to being worried about anything, and this was giving him difficulties.

"What?" I asked. There wasn't time for me to speak politely. We had people to protect, and I needed Evelyn and Dannin concentrating with me to prevent whatever damage we could. Dequasha wasn't anywhere to be seen, so I couldn't rely on her face-melting powers.

A swing of my hands had Rock Slide erupt, throwing a pair of Zarrie under the earthen attack. It didn't kill them, but the few who I missed had to dodge and take their time, breaking their rush.

I dreaded to think of the Credits repairs were going to cost. Again.

"Lousesh isn't back yet."

Fuck.

My gut clenched, threatening to bring up anything I'd eaten that morning. If Lousesh wasn't back yet, that meant Jackson wasn't here. He wasn't safe. He was still out there.

"Breathe, Kira. I'll find him." And Kyle was off before I could say anything, leaving me Healerless. But I'd been that way last time. I'd survive.

"The smaller children are all safe inside," Hirish continued, and even if he might be a mercenary orc type of dude, at least I knew then that he also had a compassionate bone in his body and it helped. Sure, it didn't help to the extent that my stomach stopped trying to turn me inside out, but it helped.

Breathe.

Focus.

Being in this place right now was what I could do to help. Just protect those people on the walls, the people inside, the people who'd become like family to me.

I lost myself in the focus it took to follow the Mana waves. My optical implants engaged as I threw myself into following the trail of Mana as it was gathered and used, the explosive way it dispersed when expended.

"Left mid, Ice Lance."

Evelyn let off a fiery shower of arrow splendor to counter the incoming ice attack, protecting the walls and the people on it who were lobbing over our own attacks, or firing directly on them.

Damn it. We'd barely recovered from the previous attack. I was severely unimpressed by their timing.

Down in the field, the Hakarta troops stayed in formation. One of them was situated directly below the gate to give our easiest point of entry the protection it needed. I had three more sets of troops in my view, although one was too far down almost to the old tax building, so close to where Mumma Wombutt had thrown us on the wall that I couldn't really focus on them and maintain my vigilance where I was.

There were several of our human ground troops out there as well and the several IRSHA members I knew were scattered in with the Hakarta troops. Except for Dequasha. Where the hell was she?

Hakarta and our own troops were assigned letters. A through D for the former, and E through G for the latter. Right wall to my side with mid, far, and close. Same on the left. Don't come at me about east and west; that just wasn't my thing. My brain didn't work that way.

"Fire incoming over Hakarta Troop B," I called out, my mind working overtime to allocate everything. "Arrow rain, Troop A. Watch the gate."

Every once in a while, when I had time or a break or just felt it was better, I used my own Mana. I had to be careful though; even the fractions of a second it took to activate a Skill could mean an attack slipping through.

But sometimes, whether it was a Water Siphon used to throw off a caster or a Rock Slide to bowl over a group of climbers, it was just more effective.

Both Ray and Dannin took my directions in stride, working in unison with Evelyn to make sure all of my spots were dealt with as I called them out.

"Fire over G. Earth under F." Earth was something I had to deal with, and often meant the next overhead attack was going to hit despite my best abilities.

"I've got F."

I didn't recognize the voice, but I glanced to my side and noticed Avery there, her expression serious as she concentrated on the line of sight I gave her.

Great. Now I didn't have to juggle so much.

Except despite focusing on incoming spells and attacks to focus on, my worry for Jackson began to push at my thoughts, trying to slip through and make me slip up.

"You've got this," Evelyn said, her voice a quiet source of confidence behind me. "He'll be okay. Let's just make it through this."

She was right. We could do this.

Molly dug her shield into the ground down below, leading E Group without her usual Healer. I didn't like that she'd gone out there, but I knew why. She was our highest Level human Tank. We needed her to use that damned shield to fend off unfriendly fire. And Sange was needed to reinforce the defense shielding.

And boy, was there a lot of defending needed. Penetrator rounds, hundreds of them fired in a second toward the wall. Energy beams, playing across hardened stone. Spells of pure force, even a fist that formed from a jackal's hand that tore at the walls.

Sange had to shift focus constantly, doing their best and listening as I called out attacks.

So instead of Sange, I could see Dale down there accompanying Molly, making sure she was warded, and taking as little damage as possible while trios of Zarrie ground troops threw themselves at us. Three of them versus eight of us. The difference in Advanced Classes against us was ridiculous.

But they only had so many Advanced Classes. And the difference between their higher-Level Basic Classes and ours was getting smaller and smaller with each day that passed.

Just wait until we got there. The afternoon dragged on, and my concentration waned more than once.

Though something nagged at me, constantly, and it wasn't my missing son. Surely the Zarrie were more organized than this. If the Hakarta were technically a rival mercenary group, I failed to see how the Zarrie would ever gain clients over them.

There was cheap, and there was incompetent. From what I'd seen so far when it came to trying to besiege our little town, there appeared to be this strange air of desperation and that belied everything I'd read about them. Well, and frankly the first experiences I'd had with them out in the wilds.

There, they'd been in command and deadly. Opponents I wanted to run away from. Cold, collected, and fierce. But now . . . I shook my head, refocusing my attention where it needed to be.

These were all things I could concern myself with later.

The first time it happened, several Ice Lances hit the far lower left wall, causing several injuries among the defenders standing on it. Shaking it so hard that I watched as one defender staggered backwards, falling off the wall and clutching a bleeding neck. Alive, I hoped.

If he was alive, he could heal. Probably. If the Skill wasn't a damage-over-time one.

When it happened the second time I wanted to kick myself. The fire shots broke through the shielding directly at the gate, latching on and burning a good portion of our otherwise-protected entrance before they could be extinguished. It was going to take a huge amount of Credits to repair that.

Still, we continued on, fighting for what we'd built. Molly's group was creeping to the fore, mowing down several of the Zarrie in their path, yet not without their own casualties. At least Molly and Dale seemed to be surviving, and when others couldn't continue, they were retrieved by our medical teams and replaced with someone else.

The points and Credits we'd put into the city's defense shielding were paying off, but I wasn't sure how much longer it would hold. It had taken an awful beating so far.

One of the biggest surprises was when I realized it was Ginali, standing atop the parapet of the tower, looking over the gate and tracking all of the combat in front of us. He'd stepped in when Dale had to go with Molly, and Kyle ran to look for my son. I'd have to remember to thank him. Once we got out of this.

The Coefficient Crafting Cartel had almost as much at stake in this as we did. They were determined to protect their investment too. Suddenly I noticed Hirish standing next to me again, his brow furrowed in that odd way. Such large eyebrows never bode well for overly expressive facial expressions.

I swear I'd seen him on the battlefield but a minute ago.

"I'll take over from here."

"You can't see their attacks before they hit," I said, waving him away.

"No, I can't, but this device can for about twenty minutes anyway." He gestured to the thing he was pulling out of his inventory. All I could think of was that it didn't look cheap. Like I'd realized before, if you had enough money, the Shop had everything.

"Save that for—" And then I realized why he was doing that.

The gates down below had just opened. Sure, they squealed in a low pitch as they were forced to swing in. Having taken damage, it took a lot more energy to get them open than it usually did.

I'd been so focused on my work, on protecting the walls that I hadn't noticed them coming home. When I dialed my optics all the way in, one body filled with Mana looked like another. I stopped seeing physical forms, just Mana waves in all of their constantly varying glory.

"Thanks," I said before I dashed off looking for my kid's patrol and my twin. He wasn't dead; I knew he wasn't. My stupid familial and parental menus would have popped up and told me, but I couldn't help that feeling, that motherly sense that something was undeniably wrong.

❖

The parking area was a mess. Hastily erected tents practically covered all of it, depending on the barrier over the settlement to protect them from overhead incoming attacks. I didn't care what people thought about twin senses or motherly instincts, but I knew my where my boy wasn't and simply headed to where I was certain he was.

My first view was of Kyle, half covered in a green, stinking glop of slime. His dark hair was matted by the stuff and red blood mingled all over his torso, creating a surreal sort of sickly green that reminded me of vomit.

Beyond him, on a gurney, was another dark head full of matted hair. My stomach clenched, trying to upchuck everything in sight, but I pushed on. I'd been through worse. I'd nursed him back from pneumonia when he was five, from breaking his leg in three places when he was eight, and I'd seen him into his teenage years.

Without noticing it, my steps had slowed, becoming hesitant even.

His usually dark olive skin was pale, sickly, and there was a large gash from the top of his head down to his chin. Even though a part of me knew the System would heal it, the other part knew that had this happened outside of this apocalypse, my son would be dead.

Hell.

If Kyle hadn't healed him—and I knew he had, because there was Kyle-shaded Mana signature running all through my kid's system—Jackson would be dead.

His entire left side was a fucking mess.

Ripped up flesh, gravel stuck all through it, traces of venom, too. Maybe they'd encountered a Bull Toad, or something worse. One of those globs that got Kylie's mom way back when we were first catapulted into this travesty.

Like gravel rash on acid, with a helping of shit Kyle couldn't cure. I'm not even sure if people were gathered around him; my brain wasn't coping with this. It didn't matter that he'd be healed eventually, what mattered was that my baby boy was lying in front of me injured badly.

Next thing I knew I was next to him, placing my hand on his chest. He didn't know I was there, not unconscious as he was, but maybe he could feel his mum standing here, murmuring to him. I started sensing his Mana, understanding what was happening and muttering orders to Kyle. He took directions with aplomb, working with me to fix the poison.

Gods. I wish I had him, had this ability when we first started. We could have saved Kylie's mum, the woman whose name I'd never know. I was sure of it.

This wasn't like it had been for Nate. Not the same thing, but working with Kyle, I knew I could help a little. Anything to make the healing easier, quicker, more in line with what the System usually did.

Don't let my baby boy die. Please don't let my baby boy die.

"Kira." Kyle's hands were on my shoulders, lending me strength I so desperately needed. He'd always been there, my entire life. We picked up the pieces and glued each other back together on so many occasions.

"It's okay. He'll heal up. I made it in time." He paused, then added, "I can't stay, even though you want me to, even though I want to. I have to help others."

Even so, I could hear what he wasn't saying. That he was telling me that he barely made it in time, that several minutes later, and Jackson would be gone.

"I know." But it hurt. It hurt that I hadn't been the one to find him, that I hadn't been the one to save him. Most of all, it hurt that I wasn't able to protect him when I'd promised him, promised myself.

His body reacted sluggishly, his healing barely speeding up after everything Kyle had done. Even so, even so, I could see how his Health ticked up.

Like Grave, the super slow music tempo my piano teacher once tortured me with. It ticked over now, wringing each and every catch of breath from me.

The tightness in my chest began to back off a little, subside, even. I'd not done much, but I'd done what I could. Maybe . . . maybe I should stay with him and make sure he knew I was there, that I hadn't abandoned my Level . . . 32 kiddo to his own fate. Damn. 32. What an amazing kid he was.

"Mum?" His voice was hoarse, and his eyes were still closed, and I wasn't sure if he was really awake yet. But his hand flailed slightly, his good one, the right one since his left side was still visibly knitting itself back together. Even the wound on his face was clearing up.

I sighed and took his hand. The relief at him surviving made me feel selfish. I'd left Hirish up there with their device to protect our town while I came down to make sure my son survived.

Whatever. I think I had a right to be selfish, just for a few precious minutes.

Leaning forward, I placed a gentle kiss on his forehead to the side of his closing wound. "Love you, my boy," I said, surprised to see a tear fall from me. Well, that escalated quickly. A part of me felt laughter bubbling, but there was no set of circumstances in which mirth was warranted right now.

He squeezed my hand gently. "I'm okay. Don't worry."

I didn't like those words, but I nodded and gave him one more kiss before pulling myself tall. "Got to get back to the wall."

Kyle nodded at me, his hands weaving Skills on the others, already targeting around him, helping lend light to the dimly lit makeshift camp, too. Helping, rather than staying still like I was.

Such a good kid.

I recognized Darren, sitting there a little shellshocked, and Nate as well. They were all going to live, so that was a bonus.

Even so, the fact that the Zarrie had taken it upon themselves to strike at all . . . that was on them. Regardless of how odd I found their behavior.

I was done playing it cool.

Chapter Thirty-Four:
Activate

Anger is one of the base emotions, and for me, right then, it fueled me. I fingered my Warhammer, wishing I could just take it and beat the living shit out of all the bastards out there who thought it would be a good idea to attack us today.

Mumma Wombutt was out there still, along with Hakarta Troop B, who were making sure she didn't take a mortal wound. Palmdale Shopping Center and the police headquarters had never looked flatter. Mumma had taken out their hiding spots, and now any attacks the Zarrie launched had to be from further away, or else out in the open.

In the open we could stop them easier, and from farther away, the volume of Skills they had available to them dropped significantly. Their attacks either didn't have the range or didn't do much damage. The Motor Inn was about to go on the chopping block from the way Hakarta B and Mumma were angling, and our little troop of what I would call snipers were sitting pretty on the top of the OfficeWorx building halfway down the parking lot.

All in all, my twenty minutes' absence hadn't killed anyone that I could tell, and the pain behind my eyes had abated somewhat. It was amazing how much stress I could cause myself with what-ifs.

I was still angry.

"Thanks."

Hirish seemed relieved to see me, and I didn't blame him. It had taken a considerable amount of self-control to pull myself away from my son. And I only had others' words for it that Wisp was indoors and safe and sound.

But there'd been no sight of Dog, so I tended to believe it.

Yet again I wasn't sure why there seemed to be so many fewer Zarrie than Hakarta. Sure, we'd found one Zarrie corpse . . . I mean, we only had like eighty of them. In the grand scheme of things, that wasn't much. But from what I'd been able to see, the Zarrie might have started out with that many, but they'd lost several of their ranks.

How, though? We weren't hunting them, and we certainly hadn't killed that many of them in these fights.

Maybe they were waiting for backup.

As I took my place again and regained my overview of the siege, I realized two things.

The first was that we were pushing them back. The Zarrie weren't stupid, and they'd attacked when we had most of our patrols out of the complex with only a handful of people left behind. At least people who were capable of defending our home from their incoming hordes. We'd had about fifteen-odd patrols out working on leveling, clearing, and maintaining the creature population.

From what I could see, Jackson's had been the last to make it back here, and I couldn't tell why. After all, he'd been relatively close to my group at the time we learned of the attack.

Though their presence hadn't increased once Jackson's group was back, so what had attacked that patrol?

Secondly, the Zarrie obviously hadn't been aided by their legal petition in any way, which made me curious as to why they'd lodged the damned thing in the first place.

The distance between the parapet now and where the majority of the Zarrie were had grown so much that I couldn't reach them with Earth Barriers, and I couldn't reach them with Implantation. And so it was that I had all of this anger at how injured my son had been bottled up with nowhere to turn to except finding every single one of those bastards who were targeting our walls.

And maybe, just maybe it helped fuel the thoughts that something was wrong. Not just "hey, my kid got injured badly" wrong, but gut-wrenching *Mana* even trying to tell me that there was more to this—that sort of wrong.

Still, not even the churning feeling in my stomach detracted from the fact that we were still under desperate attack by the Zarrie. Since Evelyn, Dannin, and Ray could target off me, this time I could pick out casters and have them do my killing for me.

It wasn't like a first-person shooter. We didn't get headshots—well, we did, but it didn't one-shot these creatures. Stupid System. Still, it definitely sent them scurrying behind their lines or risk getting taken down.

We kept hammering them, the entire thing a giant roundabout, since the moment they finished healing, they'd creep back. I was thinking of how best to switch tactics, when my Mana Sense started tingling.

And when I say tingling, I mean making me shake visibly. I wasn't sure what it was, but something in the atmosphere gave me chills.

Mana Attunement had nothing to do with it this time, either. When the two of them worked together, I felt like one of those gold-seeking sticks on constant vibration. But this was different. There was something in them-thar hills, and Brisbane was hilly as fuck.

I shook my head, focusing on taking down the few remaining Zarrie who were still too stubborn to know when they'd lost a battle. Perhaps I was a little more ruthless than I needed to be, but at the same time, if we were too nice, we wouldn't survive long.

But we had to. More so because we needed all this Zarrie, CESPOOL nonsense to disappear so we could figure out what was wrong with Carindale. One crisis at a time.

Having a second team target on top of my own trio helped really hammer those Zarrie down. In fact, I was pretty sure the first time we did that, we killed one of the buggers.

I had to give it to them. They might not be as organized as the Hakarta, but they were hardy little buggers. Dying was something they avoided with finesse . . . which only made me worry more about what the hell had killed that Zarrie all those weeks ago.

Focused as I was on two of the mages who'd inched their way toward our walls with, what I thought, was the intention of lighting them on fire, I didn't notice the one to my very far left who was aiming an Ice Lance straight at me.

Now, we did have shielding over the entire settlement bought with settlement points and loads of Credits, but it was basic grade. Anything thrown hard and fast with the ability to pierce was going to find a point where it could shatter a small section of the dome and break through.

I turned, time slowing for me in the way it did whenever heavy Mana flows were involved. The icicle hit the dome, partially shattering, yet the tip broke through the magic protecting us and hurtled what was left of the projectile toward me.

Evelyn's scream echoed through my head as she plummeted into me, pushing me aside and almost over the top of the parapet as she took the brunt of the icicle into her thigh.

She screamed in agony, and I focused on the culprit as I scrambled to my feet, readying Topsoil and Treesong together to drag that fucker into the ground so it could swallow him up.

But I didn't have to, because Mumma Wombutt crunched him under her hiney. I kid you not, she literally sat on that bastard for me, squishing him beneath her so hard that he barely managed to crawl away.

Rather than allow that, I threw Topsoil and Treesong at him, pinning him to the ground as the grasses bloomed and grew before twisting upwards to wrap themselves around him. I felt Mana flood out of me, the entire attack wasteful, but I was too pissed to care.

So pissed, until Mumma got up, backed up again and sat down.

The notification in the corner of my vision told me my revenge was done, so I turned away, my attention fully on Evelyn. She was already healing, and the fact that it was a javelin of ice meant that the damned weapon that hit her was also already melting. Didn't mean that it didn't hurt like hell.

We didn't have a Healer up here on the wall with us, and I couldn't think of a way to grip the projectile to pull it out, considering it was already melting and slippery. Ray knelt down and pushed me gently out of the way which, for our hothead, was unusual.

"I got this, don't worry." He closed his eyes briefly and icified his hand. I couldn't think of any other way to put it. Because it was icy and the icicle was wet, it froze to his hand, and he counted to three before yanking it out at two and a half.

Evelyn screamed again, her already-pale skin going another shade closer to transparent and she leaned back on her elbows, panting with the exertion it took to not pass out from the pain. I grabbed a healing potion and shoved it at her mouth. She gulped it down and it took immediate effect.

Lucky for us there didn't seem to have been poison or other nefarious elements involved with the Ice Lance. I fell back onto my butt and put my head in my hands.

Blood Dispersion wasn't even useful if I didn't have an opponent to tack it onto first. I couldn't heal someone—anyone—unless I had targeted them earlier and was actively damaging an opponent. No one on the wall was a suitable target, not anymore. At least, I hadn't thought so. And the Zarrie kept falling back out of my range.

Damn it.

"You okay?" I asked, because truthfully, almost losing two people I cared about in a short span of time just frayed the hell out of my nerves. Even if Evelyn hadn't really been in danger to start with, she'd still been hit because she'd been trying to save me. My stupid chest constricted painfully. Damn it. I didn't have time to analyze emotions.

"Yeah. Stop fussing. The wound's closing. I'm fine." She seemed irritated, and I couldn't put a finger on why. So I nodded and stood up.

To my surprise, perhaps the wombat squishing being the final blow, the Zarrie had pulled back entirely. No more were they in sight. A quick sweep of the area with my Mana Sense showed me no weird splotches of Mana, no waves or twists that would indicate a trap.

Even so, I called out to the groups outside to make a careful sweep of the surroundings and for Mumma Wombutt to come back and heal up. I didn't want anyone out there longer than they should, but we also needed to verify that they were truly gone.

The sense of urgency surrounding us was gone, and my head hurt far less than I'd expected it would. Although, in its defense, it had only managed a few hours of the usual concentration I needed to pull off for this sort of thing. In fact . . . how had the siege lasted such a short time? Was that in fact the different between a Basic-Class-ruled human settlement and a platoon of Hakarta who had several Advanced Class Levels? The sheer discrepancy that gave to newly incorporated worlds was just batshit.

I shook my head and went back to trying to figure out entirely what was wrong here.

"That didn't feel right." Ray, being the sunshine he was, piped in at the best possible moment to cement my renewed feelings of dread.

He was right, and I wished I could fathom the reasoning behind their attack this time, and why the hell they'd sought to ambush some of our patrols out in the wilderness too. Which, in hindsight was probably their best bet.

When we weren't standing behind walls, we were the easiest targets, right? But that's why we'd sent out at least one Hakarta, in some instances three, with each of the lower-Level patrols at the request of Ginali.

Things just weren't adding up in my head. I glanced around at the damage and cringed. Holy Credits, this was going to be an expensive fix. "It's fine. We'll figure it out. Right now we need to get everyone inside, keep watches on the parapets, and figure out our next move. I'm sick of waiting for everyone else to make theirs."

I wasn't a strategist. But I also wasn't an idiot. There were more upgrades we could purchase, not to mention information available in the Shop, as well as potentially expanding our city in order to make it stronger. Add to that the ability to reinforce our patrols with Hakarta, and we'd fight fire with fire. They might not be the nicest things, but the nice guy rarely won.

❖

10 Weeks Post-System Onset
10 p.m.

Wisp ran up to me, barreling into me as I entered the center. Dog sniffed at my hand while Wombie trundled past us on his way to see his mother. Or at least, I guessed that was what he did.

Disentangling my daughter from a tight embrace, I grasped her hand and headed over to the library with her.

"I don't like all this," she said, her tiny voice just that much smaller.

I couldn't imagine being a kid with all of the changes in the last couple of months. Just growing-up was such a task in itself, having to grapple with all of this sort of shit—well, that was simply ridiculous.

"I know, sweetheart. I know." I squeezed her little hand tightly, not wanting to ever let it go. "We'll be okay—we just have to figure out some things."

I pulled up a chair in the center section of the roundtable we'd created, and Wisp dragged one of the bean bags from the kids' section. She stood defiant in her choice when I raised my eyebrow, and I decided not to say anything. If it made her feel better to sit with me while the adults droned on, then so be it.

She curled up on it and then Dog curled around her, before she laid her head down against his side.

Winter made it get darker just that much earlier. Twilight was settling over us all, and I was grateful for the ambient Mana-powered lights we had these days. As I waited for the rest of the people to flock into the center, and for the rest of our little city council to flow into the library, I checked the several notifications that had popped up while I ignored them.

Level 38. That was surprising. I wonder what I'd done for the System to give me that much experience in so few hours. Whatever. I needed the strength, I wasn't about to argue. No more Skills though, not even a Skill Point until Level 39. Attributes were there though, so that was good. I'd have to allocate points later.

The next notification I brought up surprised me greatly. I thought we'd needed another hundred-odd people. And hadn't some of us died? Maybe a couple of the patrols found outliers before they brought them home. Before the Zarrie attacked.

Congratulations! You have completed a goal of the quest:

A Habitable Safe Zone

Part Three: Staying Power

You need to make it 3 months into System Onset as a Township.

Goals:

1 - Gather 3,000 total inhabitants. This may include visiting species. Current population 3,058/3,000

2 - Build up your defenses and successfully survive and remain in your growing township for 3 months from System Onset. Current staying power 10 weeks /13 weeks

Reward: 45,000 Credits for your town treasury, [unknown] reward.

Time Limit Remaining: 13 days 2 hours and 27 minutes

Good luck! You're over halfway there!

For some reason, that note of encouragement at the end didn't make me feel safe at all. I still couldn't put my finger on why, though. Even as everyone filed into the room for the meeting, I couldn't understand why I was so uneasy.

You know, apart from the apocalypse, IRSHA, the Zarrie, rampant mutations of all our favorite cuddly and deadly creatures, and the whole thing with Carindale, that is.

Dor came in and sat next to me as the rest of us got comfortable. Red ran in with his assistant Paul and put out food for us all on big trays they spaced out between us. There were a lot of us gathered in the room, but the one thing we didn't have to address right now was food storage. At least we had that.

Despite the appetizing meal in front of us, my stomach roiled. I wasn't hungry in the least until Kyle walked in and sat on my other side. He leaned over, his hand on my arm.

"He's almost back to normal now. Physically, fine. He just needs a little time to sort his emotions out."

"Do you have any idea what caused that?"

Kyle's expression shadowed over, and I realized there was a lot more to the caution I felt than I'd originally realized. He was about to say something when Lousesh stood up in the middle of the room and cleared his throat.

His booming voice was quieter than normal, with a commanding aura to it. "When we got the call to come back, that the base was under attack, we moved straight away. But we didn't get far."

He paused, looking around at all of us and coming to rest his gaze on me. I couldn't tell if he was sad, or if he was angry with me, but his next words made all of that inconsequential anyway.

"It wasn't the Zarrie who attacked us. We were attacked by a gathering of… mutations. Four Koalzillas, all of them Level-45 Elites, attacked us. We barely escaped with our lives."

No one said a thing, and the weighted silence was deafening.

Their attack had nothing to do with the Zarrie and all to do with the subversion of Mana and its effects on the creatures.

I cleared my throat, a tiny bit of guilt gnawing at me, breaking the silence. "No Zarrie in sight at the time?"

Lousesh shook his head.

So I'd lost my shit on the Zarrie for no reason? It didn't make sense to me. "This wasn't the first time either." I spoke my thoughts out loud as the pieces slotted together in my mind and looked up at our little council. "Could it be that the Zarrie were also being attacked?"

No one responded immediately, which was good in a way. At least that meant everyone was considering the possibility.

"We need to figure this out. If they were being attacked, then it puts their own sieges on us in a different light."

"They still killed people, Kira," Chris snapped, and then sighed, running her hand through her short blonde hair. She did that whenever she was irritated, I'd noticed. Sarah squeezed her wife's other hand, sapping the tension. "Sorry, but they did."

"I know. I'm not making excuses, just looking for reasons." Not that I expected the reasons to make sense.

"Okay, say they had outside motivation to take down our settlement—self-preservation motivated. Why wouldn't they have told us?" Dale crossed his arms as if to punctuate the statement.

Hirish stood up and waited until he had everyone's attention before speaking. "Actually, no. Once the Pirri Clan arrived and became a part of this settlement per the Mercenary Charter, such options grew more complicated."

"Okay, so we have three things to do, then?" I clapped my hands together to stop the sudden murmur between people and bring all the attention to the middle. My energy was flagging severely and we needed to finish this.

"First, we need to contact the Zarrie and figure out just what in the hell is going on. Second, we have to find a way to assess and categorize the true Level the mutations have been reaching. Because obviously the creatures we thought we were culling seem to be thriving and then some." I paused, glancing around.

"Third?" Evelyn asked softly, but the whole room heard. It was late now, and outside noises weren't filtering through to us at all.

"Sleep." I laughed, not actually kidding. "No, seriously. If we're mistaken and the Zarrie are just mercenary dicks, then we need a plan of attack for payback."

Dor stood, leaning on her desk, nodding her head. "Sounds like a plan, but including sleep makes it four things all you young ones have to do." Her eyes twinkled as she said the last, and some of the stress melted from me.

"Sleep it is, then," Kyle agreed. "Let's see if we can get some shut-eye; I've got a feeling it's going to be a long few days."

As our council began to filter out, Kyle helped me grab Wisp from where she'd fallen asleep in her corner. Dog eyed us warily until I petted him between his ears and he trotted along with us out to our apartment. Evelyn trailed next to me, our fingers lightly brushing as our hands swung next to each other. She'd tried to save me today. I could have lost her, and I didn't like the way that made me feel.

One day at a time. One sleep at a time. We were going to get through this. Somehow.

Chapter Thirty-Five:

Unlikely Allies

10 Weeks, 1 Day Post-System Onset

4 a.m.

Sure, those two hours of sleep I'd gotten had been enough. Bleary-eyed, with not enough caffeine or kipatchya in the world to make me move smoother, I dragged myself from our tiny apartment, wishing for the fiftieth time that we could just complete that damned expansion so I could get a house, and followed Dor as she practically ran in front of me on the way to the library. I think she'd been living in there.

Mike stood outside of the admin site, tapping his foot with what I thought was more nerves than impatience. He perked up when he saw us, but no smile graced his face this morning.

"It's only been a few minutes." His voice penetrated my fogged up brain. "We woke you as soon as we realized."

"Realized?" Hell, right then I wasn't even sure what that word meant.

Mike gestured through the glass door as he opened it, and my bleary eyes struggled to focus. Guess the System couldn't completely fix good-old still-waking-up brain.

I wasn't sure what my mind thought it was seeing when we stepped in, but I definitely did a double take.

There, right in front of us, were Hirish, Lousesh, Mon'swkinon, and two of the Zarrie.

To be fair, the Zarrie weren't just waltzing about the room all willy-nilly. They were cuffed and restrained, each by one of the Hakarta.

Two seven-foot-tall, Anubis-like, Egyptian god of the fucking dead, living, breathing Zarrie were in our library. Every bone in my body wanted to see if I could access my Cocoon ability before I hit forty. But even dragging them down into the depths of the Earth felt like an underreaction.

All of my sleepiness evaporated, but the anger I'd felt earlier still lingered, even if it wasn't as potent as it had been when I thought they'd harmed my son. They'd still killed our people.

"The Zarrie are here to talk." Hirish intoned the word *talk* with pure distaste, and I got the feeling he much preferred action.

Talk. Well, I guess one of the points we'd touched on before retiring for the night was wanting to open a discourse with them. So here we were.

"Why talk?" Evelyn beat me to it. Still in her pajamas, she tossed her long hair over one shoulder and crossed her arms in that very clear I-give-no-fucks way that she could get at times.

Mike, who was following the last of our sleepy herd into the room, cleared his throat. "It appears that the attacks on our patrols yesterday were not an isolated incident."

"So are they trying to tell us that they were victims too all along?" I didn't mean for it to come out snidely, but it did, and I cringed. Still though, the more pieces I got, the less I liked the picture the puzzle painted.

Hirish shook his head, but it was the Zarrie with sleek black fur and two white spots over his eyes who spoke up. The same one we'd healed, and met in the woods. Zyrilian. His voice was deep, but surprisingly soothing. More like someone who would read you to sleep than the barky, coarse voice I'd expected.

"Australia, this has a Class-7 inhospitable ZFQ rating by the System, verified before Mana infusion by the Galactic Council." He gestured around at the building we stood in. "This should not have been possible. You should all be dead."

"Yeah. So. Tell us something we haven't heard five thousand times before." Kyle was not a morning person on the best of days. He was usually up at this hour because he'd had an all-nighter shift. But wake him from sleep—I didn't want to be in your shoes. "What the fuck does that classification mean? Because I beg to differ—here we are."

Mon'swkinon spoke up quietly, or at least, as quiet as he got when speaking. "The creatures that lived or that live here, when combined with the potential of Mana mutation, or even of chimera effects, were calculated to overrun the humanoid population within the first fourteen days, and eradicate the remainder by the end of three months, if no outside intervention happened."

He glanced around. "IRSHA were meant to be that intervention. With our help, taking settlements and allowing those humans who survived residence within our walls, your population would be greatly diminished but you'd still have some presence here. That enough of you survived to create multiple settlements and meet the requirements of the Settlement Orbs . . . that was unexpected."

The Zarrie with sable-tufted fur took over. "The mutations out there, the chimera formations that have occurred were largely contained by you, at least around your settlements, until—"

I inspected her while she spoke.

Piola

Zarrie of the Finite Interim Commander

Soul Mage

Level 4

Commander, eh? Okay.

"Until you guys came and attacked us and made us have to defend closer to home, be warier, not to mention break the Level-maintenance cycle we'd established. We had a lot of this under control," I finished off for them.

It was just like having kids and having to remind them that we'd had everything working properly until they didn't follow directions.

The Zarrie both looked decidedly uncomfortable, and it was Piola who spoke up. "While it may appear like this, it is not. The areas beyond where you cleared grew rampant. They have increased in Level and power, and now it is truly dangerous."

There was a part of me that didn't want to believe it, but the logical portion of my brain knew. It knew those creatures hadn't been kept at bay. That it was only a matter of time before they leveled, ate the ones we'd been maintaining.

"It doesn't matter what the System calculated or thought, we're here. And we have a defensible city—to a certain extent." I took a breath, trying to suppress a yawn. "The bigger question is why should we trust this information that you're bringing us?"

"Because I was not the original commander of my division." Piola sounded defeated. "Because we lost twelve of our force before we knew what was happening and moved closer to this settlement, and have now lost a total of eighteen."

Lousesh paled, and Hirish's eyebrow practically push-upped off his face. I was no expert, but I thought they were shocked by the news.

Zyrilian continued. "We came with sixty-four, and have but forty-six remaining."

"You didn't attack with a fully forty-seven yesterday," I snapped out.

"We still had forty-nine then, and had left behind several members to guard our camp." Zyrilian scowled and his canine teeth showed prominently. "We approached your walls but your people sounded the alarm."

"Can you blame us?" Kyle said in that deadly soft way of his that meant he was as angry as possible.

Piola shook her head. "No. Not at all. We did not go about any of this correctly. We lost our three highest rankers in the second encounter. I have not led well in their wake."

I waved a hand at her, pushing my anger away to take out on something, anything, later. What I was hearing was that we were all in danger if we didn't work together. If this famous mercenary race got their butts kicked, then what chance did we stand?

A fighting one, that's what. No one was taking this safe haven from us, not even Billy the fucking koala.

"How far out were you at first?" I needed to get our bearings, figure out just how much space there was between us and the mutations from hell.

A shadow of thought passed over Piola's face. "We came down on the shore of a small lake. Not far from here, but in the wilderness enough that mutations weren't contained yet. Not to mention what emerged from the water. Tingalpa, I believe."

"Tingalpa Reservoir," Dor muttered under her breath. "Shit. That's not far from here, and I hadn't even given it a second thought. It's always been an important wildlife spot."

It was probably the first time I heard actual fear in the older woman's voice, and my stomach flipped.

"We're not the only ones close to conservation properties and reservoirs." Sienna was accessing information through the admin hub. "Carindale is in an arguably worse spot. It's right on some reserves and parkland."

Damn it. I wanted to help them; it took so much willpower not to send out multiple patrols to aid them. But we needed to come first. We'd fought too hard to not put our own survival first.

Lousesh spoke up. "We'll put together parties now, then. With the Zarrie—"

But he didn't get further than that. Kyle held up his hands to stop him. "Wait. Are you saying we're going to trust these guys now?"

Hirish stepped in. "They are victims, even if their initial task was to cause inconveniences. A temporary truce would suffice."

"How does that even—do you hear yourselves?" my twin asked. "Can you draw up a contract?"

"Of course we can." Hirish sounded insulted at the insinuation that they might not have access to that. "But it's a Dungeon World—"

Kyle threw his hands up. "And it's not legally enforceable. I get it, I get it. They're your problem if they turn on you."

The corner of Hirish's mouth lifted in a smirk as he glanced over Zyrilian and Piola. "Trust me. I'm counting on it."

Lousesh cleared his throat and continued. "We will put together patrols. Multiple Hakarta, Zarrie, IRSHA, and humans. We need the best scouts to scour the area and warn of incoming danger—and the rest need to be well equipped and ready to fight."

"Having scouts gives us time to prep," I mused out loud. Two hours sleep it was, I guessed.

"Carindale just radioed in that we should watch out for larger-than-usual mutations. That was the bulk of their message. Whatever is going on over there, they definitely think they can handle it themselves." Dor's voice was gruffer than usual.

"Good." Some of the weight I'd placed so heavily on my own back lightened. If they weren't asking for help, I wasn't a despicable human for not sending any, right?

I turned to Piola. "Guess you need to bring in more of your troops. Just don't fucking try anything."

Hirish harumphed with derision. "They can't. Don't worry about that for now."

Piola nodded. "We will contact Akins and Moke to gather the rest of our division. There is work to be done.”

"Our new camp, which is closer to here, was hit again two hours ago. It's why we came. I don't think we have much time." Zyrilian's smooth voice held a tone I believed was universal: worry.

And my gut instincts agreed one hundred percent.

What you have to understand about Brisbane is there are swaths of forest or woodland or whatever you want to call it, like . . . everywhere. And in my urgency, our urgency to take care of all of the people we had, of all of the people we loved, we'd neglected to take into account that places like oh, say, Karawatha Forest also needed to have creatures purged and regulated.

Sure, we'd headed to the opposite side and cleared out the Daisy Hill Koala Center so many times we'd lost count, but not a few kilometers away from that was Karawatha, and I was terrified of how much those creatures might have mutated and leveled.

Nourished by Shop-acquired energy drinks that weren't specifically for human consumption, my group headed out on the nine-to-ten-odd kilometer drive, acting on the intel from one of the scouting groups.

I didn't like leaving Garbo, but realistically, if we sat there and waited until these creatures had devoured everything in their path and finally made it up to us, we'd all be dead. This way, maybe we could use some the experience from killing them to make ourselves stronger.

The theory was sound, anyway.

Karawatha was accessible by taking main roads southeast, and then turning southwest in a more inland direction. I couldn't help glancing up at the sky intermittently just in case the Magon was going to stop us from doing this, too.

My group consisted of Hirish, Piola, Zyrilian, Dequasha, Molly, Sange, Evelyn, Gemma, Ray, and myself. Four Advanced Classes better be enough. The scouting report mentioned Level 48 and 50. We knew nothing about the beasts except for their appearance.

And so it was that we found ourselves out of our vehicles and off the road into Karawatha Forest, trying to thin some of the higher-Level mutations.

I hadn't even known emus were around here. Probably broke out of captivity and came from somewhere else, because why not?

Emus are pretty violent creatures. Ever tried to feed one? Use a cup or some sort of receptacle because that creature going to use all the force in its ridiculously long neck to peck the ever-loving shit out of whatever you're giving it. And if it's in your hand, you won't have one after you're done.

The thing in front of me blinked its eyes, just like an emu in that disconcerting, half-disconnected way, but where its feathered body should have ended, it extended instead. Extended with feather-colored scales and longer legs than any half an alligator should ever have had.

At least its beak remained toothless, though that was a small mercy. Instead, the edges of it were now razor sharp, and it elongated to almost the length of a crocodile's snout with cutting-edged tenacity.

Never mind where the emu came from, where did the crocodile it mutated with spring from?

Molly, ever fearless, planted herself in front of the creature, and I needed to ask her where the hell she got her damned shields from all the time. I'd hate to see her armor bill. She activated her Shield Extension Skill, grunting as she did so.

Sange cast their Barrier over all of us and then set up healing wards and rotating heals over time while I tagged the emu with Blood Dispersion, ready to let it heal us when the damned monster got through.

Implantation was a go, Planted In Place fired off. I let loose everything I could so as to make sure that beak got nowhere near any of us.

I didn't account for the fact that some ability it possessed allowed it to lengthen its neck like fucking Gumby, reaching over Molly's shield to attack those of us in the back with long, sweeping strikes. What sort of stop-motion hell was this?

Dequasha dove to the side, leaving Ray in its path, and it was only his quick thinking Ice Lance that managed to seal around the creature's head and give us a brief respite. Evelyn fired several of her arrows at close range right into its face, one arrow punching through the left eye. I watched Molly lean forwards, slamming her shield into its body and pushing it back, even as the others dispersed to the side to attack its flanks.

Even so, it still had forty percent health remaining.

With Piola and I leaching life from it, Molly disrupting its attacks every time it lengthened its neck, and Zyrilian and Gemma darting in while trying to avoid the alligator tail portion of the creature, I thought we were doing well. That is, until I realized that the incoming Mana signature close to us didn't belong to humans, but to another mutation.

Taking a deep breath, I chugged a Mana potion and glanced at my bar, and my Skills. I needed to play crowd control and get us going with the healing. The damn emu still managed to hit us—or Molly mostly—no matter what we did, and if it had reinforcements, we needed that heal over time Blood Dispersion was giving all of us.

Right now, Hirish was scouting the lay of the land, and Piola was filling in for our usual second Healer, so I guess that's what a Soul Mage did.

The very presence of Advanced Classes gave us a reduction of experience. On the other hand, it also meant we had a much lower chance of dying.

Worthwhile trade, in my opinion.

Spinning on the new incoming creature, I called out the sighting even as I triggered Planted In Place. It rooted the approaching monster, giving me a chance to inspect it.

Emugator

Level 44

Elite

First up, where were all these damned emus coming from, and secondly, how far had the damned crocodiles traveled? That was just fucked up. As was the mutation variation in front of me. Somehow there were tiny crocodile legs protruding from the chest of the emu. Useless little hands that now reminded me of a T-Rex flailing about that also had massive claws.

Worst. Mashup. Ever.

But apparently, I'd still missed something. Because when this one opened its mouth, Planted In Place as it was by my spell, a long, forked tongue darted out. Something glowed on the end, and what was already a four-to-five-foot-long tongue extended in an energy blade that barely missed Sange, who dove to the side. That broke the healing spell they were casting on Molly.

Guess that's what made it an elite.

Another twinge in my Mana Sense, another wince, and I spun around. Another monster, another emu hybrid. A third Emugator had somehow crept up on our rear without even alerting my Mana Sense. Granted, I was a little preoccupied. I hissed, throwing a Rock Slide on it, watching as the Earth heaved up and slammed down on it.

Seeing that we had our hands full, Hirish finally chose to take part. The Hakarta raised his beam rifle, opening fire from a distance as he crouched, slamming bursts of visible energy into the sneaking monster.

Zyrilian and Gemma split up, moving toward the flanks of the Emugator such that when it broke free of the Rock Slide, they were there to tear into its legs like an assault on KFC.

Meanwhile, Piola shot out what looked like a ward and leach, covering the lapse in healing while Sange repositioned themselves, farther away from that energy tongue. Meanwhile, the second Emugator's next damn trick was to shoot out venom that sizzled the fallen underbrush, making it smoke almost as if it were on fire. Didn't want that shit hitting us.

Zyrilian darted back, away from the portion of the third mutation that was too close to the second. Not a moment too soon, since the Emugator had chosen to target him, splashing the area with toxic venom.

Breathing hard, I scanned one last time for more monsters and found nothing. Knowing that we were safe for the moment, I focused on the second Emugator since the first was practically dead, refreshing my Skill with Topsoil to strengthen the grass and vines holding it still. As though realizing who was keeping it pinned, it turned its attention on me. Which was the plan.

Whenever it tried to spit at me or use its damn tongue, I took the slight rearing back it used to start the attack as a chance to rush in. Then, it was just a matter of dodging or smashing the tongue away with my Warhammer.

Ugh. Slimy, disgusting, venomous tongue.

Definitely not the kind of tongue action I liked.

It didn't take long for the rest of the team to bring down Emugator number one, who thrashed wildly the closer it came to death. That tail was obnoxious, stunning and knocking both Gemma and Zyrilian down multiple times.

My attention, distracted by Gemma and Zyrilian's latest close call as their target died and the pulse as my Implantation and Blood Dispersal turned off, resulted in the second Emugator landing its first real hit. It nicked me with a portion of the venom that coated its tongue, the glowing energy blade having disappeared at some point.

Holy fucking cuntnugget.

The pain that coursed through my left thigh as the acidic bite of the toxin ripped through my skin and muscle left me gasping for breath. Collapsing to the side, I barely "dodged" the follow-up strike.

Damn it, I needed to get that dermal underlayer implanted.

Then, all other thoughts dashed out of my brain as I fell to the ground thrashing in agony. I could practically feel the skin melting backward from all of the muscle, exposing raw nerves to the toxins.

Casting about wildly, I managed to fixate on the damned creature. The team had spun around in a well-practiced motion, Molly having used her Taunt to take its notice away from me as I lay beneath its feet. The others started firing upon it, dropping its health. Pushing the pain to the side, I tapped into Blood Dispersal first and then Blood Transfer.

Cool relief as borrowed health swept through my body, then the damn toxin hit another nerve and sent another pulse of agony, forcing me to kick and twist on the ground. A small icon in the corner of my vision told me I was poisoned and stunned.

Real helpful.

Piola knelt next to me, and I couldn't see her face clearly enough to tell what she was thinking. But I could feel it. She muttered something I couldn't discern as she held a hand over what I could feel was an ever-growing wound, and for several precious seconds the damned pain receded somewhat.

Zyrilian was suddenly there, ripping something open with his all-too-sharp teeth and handing a packet of something to his commander. Piola's skepticism was practically audible to me, but she took it anyway, hesitated all too briefly, and then sprinkled whatever that powder was onto my leg just as the damned pain began to return.

For two seconds, I thought everything was going to be fine. I thought that whatever Zyrilian had given Piola was going to work well. That is, until the fire of torment lit itself up in that entire gaping wound, and the last thing I remember was screaming until I went hoarse.

Chapter Thirty-Six:
New Threats

10 Weeks, 1 Day Post-System Onset
11 a.m.

My eyes blinked slowly open, and the first thing I noticed was the lack of pain. Relief flushed through me, and I turned my head, suddenly realizing I was lying on the ground with my head propped up by someone else's backpack, the rough canvas brushing against my cheek. Deadened undergrowth dug into my back, a single damned stick somehow managing to worm its way through my clothing to stab me between the shoulders.

I pushed myself up, only dully realizing that my teammates were all fighting something my brain wouldn't even process right then.

I didn't know how long I'd been out, but we'd moved out of the first area. The trees here were different. The clash of battle, the screams and grunts and called-out orders filtered through my ears in a dull roar, even as the all-too-familiar twisted-iron smell of spilled blood and viscera filtered through my senses.

Fingers slipped down, pushing at the smooth and healed skin of my leg. Like nothing had ever happened. No scars, no remnants, just skin that I would have had in my twenties sitting right there on my left thigh, open to the world because I only had one leg of my jeans left.

Shaking my head, I pushed myself up to standing, needing to go out there and help. The creature they were battling looked like one of those tiny blobs we'd found in the streets months ago, but it had grown, and taken a massive cane toad or something amphibian with it.

Their bodies meshed, lending it the size of a car, the toxin of a toad, and the unpredictability of the glob.

Caneglobulous

Level 49

Elite

And there were two of them.

While I had no idea how long I'd been out, I realized my Mana hadn't even regenerated completely, so it couldn't have been too long. How many damn monsters were there?

Monsters or not, outnumbered or not, the team had just fought on. Dequasha surprised me. She was half covered in grime and blood, but I didn't think any of it was hers. She looked like she was determined to make sure the monsters didn't win.

My first few steps were shaky as my eyes adjusted to the sheer volume of Mana lighting up rampantly around us. Each strand was different, each color varied. System Mana when people used it and when creatures used it, and all of the ambient versions of it hanging around us. There were just so many strands to follow that my senses would get assaulted if I wasn't careful.

No time. No damn time.

Hammer hefted in my right hand, I regained my footing completely by the time I got there, just in time to use Planted In Place, bolstered by Treesong and Topsoil to secure another incoming Caneglobulous. The creature halted, shrieking at us from the distance, and the sound gave me an adrenaline rush.

Back in the fray, I started by throwing out another Blood Dispersion on the main target of Hirish and Zyrilian. The way they fought, I knew theirs was going down first. Even so, the Hakarta and Zarrie had managed to take on a few injuries if the state of their armor was anything to go by.

Joining the humans on this team, we hammered on our own monster.

Well, not hammered in my case, since slime didn't really care much if I squished it flat. Instead, I relied on my spells, yanking water out of its body and calling out hidden attacks when I saw Mana gather.

We didn't do too shabbily, finishing ours off a minute after the aliens did theirs. By that point, of course; even more of the mutations had arrived.

The string of monsters seemed endless. Hirish seemed to delight in showing off even more techtoys, throwing down a pair of shield generators that walled off our flanks on one side. Earth Barrier guarded our flanks on the other, though I had to concentrate on making the monster-facing side particularly steep.

Didn't stop the damn toad mutations from jumping over it, but Evelyn shot them out of the sky after the first wave tried that. Zyrilian and Piola had obviously fought together a lot and started using hit-and-run tactics, the poison on their claws adding damage over time to the creatures trying to clamber over the barricades or charge our front.

We fought side by side, struggling more often than not even with the help of four Advanced Classes. I watched Hirish pull out a pair of grenades, lob them into the distance, and turn the entire area ahead of us into so much foam, trapping monsters in the hardened expulsion. It gave us a much-needed break, even as they kept firing into the group.

I really wanted a beam rifle, but when they started swapping Mana battery magazines, I realized it was probably not in the works. I didn't really want to think about how much that would cost. Better armor might be the better spend.

It wasn't a constant wave of monsters, but every time we killed, looted, and started to relax, to gain back a chunk of our resources, another set appeared. The smell of the blood, the sound of battle, or maybe just the swirling Mana around us must have drawn them.

We fought side by side for so long that I think we began to bleed together as people even in my mind. And we fought well together. We began to anticipate where one of us might flag, where a Zarrie or human might unleash a powerful Skill, when Molly might Taunt a monster toward it for us to focus fire on it. I began to wonder just how farfetched an idea it was that aliens could cooperate with humans in a normal setting, too.

The sun began to set, my pant leg didn't grow back, and I just counted myself lucky that mosquito season was over.

Finally, a full ten minutes came and went without a single damn monster appearing. Seemed as though all the daytime creatures were finally going to bed. In the twilight hours, there might be a few animals that hunted, but the real predators were going to come out later. Even if plants were my thing, I still had some knowledge about the wildlife that ate them.

"That. Was. Not. Fun."

"No. But your Level will be." Evelyn grinned at me, and I glared back. I'd lost count of the amount of time we'd been fighting, the number of creatures we'd fought back. My ability to loot was now nix with all 144-odd slots that I possessed filled with assorted pieces of slime, tongues, gallbladders, skins, and other weirdness that the crafters loved. I was way down on potions, too.

"We're the last of the patrols still out here," Dequasha piped up. "They think we've fended off the worst of it."

"For now." Zyrilian's eyes were shadowed, not the least by the fact that it was getting damned dark out here. Still, I got the feeling he'd experienced something unexpected when their camp was attacked, and now he was wary.

When a mercenary hunter who killed all sorts of shit for a living was wary of monsters, that was the time to be scared.

"Come on," I called to everyone. "Time to go back. We don't want to be out here when the nocturnal predators come out."

Those, I'd rather hunt down where they slept and kill during the day.

Our trip back to the center was uneventful, as it should be considering we'd had all the lower-Level groups backing all the way up behind us. There shouldn't have been creatures to come into contact with us, not after they killed their share.

Only the good-old Magon flying past the setting sun, overshadowing the entire area with its massive wingspan and impressive size. For those moments, we braked the vehicles and remained as motionless as we could, my heart threatening to climb out of my throat.

I checked over my stats quickly, excited to have leveled up, but a little perturbed about how much experience such large, dangerous, and mutated creatures were actually worth.

Still just shy of Level 40. I was saving that damned Class Skill Point, though.

Level 39 didn't yield anything amazing, except the feeling that I was falling short. With only two more Levels to go before I got access to the next Tier, I wanted to save my Skill Point for the penultimate Skills. I knew they did more damage or just did more than the ones below. Even if I wasn't trying to min-max my Levels, my entire damn Class being built around needing nearly all my Class Skills for one reason or another, I still wanted to do the strongest that I could.

I needed every edge I could get. With Kyle and Gemma at 42, Molly and Sange close behind at 41, and the rest of our regular group between 39 and 40, I felt like I was dragging. That wasn't all there was to it, though. It was bloody unfair they could all go out, do the killing or leveling while I was stuck in meetings half the day.

I breathed out slowly, forcing myself to calm. Harping on a lack of Levels wasn't going to help my headspace any.

Piola was quiet, contemplative even, and I found myself needing to ask her about what happened at their camp. So I did.

She looked at me thoughtfully, as thoughtful as I thought a god of death could get, and shrugged. Her shoulders were jointed slightly differently than a human's so the action had more of a ripple effect.

"We had our usual guard out, seven of us. The rest were asleep." She looked up at where the Magon had been not thirty seconds ago and sighed. "We didn't expect them to come into camp and certainly not a pack of them. We've hunted rare species, sentient and sapient alike, not to mention settlements and anything else you can think of.

"Even so, your world surprised us. Mutations that level that fast, that hard, that have more intelligence than any of us would have given credit to, are highly unusual. Most Dungeon Worlds are stable, changes in local ecology rare. It's what makes a new Dungeon World so precious. But . . . yours seemed to appear overnight."

Yay. We were special. Somehow, I managed to bite my tongue.

"We might have higher Levels than you, but in some ways, I wonder if your people are better placed to handle this." She sighed. "We are used to stability and detailed reports, known threat profiles. Yours . . . aren't."

She sounded sort of sad as she spoke, and it gave me pause, made me think that maybe she'd lost someone she cared about too. Perhaps alien races weren't all that different from us humans.

"Your mutations and the chimera effect on some of those combined creatures is due to the levels of Mana saturation in oddly placed parts of this continent. These mutations are all unique." There was something else in her expression now, that I only caught by a glimpse of dimming light. She was eager to find more of these and hunt them down. I just couldn't place whether that was because of revenge or because she loved the hunt.

Dequasha cleared her throat as we approached the gates. "I think all the other high-Level patrols have returned. Everything they encountered got cleared, but they're concerned about the amount of creatures they encountered. Meeting is being held now."

Having Dequasha communicate directly with Mon'swkinon was a lot easier than having to listen to the communications arrays that we had, yet at the same time a little eerie.

The gates opened in front of us, letting us in to our home. Even with a perfunctory glance, I could see the exhaustion seeping out of everyone. These had been a long couple of days, and no one trusted Piola and his people yet. Sleep was not going to be easy, and I wouldn't blame them.

Even if we were united right now, there was always the chance that they'd turn on us. They were alien, after all, and not contracted to anyone who had a real stake in Garden City. All we could hope was that the Hakarta could hold the Zarrie to the agreement between them. I had a lot of faith in Hirish.

I needed to.

I'd almost died out there today. Come so close to leaving my kids without their mum. How could I be so stupid? And yet . . . staying back was selfish. While I might not be the strongest, I did have aspects to my Class that helped.

Staying home with my kids was selfish to those I could help save. Going out and risking my life was selfish to my kids who'd be left behind if I died.

And there was no way to resolve the conundrum.

The night was warm for a winter's night, sitting at around ten degrees Celsius. The cold bit at my bare leg, draining body heat. So I headed inside to grab a spare set, determined to get myself a Dermal underlayer tomorrow from the Shop before I headed out. Right now, I just needed a pair of trackies to keep me warm.

Wisp was curled up by herself on her cot when I got in, and she turned as she heard me enter. "Mum!"

Her hands wrapped around my waist, and I noticed that she'd grown. Not a huge amount, but maybe five centimeters. The apocalypse hadn't changed all that much. My kid was still growing up whether I wanted her to or not.

"Why on Earth do you only have one leg in those jeans. You didn't leave like that!" She glared at me, like she knew I was going to give her some tall tale, or try to cushion the blow somewhat. But, you know, she was almost nine, and I'd had enough secrets for a lifetime.

"Got a little too close to an emu crossed with a gator." I pulled my trackies on, immediately feeling warmer.

"That's a really strange pairing." She pursed her lips like she was thinking about how that even worked. I couldn't blame her. It had been decidedly odd.

"Come out with me? There's going to be loads of talking about boring stuff, but Jackson and I'll be there."

Wisp smiled. "Wouldn't miss it for the world."

Such a brave kid.

The din when we got outside surprised me. With the open space, I'd expected it to be quieter. I guess with the sheer number of people we had going out in Adventurer groups now, this was to be expected.

Including our Zarrie and Hakarta forces, not to mention the groups IRSHA sent out with us, we had nearly five hundred bodies out there in that carpark packing it pretty thick.

Ray pushed through to me, his expression frazzled. "We lost fourteen of our people, but also managed to pick up forty-seven new residents."

I didn't hear him past fourteen, not really. Fourteen people? Who? Did I know them? How did they die? All the questions and my own close call served to twist my gut so much I wanted to throw up.

That someone like Ray could say that from one heartbeat to the next, it showed me just how different things were.

"Sorry." I held up a hand to stop him. "Repeat that?"

He glanced at me with an odd look for a moment before repeating himself. "I'm working on getting the new people settled in. But Kira, we're out of space."

Fine. That was something I could address. Something I could control—as much as anyone other than the damned System could control anything.

I clapped my hands as loudly as I could, which wasn't overly loud, and frankly, if Hirish hadn't seen what I was trying to do and yelled out "Shut up!" in a hugely booming voice, I don't think I'd have gotten anyone's attention.

"Ray, Red, Dale, and Sienna will organize the groups of you that have specific resupply needs. Stay out here with them and get that sorted. The rest of the council will be deliberating for the rest of the evening."

Paul, our amazing chef, tugged on my arm and I smiled as he whispered to me. "All set up in the food court."

Food. Nothing like a full stomach to make us sleepy. I raised my voice to make sure everyone could hear me. "Paul assures me there is plenty of food waiting in the food court. Just head on in and line up. Get a good night's sleep."

❖

10 Weeks, 1 Day Post-System Onset
7 p.m.

Even as everyone filed in, there was one question I needed to ask Dor and Sienna. Lowering my voice, I summoned the courage. "Any word from Carindale?"

Sienna shook her head. "Not since early this morning. Didn't you say they were mostly Adventurers?"

"Yes." She did have a point. Still, though. "But their Levels were even lower than ours."

She smiled at me, understanding in her eyes. "They made it to the settlement and the claimed the orb, gathered the requisite thousand people. Whatever trouble they're in, if they're indeed in any, they can at least handle themselves to some extent."

"She's right, love." Dor smiled softly at me. Or maybe she was just tired. "We have enough crap to clean up here first. Once we've done that, we can worry about saving the rest of the country, eh?"

I nodded. They were right. Didn't make me feel any better, though. Maybe Kyle had rubbed off on me, or perhaps it was the fact that the plants in this Dungeon World were mutating so far outside of my Earth plant understanding that I felt I had to save something.

I didn't know. I just knew that we all needed to survive.

Everyone I needed was inside now, along with the Zarrie, IRSHA, and Hakarta. Wow, look at us playing nice with aliens. I could practically feel everyone else's fatigue as well as mine.

"I know it's late, and everyone wants to sleep, but we have a crowding issue here."

"This is fine as a headquarters," Hirish began and then smiled when he realized what I meant. "You mean the base you have here."

"Yep. Garbo really wasn't ever meant to house thousands of people permanently. It was simply the safest place I could think of that didn't involve crossing a river." I shrugged, suddenly a little cold as the alien energy drink finally wore off and returned my body to it's far-too-sleep-deprived state.

"We need to expand our borders, and the only way we can do this is by asking that those people who have the funds, purchase their own property. Once they do, as long as we own eighty percent within a specific boundary, I believe we can then increase our border protections." I looked back at Sienna, who nodded.

Dale crossed his arms as he cleared his throat. "So we'll pick a direction and expand?"

"Exactly." Relief rushed through me. I had no idea if I was making sense.

Sienna stood up, drawing attention to herself. "I'll sketch out the best and most advantageous way for us to begin expansion. Shouldn't take more than a couple of days to get info files ready for those people capable of purchasing their own house."

Great. That was the first thing off the agenda. Next, I looked at Piola, but Hirish beat me to anything I was going to say.

"That sounds like a plan," Hirish inserted, his gaze never leaving Piola. "The Zarrie have agreed to donate the amount needed to repair those facilities to the treasury."

Piola simply nodded, but her gaze focused on the Hakarta with a sharpness I'd not seen from her since meeting her. Something to keep at the back of my mind, considering historically it appeared these two species were rivals.

"Fantastic—that means repairs and border extension will be done soon, then." I ticked things off mentally in my mind, trying to keep my mood upbeat so that the Zarrie-Hakarta staring match wouldn't devolve. "Is everyone who doesn't quite understand the Shop getting the walkthrough they need for protective or enhancement gear, Gemma?"

"Just come to my tutorial tomorrow and do the playthrough." She laughed at her own joke and quickly sobered up. "Sure. They'll be fine. I've got this."

If there was one human who had utilized what the Shop had to offer to the fullest, it was Gemma. In the wake of Jules, she'd sought to make herself as invulnerable as possible. And I couldn't blame her.

I took a deep breath. Now for the part I didn't want to address. The damned massive elephant in the room. "We lost fourteen people today. I don't know their names. I'm dreadful with names, but I feel we need to officially thank those who sacrificed for our town to keep going."

Evelyn was suddenly there, just to the left behind me, and I flashed her a grateful half smile. Death. I think the amount we'd witnessed so far was starting to numb us to it.

Ray pushed himself up of his chair, his expression somber. "I'll take care of that. Should we compensate them if they had a family?"

The question hit me out of left field, sucker punching me in the gut. It felt like all the wind had whooshed out of me. Did we do that? What if they'd had kids, a partner?

They'd had dreams, friends probably . . . shit. I only partially noticed as Evelyn stepped around to speak to Ray. It helped shake me out of the sudden spiral of angry helplessness I felt.

Composure. I needed to focus on the anger, on the helplessness and what I could do; no, what we *all* could do to make sure those deaths weren't in vain.

I lowered my voice as Evelyn spoke to Ray, making sure only they could hear me. I didn't even know if anyone in this room had lost someone.

What sort of settlement leader was I?

"Make sure their partners, family . . . make sure they know that loss wasn't in vain." My voice came out hoarser than intended, and I blinked back the tears angrily.

Humans were not weak, and we were going to prove just how wrong the System was.

Clearing my throat, I spoke up again. "We need to compile a listing of all the mutations and monsters we encountered today and what their abilities entail. The better the description of everything, the better chance others have upon encountering a similar creature."

"Sort of like a database of mutation information?" Kyle actually looked eager for this. "Weaknesses, aversions, powers, that sort of thing?"

"Knock yourself out." I paused, smirking at him. "You know that means you'll have to talk to the patrols, right?"

He shrugged good naturedly. "I got this."

This time, Dor stood up and walked around the desk she'd sat behind to lean against the front of it with me. "Now I, as the Den Mother, get to tell you all the things no one wants to say, and even fewer people want to hear.

"Today will help with the overpopulation and might even allow you some respite, but it's not going to last long. While the patrols can probably keep this up for several days, maybe a couple of weeks, eventually you're all going to be over-exhausted, and make mistakes."

Hirish glared at Dor, but she ignored him.

"So whatever you do, whatever we decide, those mutations and their Levels need to get under control quickly."

That was the problem right there. Garden City was in a pretty good place. We had walls, we had in-built defenses and shielding. Our teams could take out monsters at the Levels we faced today—we'd shown that.

But if we were going to go out every day, all day, it would wear us down. And if they approached our city, devouring each other and consequentially leveling on the way? Well, we'd never survive a siege.

In those, Mana became a problem. Monsters might use Mana, but they mostly relied on fang and claw and muscle. Things that didn't run out that easily.

The room went quiet for a while and this time, well, this time I let out that sigh. Shit—was what I wanted to say, and I was glad when Kyle spoke up for me.

"So, how about that alliance?"

Hirish glared at Piola some more and the Zarrie finally chuckled and turned to me. "We, the Zarrie, make a blood oath not to harm the humans or their deemed allies on this planet for the duration until our combined threat is controlled and or nullified, plus two Earth weeks."

Hirish cocked his head to one side. "We, the Hakarta, make a blood oath not to harm the Zarrie or their deemed allies on this planet for the duration until our combined threat is controlled and or nullified, plus two Earth weeks."

They cross-locked their hands, cringing at the same time as the sharp pin held by Hirish pierced both of them. Mana flurried around them like a small vortex producing a signed in blood-binding contract.

SYSTEM MESSAGE

42nd Hakarta Division and Zarrie of the Finite have signed a blood pact.

Parties:

Finite Zarrie Clan - Interim Commander: Piola

The 42nd Hakarta Division — Pirra Clan

Subject of protection: Kira Kent and the Settlements of Brisbane, Continent Australia (Class 7 Inhospitable ZFQ)

*Penalty for breach: -25% Credit penalty, Reputation loss. Depending on extent —
bounties may be levied for specific clans.*

Well, that was one problem solved, I guess.

As if to punctuate the moment, there was a loud caw-roar from outside, strong enough to shake the air. Reflexively every single being in the library looked up, as if we were scouring the sky for the damned creature.

But the library ceiling was decidedly tame in comparison. A collective ripple of relief ran through the room. It did nothing for the cold sheen of sweat at the nape of my neck from sheer panic at hearing the sound.

Maybe the Magon was giving us an omen.

Great time to remind me that there was also a mutant dragon itching to eat us all.

I rubbed at my temples to bring my thoughts back into order. We had an interspecies alliance that could backstab us if the benefits ever outpaced the penalties of their Contract, a settlement filled to the bursting, another human settlement close by that is giving me the creeps just by existing and, most importantly, more mutations Leveling so fast I had no idea how we were going to keep up.

Not to mention I also had a teenager and a tween to parent. I wasn't sure what the bigger challenge was.

Just another post-apocalyptic Tuesday.

Author's Note

Hi there! K.T. Hanna here.

I want to thank you for reading *The System Apocalypse: Australia – Flat Out*. I really miss my hometown of Brisbane, especially because I haven't been able to visit since COVID hit. I hope you enjoyed the Koalzillas as much as I loved writing them.

If you enjoyed the first two, then you're going to love the next books. Writing in Tao's world has been a fantastic experience and I can't wait to show everyone else just how amazing Kira can be.

If you enjoyed the book, I ask you, please take a moment to leave a review. **Reviews** are an author's lifesblood. Without them, our books sink into obscurity. With them, most algorithms allow well reviewed books to self-promote in some way.

Want to find out more about my books? Here is how you can keep in contact with me:

- Sign up for my Reader's Group and get a short story for free! http://login.somnia-online.c/
- If you'd like to contact me, my email is: kthannaauthor@gmail.com I'll do my very best to get back to you
- If you'd like to my books prior to publishin: previews of what I'm writing, or art I'm commissioning can be found on my Patreon! https://www.patreon.com/KTHanna
- I can be found in my FB reader group fairly often, and also on Twitter & Instagram.

-KT

About the Authors

KT Hanna

KT Hanna has such a love for words, a single one can spark entire worlds.

Born in Australia, she met her husband in a computer game, moved to the U.S.A. and went into culture shock. Bonus? Not as many creatures specifically designed to kill you.

KT creates science-fiction, fantasy, and LitRPG like it's going out of style, with a dash of horror for fun! She plays computer games, and ferries her daughter everywhere, all while looking after her cats, dogs, and her husband.

No, she doesn't sleep. She is entirely powered by caffeine, Chipotle, and sarcasm.

To find out more information about the author's other series, visit their website: https://www.kthanna.com/

Tao Wong

Tao Wong is an avid fantasy and sci-fi reader who spends his time working and writing in the North of Canada. He's spent way too many years doing martial arts of many forms, and having broken himself too often, he now spends his time writing about fantasy worlds.

For updates on the series and other books written by Tao Wong (and special one-shot stories), please visit the author's website:
http://www.mylifemytao.com

Or visit his Facebook Page: https://www.facebook.com/taowongauthor/

Subscribe to Tao's mailing list to receive **exclusive access to short stories in the Thousand Li and System Apocalypse universes.**

Acknowledgements
from KT Hanna

I have a lot of people to thank. Even those who don't contribute directly through the writing craft keep me going and help me write my best stories.

Love of my life, Trevor, and my little Bria. It's his fault I found the genre, and her fault I never give up on writing.

I wouldn't be here without the following friends:

Jami Nord & Owen Littman

Amanda W.

Quinton Shyn

Dawn Chapman

Bonnie Price

Andrea Parseneau

Cait Greer

M Evan Matyas

Dave Willmarth

Charles Dean

Daniel Schinhofen

Jay Boyce

Michael Chatfield

Luke Chmilenko

Tao Wong

And of course my family:

Mumskin & Papilie, Tracey, Bev, & Robbie.

The entire Rainbow Room.

Kristen, Everlosst, Hydrael, Kai

And every one of my Patrons, not to mention my FB Group. You all help me maintain a level of sanity.

About the Publisher

Starlit Publishing is wholly owned and operated by Tao Wong. It is a science fiction and fantasy publisher focused on the LitRPG & cultivation genres. Their focus is on promoting new, upcoming authors in the genre whose writing challenges the existing stereotypes while giving a rip-roaring good read.

For more information about latest releases and new, exciting authors from Starlit Publishing, visit our website or sign up to our newsletter list: https://www.starlitpublishing.com/

For more great information about LitRPG series, check out these Facebook groups:

- GameLit Society

> https://www.facebook.com/groups/LitRPGsociety/

- LitRPG Books

> https://www.facebook.com/groups/LitRPG.books

Glossary

Ecological Chain Specialist Skill Tree

Basic Class: Pest & Pathogens Unit: Microbiologist / Plant Pathologist / Entomologist / Hydrogeologist / Molecular Biologist - Abbreviated as: Ecological Chain Specialist

Earth Baricade		Seismic Awareness		Blood Transfer
Water Siphon	Mud Slide	Rock Slide		Mana Transfer
Treesong		Top Soil	Planted in Place	Impalantation
Vine Defense		Stone's Throw		Blood Dispersion
Cocoon		Ecological Outreach		Mana Dispersion

Ecological Chain Specialist Skills

Tier One (1-9)

Earth Baricade (Level 2)

Effect: Earth Barricade allows you to command the earth beneath your feet for the sole purpose of defending you and your allies. Size and strength of the barricade depends on level of spell and caster.

Mana Cost: 20

Mana Attunement (Level 2)

Effect: Using your affinity for the world around you, you can tap into the earth and coax it to warn you of any incoming threats. Radius and specific information increases with spell and caster level.

Range: 200 meters

Blood Transfer (Level 1)

Effect: Due to your devotion to understanding the world and mechanics of biological evolution, you are able to tap into the blood of your opponents and redirect that damage to heal yourself. Only usable on self. Caution: best used on enemies. Self heal only, damage and heal amount depended on level of spell and caster.

Mana Cost: 5 mana per second

Tier Two (10-19)

Water Siphon (Level 2)

Effect: Moisture is in almost everything, humans, intergalactic species. This ability allows you to siphon the water out of anything that contains it. Level of effectiveness dependent on caster and spell level.

Mana Cost: 60 Mana per Siphon. 25% water per application. Application duration—30 seconds.

Caution: Target will be immune to the effects of Water Siphon for 15 seconds after this application.

Rock Slide (Level 1)

Effect: Rocks are a strong part of the ecosystem around you. With the right level of encouragement you might even be able to use them to attack, or defend. The choice is yours. Strength and durability dependent on spell and caster level.

Mana Cost: 30

Mana Transfer (Level 2)

Effect: Due to your devotion to understanding the world around you and how to preserve and bolster it, you can tap into the mana saturation around you, bolstering your regeneration on a constant basis. Strength and capacity is dependent on spell and caster level.

Mana Cost: 20 Mana – 30 seconds of regen increase.

Tier Two Hybrid ability (20)

Mud Slide

Effect: Proficiency with Water Siphoning and coaxing the ground to do what you want, enables you to pull forth a mudslide. Usable twice per day. Usage, severity, and impact dependent on caster and spell level. Caution: Make sure you understand the lay of the land before engaging this ability.

Mana Cost: 65

Area of Effect: 3-meter radius from targeted casting. Damage minimum 2x caster Level per target.

Tier Three (21-29)

Treesong

Effect: Your affinity with nature and the life around you allows you to be at one with the trees. Sort of. The System and Mana have made vegetation come alive. Duration of Skill varies dependent upon strength of Mana Affinity.

Command Vegetation to attack your enemies, or just leave you and your friends alone. Assistance arrives with a price. The more time you spend in the clutches of Treesong, the more likely the voices will speak to you voluntarily.

Mana Cost: Commands: 12 per second

Requests: 60 per request.

Topsoil

Caution is advised. Too much power could go to their heads. Too little could shrivel what you hoped to help thrive. Practice makes perfect—Mana Sense lends understanding.

Effect: Supply nutrients to those plants around you and they will be more likely to come to your aid. Increases nutrition levels and ambient Mana levels by 15% on each use. Requires a period of 72 hours for nutrition levels and ambient Mana to collect. Repeated uses within the collection period will extend timeframe and provide a prorated fraction more level increase in effects.

Mana Cost: 10 Mana per second of Topsoil Treatment per plant.

Implantation

Duration: 10 seconds Effect: Implant a mana bomb into the chest of your enemy. The damage done to the enemy during the implantation phase will dictate the area of effect explosion of mana and health over your party once the detonation is complete as well as the damage inflicted by the bomb on your target. Should the target die before the bomb can complete its countdown, all benefits are forfeit. Use this wisely.

Damage: 25% of damage caused is inflicted on your target, 75% of damage caused is distributed as health and mana to your party/group. Higher levels of this ability will increase the impact levels and mana cost.

Recast: 240 earth seconds

Mana Cost: 25 mana

Tier Three Hybrid Ability (30)

Planted In Place

Exactly what it sounds like. Call on the roots and branches, vines or leaves, of the plants around you to aid in your adventures and root your enemies in place. Effect: Employs vegetation to grasp a single target with roots, branches and vines. Length of rooting dependent upon strength of vegetation used and ambient location.

Mana Cost: 30 mana per instance

Tier Four (31-39)

Vine Defense

Effect: Increase your Target's armor by 100% for 15 seconds by calling on the resilience of nature.

Note: Applying Topsoil and Treesong can boost the increase to 150%.

Caution: Fully effective only in vegetation-dense surroundings.

Mana Cost: 75 Mana (+cost of Topsoil and Treesong)

Stone's Throw

Similar to Rock Slide, this ability allows you to form any single type of earth, from dirt to pebbles, into a projectile to be thrown at your opponent. Must have requisite materials on-hand for Stone's Throw to be used.

Be wary of where you choose to use this.

Effect: The Stone's Throw will cause 180 damage. If the stone breaks on impact, it has the potential to cause another 25% falling damage to those it cascades over.

Mana Cost: 75

Blood Dispersion

Due to your devotion to understanding the world and mechanics of biological evolution, you are now able to corral the lifeblood of a target to aid your party. Damage done to the target is absorbed by this Skill and dispersed as health to you and your allies.

Effect: 5% of net damage done to target is returned as health to all members in the party within a 20 meter range.

Mana Cost: 95

Preview Tao Wong's other series: The System Apocalypse

System Finale (The System Apocalypse Book 12)

I almost prefer the torture sessions to this. At least when they're sticking flesh-eating worms under my skin or extracting bones from my extremities, the results are focused, and the intentions of my torturers are easy to guard against.

This is just so much more insidious.

"Well, what do you think?" Merdof asks impatiently.

"A little too bitter," I answer at last, swallowing the lump of chocolate.

"It's chocolate. Of course it's bitter!"

"It's only sixty percent cocoa. You added a bunch of sugar and milk to it too, to give it creaminess, but still managed to make it too bitter. I'd expect it to be that bitter and rich at around eighty or ninety percent," I reply, pocketing the remaining piece of chocolate.

"You're still taking it."

"Of course I am. It's chocolate." I lean back in the chair, fixing the man across from me with my stare. I'm told it's unnerving when I just look at people. Something about the simmering anger or the way a part of me—the part that has blossomed and grown thanks to the System and a lot of Intelligence points—runs the numbers and angles if I need to take someone apart.

Maybe it says something about my life that the need is all too common.

"What?"

I shrug, letting my gaze roam over the industrial kitchen we're in. It looks similar to what I'd expect a full-sized industrial kitchen would look like, with multiple stoves, burners, gleaming metal appliances, and kitchen sinks. Of course, the sinks are sonic disruptors, and the stoves are convection ovens that generate heat via Mana Stones, but outside of those details, a typical commercial kitchen.

"No, seriously, what?" he asks.

"Just trying to figure out your play."

"Chocolate."

I give him a flat stare and he shrugs.

"You're a smart human. You know what the play is."

"Yeah, I do. Good cop, bad cop." I raise one stump of a hand, the fingers and wrist still growing back from the latest session. "Torture, pain, mutilation, and death." I raise my untouched other hand. "Chocolate, friendly conversations, and betrayal."

"Exactly."

"But what makes you think I know anything worth all this effort?" I shake my head. "We've been at this for what, nearly a year now?"

I've kind of lost track of time. The Administrators cheat a little, twisting how much time passes in this dimensional plane they're keeping me in. I know, via the Administrative Interface I still have a modicum of access to, that I'm still attached to Xy'largh and time compressed, but I don't know exactly how much.

"In your Earth years, yes." A pause, then the grin again. "Just over, in truth."

"Can't be cheap. I know the System doesn't like when you waste so many resources putting up a time compressed zone. Hell, our experience gains have been hammered because of it."

"But still good, do you not think so?"

"In a sense."

I have to admit he's right. One of the reasons why they let me have my System access is to let me code solutions for the System. I'm still gaining experience from it, though it's incredibly heavily discounted. But considering when I'm not being tortured, I have nothing better to do half the time, I've been a good little worker bee.

It amuses me that the other Administrators thus far have yet to patch the cheat Mikito and I found. It's not as if it's not staring all of us in the face when we access the System Ticketing Board. Sometimes, I wonder if they're using it to track her. I can't think of how, but for all my skill and ability to absorb information, the System literally runs everything in our lives, and I've had only a few years to work out how to use it. Some of the other Administrators have had literal centuries.

"You are correct, however," Merdof says. "Every day that you delay us, it grows harder to justify keeping you alive."

"Then don't." I shrug. "I mean, I'm not exactly wanting to die, but considering my other options…"

"And what if I said that rather than death, the other hand gets you? For eternity."

"Eternity's a long time."

"We have Skills."

I grunt, closing my eyes for a second. It's a sign of weakness, of them getting to me. A year ago, I wouldn't have even given them that much. A year ago, I was all piss and vinegar, ready to take everything they could throw at me with the confidence that I'd come out swinging.

A year ago, I hadn't been put through hell and back.

Truth is, pain—constant pain—and the things it does to a person is impossible to predict. You never know how you'll react, what you'll do when your daily existence can change on a whim. One moment, you're working on a new ticket, the next, you're screaming your head off.

And I do scream. I might not have broken, I won't break—at least not yet, though the gods know what it'd be like a thousand years down the road—but I do scream. Holding it in is worthless, since by that point, they've stripped everything from me anyway—skin, organs, dignity....

A year ago, I would have not given them this much. But all this time has stripped me down, burnt out foolish egoistical things like not screaming. Sure, I'll think about telling them all I know. I'll flinch. They know it, I know it, so why bother hiding?

But...

"I guess I'll be screaming a long time then."

A grim nod. "He's not your friend."

"I never thought he was," I reply.

"The Prime Administrator will not save you," he continues.

"Didn't figure him to."

"And we will capture your friends."

"I'm sure you will try." I return his heated gaze with my own, taunting him.

He stands, fast and hard, and the mask falls away. I'm not surprised. They keep changing the good cop, hoping at some point they'll find someone that works. They've tried it all—big and ugly but friendly to thin and cute and perky. At least five different sexes at last count, just under a dozen races. Some don't last more than a few days, others like Merdof last months.

They all break eventually.

I guess if I had a skill, it'd be pissing people off.

He claps his hands and they come, dragging me out. I could fight, but what's the point? The bracers on my hands short-circuit any of my Skill use. And the moment I try, they'll drain me of Mana, shut down my link to the System, and beat me even more.

More importantly, I've never managed to kill the guards before I'm caught.

So I wait for the time when my friends come and rescue me.

And even if they do drag me into the room—gods, the room—and truss me up for my latest round of torture, I wait. Knowing that somewhere, sometime, they'll come for me.

I just have to hold out.

Read the rest in the last book of

the System Apocalypse series:

System Finale

Available on March 1ˢᵗ, 2022.

https://readerlinks.com/l/1946286

To learn more about LitRPG, talk to authors including myself, and just have an awesome time, please join the LitRPG Group:

https://www.facebook.com/groups/LitRPGGroup/

www.ingramcontent.com/pod-product-compliance
Lightning Source LLC
Chambersburg PA
CBHW050848210726
48290CB00004B/1140